Hail Mary

Copyright (C) 2023 Kandi Steiner
All rights reserved.

No part of this book may be used or reproduced in any form or by any means, electronic or mechanical, including photocopying, recording, or by any information storage and retrieval system without prior written consent of the author except where permitted by law.

The characters and events depicted in this book are fictitious. Any similarity to real persons, living or dead, is coincidental and not intended by the author.

Published by Kandi Steiner
Edited by Elaine York/Allusion Publishing
www.allusionpublishing.com
Cover Photography by Ren Saliba
Cover Design by Kandi Steiner
Formatting by Elaine York/Allusion Publishing
www.allusionpublishing.com

Hail Mary

KANDI STEINER

To the girls who love
tattoos,
video games,
fucking shit up,
and hot, cocky, *infuriating* playboys.

This one's for you.

Chapter 1

**THEN
MARY**

Asking for *Halo 5* for my fifteenth birthday was the biggest mistake of my adolescent life.

First of all, my mother about fainted when I did. It was hard enough to get her to even allow me to have an Xbox with a few single-player fantasy games, and that was because she thought it was a phase I would grow out of. But asking for an Xbox Live subscription and a game I could play with people around the world where our main goal was to kill each other?

My poor mother didn't know what to do with that.

"What about cheerleading? What about hanging out with your *friends,* shopping at the mall, boys?" She'd asked each question more frantically than the last, all the hope dwindling in her eyes.

Fortunately, I had Dad, who I think knew from when I was a young age that I was not going to be what he and Mom pictured.

Mom wanted a cheerleader and debutante just like her. She wanted her daughter to rush the same sorority she'd been a part of in college and dreamed of planning a huge wedding day with a fluffy white dress.

Dad wanted me to be in acquisitions, just like him and my older brother, Matthew, who was in college and destined to follow in his footsteps. To be fair, I *did* get my sass from my dad, and my *take no shit* attitude. But using those skills to be ruthless in a business merger was not exactly on my radar.

No, what they got instead of all that was an emo kid with a love for doodling and a dream of being a tattoo artist.

But that's not even why *Halo 5* was the beginning of my demise. Because as much as Mom hated it, Dad encouraged her that it was fine for me to play. *Good for the brain muscles,* he jokingly said over dinner as Mom angrily chewed an asparagus sprig.

And so, on my fifteenth birthday, I ripped open the present shaped like a video game first and squealed with delight, abandoning all my other gifts and running back to my room to play immediately.

It took me a while to figure the game out, but not too long to realize that I was *years* behind most of the people I was playing live with. Not that that deterred me. I was a teenager on summer break with all the time in the world. And if there was anything I loved more than drawing or gaming, it was a challenge.

I played as much as I could those first few weeks of summer vacation, leveling up and honing my skills. It wasn't unusual for me to still be awake when Dad's alarm went off for him to go into the city. He'd pop his head into my room, smile, and warn me to at least pretend I was sleeping when Mom got up.

I *loved* that summer. I loved the feeling of a winning streak, of staying up until the sun rose, of surprising my team when I spoke into my headset and they realized I was a girl. At school, I was a nobody, a loser, just another overweight teenager with acne and bad teeth and baggy clothes who lost more and more friends as she discovered her true interests.

But online? I was a bad ass.

I was almost a *god* — or god*dess* — when I was playing *Halo*. I controlled what I looked like, who I played with, and what a huge part I was of our team's victory. People *wanted* me on their team. They wanted to play with me. They wanted to *be* me.

Everything was going great.

And then, a month and a half after my birthday, when summer was in full swing but school was looming on the other side of it, I was popped into a game with the absolute last person I ever expected.

Leo Hernandez.

Anyone who went to my high school knew who Leo was. Every girl knew his messy hair, his crooked smile, his lean, muscular body, his golden skin and infectious laugh. Every boy knew his speed and agility, the ease with which he excelled on the football field and off it, too. He was a star athlete with a dad who used to play in the NFL. He was popular. He was funny. He was rich.

He was the kind of boy who could smile at you and make you feel like the only girl in the world.

Little did I know he was also the boy who would ruin my life.

I knew it was him as soon as his username popped up: *leohernandez13*. Sure, there had to be other Leo Hernandez's in the world, but that 13 gave him away. It was his jersey number since he played Pee Wee, and if there was any doubt left that it was him, it was obliterated when his familiar voice rang out in the chat.

"Who's ready to teabag some newbs?"

I stayed quiet the entire game, internally freaking out that I was playing with Leo even though I wished more than anything to be unaffected by him. I couldn't help it. I was a teenage girl, and the first time I'd seen him rip his jersey off after a football game had been my sexual awakening.

Of course, like most of the student body, he had no idea who I was.

At the end of our game, Leo denounced everyone on our team for "sucking ass."

Except for me.

And then he changed my world with three words.

"*Octostigma*, wanna squad?"

Octostigma was my username, one I'd patted myself on the back for thinking of because it was so cool and creative and elusive, and *no one* had even remotely the same one. It was combining two things I loved — octopus, the coolest animal on the planet, and *stigma*, which was the ancient Greek term for *tattoo*.

Hearing Leo Hernandez say that username, hearing him ask me to play with him?

Another awakening.

Everything happened fast after that. He added me as a friend, barked out a laugh of surprise when he found out I was a girl, and then we played several rounds on the same fireteam before he had to go to bed.

But the next night, when he logged on, I was immediately invited to play with him again.

It went on like this for about a week before, one night, he declared, "I'm bored with this. Do you have the new *Resident Evil*?"

"No."

"Can you get it?"

"Maybe."

"Let me know when you do."

With that, he exited *Halo*, and I saw the notification pop up that told me he was playing *Resident Evil: Revelations 2*.

I was not above begging my mother at the breakfast table the next morning. In fact, I quite literally fell to my knees.

"Games are expensive, and you just got one for your birthday," she said.

My dad gave her a look over his Sunday morning paper, which said without words that her telling me a game was expensive was comical considering what she spent on a pair of shoes weekly.

"Please, Mom. I'll do anything."

"Anything?"

"Anything," I said earnestly.

Mom looked at my dad and then back at me. "Next season, you'll be introduced to society."

And I shit you not, I didn't even groan or roll my eyes. "Done."

It was that easy. Agree to be a deb and I got the ticket to my crush. Two days later I had *Resident Evil: Revelations 2*, and when I signed on, Leo was already there.

"Stig! You got the game," he announced when our headsets connected.

I tried to ignore the way my stomach flipped at the nickname he'd given me, at the fact that he seemed happy I was online. "Don't get too excited," I told him. "I've never played before, which means I'll undoubtedly *suck ass*."

He laughed at me using his verbiage. "I'll teach you."

And that's all it was for a while, him teaching me the ropes of the game in Raid mode with the only conversation between us being me asking questions or him giving tips. But eventually, when I had the hang of it, the intimacy of playing a game with *only* Leo and not a squad full of other strangers hit me. And when we didn't need to talk about how to play the game anymore, we started talking about other things.

"So, how old are you?" he asked me during a raid one Sunday night.

"Fifteen. You?"

"Sixteen," he lied. I knew it was a lie because his birthday wasn't until October, but I let him lie because I liked the idea of him lying to impress me.

"Cool."

"So, you're a sophomore?"

"In a few weeks when school starts," I said, pausing when we came upon a cluster of zombies that required concentration. When we made it past, I continued. "Not really looking forward to that, to be honest."

"Why?"

"School sucks."

He chuckled. "Yeah." A pause, then, "Do you have a boyfriend?"

My skin burned so fiercely I took one of my cold hands off my controller and pressed it against my cheek. "No."

"*No?*" Leo laughed. "That's insane. How do you not have a boyfriend?"

I snorted. "The boys at my school are not into girls like me."

"Are you kidding?" He made a clicking sound with his tongue. "Then they're idiots. If there was a girl at my school who played video games? I'd be all *over* that."

"You have no idea what I look like."

"So?"

Heat full on invaded my body at that, like I had an inescapable fever.

"Are you hitting on me, *LeoHernandez13*?"

"Maybe I am, Stig."

My stomach did a backflip. "You're only saying that because you don't know who I am."

The conversation stalled as we hit the end of a raid, all focus on slaying zombies and other creatures. When we were back in the lobby, Leo said, "So what do you do when you're not gaming?"

"Draw."

"Draw what?"

"I don't know. Animals, flowers, tattoo designs, just—"

"Wait. *Tattoo designs*?"

I bit my lip against a smile. "Yes."

"Do you have any? Tattoos, I mean?"

"I'm fifteen."

"Fair. I thought maybe you had cool parents."

I snorted. "Far from it, unless you think a dad who works in acquisitions and a mom whose job is keeping up with the latest gossip at the club is cool."

"I've heard worse alternatives. So, you game and you draw. What else should I know about you?" He paused. "Maybe… your name?"

I swallowed, anxiety zipping down my spine. I knew he wouldn't know me even if I gave him my full name and a picture, because Leo was in the top two percent at our school, popularity wise, and I was at the very bottom of the barrel. But still, there was something powerful about anonymity. As *Octostigma*, I was cool, mysterious — the fun girl who plays video games. Maybe my voice was hot. Maybe the elusiveness was all part of it.

But as Mary Silver, I was a loser.

"You can just call me Stig."

It went on like this for the rest of the summer. I couldn't wait to log on, couldn't wait to see the notification that *LeoHernandez13* was inviting me to play with him. We'd kill zombies and laugh and fight over upgrades and who was better at what skill. In the lobby between raids, we'd talk, and the more we did, the deeper the conversations went.

I told him about the god-awful deal I'd made with my mom in order to get this game, and he laughed, asking what kind of dress I'd get for the debutante ball and if I was as good at dancing as I was at slaying zombies.

But his voice softened when he told me about the pressure he felt from his own parents, namely his father.

"He wants me to follow in his footsteps and go to Southern Alabama to play, but I love New England. I love Boston. I just... I can't imagine leaving."

"You don't have to."

He laughed. "You don't know my dad. I'm his pride and joy. It'd crush him if I didn't go to his alma mater."

"But it's your life," I reminded him. "He can't live both his *and* yours, too. Besides, wouldn't he be proud of you no matter where you decided to play football?"

"You make it sound so simple."

"Years of disappointing my parents and still having them love me."

There was a soft laugh through the headset, and then silence. "Hey… I know this is kind of against all the rules our parents set up for us when we started playing live video games but… do you think I could have your number?"

Butterflies.

Butterflies *everywhere*.

"Sure."

When I gave it to him, he freaked out.

"Wait, 781… that's Weston! That's where I live!"

Shit.

Panic zipped through me. I hadn't thought about him putting two and two together when I gave him my number.

I bit my lip in lieu of answering.

"Why didn't you ever tell me?"

"You didn't ask."

"Well, that's because I assumed you were in, like, I don't know, Canada or something."

"Canada?" I laughed.

"What school do you go to?"

That killed my laugh. "Uh… it's a small private school, you wouldn't know it."

"I go to a private school, too."

Sweat prickled the back of my neck. "I have to go. Mom is yelling at me to go to sleep. Wants me to get on schedule before school starts. Bye!"

I logged off before he could respond, my heart hammering in my chest. I flopped back on my bed and closed my eyes. *Stupid, stupid, stupid!*

But then, my phone buzzed, and a text from a new number came through.

Unknown: Sweet dreams, Stig.

I thought that was it, but after I brushed my teeth and crawled into bed, there was another one waiting for me.

Leo: I'm really glad I met you.

The next morning, my phone rang at seven AM. I answered blearily without even checking who it was, because I *never* got phone calls, let alone that early.

"Rise and shine," Leo said.

I bolted upright.

He called me?!

"Um... hi?"

"Figured I'd help your mom in her quest to get you ready for the school routine," he said. His voice sounded even warmer over the phone, more crisp than over the headset I was used to hearing him in. "Plus, I have football practice, and it just feels fair that you should have to get up at the same time as me since you kept me up so late."

"I kept *you* up?"

"All summer long. You really are a bad influence."

"Says the one who asked for a stranger's phone number online."

"And I don't have a single regret."

I flushed, flopping back onto my bed and covering the phone so he wouldn't hear my ridiculous little squeal.

"Hey, Stig?"

"Yeah?"

"Draw me something."

"What do you want me to draw?"

"Anything," he answered quickly. "Show me a part of who you are."

"Why?"

A pause. "Because I like you."

My eyes widened, heart hammering so loud I couldn't hear myself when I responded with a weak, "Okay."

"Okay," he said.

And even though I couldn't see him, I knew he was smiling.

Chapter 2

MARY

We talked every day, and every night, for the next two weeks.

I woke up to good morning texts that made me squeal and thrash in my covers, they made me so happy. At night, it seemed we spent less and less time playing games and more time on the phone, talking for hours until our throats were hoarse.

The first time he sent me a picture, I dropped my phone. Literally. It was just a selfie of him after summer practice, his hair a sweaty, matted mess, his lips chapped, skin red. But his smile was wide and blinding and all for me.

I didn't send a picture back, and he didn't push.

I loved playing Xbox with him. I loved when he texted me some stupid meme or told me a funny story about his family. I loved when he asked me if we were ever going to hang out in real life and then let me change the subject.

But my favorite nights were the ones he'd call me and we'd just lie there and talk.

Most of the time we laughed. Sometimes, we got so deep that I confessed things to him I never had to anyone else, and he did the same. Like the night I admitted I was afraid of never being enough for my mom, or the one where he told me he couldn't picture a life without football, and getting injured was his biggest fear.

Through it all, I drew for him.

"Are you ever going to show me what you're drawing?" he teased me every chance he could. "I'm starting to think you're a liar and you don't draw at all."

That's when I sent him a picture for the first time — a pulled-back view of a page of doodles in my sketchbook.

He fawned over it for days, pestering me even more to show him what I was making for him.

"I'll show you when it's ready," I kept promising.

The truth was, I was trying to work up the nerve to show him *in person*.

School started, and any balloons of hope I had that maybe this year would be different after what felt like a life-changing summer were popped immediately when I didn't even make it through the first day without multiple insults and being tripped in the cafeteria. Sometimes, I wished I was the invisible type of loser, the one who could escape all the bullying.

No such luck.

The words didn't hurt me — at least, not anymore. After years of enduring them, it was like being pierced through my skin with hundreds of needles until I was so used to the feeling that it felt normal. I'd become numb to all their insults — *goth, loser, nerd, fatty, crater face*

— whatever they threw at me, it was easy to roll my eyes at.

But when they shoved me, tripped me, threw their food into the garbage and laughed as it splashed up on me... those things were harder to brush off.

I felt each attack chip away at my already-scarce confidence, making me want to hide like a turtle in a shell. When it came to high school, excitement was the furthest thing from how I felt.

I just wanted to survive.

I didn't know when it happened, when I somehow went from a normal kid with a small but great group of friends to someone living life on the outside. I guess when my friends became more interested in boys than gaming, when they started wearing soft eye shadow and pink lip gloss and I opted for dramatic cat eyes and painting my smile burgundy, when they all slimmed down and I filled out — in every curve.

Somehow, somewhere along the way, I ostracized myself.

But this year would be different.

Because this year, I'd have Leo.

The first time I saw him at school, he was clowning around with some other players on the football team in the cafeteria before first period. I watched him with a smile before one of my only friends, Naya, elbowed me in the ribs.

"Why are you smiling at those assholes?"

I shrugged her off, frowning as I went back to doodling in my notebook. "I wasn't."

Naya loved anime and cosplay the way I loved video games and drawing. She also had a bearded dragon as a pet and an intolerance for jocks or anyone deemed popular in our school.

"Yes, you were."

"Shut up," I mumbled, and then I ignored her, focusing on my notebook until my phone buzzed with a text.

> **Leo:** You're right, school sucks. I miss summer days with you.

Every nerve in my body lit up as I read the text over and over, my eyes skirting to where Leo was across the cafeteria. He was laughing at something the quarterback had said, and then Lila White ran over and flopped down into his lap.

He wrapped his arms around her easily, but not in the way that made me feel even a little bit jealous. It was the way that said without words that he was uncomfortable, that he was just letting her sit there because he didn't want to answer questions if he pushed her off.

I smiled.

I liked that I knew him like that, that I could see right through his façade.

> **Me:** Call me tonight and we can pretend summer never ends.

As soon as I sent it, I watched him hastily dig his phone out of his pocket. He lit up with a smile as he read the text, and then he thumbed out a reply before tucking it away.

Later that night, I asked how his day was.

"Exhausting."

"Practice?"

"No, football is my release. It's the rest of it that wears me out."

"Like, classes?"

"Kind of. I don't know. It's like..." He paused, and I wished I could see him, could watch his body mannerisms in that moment. "Sometimes, I'm hanging out with all these people, all my *friends*, and I just look around and realize that I don't really know any of them at all, and they don't know me. Aside from football, I mean."

"You could tell them more about yourself," I offer. "Ask them to be real with you, too."

He laughed. "Yeah, right. The way they see me at my school, I'm just the class clown, you know? The jock who makes people laugh and has girls lining up at his locker."

I swallowed. "A whole line, huh?"

"Don't be jealous, Stig," he said, humor etched in his voice. "None of them compare to you."

"Oh, fuck off."

"I'm serious! They don't."

"*Anyway*," I said playfully, but mostly because I needed to change the subject before I melted into a puddle on the floor. "So, you feel like you have a role to play?"

"I guess so. Or maybe, as tiring as it is to play the role, it feels even more exhausting to try to change it."

"For what it's worth, I like you best when you're real, when you're open. You're funny, yeah, but... you're more than that."

Leo was silent for a long moment.

"I wish you'd tell me who you are," he said softly.

I swallowed. "Soon."

Another week passed with me living on the outskirts of Leo's life, in his periphery — there, but never really seen. I was happiest when he texted or called me. I was the most miserable when I was close enough to touch him and still somehow invisible. And it was in that time that I somehow found the courage I'd been searching for. Anxiety and fear still niggled at the back of my brain, but they were drowned out by the glowing orb of hope that whispered two words continually into my ear.

What if?

And so, on a crisp fall afternoon, I carried a notebook full of drawings tucked under my arm as I walked across campus toward the football field.

Practice would be over in twenty minutes, and I decided I was finally ready to tell Leo who I was.

Chapter 3
MARY

My armpits were swamps as I stood there on the track that circled the football field, clutching my notebook to my chest and watching as Leo wrapped up practice with his team. Everything inside me *screamed* to turn around and bolt, but I fought against instinct.

My poor body was trying to save me, and I wouldn't listen.

Instead, I stood as tall as I could, fingers trembling and heart racing. And when Leo was jogging past me with some of his teammates, I called out his name in a weak, cracking voice.

He slowed, head whipping in my direction, his damp, messy hair flowing like a slow motion commercial when he did. It stole my breath, seeing him that close after all the nights we'd spent together on the phone. His eyes were more golden than I'd ever realized, his jaw more defined, body glistening with sweat.

I waited for it, for the moment he looked into my eyes and just *knew* that it was me, that I was the girl he'd talked to every day and every night for most of the summer. I waited for his smile to spread, for him to run toward me and scoop me into his arms just like all the stupid movies had prepared me for.

Instead, he frowned, confusion etched in his brows as he slowed to a stop and walked a few hesitant steps toward me. "Yeah?"

I tried to ignore the way my heart sank, the way my nerves doubled when a few of his teammates stopped, too, looking at Leo, then me, then each other with this look that said *oh, this ought to be good*.

"H-hi," I breathed, swallowing and reminding myself to force an exhale.

Leo still looked confused, but he offered a small smile of mercy. "Hi."

"I'm sorry to bother you, I just..." Every word I'd planned to say flew out the window in my panic, but I knew I didn't need words. He'd know who I was without me having to tell him.

Because I was going to *show* him.

"I drew you this," I said, thrusting the sketchbook toward him.

My smile was confident, wide and gleaming, because I just *knew* he was going to get it. Who else would be *drawing* him something? Besides, he knew my voice. He knew *me*.

Leo looked back at his friends who were fighting off laughter, his brows still bent together when he turned to face me again. "Um... okay?"

He took the sketchbook from me, and a teammate behind him said, "Go on, what is it, Hernandez?"

Leo glanced at me before hesitantly opening the book to the first page. It was the simplest of the drawings I'd been curating for him since the night he asked me to, a fine-line sketch of things that made me think of summer — wildflowers, bumblebees, a rushing river.

When it didn't hit him after seeing it, when he just screwed up his face and glanced at me before flipping the page, my heart sank.

His friends watched over his shoulder, and when the page was flipped, they started laughing and yelling and hitting each other before one of them ripped the notebook out of his hands.

"What the hell? Did this crooked-teeth freak draw you *porn*?"

My cheeks flushed with a furious heat, and I made a mental note to never smile again. "It's not porn," I argued.

One of the guys flipped the book around toward me, showcasing the curvy girl who I felt looked like me. She was in a hoodie and leggings, what I usually wore when I played, and a boy in a football jersey held her in his arms, wrapped around her as they looked up at the stars.

The boy was supposed to be Leo.

If you looked closely, in our hands, there was a single Xbox controller — one we held together.

But Leo *didn't* look closely. In fact, he barely looked at all before he ripped the book away from his cackling friends and shoved it back into my chest.

"Look, I don't know what the hell this is supposed to be, but I don't want it."

His eyes locked on mine.

And what I saw reflected in them tore me to shreds.

He knew.

He *knew* it was me. It was written in every feature — the pity in his eyes, his furrowed brows, his rigid stance and heaving chest. And right then and there, I recognized the truth.

He knew it was me, and he didn't like what he saw.

"*You have no idea what I look like.*"

"*So?*"

How stupid I was for believing he meant that.

He couldn't even hold eye contact for more than a moment before he looked down at the ground between us, the book still extended toward me.

My throat burned as I snatched it out of his hands, willing the tears flooding my eyes to stay put and not release down my cheeks. "You're a liar, and a jerk, and I hope one day someone hurts you as bad as you just hurt me."

His friends broke out into a chorus of laughter, and one of them said, "Ohhh, you hear that, Hernandez? This fat, pimple-faced freak called you a *big bad jerk*!"

The boy's voice mimicked that of a little kid with those last few words, which made everyone crack up all over again.

And Leo didn't say a word.

He didn't stop them, didn't tell them to shut up and leave me alone, didn't defend me or even show an ounce of mercy. And when his friend threw an arm around him, leading him and the rest of the pack away from me, Leo looked back only once.

I thought I saw him mouth that he was sorry.

It only made me fume more.

A blink released the tears I'd been holding back, and they burned the memory into my brain forever as they seared down my cheeks.

I waited until I was home, until I was behind my bedroom door that I slammed vehemently. Then, I screamed and ripped at the pages of the notebook

"I *hate* you, Leo Hernandez," I seethed, tearing page after page. "I hate you, I hate you, I *hate* you."

Yanking the pages out of the notebook wasn't enough. When they littered my floor, I picked them each up and shredded them into tiny morsels until my bedroom floor was covered in paper snow. My chest was heaving by the time I finished, and then I collapsed right there in the middle of the pile.

And I cried.

No, I *sobbed*, until my lungs gave out and there were no more tears left in my ducts. Mom hesitantly knocked on my door, but I told her to go away, and I told Dad the same when he got home from work. I didn't join them for dinner. It felt like I'd never eat again, never sleep again, never be the same person I was before Leo destroyed me.

I tried to find reason, tried to remind myself that I was a high school girl and these emotions would pass. That's what Mom always told me when I was being dramatic. But nothing could pull the hurt, the *rage* from my heart — not this time.

That day fundamentally changed who I was.

The weak cage I'd tried to live in to please my parents, to be what they and everyone else in my life wanted me to be, was completely obliterated. I clawed at the bars, bending and warping them until I could step through. And on the other side, I was untamed, unfazed, unstoppable.

I decided right then and there that *nothing* and *no one* would ever hurt me again.

That evening, when Leo logged on and tried to request for me to play with him, I unfriended him. He called me immediately after, and when I didn't answer, he sent a text that I didn't even bother reading.

I blocked him on everything.

I unplugged my Xbox and made a plan to take it and all my games to GameStop and exchange it for a PlayStation, instead.

I shut the world out.

I shut who I used to *be* out.

And that night, when sleep wouldn't come, I didn't know a lot of things.

I didn't know how much worse things would get at school the next day. I didn't know that it was possible for an already-fractured heart to break even further. I didn't know that those asshole friends of Leo's took a picture of my drawing when I was busy looking at Leo. I didn't know they'd make copies and plaster it all over school with my hideous freshman school photo, that *pimple-faced porn freak* would become a nickname I'd never escape in all my high school years. I didn't know that Leo would laugh with them, that he'd never so much as look my way again, that he'd pretend I didn't even exist.

The biggest surprise of all?

I didn't know that six years later, when I was no longer even a semblance of the girl I was that summer I turned fifteen — Leo Hernandez would be my neighbor.

And a year after that... my roommate.

Chapter 4

NOW...SEVEN YEARS LATER
LEO

"Coach! Coach!"

I turned, setting my cup of Gatorade down on the folding table just in time to save it before I was run over by three eight-year-old kids in full padding. I scooped one up under my arm while the other two collided with my legs, their little hands around my waist.

"Did you see that?!" Keon said, pointing back at the field. His helmet was a bit too big for him and his head wobbled with the weight of it when he looked back up at me. "I hit him with the stiff arm, just like you said!"

"Did not!" Jordan combatted, releasing his grip on my waist only long enough to shove Keon backward a bit.

"Did, too!"

"I tripped."

"Yeah, because I *pushed you*. With my stiff arm."

"Yeah, but I tackled you, Keon," the little tyke under my arm pointed out, wiggling until I set him back down. "So that stiff arm doesn't really matter."

"I got twenty yards!" Keon combatted.

"Nuh-uh!" the other two said in unison, then they were all fighting, and I chuckled, bending until I was down on one knee and at their level.

"Alright, alright," I said, grabbing two of them by their shoulders. I gave them each a look until they quieted. "Keon, that was a damn good run. You should be proud of it."

Keon beamed.

"But," I added quickly. "There's a difference in someone who thinks he's good and someone who *knows* it — the main one being that when you know it, you don't need to brag about it."

"Yeah, Keon," Jordan said, crossing his arms.

"And Jordan, that was some great defense out there, but don't be too proud to admit when you could have done better. Why do you think Keon was able to shove you off so easily with that stiff arm?"

Jordan looked down at his cleats. "Because I didn't wrap him up."

"You didn't wrap him up," I echoed.

"But I did!" Mason beamed.

I swiveled until my eyes were on him. "Twenty yards later."

That quieted them all, though Keon wore a smirk.

"Look," I said, pulling them all in a bit closer. "You all did good. But you all could have done better. And I hate to break it to you, but that's football. In fact, that's football *on a good day*. Most of the time, you'll make mistakes that you know you shouldn't make, and then you have to dust yourself off and get right back on the line for the next play."

I pushed my finger into Keon's chest.

"The most important thing is that you stay humble, remember why you love this game, and put your team above your own personal stats. Instead of ragging on each other, cheer each other on. Jordan, that was a hell of a run Keon had, wasn't it?"

Jordan smiled at Keon, nudging his shoulder. "Yeah."

"Yeah. And, Mason, you wouldn't have been able to take Keon down if Jordan hadn't slowed him with that attempted tackle, huh?"

"Probably not. He's so fast," Mason said.

"And it was a great tackle," Keon said to Mason before I could prompt him. "You really wrapped me up, I couldn't break it even if I wanted to."

"See?" I said, thumping each of them playfully. "Now that's what makes you stronger as a player and team right there."

Coach Henderson's shadow washed over the four of us, and I stood to join him as he nodded toward the field. "Alright, you three, back out there."

"Yes, Coach!" they said in unison, and then they were jogging back out to play, laughing to each other instead of fighting.

Coach Henderson was the head coach of the Pee Wee team I'd been assisting him with since my sophomore year at North Boston University. It started as an accident, really — just me stuck on campus over the summer and bored, looking for something to do that wasn't conditioning. That was about all we could do during the summer without breaking the rules of college ball. There were no *real* practices until fall camp.

Henderson had seen how antsy I was and offered me this unpaid job — one I took without thinking twice.

"They're going to miss you next year," he commented as the kids lined up for another play.

"Ah, most of them will be moving on to the next level, anyway," I said. "And those who aren't won't be thinking of me."

"You'd be surprised. You've really made an impact with these kids." He paused, shaking his head. "Though I find you giving them advice on being *humble* quite comical."

"Hey, I'm as humble as they come," I said defensively.

"Right. What was it you said in that interview after the championship game last year?" He tapped his chin. "Oh, that's right. *I've broken two school records in my three years here, and by the time I leave, I'll break them all.*"

I blinked. "What? That's just facts. NBU has never had a running back like me and you know it."

He smirked and shook his head, clamping a hand on my shoulder. "Maybe just practice a bit of what you preach, eh, kid?"

I shrugged him off, but smiled, because maybe he was right. Maybe I could use a slice of humble pie on my plate now and then. But that just wasn't how I rolled. For me, the key to success had always been cockiness.

Play like hell. Rub it in every defender's face when they can't stop me. And remind anyone who asks that I'm the best there's ever been.

It didn't matter if it was true or not. When you said something enough, you started to believe it. And when you believed it, you became it.

Those were my father's words, and I held them like a creed.

My dad, Nick Parkinson, was and still *is* the best receiver to have ever played at Southern Alabama University. He was also a beast in the NFL until an injury ended his career, but not before he'd made enough cash and connections to set up a place for him in the sport forever. Now, while he spent most of his time as a commentator on television or an advisor for young players, he lived out the rest of his dream through me.

When Coach blew the final whistle of practice, I helped pack up before hitting the gym on campus. Some of my teammates slacked during the summer, only showing up for the bare minimum of what was required of them. But I wouldn't be caught dead doing the same.

Summer was what separated the good from the great, the college athletes from the ones who would go pro. I used every bit of my time working toward my ultimate goal.

To play in the NFL, just like my dad.

I was drenched in sweat by the time I climbed in my car to head to my campus home — affectionately known as The Snake Pit. It was the team house, bought in the 80s and passed on through generations and generations of players. It was home base, the house we partied at when we won and strategized at when we lost. It was old and decrepit and — now that our responsible, clean, and organized quarterback had graduated and gone pro — a lot messier than it used to be.

But it was home.

As I drove, one arm on the steering wheel and the other hanging out my driver side window, I soaked in the warmth of summer, the feeling this *particular* summer brought me. It was the last one of my school career, one final summer before senior year at North Boston University.

Before my final year of college ball.

We were champs now, coming off one of the hottest seasons in our school history. Going into the start of the season with that number one rank would be sweet, but it would also mean we had a target on our back — one I had full plans to make impossible to hit.

On the backend of the blissful, exciting feeling this summer brought me, there was a dark edge, a bottomless pit that would gladly swallow me up if I stopped running long enough to let it. It was an abyss created by a girl years ago, an endless hole left in the very center of who I was after the one and only person I'd ever felt a genuine connection to in my life ghosted me.

And I didn't even know her name.

I swallowed, shifting in the driver seat and taking my opposite hand to the wheel. Thoughts of that summer always made me squirm. I couldn't even remember who I was back then, and yet I knew that the realest I'd ever been with anyone, at any point in my life, was that summer.

With a stranger I met playing video games online.

It was so cliché and embarrassing that I'd never spoken it out loud to *anyone*. I couldn't. I had a reputation for being a playboy, a smart ass, a clown, a powerhouse, a fucking *star*. I loved that role. I *created* that role for myself. And I knew if I ever admitted to anyone what had happened that summer in high school, I'd become the joke itself instead of the joke*ster*.

No, it'd go to the grave with me.

And if I didn't ever learn to fucking let it go, it might be what puts me *in* said grave.

Whenever that darkness crept into my mind, I was always tempted to succumb to it. Part of me thought it might bring relief, to just slip into the unending spiral of questions that assaulted me seven years ago and begged for me to let them back in every day since.

I could beat myself up for an eternity wondering what went wrong, what I did, what happened. I could dive headfirst into anxiety that something bad had happened to *her,* that she had been kidnapped or sent to a boarding school by her parents or, the worst possibility, that she was dead.

I didn't know her name, but I knew *her*.

I knew the way she laughed when she was exhausted from staying up all night with me. I knew she never backed down from any challenge. I knew she was unapologetically and fearlessly herself, no matter what her parents or friends or anyone else thought. I knew she was funny, and adorable, and cool as hell. She played *video games*, for fuck's sake.

And I knew she knew *me*, at the most vulnerable and honest level, and she liked me. She cared about me.

Or maybe she didn't.

Maybe she never did.

Maybe she wasn't a kid like me at all. Maybe she was some weird creep living in her parents' basement at the age of thirty pretending to be a teenager so she could prey on young boys.

Even as I thought it, I knew it wasn't true. But sometimes it made me feel better to pretend that was the case, because the alternative was that she had just... left me.

And I'd never know why.

One quick shake of my head sent the shadow of all those thoughts scurrying away as I turned onto my street. I let out a heavy sigh as I pulled into the driveway, hopping out and grabbing my duffle bag out of the trunk. I slung it over my shoulder, locked my car with a click of the key fob, and was ready to head inside and take a shower before sitting down for a round of video games with my roommates.

But a glance across the street stopped me in my tracks.

Mary Silver stood in her yard with her hands hanging on her full, enticing hips, her gaze fixed on her house while some stocky older guy in a grimy t-shirt and worn jeans rattled on beside her. I could only see her profile, but I noticed how her brows were furrowed, how she was gnawing the corner of her plump bottom lip.

Mary had moved into that old house across the street from us last year — along with Julep Lee, our coach's daughter and, now, our previous quarterback's fiancée. Holden and Julep pretending like they didn't like each other provided many nights where Mary joined her roommate here at The Snake Pit for parties, and every time she walked through our front door, I ached with the need to touch her.

I couldn't help it.

Esa gata se vé riquísima.

The girl was *fine*.

I was used to being surrounded by a certain kind of female — cheerleaders, athletes, sorority girls. But none of them looked like Mary. Where they were typically lean and toned, Mary was curvy and soft, with thighs and hips and breasts that called to me as if she were Aphrodite reincarnated. She was covered in tattoos, the ink sprawling her skin from her neck to her ankles, and she had more piercings than I had touchdowns last season.

I'd been immediately intrigued by her from the moment I first saw her.

I'd also been immediately shut down.

She was immune to my charm, to the cocky lines I delivered with ease that usually had girls falling at my feet and, more often than not, dragging me to the nearest bedroom.

No, Mary seemed vexed by my very existence.

Naturally, that made me want her even more.

I watched as she shook her head, her long, golden hair gleaming in the sunlight as she did. Whatever was happening with Bob the Builder there by her side, it wasn't good.

It also wasn't any of my business.

But that didn't stop me from dropping my duffle bag on the ground by my car and walking across the street.

Chapter 5

MARY

"**M**onths?!"

I repeated the word back to the stout, almost too-muscular man staring back at me with an expression like he was bored with my concern. He was chewing on some sort of seed, and he spit out a shell before nodding and looking back at the house with one hand on his hip and the other holding his clipboard.

"It's very possible," he said with a thick New England accent. "I know that's not the news you or your landlord want to hear, but... the pipes are a mess."

"Clearly," I said, pinching the bridge of my nose as I recalled the flood inside the house. I'd come home to it after a late night at the tattoo parlor and had spent most of the early morning hours mopping up what I could with every towel in the house.

"It's going to take a while to assess the damage entirely, clean up enough of the mess to get to the root of the problems, and then fix said problems. Of course, you're going to need new floors, and then there's the walls, the ceiling..."

He must have noted the way my face crumpled more and more as he spoke, because he quieted, clearing his throat.

"The good news is it's fixable," he offered pathetically.

"Right. You just need to gut the entire system."

The man gave me an apologetic smile. "Ah, don't beat yourself up. Happens all the time with old houses like this, especially with the summers getting hotter and hotter. These pipes just can't take the expansion of the water when it gets hot like this after an already-brutal winter."

I wanted to beat my head against the nearest brick wall.

"I spoke with your landlord, and she wants this resolved just as quickly as you do."

"Mm-hmm," I said flatly, trying not to laugh as I pictured Miss Margie doing anything quickly. She was a doll, and an absolute saint for renting the house to me for the low price she did. But she was also a nutcase and moved at the pace of a snail on vacation.

It had been tight since Julep moved out. That traitor of a roommate had booked the first flight to Charlotte after her boyfriend — er, *fiancé* — was signed to the Panthers in April. Not that I didn't know it was coming, and not that she wasn't an angel for still paying her half through the end of our lease, but I'd been floating it all on my own ever since.

I was doing it. I was capable. But it wasn't easy, and I had been actively looking for a roommate to help make things easier for a few weeks now.

So much for that.

Now, I was homeless with no money saved and a paycheck that just barely helped me scrape by as it was. And, unlike many of the college kids who lived in this old neighborhood, I couldn't just call up my mom or dad and ask for money.

I mean, I *could*. But I wouldn't.

My pride, among other things, wouldn't allow that.

I was still standing with my arms folded, subtly pinching the inside of my rib cage just in case this was a nightmare I could wake up from, when someone sidled up beside me and nearly made me jump out of my skin.

"What's the problem?"

I pressed a hand against my heart from the scare, eyes wide until I turned and found Leo Hernandez standing beside me with concern etched into his brow.

Leo fucking Hernandez — North Boston University's star running back, most unobtainable bachelor, and number one on my *people I would murder if I could get away with it* list.

Also, my neighbor.

That had been a comically ironic discovery after I'd signed the lease with Julep last year. Had I known *before* signing, I'd have steered clear of this house, this street, hell — this entire neighborhood.

He looked like he was fresh from summer practice, sweat soaking the edges of his hairline and making his gray NBU football t-shirt stick to his chest. His hair was boyish in its length, messy and sticking up in a thousand different ways where it wasn't stuck to his forehead. His hazel eyes and warm brown skin were too much for most anyone attracted to males to resist, and when you combined it with a body built by years and years of football, it was the most unfortunately irresistible combination.

I used to think I loved him.

But that was before I hated him.

He folded his arms over his muscular chest, and it was then that I realized he'd ripped the sleeves off his shirt, showcasing his upper outer rib cage and every inch of his arms. I glanced at his bulging biceps for only a moment before I scoffed and rolled my eyes.

"Nothing that concerns you."

"As your neighbor, I beg to differ."

"This your boyfriend?" The man with the clipboard asked, pointing at Leo. "I can explain it to him, if you'd like."

I ground my teeth, both at the insinuation that I would ever date a pig-headed asshole like Leo Hernandez and that, as a woman, I needed a man whom the contractor could explain the pipe issue to in order for me to fully comprehend.

"He's no one," I grumbled, angling my body so that Leo was cut out of the circle that had somehow formed. "I'll speak with Margie about next steps. Thank you for your time."

The man looked between me and Leo a few times before shrugging, then he ripped off a copy of the assessment from his clipboard and handed it to me. "I recommend getting anything you care about out of there."

"Right," I said, again annoyed that he even felt the need to say that, as if it wasn't common sense.

He left along with the small crew he'd brought with him.

Leo, however, was still standing behind me once the truck pulled away.

"Did a pipe burst or something?"

"Go away," I clipped before heading for the house.

He was on my heels. "It sounds pretty serious."

I ignored him, opening the front door of the house and attempting to slam it in his face. But he caught it, and then he dipped his head through and whistled at what he saw.

It was a fucking mess.

Not just one pipe had burst. It was as if one gave out and the rest of the pipes decided they were tired, too, so they threw in the towel and joined the first. There was a giant hole in the ceiling where water had built and caused it to collapse, and if that were all I had to worry about, maybe I could have stayed. But the entire system had gone. Water was everywhere, and so was debris, and I just stared at it all with Leo at my side.

"You can't stay here," he said, assessing the damage with his thick brows bent together. His dark, messy hair was still half-stuck to his forehead, his lips a bit chapped from the sun as he looked around. How he made sweat and sun-damage so appealing was beyond me, and I filed it as just another reason to hate him.

And I already had plenty.

"Wow, where would I be without you to point out the obvious?"

He shook his head. "Do you have a place to go? Need a ride or anything?"

I made an exasperated noise in my throat and pushed inside, not caring at this point that he was still standing in my doorway. "My car isn't an issue, idiot. And I'm fine. You can leave now. Thank you for the neighborly concern."

I shot each word out like pellets from a gun chamber, surveying the house and trying to decide where to start, what I needed to get out, and what could possibly remain behind. The fact that I didn't have anywhere to move any of it was an issue I would deal with once Leo got out of my hair.

"You can stay with us."

I laughed — and not an amused laugh, but one that was laced with bitter anger and resentment.

"I'm serious," Leo said, pushing inside and carefully side-stepping where the ceiling had collapsed. "You don't even have to pay rent. Holden's room is free now since he and Julep moved to Charlotte."

I spun on my heels. "You really expect me to move in with you and two other football players?"

He shrugged, a cocky smirk playing on his lips. "What I expect is that you don't have as many options as you're acting like you do."

I clamped my mouth shut, jaw aching with how hard I ground my teeth. He was right. I didn't have a single option, really, other than stay a few nights at a hotel and try to find a cheap interim place on Craigslist. And even those options meant I'd have limited funds for things like food and gas after the fact. I was *trying* to work on a savings, but as an apprentice slash shop assistant, I didn't have much to make ends meet, let along stash aside for a rainy day.

I didn't think Margie would charge me rent while she fixed the place, but I also didn't think she'd let me completely out of the new lease I'd *just* re-signed.

Even if she did, I didn't have anywhere to go. And with fall just around the corner, I'd be fighting against the rush of NBU students trying to find places, too. I'd dealt with that nightmare time and time again already. The thought of having to face it again now made me want to fall into a heap on the floor and cry.

"Hear me out," he said, approaching me slowly when I didn't immediately respond. "You get to stay for free. It's right across the street, so you don't have to move all your stuff into storage or across town. You don't even have to change your mailing address. You have me and the other guys to help you move. You have your own room. We're clean…" He paused. "Ish."

I rolled my eyes.

"Did I mention it's free?"

I chewed my lip, hating how many good points he had. It wasn't like I didn't know the guys, either. I'd spent enough time partying or hanging out at The Pit now, thanks to Julep, that I felt like an adopted little sister.

It would be nice to not have to worry about paying rent for a while, to possibly get *some* sort of savings started…

I shook my head for even considering it, mentally slapping myself. This was Leo Hernandez, for God's sake. This was the prick who'd made my entire high school existence absolutely miserable and then completely forgotten about it because that was how little it mattered to him.

How little *I* mattered to him.

"I'll be fine," I said, turning on my heels.

His hand shot out, catching me by the crook of my elbow. Heat shot through me just as much as revulsion as I pulled away from the touch.

"Come on. Let us help you out. You're Julep's friend, and therefore, a friend of ours."

I narrowed my eyes at him. "Since when are you nice?"

He feigned offense, pressing a hand to his chest. "Me? I'm always nice. I'm the nicest guy you'll ever meet."

I blinked at him, ignoring the urge to refute that statement in a law-based manner complete with evidence and a jury of women I knew would find his ass guilty.

"Just... think about it. Here," he said, holding his hand out. "Give me your phone. I'll put my number in, and I promise not to say another word about it. But if you change your mind, one text and we'll be here helping you move everything out and across the street. We won't have anyone else in that room until fall, so you have at least a couple months, and it should all be fixed by then, right?"

I couldn't do anything but look at him and slowly blink again.

I loathed his existence, and yet in that moment, I saw a glimpse of the boy I used to know.

The boy I thought I knew, anyway — the one who was crushed under the pressure of what he thought he should be, who laughed in a particular kind of way when I surprised him, who had deep thoughts and feelings that he didn't share with anyone but me. I saw the boy who cared about the girl he stayed up with every night online.

"Phone," he said, wiggling his fingers.

I blamed the lack of sleep and the supreme yearning to get him out of my house for my actions next. I dug my phone out of my pocket and handed it to him. For a split second, I panicked, thinking that when he tried to text me, he'd be blocked. But I'd gotten off my parents' phone plan a couple years ago — another way of me asserting my independence — and so it would be a new number altogether, and a new area code, too.

He put his number in, sent a text to himself so he'd have my number, and then gave it back to me.

"One text," he said, and then true to his word, he turned and left.

"Fucking shit hammock," I muttered under my breath once he was gone.

I was exhausted, and angry, and stressed the fuck out. All I wanted to do was take a hot shower, get in my pajamas, and pack a bowl.

I didn't care how desperate things were. No way was I moving into The Pit with a house full of disgusting football players, especially not with Leo Hernandez being one of them.

•••

Three days later, I sent a text.

Me: Don't make me regret this.

One minute later, Leo wrote back.

Shit Hammock: That's a weird way to say thank you.

And within the hour, my house was full of football players hauling my belongings across the street.

Chapter 6

MARY

I hung my hands on my hips, staring at all my stuff crammed into Holden's room.

My room, now.

It was smaller than mine across the street, but still more than adequate. It had built-in bookshelves I could use for my tattoo machine, along with the needles, tips, tubes, and grips. The rest would be used to display my art. There was a small desk against the wall facing away from the window. I'd set up my gaming system there. The closet was actually *larger*, which was the biggest blessing of all. And though I was downgrading from a queen bed to a full, at least it was dry in here. I also had an en-suite bathroom and a window that overlooked the garden out back, one Holden had nurtured when he lived here.

I wondered who took care of it now.

"This isn't terrible," Giana said, startling me as she slid past me and right into the room. Her arms were full of my clothes that I was certain weighed more than she did, and she plopped them down on the bed before sitting next to them and catching her breath. She mopped her curls out of her face with one swipe of her hand and shoved her glasses back up the bridge of her nose. I marveled at how she'd shown up to help me move in a plaid skirt and thigh-high socks with whiskers at the top of them.

Riley came in after her, two boxes balanced in her arms. One of them had my textbooks and tattoo books in them, and the other was everything from my bathroom. The fact that she carried both of them like they were just a couple of pillows reminded me of all the strength packed into that tiny package.

What was it that her boyfriend called her?

Mighty Mouse.

She was in her usual athleisure, sporting NBU Football across the chest of her crop tank top. I wondered if she'd had that specifically made for her, since she was the only female on the team, and I doubted the staff had a crop top on the menu for team swag.

"I think you have more makeup than the entire Kappa Kappa Beta sorority house." She huffed once she set the boxes in the corner of the room.

"Makeup is to me what football is to you," I said.

"Wouldn't that be tattooing?" Giana argued.

I shrugged. "I don't know, they might be tied for first place in my heart."

I met Riley and Giana through Julep last year. Riley was the North Boston University football team's kicker and Giana worked for the team's Public Relations department. They were both dating football players, and I half-blamed them for not helping me talk sense into Julep when she was falling for Holden.

Then again, Julep was engaged now, so I guess it was me who was in the wrong.

I couldn't help it, projecting my own feelings toward football players onto my roommate when I saw so clearly that she was falling for the guy. Football players had ruined my life in high school, and as far as I was concerned, they were all assholes.

No matter how my three friends tried to prove that theory wrong.

I laughed internally, not missing the joke of me now *living* with three football players.

"I'm glad you took Leo up on his offer," Giana said after a moment. "I would have forced you to sleep on mine and Clay's couch otherwise."

I wrinkled my nose. "Yeah, no, thanks. I don't want to know the smutty book scenes that couch has been used to reenact."

Clay was the safety on the team, and he and Giana had been dating two seasons now. Of course, that first season, they were technically only *pretending* to date, but it still counted.

"You think the couches *here* are any better?" Riley popped a brow.

I buried my face in my hands. "I'm already regretting this."

"Regretting what?" a deep voice called behind me, and then Kyle Robbins was sliding into the room. He flopped onto the bed next to Giana, making her bounce into the air like she weighed nothing. "This is going to be the best time of your life."

"Ew, Kyle, you're sweaty! Get off," Giana said, pushing him away.

Kyle Robbins was the definition of a douchebag — at least, in my experience with him. He made the most of the Name, Image, and Likeness opportunities he had as a college athlete, signing every deal offered to him no matter what the brand was. I had to unfollow him on social media because I swore if I saw one more sponsored post that he tried and failed to make seem natural, I was going to roll my eyes so hard they fell out of my head.

Sometimes I wondered how he was even on the team after all these years and all the shit he'd pulled — including ostracizing Riley her first year and nearly fighting Holden over Julep last season.

But when he got on the field, it was easy to see why he never had to worry about losing his position on the team. He was a beast — tall, strong, and freakishly fast with hands that never missed a ball thrown within ten feet of him.

"Oh shit, is that... a *PlayStation*?" Kyle asked, his gaze on my console before he arched a brow at me. "You game?"

"Hell yeah, she does," Giana answered for me. I smirked a little at how proudly she said it, her chest puffed and chin high. "And she's a bad ass, too. I've watched her play."

"Huh," Kyle mused. "We need to get you on Xbox, then we can really see how good you are."

"Xbox is for twelve-year-old boys or grown men who live in their parents' garage who don't know how to play anything but First Person Shooter games," I shot back.

He chuffed. "Let me guess, you're more into RPG?"

"Games that require a little brain power instead of just a happy trigger finger? Yeah, I am."

Kyle smiled, leaning back on his palms. "If you were a dude, I'd rag on you. But I'm honestly impressed you game at all, so I'll let it slide."

"Gee, thanks. My whole life has been made with your approval," I deadpanned.

"I think we got the last of it," Braden Lock said, and he somehow managed to fit himself into the room with the rest of the zoo.

He had his arms full of clothes, too, and instead of tossing them on the bed, he moved to the closet and hung them all up as if the two-dozen hangers full of dresses and jackets and jeans didn't weigh more than a pound. He leaned his hip against the wall then, folding his arms and looking around.

Where Kyle was a clown, Braden was a teddy bear. He was short for a football player, five-eleven if I had to guess, and he spent his free time volunteering at our local homeless shelter as opposed to making deals with sneaker companies.

"I'm glad you got this room," he said, his eyes washing over the space. "Holden was the cleanest of us all when he lived here."

"Speak for yourself, Lock. My room is immaculate," Kyle argued.

Braden snorted. "Immaculately clouded with cologne. Hate to tell you, bro, but you can't cover up your farts no matter how much of that shit you spray."

Giana and Riley laughed as Kyle grabbed my pillow and threw it at his roommate.

Our roommate?

"Hey, uh, Mary?" a new voice said, and I closed my eyes on an internal groan because I'd know that voice anywhere — even if it had aged and deepened from when it used to fill my headset years ago. "Where does *this* go?"

I turned toward the hallway, the rest of the crew craning their necks to do the same. At the end of it near the top of the stairs stood Leo.

He was leaning against the wall, one leg crossed over the other and a casual indifference in his stance. His lips were curled up on one side like he knew every secret you never told. One hand was in the pocket of his joggers, his arm relaxed, and yet his bicep bulged like he'd just finished working out. And in his other hand...

Was my fucking dildo.

My eyes nearly popped out of my head as panic and embarrassment ripped through me, but I didn't let either one of those emotions latch on before I was storming the few steps toward him and yanking it out of his hand.

"What is *wrong* with you," I whisper-yelled through my teeth.

"Hey, you told us to get everything out of the nightstand. I figured that was the most important item." He nodded at the device clutched in my fist, and my neck heated even more as I tucked the thing behind my back and out of his view.

"What is it!?" Kyle asked, and then I turned just in time to find him and everyone else in the doorway, one head popping over the next like a bunch of fucking nesting dolls. All their eyes caught on the neon pink sex toy before I could turn and put it out of their view.

Kyle whistled at the same time Giana and Riley laughed. Giana's laugh was a little shy, her cheeks turning pink. Riley seemed impressed. Braden was the only one kind enough to pretend like he didn't see it as he dipped back into my room.

"Damn. Wouldn't want to be the man to compete with *that*," Kyle said with a smirk.

"Does that have multiple rotating levels?" Giana asked with an arched brow. "I think I read about one of those in a motorcycle club series last year."

I let out a frustrated growl before slapping Leo's shoulder with the only weapon in my hand before I realized what I was doing. "See what you did now?"

"What *I* did?" His mouth was hanging open. "You just hit me with your dildo."

That made everyone down the hall burst into a fit of laughter, but my cheeks only burned more. Normally, I'd have something to shoot back at him and deflate his ego, but I was currently going against every fiber in my being and moving into the same damn house with the one boy I hated. Add in the fact that, although I knew this teasing was harmless, it also poked the very sensitive bruise left behind after years of being bullied in high school.

My nerves were frayed. My brain was scrambled.

I was quite possibly making the worst decision of my life.

It was an easy one to make when the alternatives were so depressing — live in a hotel until I ran out of money, sleep on someone's couch, or, the worst of all, move home.

I swallowed, not even wanting to consider that a viable option.

But this...

This didn't feel like the right one, either.

"This was a mistake," I said, my voice a bit too quiet, and already I was marching down the hall. "I can find a hotel. I—"

My sentence was cut short when I was wrapped up from behind, and I squirmed in Leo's grip pointlessly as he carried me back toward the bedroom.

The fact that he could even *lift* me like this made it hard to say a word — I was not tiny the way Riley and Giana were — but the fact that I was pressed up against every inch of him with his arm porn wrapped around me sealed the deal. I felt those biceps like a straitjacket and a warm hug all at once, his chest and abs pressed against my back and ass in a way that made it impossible not to blush.

"Relax, *roomie*. We're just giving you a hard time."

His voice was right in my ear, his breath warm on the back of my neck, and I hated how chills broke out over my skin at the combination.

"Not as hard of a time as that guy in your hand, I imagine, but— *oof!*"

I cut his smart-ass remark short with a drive of my elbow into his gut.

"It's how we show love," Kyle added with a grin when I was carried through the threshold of my room against my will.

"Put me down," I said through my teeth.

Leo carefully set my feet back on the ground, my backside running down the length of him in the process. I ignored the heat crawling over me as I put distance between us and crossed to where my new nightstand was. I opened the top drawer and shoved the hot pink monster in there before slamming it shut and turning to face the room.

"If this is going to work, we need rules," I said.

"Rule number one: No hitting roommates with supersized sex toys." Leo held up his pointer finger with a mischievous smirk on his lips.

I ground my teeth, fingers curling into fists. I was ready to pull my toy back out and hurl it at his head before calling a moving company regardless of whether I could afford it or not. There had to be a seedy hotel in this city that could serve as a makeshift home for a couple of months without bleeding me dry.

Anything was better than this.

It was a mistake, one I made in a moment of desperation when it seemed like there were no other options. I was already moving to grab the first box off the floor and hike it back across the street when Braden put a hand on my shoulder, stopping me.

I looked up to find his soft blue eyes under bent brows, and I couldn't explain how or why, but just that one look made me release a slow, easy exhale.

"Hey," he said, squeezing where he held me. "Don't let these clowns get under your skin. Their humor off the field is almost as bad as their game on the field."

That earned him a snort from both the guys.

"We want to help," he said loudly enough to drown them out, and at that, he stood and pinned his roommates with a glare. "And if setting some ground rules will make you feel more comfortable, we're all ears. Right, guys?"

Kyle's cocky grin faltered a bit, and he nodded. "Of course. He's right, Mary — we don't want to make this any more difficult for you than it already is."

I relaxed a bit, and then all eyes were on Leo, who was watching me with an unreadable expression. It was almost like... *studying* me.

Like he just realized I looked familiar, but he couldn't place why.

"Leo," Braden scolded.

Leo shook his head, like he'd been snapped out of a daze. But his eyes wouldn't leave mine. He cleared his throat and then swept his hand over the room. "The floor is yours."

I straightened, smoothing my hands over my jeans. Then, I sighed, pinching the bridge of my nose as I closed my eyes. "I'm sorry. I know you guys were just joking around. And normally I'd be firing it right back, but I'm just... a little stressed."

"Understandably so," Riley pointed out.

I nodded, dropping my hand to my thigh. "We don't need rules. Well," I amended. "Maybe a couple. Like... just don't come in my room without my permission. Don't touch my stuff. Don't hit on me, even if it's a joke. Clean up after yourselves, especially in the common areas."

"Looking at you, Robbins," Braden chirped.

"Fuck off, I pick up after myself."

"Tell that to the pile of clothes by the front door that's started growing its own habitat," Riley chimed in.

"Hey, this is a roommates-only discussion, Novo," Kyle snipped. "Why don't you go play with your boyfriend."

"Gladly," she said, hopping off the bed. She crossed the room and wrapped me in a hug. "Please call me if you need help wrangling these guys. I've had plenty of practice the last three years." When she pulled back, she leveled her stare with me, dropping the joke. "Seriously. I'm here if you need me."

"Me, too," Giana piped in, and then her arms were around me and Riley both. "I left some new books for you on the shelf. They're my favorite comfort reads. Thought they might be nice for the adjustment period."

I sighed on a smile, hugging the two weirdos back. I wasn't really used to having friends — at least, not more than the ones I made playing games online. But I was really glad in that moment that Julep had changed that, and had introduced me to Riley and G.

"I'll be fine," I assured them.

"Yes, you will be. And this will all blow over soon. You'll be back across the street in a fixed-up house before you know it," Giana said.

Riley nodded toward the room. "Until then, feel free to use whatever means necessary to set these guys straight."

"We are still here, you know," Braden teased.

Riley smiled at him and leaned up on her toes to kiss his cheek before looping her arm through Giana's. They waved goodbye with a few more digs at Kyle on their way out.

My gaze snagged on Leo, who was unusually quiet, his arms folded as he watched everything take place. When the girls were gone, I cleared my throat.

"I think I just want to start unpacking."

"No more rules?" Kyle teased.

"Basically, she's saying be a decent human being. Think you can manage?" Braden asked, socking Kyle's arm as he passed. Kyle jumped up and started chasing after him. They were barreling down the stairs when I heard Braden call out, *"Welcome to The Pit, Mary!"*

And against all the stress wound through my body, I cracked a smile.

Until I remembered Leo was still in the room.

He pushed off the wall to stand, crossing the room and tucking his hands in his pockets. I resisted the urge to look down at where his pockets were in those dark gray joggers because they should have been illegal, for what little they left to the imagination. Why was he even *wearing* joggers, anyway? It was seventy-five degrees outside. He was sweating.

Don't think about his sweat, Mary.

"Hey, I'm sorry if I made this harder on you. I meant what I said the other day when all this went down. You're our friend, and we want to help."

I snorted a bit at the word *friend*, which only made Leo furrow his brows more.

"I'm serious."

I hated the sincerity in his eyes more than I hated him teasing me with my bright pink dildo.

"It's fine," I said, waving him off and crossing my arms over my chest. I looked around at the room so I didn't have to look at him. "I just want to get started unpacking."

"Want any help?"

"No."

I answered a little too quickly, a little too aggressively, but I didn't redact the sentiment. It was already going to be hard enough existing in the same space with Leo, I didn't want him thinking I wanted any kind of friendship.

"Alright," he conceded, running a hand back through his hair. "Well, when you're settled, I can show you around a little, give you the lay of the land. The washer and dryer are pretty old, need a little TLC when you want to use them."

"I'm sure I can manage."

He nodded. "I'll just leave you alone, then."

"Finally, I get my wish."

Leo smirked, but that damn question was still in his eyes as he turned and left me to it.

When I was alone, I flopped onto the bed and stared up at the ceiling.

I probably needed to call my parents and tell them what was happening, but just the thought of it made me want to pitch myself off the roof. I could hear Mom's condescending remarks already, could hear the way she'd belittle me and my choices before crying on my dad's shoulder to get his sympathy, as if to ask *what did I do to deserve a wild child disappointment like Mary?*

Dad wouldn't be mad. He'd likely barely react other than to ask if I was okay and if I needed anything. He'd probably wire money into my account without a word and then I'd have to pay the fees to wire it back to him because I'd refused to take anything from them since the day I moved out. Mom would then demand I come home, and he'd calm her, assuring her that I was an adult who could make my own choices, who knew what I was doing.

That was almost worse.

Because my father gave me his trust even when I didn't deserve it, and the truth was, I had *no idea* what I was doing.

All I knew for sure was that I didn't want to do anything Mom had pictured for me. I didn't want to go to college, or be in a sorority, or marry the first guy with a promising career path who came from good money. I didn't want the house and the yard and the two-and-a-half kids.

Still, I didn't necessarily want to be rooming with three smelly football players because I could barely afford gas in my car and a can of tomato soup, either.

I sighed, closing my eyes.

Temporary, I reminded myself. *This is all temporary.*

Then, deciding I was *technically* an adult and my parents didn't need to know everything, I peeled myself off the mattress and got to work.

Chapter 7
LEO

"Behind, behind," I yelled into my headset, and then I was getting lit up. "*Mierda!*" I turned my Legend around to fight back, thumbs pressing wildly on my controller. My screen was continually flashing red, the sound of gunfire popping off in my headphones.

I stuck my tongue out of the corner of my mouth in concentration, ignoring my character's depleting health until I hit the ground.

"Bleeding out," I called as I put up my shield, cursing when I saw how close I was to being eliminated. "Fuck. I'm knocked, but he's one shot!"

My teammate, BlueChip206 also known as Warren from Florida, got to me a second too late, but the fucker who had taken me out was still there.

"One shot, one shot!" I repeated, watching the scene unfold and powerless to help with my guy laid out on the ground. Once Warren took him out, he could revive me.

Except Warren was firing at him and he still didn't die.

Then, Warren got knocked, too.

The game ended, and I sucked my teeth, scrubbing my hands through my hair.

"He was not one shot, dude," Warren said with a huff.

I laughed a little at that.

"Alright, man, I'm getting off," he added a moment later.

"See ya," I replied, and then I checked the time on my phone. It was late, but I felt restless tonight. Always did in the summer. In the fall, I knew exactly who I was, what my purpose was, where to be and what to be doing. Summer made me feel a little aimless, like I was stuck in some sort of limbo waiting for my life to start again.

Everything had centered around football for me for so long, I didn't know what to do without it.

So, I prepped for one last game of *Apex Legends*. Might as well enjoy the late nights before early practices started.

A notification popped up assigning me my new teammate, and I was scrolling through the Legends deciding which one I wanted to play with next when I saw the username.

It made my stomach drop, my eyes scanning it beginning to end.

Octosquid68.

The breath that had hitched in my throat slowly deflated, my heart still racing even as I stared at the name and realized it wasn't what I thought. I didn't know why I even thought it would be. I hadn't seen that name on my screen in years.

Still, anytime I saw one that even resembled hers, it stopped me in my tracks.

A flash of something crossing the living room caught my attention, and I turned just in time to see long blonde waves of hair disappearing into the kitchen. I looked at the screen, then back at where Mary was visible through the little cutout window in the wall between the dining area and kitchen, and ultimately shut off the console with my heartbeat still a little unsteady.

Checking on our new roommate sounded like more fun, anyway.

I made my way to the archway that separated the rooms, the old house showing its age with the lack of open-space concept. I leaned against the frame, watching as Mary unloaded the small cooler we'd filled with what little she had in her fridge across the street.

I knew I needed to announce my presence, but I couldn't help but take a moment to just appreciate the view. I hadn't known Mary well over the last year of her being our neighbor across the street — not for lack of trying, but more because she made it very clear she wanted nothing to do with me or anyone else on the team. Still, I'd hung out with her enough to know she was always dolled up — dresses, boots, tattoos on display, and makeup like a movie star. Not like Julia Roberts movie star, but like Olivia Wilde. A little dark, a little edgy.

Always hot as hell.

But right now, she wore impossibly tight black leggings that hugged every curve of her hips and ass, and she was bent over, offering it all on a silver platter as she unloaded condiments from the cooler into the fridge.

I cleared my throat. "Need any help?"

She paused, one hand still on the cooler as she peered over her shoulder.

And *fuck* if that didn't make the view even harder to look away from. Now not only was she bent over, but she was bent over and looking back at me with those kohl-lined green eyes and pouty fucking lips.

"Does it look like I can't handle unloading a cooler?"

I bit back the urge to tell her I didn't think there was much of anything she couldn't handle.

Instead, I stepped fully into the kitchen, reaching over her head for a beer out of the fridge door before I hopped up to sit on the counter. I cracked the top on the can, sucking half of it down in one pull.

Mary just stared at me, offering one solo, slow blink before she shook her head and got back to what she was doing.

"Are you all settled in your new room?"

"As settled as I need to be for this temporary situation, yes."

I paused, something familiar about her voice striking me like a lightning bolt to the gut. It had happened earlier that day, too, and I couldn't explain it. I'd talked to Mary dozens of times since she and Julep moved across the street. Of course, her voice sounded familiar.

But it almost felt like something more than that.

I shook my head, blaming the weirdness on the heat stroke we all incurred moving Mary's shit.

"I'm sorry about earlier," I said after a moment, and I meant it.

It had all been fun and games until I'd seen regret in her eyes. For reasons I couldn't explain, it made me a little ill to think about her spending the night at some

Hail Mary

cheap motel with God knows who in the room next to her. I was glad she took me up on my offer — that we could help while they fixed up her place.

"Clowning around is kind of my default mode, but I know shit like that can be ill-timed. I didn't mean to upset you. I'm sure this is all—"

"It's fine," she said, cutting me off. "You can go back to your game now."

I smirked at the sassy interruption. She was already more herself than earlier. "Game's over. I think I'll hang out here, instead."

She didn't have to turn around for me to know she was rolling her eyes.

I didn't know why I loved to get under her skin so much. Probably because I was used to a very different reaction from most of the girls I encountered. The past three years had been easy for me. If I wanted a date, I could have one with the snap of my fingers. If I wanted a girl in my bed, I had a phone full of numbers I could shoot a text to and get just that.

But Mary Silver didn't give me anything other than slightly heated indifference.

It was sick how much I liked it.

That prickly nature wound me up in a way nothing else could. I liked that she wasn't simpering, that flirting with me seemed to be the furthest thing from her mind. Her sharp wit was just icing on the cake.

"We should game sometime," I said.

She froze, only for a second, but enough for me to notice before she grabbed a container of yogurt and slid it into the back of the fridge.

"Kyle told me you have a PlayStation."

"I doubt we play any of the same games."

"I could teach you."

She whipped around, narrowing her gaze at me with one eyebrow arched.

I threw up my hands with a laugh. "Or you could teach me, I didn't mean to assume."

She was still glaring at me as she turned back around.

"I'm not really into Battle Royale games," she said. "Or those weird ass faces you were making out there."

"I don't make faces."

She shut the fridge door and slowly stood, hands bracing on her knees as she did. "Oh?" She squinted her eyes, tongue sticking out of the corner of her mouth first before she started rolling it like she was trying to wet every inch of her lips. Her hands were braced in front of her holding an invisible controller, and she made sharp, shifty movements, looking like some kind of deranged animal.

Abruptly, she stopped, her face deadpan again.

"So you just look like that normally?"

I blinked at her, then barked out a laugh. "I wish I would have recorded that."

She didn't humor me with so much as another glance in my direction before she picked up the empty cooler and started walking toward the stairs. I hopped off the counter and followed.

"We can store that in the garage," I offered.

"It's fine, I have room in the closet."

"I find that hard to believe after the heaps of clothes we carried over today."

She sighed, still holding the cooler at the foot of the stairs as she turned to face me. "Is this how it's going to be until my place gets fixed? You buzzing around me like a gnat?"

I had a quip locked and loaded, but there was something about the way she looked at me in that moment that made it evaporate on my tongue. It was the same way she'd looked upstairs that had made me pause earlier — a softness in her eyes that wasn't normally present, defeat slumping her shoulders.

It felt... familiar, in a way I couldn't explain.

"I feel like I know you."

She arched a brow. "Trust me — you know absolutely nothing about me."

"No, I mean like I feel like we've met before."

Her lips tightened into a line, and with her hands still holding the cooler, she flicked her head back to get the fallen strands of hair out of her face.

I narrowed my eyes when she didn't answer. "Have we?"

She finally looked away from the stairs and directly at me.

I swore I shrank a few inches.

"Don't you think you'd remember if we had?"

The corner of my mouth kicked up at that. "Fair point. No way I'd forget meeting someone with such large..." My eyes trailed the length of her, appreciating the ample curves of her bust, her hips, her thighs. When I met her gaze again, she had an eyebrow quirked with a warning in her glare. "Tattoos," I finished.

Her lips flattened even more, and then she turned and headed up the stairs.

"I really would like to see them all, you know," I said, leaning against the bottom railing as she climbed.

"Go to bed, Leo."

"Come on, tell me about them. Just one."

"In your dreams."

"Yes, actually, among other things. Want me to detail them?"

She paused, turning on her heel to look down at me. "You're insufferable."

"I've been called worse."

She shook her head, but under her annoyed expression, I thought I saw hints of a smile.

"I'm too tired to deal with you," she said, turning to climb the last few stairs.

"Need someone to tuck you in?"

"Good*night*," she called when she dipped out of view, and I stood there at the bottom smiling even after I heard her door click closed.

Chapter 8

MARY

The first dust of dawn was falling over the city of Boston when I shook out my yoga mat on the back patio. It was surrounded by the lush garden Holden had grown in his time here, and I closed my eyes, inhaling the scent of flowers and herbs and vegetables as I wiggled my toes on my mat.

Usually, I'd wake and bake sometime around eleven, maybe even noon, before I'd settle in for a yoga session. But that was because under normal circumstances, I was at the tattoo parlor until two or three in the morning. I'd been off the last couple of nights to get my current situation under control, and it felt like a piece of me was missing.

I couldn't wait to get back tonight.

Still, even without being at the shop last night, I couldn't believe I was up this early. I blamed the lack of sleep in a new place.

Holden's bed was comfortable enough, and the house was quiet once the boys went to bed. But it felt like trying to sleep in a tree knowing creatures lurked in the forest around me. I was on edge, too aware, like I knew I didn't belong there. It was just... *strange*, and I couldn't fully relax.

I'd given up somewhere after midnight, tossing the covers off and deciding to wander the house. I used to have trouble sleeping when I was a kid, and I swore Dad was connected to me in a way no one else in the world was because he would sense it. He'd knock softly on my door, and then he'd tell me to put my shoes on and we'd go for a walk.

We never talked, just walked side by side around the block a couple times. It wouldn't take long to quiet my mind, still my heart, and find myself a bit more relaxed.

I always slept better after those walks.

Of course, last night, I didn't feel safe walking the neighborhood at midnight, even if we were in a relatively safe suburb. Instead, I walked around my new home, slowly taking in the eclectic décor as I ran my fingers down the walls. The Snake Pit had character, that much was easy to see. There were so many remnants of the past football players who had lived there — pictures, knick-knacks, scuffs on the walls.

Everyone who lived here left a small piece of them behind.

I still felt a little wound up when I finally ambled back to my bedroom, but I did manage a few hours of sleep before my body woke me with the desire to get on my mat.

With my eyes still closed, I inhaled, sweeping my arms overhead and stretching up to the sky. On an exhale, I folded, fingertips touching my toes as every kink in my back and hamstrings let go with a sigh. On a halfway lift, I inhaled, folded once more, and then easily stepped back for my first cobra into downward dog. It took me a few salutations to get fully ready, to really slip into the session.

I was on my third one when a *slap* sound had my eyes popping open.

I peered up and found Braden.

Shirtless.

"Mind if I join you?" he asked, his mat already laid out beside me.

"I didn't realize you practice."

"Good for mobility," he said simply, and then he was quiet, which I appreciated. I was worried for a moment I'd have another Leo on my hands. Instead, Braden moved through his own practice next to me, the only sound was our breaths as we flowed.

Once we were back in the rhythm, my brain decided to be an asshole and filter through the memory of last night. Leo pinning me with that curious gaze again, the way he'd said he felt like he knew me.

It was like a knife twisting in my gut.

Part of me wanted him to know, wanted him to remember what he'd done to me, to give even one small shit about the girl he hurt all those years ago.

The other part of me didn't want a single damn thing from him other than to be left alone.

I'd worked hard on letting go of what happened between us — both the good *and* the bad — and I didn't want to be reminded.

I wondered how impossible that would be now that his room was two doors down from mine.

And okay, so if I was being completely honest with myself, I hadn't truly done *that much* to let go of what had happened. In fact, I'd maybe done the opposite, holding on to those wretched memories and using them to form a block of protective ice around me.

I'd learned to live *despite* what happened to me. And maybe that made me stronger than if I'd just forgiven and forgotten.

Shaking off the thoughts, I sank back into my practice, and for the next forty minutes, it was just me, my body, and my breath.

It was around six thirty when Braden and I rolled up our mats and tucked them under our arms, walking back into the house. As soon as we shut the back door behind us, my nostrils were invaded with a sweet, mouth-watering aroma.

Braden moaned. "Fuck yeah, pancakes!"

He took off in a run, abandoning his mat at the door. He slid to a stop at the end of the hall and paused, turning back to me.

"Come on," he said, beckoning.

I didn't know why I felt so nervous, like I was intruding on something not meant for me. But I offered as best of a smile as I could before placing my mat next to his and following — albeit at a much slower pace.

More and more sound found me as I made my way toward the living room. Rap music, dishes and silverware tinkering, soft sizzling, and then a chorus of laughter. I saw a glimpse of Kyle through the kitchen window, a goofy grin on his face and his hair mussed as he flipped a pancake.

He was shirtless, too.

I didn't let myself take in his tall, lean build, or the muscles that lined it as I slowly made my way into the kitchen, pausing at the frame just like Leo had last night. And there all three of them were — Kyle making pancakes, Braden pulling plates from the cabinet, and Leo pouring coffee.

Every single one of them without a goddamn shirt.

It was really hard to remind myself in that moment that I hated football players with all those muscles gleaming back at me, the top edge of their boxers peeking out over the band of their shorts. Kyle wore tall tube socks, Braden was barefoot from practice, and Leo had on a pair of house slippers that should have made me laugh but somehow just made him look cozy in the way that had me itching to know what it would feel like to have him curled around me on the couch with the snow coming down outside.

I mentally slapped myself, and just in time for Leo to pop his head up and find me in the doorway. He had a sleepy sort of smile on at first, his hair curling around his ears, but when his eyes trailed the length of me in my leggings and sports bra, something heated his gaze.

"Well, good morning, roomie."

I folded my arms over my middle, wishing I'd stopped to put a shirt on. "Hi."

"You made it up just in time for my famous pancakes," Kyle said.

"She's been up for hours, dumb-dumb," Braden interjected. "We just finished yoga out back."

"You going to do Pilates next?" Kyle teased him.

Braden made a face before socking him on the arm as he passed. "Maybe. Both are great for mobility. Great for picking up girls, too, in case you didn't notice that I'm vastly outnumbered when I go to a class."

"We don't notice because, unlike you, we don't need to encroach on a women's fitness class to get laid," Leo shot back.

Kyle burst into a fit of laughter while Braden made a *ha-ha* face before grabbing a piece of bacon and hurling it at Leo. Leo opened his mouth and snagged it out of the air, chomping on it with a grin.

"You couldn't handle the mental side of yoga, anyway," I chimed in, sliding just a bit farther into the kitchen and leaning my hip against the counter.

Leo's eyes landed on me, pinning me to where I stood. It was then that I noticed a few chain necklaces around his neck — a cross, a plain gold chain, and was that a saint?

I almost snorted at that.

"Oh yeah?" he challenged. "And why's that?"

"Because you'd have to drop your ego, and we all know you cling to yours like a life raft in the middle of the ocean."

A laugh fizzled out of Braden and Kyle both.

"I'm as humble as a priest," Leo said, pressing a hand to his chest.

"And as full of shit as a porta-potty."

Kyle and Braden let out mixed sounds of laughter and jest as Leo stared at me, an amused smile curling on his lips. I blinked and looked away, hoping he could see I was bored by our interaction.

At least, that's what I wanted him to think.

The truth might have rested more in the fact that if I stared at him any longer, I'd start tracing those flecks of gold in his eyes, start remembering how that voice used to sound on the other end of the phone every night.

"Ladies first," Kyle said, plating a couple pancakes for me. "This one I made especially for you. Welcome to The Pit, roomie."

When he handed me the plate, I looked down to find a smiley face made out of chocolate chips staring back at me from the top pancake.

And the first genuine smile in days found my lips.

I arched a brow when I looked back up at him. "I thought you were a douchebag."

Something softened his face then, like that actually hurt to hear, but he quickly laughed it off with a shrug. "I am. But I'm trying to make up for being an asshole yesterday. There's a difference between the two, you know."

"Yeah. Kyle's a douche," Braden said, piling a stack of pancakes on his plate. "But Leo's an asshole."

"And Braden's a pussy," Leo quipped.

I instantly flung my arm out, swatting his chest with the back of my hand and a loud *thwap*. "What the hell is that supposed to mean?"

Braden snickered while Leo stared at me open-mouthed, rubbing the spot I'd just hit. "I was just—"

"You were just using female anatomy as an insult because in your Neanderthal brain, pussy is less than dick — weaker, not as important."

"On the contrary," Leo said, his lips curling as he stepped a little closer. "I think pussy is the most powerful thing in the world."

"So you were complimenting him?" I challenged.

Braden shook his head, slipping in between where I was glaring at Leo, and he was smiling like the Cheshire cat.

"Alright, alright," Braden said, holding a hand up to me and his plate of pancakes against Leo's chest. "Break it up. We don't need a fight this early in the morning. Besides, like I said, Leo's an ass," he said to me with a shrug. "We don't take anything he says too seriously."

Braden popped a piece of bacon into his mouth with that, exiting the kitchen and heading toward the living room with his food. I turned my glare back to Leo, ready to square off, but all the humor had faded from his expression. He almost looked a little... *sad*.

I thought about when we were younger, about the nights we talked until we were hoarse and bleary-eyed.

"Sometimes, I'm hanging out with all these people, all my friends, and I just look around and realize that I don't really know any of them at all, and they don't know me. Aside from football, I mean."

An unwanted emotion caught in my throat, my brows bending together as I watched Leo. But he didn't look at me again. Instead, he took a breath and put his cocky smirk back on his face before clapping Kyle on the shoulder as he plated his last pancake.

"Thanks for breakfast, man."

"Thanks for the coffee. I swear, no one makes it better than you."

"*La jefa* is the only one, and she'd disown me if I didn't live up to her legacy now that I'm on my own."

"*La jefa*?" I asked as Leo filled his own plate, and we all plopped down on the couch to eat. There *was* a folding table that could serve as a dining table, but it was currently sticky from what I could only hope was beer and not the alternative.

"The boss. In other words, *mi madre*." Leo winked, and then the attention of my roommates shifted to the television where Braden had just turned on ESPN.

I smiled, but again, something pulled at my chest. Because I knew probably better than his roommates how special Leo's relationship was with his mom. She and his dad had split up when she was pregnant with him, and so she'd given him her last name instead of his dad's when Leo was born. And while his father pushed him to follow in his footsteps, his mom always gave him space to be whatever he wanted to.

Of course, Leo didn't play football because of his dad. He played it because it was in the very fibers of who he was. Still, I wondered what it was like to have even one parent who supported you in that way.

My dad tried, he did. He was gentle with me in a way that Mom never could be. Still, I saw the disappointment in his eyes when I told him I didn't want to go to college, when he realized I meant it when I said I wanted to be a tattoo artist.

He didn't stop me, but he didn't support me, either.

That hurt just the same.

I looked down at the smiley face that was melted into my pancakes now, and then up at the three shirtless boys chowing down on their massive stacks that could have fed a family of four each.

For the first time, I felt myself take a real breath and relax.

"Thank you," I said out of nowhere, and all the guys swiveled their heads toward me. "For letting me stay here. It… it's really kind of you. And I…" I swallowed, looking down at my plate. "I don't know what I'd do otherwise."

Kyle reached over from where he sat on the couch and thumped my knee. "Hey, we're happy to have you."

"Just remember how thankful you are when our mess starts to creep in," Leo added. "We might have spent two hours cleaning before we started moving you in yesterday."

"*I* am always clean," Braden argued.

And then they were bickering again, tossing bits of food at each other and slinging insults like it was their love language.

I smiled.

Maybe it really was.

Chapter 9

LEO

"The twenty-seven exes of Leo Hernandez," Coach Lee read off loud and proud, as if I wasn't seeing the words on his computer monitor. Just under the headline was a picture of me at one of the parties we'd had at The Pit after winning the championship game last season. I had two girls under each arm, and though their faces were blurred, their scantily clad bodies were not.

Coach lifted a brow at me while Giana covered a little cough with her fist in the corner, pretending to write something in her notebook so she didn't have to look at me. I hadn't seen her since she helped us move Mary in last week, and I had been glad for it, for the break from doing press.

I had a feeling that was about to change.

"The number is *probably* closer to thirty-seven, if we're being picky here," I said with a smirk. That was my defense mechanism, like the old black and white movie my mom used to watch when she was having a bad day — *Singin' in the Rain.* I lived my life like Donald O'Connor.

Make 'em laugh, make 'em laugh...

Coach wasn't having it, though, and his stern expression said as much.

I sighed, sitting back in my chair and folding my arms over my chest. "It's a sorority-run blog. It's not like it's the Associated Press."

"No, but one of the girls made it into a video which has now gone viral," Giana said, and when I looked at her, she cringed, like she was sorry she had to be the one to break the news. "And this morning, it showed up on the *College Sports Network* when they were talking about predictions for this upcoming season."

"And the only prediction they have for *you* is that you'll get a girl knocked up," Coach clipped.

"Coach, come on," I said, leveling a gaze at him. "You know me better than that. I'm careful. I'm—"

"Wasting your talent on the field by acting like an amateur off it?" he shot back. "Yes, you are."

I zipped my lips closed, settling into my chair even more when I realized I wasn't getting out of this lashing. Coach Lee was as severe as he was untouchable as a head football coach. He'd come in guns blazing as our new coach last season, a legend out of Alabama with a reputation that far preceded him. My father was ecstatic when he heard the news, because in his eyes, anyone who played or coached in Alabama was in a league above the rest.

Coach Lee came in, and in one season had taken us all the way to the championship game.

We brought the trophy home, and I knew a lot of it was thanks to him.

But he was also a little too condescending for my taste, and no matter how many times I'd hung out with him outside of practice, whether it be at The Pit or at some family event with Holden and Coach Lee's daughter, it seemed his opinion of me never changed.

Then again, I guess I wasn't helping matters by playing into the role I'd created.

"Leo," Giana said softly, calling my attention to her. "You're an amazing player, and you know how to charm the wings off a bird. Whenever I call on you for press, I know you're going to hit it out of the park."

"And *I* know when I call on you for a run, you're going to get the first down or wreak havoc trying," Coach added. He leaned forward, resting his elbows on his desk and folding his hands together. "But here's the thing — it doesn't matter how well you do on the field. If the GMs think you're a liability, they won't think twice about skimming right past your name when it comes time for the draft."

I snorted. "And getting laid makes me a liability?"

"Your attitude makes you a liability," Coach snapped, his tone one that demanded I remember my place. "The way you strut into practice late, spend your time on the sidelines at every game making eyes at girls in the stands, and all your extracurricular activities that get more attention than you think."

I stayed silent, resisting the urge to point out how I volunteered with Pee Wee football every summer, how I mentored high school kids in the fall, how I got straight fucking As in all my classes in a major that was twice as hard as the bullshit ones most of my teammates declared. The truth was none of that mattered, because to the media, it was boring.

They'd rather play my same cocky remark during a post-game interview over and over on the highlight reels as they debate whether I have a shot going pro or not.

But that was the thing — I *knew* what they wanted, what got their attention and put me on their programs. It was fine to be a great running back, but we had a nation full of those. There were also plenty of kids volunteering and acing their classes.

If I wanted to stand out, I had to give them a reason to remember my name.

And if there was one thing I was good at besides football, it was causing a scene.

The way Coach and Giana were looking at me now, though, I guessed I'd taken it a little too far. It was one thing to have general managers know your name. It was another entirely to have your name at the top of their mind when they thought about players they *didn't* want to draft.

"Maybe just... tighten up a little this season," Giana recommended. "Focus on football and not so much on the girls. I can set up a couple volunteer opportunities, and we can get a one-on-one interview for you before the opening game."

"No."

My response surprised them both. "No?" Coach repeated with a warning edge to his tone.

"I hate that shit. They just want to probe into your family or personal life, get some sob story out of you so they can plaster it all over the news. Look at how they treated Holden last season when he was inching toward the draft. You couldn't turn on *SportsCenter* without seeing pictures of his dead family flashing on the screen."

"And look where he is now," Coach said without hesitation.

I sighed, sinking even farther into my chair.

"It doesn't have to be super personal," Giana offered softly. "Just... open up a little. Show them you're more than the cocky running back they think you are."

I wanted to roll my eyes so badly, but I refrained. "Fine."

Coach and Giana shared a look before he dismissed us both with a nod. Giana stood, and I bolted out of the office first with her on my heels.

"Hey," she said, catching the crook of my arm. "I'm sorry about that back there. I wanted to handle it with you myself, but..."

"I know."

She nodded. "It's just... I think he sees a lot of potential in you, Leo. He knows you can be great — you already are."

I sighed, but knew she was right. Coach Lee didn't know how to show his love to his players only to come down hard on us. I'd seen that firsthand with Holden last season, and with any other player he thought had a chance. He was much harder on me, Clay, Kyle, Zeke, and Riley than any other seniors. He thought we had potential.

Still, it thoroughly pissed me off that he couldn't see past the superficial bullshit and realize I was already doing all the things he wanted me to. I was a part of our community — not because they asked, but because I wanted to be. I was doing well in school. I was performing on the field.

So what if I was confident in my interviews? They loved that shit. That's why my clips got more airtime than anyone else's. And who said this kind of publicity was bad? Isn't *all* publicity good, in a way?

"How's it going with Mary?"

I blinked at the rapid change in subject, and a flash of Mary and her big green eyes hit me like a ball out of left field.

"Good," I answered. "I think she's feeling more comfortable than last week."

"You guys are being nice to her?"

I smirked. "*Very* nice."

Giana narrowed her eyes. "Don't be cute."

"Impossible not to."

"I'll see you later," she said with a roll of her eyes. She pointed her pen at me as she backed away. "Angel behavior, got it?"

I drew a halo around my head before pressing my hands together in mock prayer. She turned with a smile, and then I dropped my hands, a long exhale leaving me.

I was already dreading the interviews Giana would set up, the inevitable questions that would come. No matter how G tried to keep them on track, I knew from experience that reporters wanted the dirt. They'd ask about that article, and about the girls in my life — emphasis on the plural.

If I told them the truth, they'd be let down.

They loved to believe I was this big player, fucking anything with tits that walked past me. *That* said athlete. *That* said cocky son-of-a-bitch.

If they knew that of those twenty-seven girls in that article, I'd only slept with four of them?

They'd be much less interested.

Did I love the attention girls gave me as a college football player? Hell fucking yeah, I did. Who was I to turn down a girl who wanted to dance at a club, or makeout at The Pit, or take a body shot, or wear my jersey to the games?

But something soft about me that I wouldn't admit to anyone other than my mother was that I needed to feel a connection to a woman before I wanted to fuck her.

I had no problem making out, or even hitting second base with someone I didn't have feelings for. I was a man, after all, and I much preferred a random girl's mouth to my hand. But when it came to stripping down — literally and figuratively — I was a lot more picky.

I needed to feel something.

I couldn't lay a stranger down and look into her eyes in a moment so intimate, in a situation where I felt so vulnerable, and not know a single thing about her or feel like she didn't know me. I couldn't fuck a girl and then immediately put my clothes on and leave, or ask her to do the same.

I needed to relate to her, be intrigued by her, be *comforted* by her.

And for that, I blamed the first girl who ever made me feel that way.

I dragged my ass down the stadium hallway, passing by the locker room and heading straight for the weight room, instead. I barely warmed up before I set up at the angled leg press, stacking three-hundred pounds of plates on the machine before I sat down and huffed out the first set of reps. I felt some of the tension melt out of me, but my thoughts didn't quiet.

I let my head fall back against the bench, staring at my sneakers as I caught my breath.

I didn't even know her name.

That was what bothered me most all these years later. It made me sick that she ghosted me. It coiled my guts to think that something might have happened to her. It made me furious that I didn't push harder to meet in person, to put a face to the girl who had permanent residence in my head and my heart.

But not knowing her name?

That meant I didn't have a prayer of ever finding her.

I shook my head. "Stop being such a fucking pu—"

The word died on my lips, and I paused before a little laugh exhaled out of me remembering how Mary had slapped me the last time I'd used that word as an insult.

Pulling the latches at my side, I focused on my core and my breathing as I repped out another set, and then I locked the weight back into place, legs burning.

I didn't want to think about my past anymore, about the fact that I was hung up on someone who likely never thought of me now. She would be in college, too — or maybe graduated already. Or maybe she didn't go to college at all.

Maybe she had a boyfriend. Maybe she was already married and knocked up.

I'd never know.

"Let it go, man," I urged myself, and then I unlocked the weight again, prepping my breath before I brought my knees to my chest and then powered them straight again. Over and over, I pushed until my heart was racing and my legs were on fire.

And finally, my thoughts drifted away.

For the next hour, it was just me and the weight room. I was the only player in there, and I didn't even put on headphones like I typically did. I savored the silence, savored the way my body took the pain and pressure off my heart.

One day, I'd wake up and not even think of her at all.

One day, I'd meet someone new, someone who made me feel the way she did, but stronger.

One day.

Until then, I had football.

That was all I needed.

●●●

I was exhausted by the time I dragged my ass back to The Pit. Between the early morning conditioning, the whipping from Coach, the punishment I self-inflicted in the weight room and an entire afternoon of Pee Wee practice, I was ready to collapse before I even made it through the door.

When I did, I ran smack into Mary.

I opened the front door and blew through it, and when I turned to the left to immediately toss my gym bag onto the disgusting cushion under our bay window, I collided with her, knocking her so hard she nearly toppled over the arm of the couch. My bag and her purse both crashed onto the old hardwood floor, but I focused on making sure she didn't join them.

My hands shot out, catching her by the hips just as the back of her knees hit the couch. She angled back with a surprised squeak, arms windmilling, but I kept her from going down, pulling her back up onto her feet.

Her eyes were wide when she was upright again, chest heaving a bit like I'd scared the shit out of her. I guessed I probably had, swinging through the door like a bat out of hell and nearly tackling her. I kept my hands braced on her waist, making sure she was steady, and her hands had found my shoulders once they stopped flailing about.

Now, we were about two inches apart, and I took the lack of distance as an excuse to soak her in.

I was so used to being kept at a distance, but now, I could see every curve the burnt orange dress she was wearing hugged, and every little tattoo peeking out from under the fabric. I noted the flowers wrapping her shoulders, the little bumble bee nestled under her collarbone, the impressive sternum piece that spanned her chest and disappeared under her dress. She wasn't wearing a bra, either, her breasts gaping enough for me to see how that tattoo dipped between them. I followed the black lines of that ink until I couldn't see any farther, and then lingered on the outline of the metal piercing her nipples.

Fuck me.

My eyes dropped to where my hands held her hips, continuing down to where the ink began again under the hem of her dress, coloring her thighs and knees and shins all the way to her black boots.

I took my time trailing my gaze back up, and when my eyes met hers, she lifted her chin marginally, as if I were a predator and she wanted to prove she wasn't afraid of me. Her septum piercing glinted in the light, and I noted how her throat constricted with a thick swallow before she pressed her hands into my chest and shoved me away.

"Can you watch where you're going?" she said, annoyance evident in her voice. Then she looked down to where the contents of her purse had spilled out, sighing as she dropped to her knees to start picking it all up.

I was really tempted to stand there and enjoy that view, but good sense found me and I bent to help her.

"Sorry," I said, scooping up a lipstick and mascara and dumping them into her bag. "I didn't expect anyone to be home."

We finished gathering her belongings off the floor, and I held out a hand to help her stand. She looked at it, scoffed, and used the couch, instead.

"Where are you off to?" I asked.

"I'm sorry, are you my daddy now?"

"In every single one of my dreams."

Mary folded her arms over her chest, that usual bored expression she loved to wear settling in and erasing any trace of that curiosity that had been there before. I'd felt it, though — the way her breath hitched when I had my hands on her.

It gave me the confidence to pin her with a cocky grin that told her I saw right through the act.

She flattened her lips. "You look like hell, by the way."

"And you look like a snack," I shot back. "We haven't given you a proper tour of the house yet, have we? We could do that now, start with my bedroom…"

I thought I saw a flicker of something in her eyes — amusement, maybe? Desire? The temptation to say yes to my offer just to see if I made good on it?

But she just shook her head, pressing her tongue into her cheek as she scrutinized me. "That *actually* works for you, doesn't it?"

She looked almost sorry for me as she pushed past, and all the playfulness died with that look. I closed my eyes, internally groaning at the idiotic comment as my hand shot out, catching the crook of her elbow and spinning her back around before she could reach the door.

"Wait," I said.

She shook me off. "Stop touching me."

"Sorry." I threw my hands up in surrender. "For the bedroom comment, too. It's been a long day and I was just—"

"Joking. Yes, I'm aware," she said, folding her arms over her chest again. I thought she was going to lay into me, but she just fell silent, her eyes flicking between mine.

I shifted under that lingering gaze.

"What happened?" she asked.

"What do you mean?"

"You said it's been a long day. What happened?"

I sighed, raking a hand back through my hair as I looked away from her and out the bay window. "Just some media bullshit."

Mary frowned. "What'd you do?"

I chuckled. "Why do you automatically assume I did something?"

All she did was arch a brow.

"Some sorority girl wrote a story about me being a player, essentially," I said, shrugging. "*The twenty-seven exes of Leo Hernandez.*"

"Twenty-seven, huh?" Mary let out a little whistle. "Impressive. All in the same sorority?"

"Of course not. I'm not a monster." I grinned. "I try to keep it to five per house."

It was a joke, one that came so easily from me I was almost surprised. Almost being the key word, because it was easier for this front to slip out than anything close to the truth.

It was clear to me that the way I presented myself was exactly how Mary saw me, too, when she rolled her eyes.

"So, the article is accurate, then?"

"What do you think?" I challenged.

She tilted her head a bit to the side, and again, I felt myself want to fidget under the weight of her gaze. The longer it lingered, the more I felt like she was stripping me down without my permission.

"I think you've gotten really good at playing the part."

Her words shocked me silent, all traces of humor leaving me at the sound of them. "What part is that?"

The corner of her mouth tilted up, but then she dropped her gaze, fishing her keys out of her purse. "I have to run. I have some laundry in the dryer, but I'll take care of it later." She pointed a key at me, then. "Don't touch it."

"What, you don't want us to do something nice for our new roommate like fold her clothes?"

"I don't want one of you perverts stealing my panties."

"Oh, now *there's* an idea…"

"Leo," she threatened, poking that key out even more.

I chuckled. "Don't worry, your thongs are safe. Now, your hot pink friend upstairs, on the other hand…"

Mary sucked her teeth before turning on her heels and swinging out the front door. "GOODBYE."

I smiled until she was gone, thankful she left on a more playful note.

But once she was gone and the house was silent, that smile slipped.

And her words replayed in my mind for the rest of the night.

Chapter 10

MARY

I never thought I'd be so happy scrubbing a toilet, but here I was with rubber gloves, bleach, and a giant ass grin on my face.

Because today, I would get to tattoo *skin*.

Not fake skin, not a grapefruit, not *my* skin — but a real live human being who trusted me enough to lay permanent ink into their body.

It was all I could do not to hum and skip around the shop as I cleaned, making sure it looked pristine from the moment the client walked through the door all the way back to the bathroom. I sanitized the iPads at the front desk, tidied up all the artist stations, swept and mopped and ordered the supplies we were running low on. All the while, the shop buzzed with conversation between artist and client, bass-heavy deep house music playing as a background to all of it.

"Mary, do you know where the—"

I handed a fresh bottle of black ink to Tray before they could finish their sentence, and they chuckled, taking it out of my hand.

"Don't know where we'd be without you," they said, the light gleaming off their turquoise hair.

"I'm sure you'd find someone else who could stock the shelves."

"Maybe. But no one else who could organize our lives the way you do."

With one last smile, Tray skipped over to where their client was waiting, and I beamed under the praise even if I knew it was superficial. *Anyone* could do my job, really, except for the tattooing part. But that was only really starting today.

Today.

I was tattooing skin today!

With more pep in my step, I continued through the shop, stopping by each artist station to make sure they had everything they needed for the week.

I was used to these duties — they were the same ones I'd had since I started as an apprentice at Moonstruck Tattoos over a year ago now. In the time I'd been here, I'd spent half my hours cleaning the shop like it was my home, and the other half studying every artist in here, notebook in tow, my eyes trained on their hands and watching their every movement.

My boss and the owner of the shop, Nero, was my favorite to shadow.

Not only was he skilled in a way I aspired to be, with steady hands and perfect lines and shading that made me physically drool, but he was also so comfortable in his work that he could answer my questions without a hint of annoyance in his voice. I'd peer over his massive shoulder and ask why he chose a specific needle, and he'd answer in full detail without breaking concentration with his art. I never had to wait for a break or worry I'd mess him up when a question popped into my head, and if anything, he'd give me a look of disappointment if too much time went by *without* me asking a question.

The rest of the artists?

Well, they all had their own ways of teaching, and most of them preferred me to stay unseen and quiet until they were done with their work before I asked anything.

I'd first come around Moonstruck as a fresh-skinned eighteen-year-old just desperate to get some ink on me. I'd still lived with my parents then, and Mom had *actually* fainted when she saw my first one — a little heart on my ribcage that I thought I would be able to hide.

And I had, until she'd accidentally walked in on me changing one morning.

After that, the rule was no more tattoos while I lived under their roof.

Naturally, that meant I had to leave.

My first apartment was a shanty that Dad didn't really want me moving into, but I told him he didn't have a choice. I worked day and night at a restaurant, hosting and bussing at first before I finally got bumped up to waitressing and could make some decent tips.

And any time I wasn't spending *making* money, I was here — spending it.

I had a little piece of every artist who worked here on me, some more than others, and once I learned enough from them to feel confident trying it on my own, I was tattooing any piece of my skin I could reach.

Finally, maybe more out of pity than anything, Nero offered me an apprenticeship.

I'd never said yes to anything so fast.

In my year tenure, I'd learned that what made the difference between a good tattoo artist and a great one was style.

You had to have a voice, a vibe, an aesthetic — one that called to a certain kind of clientele. If you failed to have a style, you would end up doing the kind of tattoos brought in off the Internet, the ones with no artistic freedom. *Hey, can you do this exact lotus flower on my wrist? How about the word 'breathe' in a script font you just trace from the stencil?*

Not that there was anything *wrong* with those kinds of tattoos — in fact, I was over the goddamn moon about the fact that I got to do a flower and script tattoo on a willing client today. I didn't care that it wasn't my design, that it was one from Pinterest.

Because I would be the one driving the needle.

Still, I longed for the day when I'd have a chair at this shop, when clients would seek me out because of *my* art, my vision, my style.

I just had to figure out what exactly my style *was*, first.

I peeled off the rubber gloves when the bathroom was sparkling, putting all the supplies away before I slipped into the back and grabbed my water bottle. I downed half of it before I heard Nero chuckle.

"You're drinking that water like you're about to hike the desert," he commented from where he was at the computer, finalizing the design I'd be working with. It was a Saturday, one of our busiest nights of the week, and every artist was either with a client already, or scarfing down a quick snack before their next one came in. Nero had the ability to be picky with his time, and he only did larger pieces now, a minimum of four hours work. His client had canceled today, and so he'd taken on a last-minute request from some girl on Instagram.

Some girl on Instagram who was willing to let an apprentice mark her for life.

God bless her.

"With how dry my mouth is, it feels about the same."

He smiled, a toothy grin just barely visible through his thick beard. Nero was what I imagined the Roman ruler he was named after would have looked like if he was taller, beefier, covered in tattoos, and so full of metal he'd never get through any airport without a good pat down. His dark hair was pulled back in a messy bun near the nape of his neck tonight, his beard neatly trimmed where it framed his jaw.

"You'll be fine. I mean, look at this shit," he said, holding his palm toward the computer screen. "If you manage to fuck *this* up? You might as well change careers tomorrow."

"Gee, thanks. Now I feel absolutely zero pressure."

He just shook his head, eyes on the screen. "'*No is a full sentence,*'" he read. "Who would get that tattooed on them for life?"

"Someone who has said yes one too many times and paid the price for it," I replied.

"Could never be me." He took a long hit from his pen, and the sweet, pungent scent of marijuana filled my nostrils before he handed it to me.

Maybe *this* was another reason Nero was my favorite.

I took a pull, feeling a bit of calm come over me as the smoke left my lips. I handed it back to him after just one hit, though, because one would center me, but any more than that and I'd risk losing my focus.

"What if we tied in the poppy to the end of the script," I offered, stepping up behind him with my eyes on the screen. "See where the e trails off? What if we turned that into the bottom of the stem, the poppies blooming out of the words."

Nero considered. "I mean, *I* like it — but the client sent in this exact picture."

"It's going on her forearm, right?" I pointed at how it was laid out currently. "That's going to look funky, too block-like instead of lengthening. What if we just showed her the options side by side? I bet she'd see it then, how this is a better layout."

He smirked up at me, pushing back from the computer to let me take his place. I was slightly blushing as I slipped in and made the edits on the iPad, connecting the design and the script and making the poppies a little bit my own, too — dainty, airy, dreamy. When I finished tweaking, I crooked my gaze up to look at my boss.

"It's better," he agreed. "But you still have to convince *her*."

"And you think I can't?"

Nero's eyes landed on me then. "I think if anyone can, it's you."

His dark eyes lingered for a moment in a way that made my neck heat. Nero was an attractive man — there was just no way around noticing it. But he was also married, with a tattoo shop his wife named, and *her* name sprawled across his left pec.

I wasn't an angel — that much I could easily admit. I liked having a guy's face between my legs for a night or railing me in the morning before breakfast. And most times, we didn't talk enough for me to know if they were in a relationship or not.

With Nero, the age gap didn't bother me, but as Giana would say, I wasn't into love triangles or the cheating trope. I *knew* he was married, and he was also the one who signed my paychecks.

He was my boss and my boss only — that was a firm rule.

Before I could reply, my phone rang, Julep's face lighting up the screen. I smiled at the picture of my former roomie, ducking out the back door and into the alleyway as I accepted the video chat.

"*Damn*, girl — you trying to get a daddy tonight?" she said in lieu of a normal greeting, her eyes catching on my cleavage before she waggled her brows.

"Mommy, actually. I'm tattooing my first skin. Here's hoping she loves my work and leaves a big tip."

Julep's mouth popped open at that. "Shut up! Are you freaking out?"

"Very much so, but trying not to, so please — distract me."

"You'll crush it," she said with full belief, and my icy heart warmed a bit at the sight of the smile she wore so effortlessly. The way her skin glowed, how her eyes didn't carry so much weight anymore... it was enough to defrost me. She'd really turned a corner since the first time I'd seen her strung out in our living room on moving day. That ragged girl with the dark circles under her eyes was nothing more than a memory now, permanently banned now that Julep had found true happiness with Holden.

I narrowed my eyes at the screen. "Where are you?"

Julep looked around her before sitting back with a sigh. "Waiting outside a nursery while Holden decides which seventeen plant babies he's going to bring home with us. I told him he had to narrow it down from thirty."

I cracked a smile. "He's having a heyday now that he's in warmer climate, isn't he?"

"You would not believe the amount of squash and watermelon we have in our backyard."

"Tell him his peonies are still thriving at The Pit."

"This far into June? He'll be tickled pink." She raised a brow. "Speaking of which, how's that been going? It's been a couple weeks now since you moved in, right?"

"Tomorrow makes two," I said, leaning against the brick wall of the building. "And surprisingly… it hasn't been too bad, yet. I feel like the guys have been on their best behavior, roommate wise. They're not as gross as I suspected."

"Color me surprised." She paused, seemingly weighing her next question. "Has Leo left you alone?"

I snorted. "I don't think he's capable of such restraint."

"You never told me why you hate him so much."

I shifted, cracking my neck. "For the same reason I hate all football players. They're cocky playboys with an attitude like they own everything. It's infuriating."

"Yeah, but you don't act the same way toward Holden, or Zeke, or Clay, or even Kyle."

Suddenly, my mouth was dry again. "He just… dated a friend of mine and broke her heart," I lied. "But it's fine, she's moved on and Leo has been tolerable." I paused. "I *would* like it if they'd wear more clothes around the house, though. I swear to God, Julep, I've never seen so many naked muscles in my life."

She barked out a laugh at that. "Hey, gives you an excuse not to wear pants. If they're comfortable naked, why shouldn't you be?"

Before I could answer, her eyes shifted to somewhere behind her phone and she lit up with a smile. "Gotta go," she said as she stood, shaking her head. "He's got two carts full. Two *carts*, Mary."

"Good luck with that."

"And good luck with your *skin*," she said with a little squeal. "Take pictures!"

Julep blew me a kiss through the screen before the call ended, and I smirked, tucking my phone into my back pocket before making my way inside the shop.

My stomach was a little uneasy from the lie I so easily gave one of my only friends, but it twisted even more at the thought of telling her the truth. I wasn't sure if it was because I felt pathetic for still holding a grudge all these years later, or because it would hurt to relive the pain out loud. It was enough to see him day in and day out and know that, even with me *living in his house*, he didn't recognize me. But to speak the words into the universe, to admit to someone what happened?

It made me sick to even consider.

For a second, I let myself wonder what *would* happen if I told him, if I waited for him to give me some smart-ass remark about what a great, humble guy he was and then threw his cruelty right back in his face. Would he wave it off with a laugh? Call me sensitive and a weirdo for even remembering it? Would he call me out for not telling him? Call me a creep?

Would he be sorry?

I laughed out loud at that thought because I knew with full certainty that he didn't even *remember* what he'd done to me, it had been that insignificant in his life.

I had been that insignificant.

With another drop of my stomach, I swallowed, shaking the thoughts away just as the front door opened, our little shop bell ringing.

Nero caught my gaze with a smile. "Bet that's your skin."

And for the rest of the night, excitement and nerves were the only thing I felt, Leo completely out of my mind.

※ ※ ※

I woke the next morning at an ungodly hour.

Okay, it was nine — but after having my first skin and being at the shop until after two, it was an ungodly hour for *me*.

Still, I was somehow unusually awake as I threw the covers off, the energy from last night still buzzing through me. The client had been an absolute sweetheart. Not only did she hug me when we met as if we'd been friends since middle school and she hadn't seen me in years, but she'd quite literally jumped for joy when I showed her my amendments to her design. And suddenly, I wasn't just doing a tattoo that had been done a hundred times on a hundred different people.

I was leaving a piece of me, of my art, on someone else.

It was her first tattoo, but she handled it like a champ, and she was encouraging *me* the entire time rather than me having to do much comforting her. In the end, she cried not from pain, but from how much she loved the little piece on her forearm, and I saw the way Nero crooked a smile at me when the girl wrapped me in another fierce hug.

I'd done it.

I'd tattooed my first client and I couldn't have asked for it to go better than it had.

When I ambled into my en-suite bathroom, I chuckled a little at my reflection. My hair was a matted mess, eyes dark from where I hadn't been successful in taking all my makeup off last night. Still, I looked happy in my chaotic, sleep-deprived state, and I gave myself nothing more but a quick sweep of a hairbrush through my locks and a cold splash of water to the face before I was ready to venture downstairs for some coffee.

I had my hand on the door handle when I paused, glancing down at my bare legs. I was in a pair of boy shorts that hiked themselves up my ass without me trying — mostly because my ass was so big, it ate every piece of underwear I wore, regardless of size. You couldn't even *see* my panties, really, under the oversized Cold War Kids t-shirt I wore.

I glanced over my shoulder at the dresser, debating sweatpants.

And then, I remembered what Julep said last night.

If I were at our house across the street, I wouldn't think twice about walking out like this. And the guys all insisted on how they wanted me to feel at home, to not walk on eggshells.

With a shrug, I opened the door and headed downstairs with a *fuck it* attitude. It was too hot for sweatpants, anyway.

I skipped down the stairs, humming happily to myself as I rounded the bottom of them. I smiled at the sight of the guys all piled on the couch, Braden and Kyle playing a game of Madden while Leo ate a gigantic bowl of cereal and watched.

They were all focused on the screen as I sang, "Good morning."

I leaned a hip against the back of the recliner chair, folding my arms and watching as they lined up for the next play.

"Morning," Braden said without taking his eyes off the game.

"Coffee's still hot," Kyle added, but he *did* take his eyes off the screen.

And then, the controller went limp in his hands.

Braden celebrated a victorious play with Kyle distracted, but then he followed his roommate's gaze, and I flushed when their eyes landed on my legs. Braden's eyebrows shot up. Kyle crooked an appreciative smile.

Leo, on the other hand, looked like he was two seconds away from committing homicide.

His jaw was set, brows a hard line over his warm eyes as he took in the sight of me. He didn't stare too long before his glare was on his roommates, and he smacked the back of Kyle's head.

"Ow!" Kyle yelped, making a fist and laying it into Leo's bicep in retaliation. "Fucker."

"Pay attention to the game," he said.

Kyle made a face. "You're not even playing."

"Neither are you."

Braden looked to Leo, who was glaring at me again, before he gave me a curious smile over his shoulder.

Then, the next play started, and I continued on to the kitchen, pretending like nothing was out of the ordinary.

I reached into the cabinet above the coffee pot, pulling out an NBU mug and filling it to the top.

"God*damn*, I didn't realize she had so many tattoos," Kyle said from the living room, low enough he probably thought I couldn't hear him over the TV.

"Did you see that one on her inner thigh?" Braden whispered back. "That shit had to hurt."

"That girl is *nasty*," Kyle said, but he said it in a way that made me feel strangely... honored? Like nasty was a good thing.

Was it?

I didn't have time to contemplate more before the clattering of dishes in the sink made me jump. I whipped around, finding Leo angrily rinsing his cereal bowl and spoon before all but throwing them in the dishwasher and slamming it shut.

"Jesus," I said, a hand to my chest as I caught my breath. "Scared me."

I smiled with that, wrapping my hands around my fresh mug of coffee. I typically liked a sweet creamer in mine, but I didn't have the spare cash for such luxuries at the moment. My heart squeezed with the memory of having coffee with my dad in the mornings when I visited home, how he always had the best creamer even though he drank his black.

He did it for me.

"What did the dishwasher do to make you so mad?" I teased as I leaned against the counter.

A muscle in Leo's jaw popped as he turned to face me, and this time, he let his eyes wash all the way over me, from where I knew my nipple piercings were visible under my t-shirt to where the hem of it dropped off and left my legs in full view.

"Did you forget pants this morning?"

I hiked up my shirt, which had his eyes flaring as he took in my black boy shorts. "I have pants on."

"Those are *not* pants," he argued.

An unattractive snort left me as I dropped my shirt back down. "Wow. You really are going for that daddy title, aren't you?"

"I'm pretty sure Kyle has a boner right now."

"That's unfortunate."

"Look, I'm not here to tell you how to dress, I just—"

"Really? Because that's exactly what this feels like. And *you three*," I said, pointing at him first and then toward the living room. "Are naked from the waist up every single day, so you have zero room to talk."

A smirk painted itself slowly on Leo's lips, and he folded his arm over his bare chest — which was proving my point so well I couldn't contain the pleased purse of my lips.

"Ah," he said. "So that's what this is. Giving us a dose of our own medicine."

"We're roommates," I said. "And we're all adults. I think we can handle seeing skin, if it makes the other more comfortable. Don't you agree?"

His jaw ticked again, like he didn't feel safe to answer that question.

"You're different this morning," he stated instead.

"Why, because I'm pantless?"

"Because you're smiling."

My cheeks flushed for some reason, and I looked down at the mug in my hands, another wide smile surfacing on my lips without any power for me to restrain it. "It was a good night."

I peeked back up at Leo just in time to see him swallow hard. "Did you have a date or something?"

"Ew, no," I said with a wrinkle of my nose, waving him off. "Who has time to date? I had my first skin last night."

That made him arch a brow.

"My first tattoo on someone who's not me. Or a grapefruit."

At that, Leo's entire face lit up, and he flashed one of those goofy boy-grins that made my stomach hurt because it reminded me so much of him in high school. "No shit? That's bad ass. Did you take pictures?"

For a moment, I was fifteen again, that boy's excited voice in my ears as he told me about football camp, about how pumped he was for the season.

About how ready he was to meet me.

I blinked, pulling my phone from where I'd had it tucked in the back of my shorts. Leo popped another brow at that, like it was a magic trick, but then his eyes were on the screen when I showed him the final piece from last night.

"Wow," he said, taking my phone and zooming in on the picture. He studied the tattoo like he actually gave a shit.

That made my stomach hurt, too.

"This is really good, Mary," he said, peeking up at me from where he still held my phone.

I reached out and snatched it back. "It's not a big piece or anything, and the script was from the computer. I just added the poppies. It's not really—"

"It's fucking awesome," he said, cutting me off.

My eyes met his, finding him looking back at me with reverence.

"I'm sure that was scary, but you did great. Congratulations."

I swallowed, my voice quiet when I responded, "Thanks."

Leo kept his eyes on me as I tucked my hair behind one ear and took a sip of my coffee. I hated that he didn't look away, that he didn't feel the need to the way I did. He was so fucking confident he would stare the hottest person in the world right in the eyes and make *them* feel inferior somehow.

"Have you heard anything about the house?" he asked after a moment.

"Trying to get rid of me already?"

"Might be trying to save my sanity, because if I wake up to this every morning," he said, waving a hand over where I stood. "I'm bound for the looney bin."

I rolled my eyes. "Shut up."

"I'm serious!"

"Margie said they should be getting started soon," I said, ignoring him and the way my chest fluttered at the thought that maybe I was a temptation to Leo Hernandez.

Then I gritted my teeth with annoyance at myself.

Who cares even if I am? He's a prick, remember?

"Apparently, they were in the middle of another project. But by the time they assess fully, remove all the damaged shit in there, fix the pipes, redo the walls, the floors, the ceiling..." I sighed, thumbing the handle of my coffee mug. "I don't know what we're looking at, time wise."

Leo almost looked like he felt sorry for me. "You can stay here as long as you want, as long as you need to."

"Not true," I argued. "Eventually, you're going to have another teammate in the room I'm squatting in now."

"Then you can stay in mine," Leo quipped back, and he crossed the kitchen into my space with a salacious grin. "My bed is the best in the house."

"And you'd be where, on the couch?"

He shrugged. "I guess — until you realize you want me in there with you." He stepped even closer. "I'm a great big spoon." His voice lowered a bit then, his eyes raking over me inch by inch. The golden flakes in them dazzled in the light. "An even better fork."

I wanted to snort, to press my hand into his chest and push him away like he annoyed me. Because he did. And if it was just him saying those words, maybe I could have.

But it was the way he said them, all rugged and daring. It was how he stepped into my space, how I could smell his body wash and feel the heat from his skin.

He pissed me off.

But he also turned me all the way on.

I fought the urge to squeeze my thighs together against the sensation building there, like if I ignored it, that would make it easier to pretend like it didn't exist. My nipples hardened under my shirt without my consent, the metal in them heavier somehow as I kept my gaze locked on Leo's like he didn't intimidate me.

Like I was bored instead of wanting.

"Mary! Come play with us!" Braden called from the other room.

Leo was still staring at me.

I stared right back.

"Mary doesn't play Xbox," he called over his shoulder. "Or any of our *lesser than* games."

There was a challenge in his eyes, and I met it with my own as I pushed off where I was leaning against the counter and slipped past him. My ass rubbed against his hip as I passed, careful not to spill my coffee, and that became even more of a chore as Leo sucked in a groan under his breath.

I plopped that half-covered ass down right in-between Kyle and Braden once I made it to the living room, and I snatched the controller out of Kyle's hands.

"Anything but football."

"*Halo?*" Braden offered.

My eyes shot to Leo, who was standing behind the recliner now so he could see the screen. I waited to see if there was some sort of recognition on his face when the game was suggested, but I didn't know why I did. He didn't so much as blink, just wore that same cocky smile as he waited for us to start the game.

I ground my teeth together, and I no longer had to pretend to be annoyed. "How about COD, instead?"

Braden smiled, seemingly impressed by that alone, which made me want to roll my eyes. But he keyed up the game, and I ignored Leo standing in the corner as I proceeded to surprise every single one of them.

We played co-op mode, and Kyle and I had no sooner finished our first round before Braden was yanking the controller out of his hands so he could play with me next. Sunday morning slipped by like that, until I grew bored with the game of making Leo eat his words and stood, stretching.

"I'm going to shower," I announced, reaching my hands up to the sky before twisting my body left and right to crack my back.

Leo, who had been quiet most of the morning, stared at where my shirt rode up over my panties as I did.

When I dropped my hands and the shirt fell back into place, his eyes found mine, and I smiled. "As long as it's okay with you, *Daddy*."

Kyle and Braden exchanged looks, and Leo grinned. "I'll allow it, since you've been such a good girl."

I rolled my eyes. "Someone needs to mow the lawn," I said as I grabbed my empty mug off the table. "I'll start the dishes, but I scrub toilets too much at the shop to do it here. One of you needs to hit the guest bath. And for God's sake, *please* take care of whatever *that* is," I added as I rounded into the kitchen, pointing behind me to the pile of gym bags overflowing with smelly socks, shorts, sneakers, and who knew what else that cluttered the front bay window.

As I rinsed my mug and set it in the top rack of the dishwasher, I heard Kyle say, "Maybe we should call *her* daddy."

Chapter 11

LEO

Our poor new QB1 looked like he was ready to shit himself.

The sun beating down on us only made Blake Russo sweat harder as he looked around at the team waiting for him to tell them what to do. It'd been another long summer day for all of us — a two-hour workout in the morning consisting of weightlifting and conditioning that made us all want to vomit, followed by classes. And now, those of us who wanted more torture were on the field for player-led skills and drills.

Except, typically, it was the quarterback who led us.

Holden wore leadership like it had been infused into his DNA at birth. Blake, who was stepping in to take his place this season after impressing all of us when Holden was injured last year, was getting there. He was working on it.

He just didn't quite have the same demanding severity that our old Captain did.

I grabbed a water bottle and squeezed it over my head, cursing at the bite of the cold but loving it all the same. Riley grabbed it out of my hand next and did the same, shaking the water off her hair as she looked from me to Blake across the field.

"Think we stand a chance this season?"

"What kind of thinking is that, Mighty Mouse?" Zeke asked, smacking her ass from behind as he joined us. She swatted him away.

"I'm just being realistic. We're a championship team with a target on our back now," she said.

"And he's not Holden," Clay finished her thought, folding his arms over his chest. We stood there just like that in a line of cautious stares aimed across the field at our new quarterback.

"He kicked ass last season," I reminded them. "If it weren't for him stepping in when Holden was injured, we wouldn't have even made the championship bowl game — let alone won it."

My teammates made various faces that said *fair point*.

For a moment, I watched them with an uncomfortable nostalgia swimming in my gut. We'd all walked onto the team as freshmen together and had been through so much the last three seasons, I knew we had the kind of friendship that was forged in fire.

I could still remember when Riley walked into our locker room that first day of fall camp like she had something to prove — and she did. I remembered her slowly gaining our trust, kicking Kyle's ass in a game of five hundred that would go down in our team's history, and finally giving in to her feelings for Zeke.

Zeke, who had the highest returning yards of any special teams punt returner in the last season. On top of that, I'd watched him go from a kid who struggled so much in school that he just wanted to give up on it completely, to one who tutored the freshmen we had now who were in the same position he once was.

Clay had always been a beast on the field, and he'd had that same easy ability to lead just like Holden. But in the past year, he'd dedicated himself to weights and conditioning, to his diet, and he now had the build of an NFL player. He didn't look like a kid anymore, like a college athlete. He looked like a pro. And I knew by this time next year, he would be — just like Holden.

My thoughts drifted to Coach Lee, to the look on his face when he showed me that stupid fucking article.

When he thought of us, of our crew, where did he place me? Did he see my growth, my potential?

Or did he only see wasted talent?

"I think he just needs a little support," Clay said, and he clapped Zeke on the shoulder, stepping forward like he was about to jog over to where Blake stood with the team.

"Wait," I said.

He turned, his eyes meeting mine along with the rest of them.

"I got this."

Clay and Zeke exchanged looks before Clay waved his hand over the field as if to say *after you*.

I nodded, jogging over to where Blake stood. I nudged his arm when I reached him. "You good, Cap?"

Blake tried to smile but it fell flat. "I'm not captain yet."

"And you won't be if you keep acting like you don't belong in that QB1 spot."

"Maybe I don't," he said, his eyes snapping to mine. He was shorter than Holden, softer somehow — and yet, I had seen what he could do, what he was capable of when he turned his brain off. "Coach brought in a freshman QB, remember? Maybe he'll be the one out here once fall camp starts."

"Is that what you want?"

He hit me with a look that said *what do you think?*

"Stop acting like he's already here, like he's already better than you. You haven't even seen him play. Besides, *you* are the veteran," I reminded him, pointing my index finger into his chest. "*You* are the one who led us to a winning season last year. That kid might have talent, but he doesn't have anything on what you have."

"Which is?"

"*La experiencia*," I answered easily. "Experience. Skill. And a whole team who has your back."

Blake nodded, the corner of his mouth lifting. "You're right."

"Aren't I always?"

He laughed at that, and I clapped him on the back before turning my attention to where the team had been resting and waiting for direction.

"Alright, fam. You know the drill. You're here because you want to get better, because you don't want to waste a single second of this summer while our opponents are out there training for their number one goal — to beat us. They want to see us lose. They want to see us tuck our tails and limp back out of the spotlight where they liked us. But is that what we're going to do?"

"Hell no!" Clay said from the back, and the rest of the team shot out various agreements.

"Hell fucking no," I echoed. "No one is here to hold our hands. Coach can't work with us over the summer except to direct our strength and conditioning staff to get us into shape. But we all came here to work together, and we know what to do." I grabbed a ball off the field and shoved it into Blake's hands. "Blake will take offense. Clay, get your defensive players on the backfield. Zeke and Riley, work with special teams and the kicking unit. And if you're training and you think of something we need to work on, speak up," I said to the rest of the team. "I don't care what year you are or what experience you have. In fact, usually, you see more when you're on the sidelines. So let's work together. Let's *get better* together."

Clay barked deep and loud like a dog, and the rest of the team beat their chests and nodded and bounced up and down like they were ready to kill.

"Hands in," Zeke called, and everyone piled their hands one on top of the other. "Family on three. One, two—"

"*Family!*"

As soon as the word was chanted, the team broke out into the various parts of the field, ready to work.

Blake grabbed my shoulder, squeezing with an appreciative smile. "Thank you," he said, and then he leaned in a bit closer. "Keep acting like that, and it's going to be *you* wearing the Captain badge on your jersey this year."

I shrugged him off with a joke before we jogged side by side over to work offense together.

But in the back of my mind, a new goal bloomed.

One I would pursue relentlessly.

●●●

I was in just as much disbelief as the rest of the team when I turned down the offer to go out after we wrapped practice. They swore it was just to grab pizza and a couple beers, but I knew how quickly that could turn into being out all night long and dragging ass into conditioning in the morning.

For the first time maybe ever, I didn't want to.

I was tired, and sore, and smelly as hell. I knew I could have a girl in my bed by the end of the night if I went with them, that I could take out some of my pent-up frustration and have a little fun. But it wasn't just the article and Coach's words in my ears that stopped me.

I felt focused on football, on my classes, and now — on leading our team.

So, I did what Holden would do. I listened to that smart voice inside my head that said *go home, get some rest*. And I didn't feel like I was missing out. In fact, I was *relieved*.

All I wanted was a shower, sweatpants, *tostones,* and a night to unwind before I woke up at five thirty tomorrow morning to do it all again.

The house was quiet when I threw my bag onto the bay window. I did a double take, though, because for once, I wasn't *adding* it to an already-steeping pile of shit. Instead, it was empty — and there was a new, thick, navy-blue cushion with a stack of books in the windowsill. One glance at that book stack let me know they had to be from Giana's collection, and I smirked, wondering if Mary read them, too.

With that smile still in place, I lugged my bag back onto my shoulder and hiked it up to my room, instead.

I could have stayed in the shower for hours, letting that hot water massage my sore shoulders and back. After a while, I ran it cold, knowing that was likely what my body needed more than heat, anyway. Then, I toweled off and tugged on my NBU sweatpants, hair still a little wet as I padded down the stairs.

I flicked on the television as I passed through the living room, turning on ESPN before I swung into the kitchen and pulled out all the ingredients I needed: plantains, garlic, vegetable oil, olive oil, salt, tomato, parsley, and freshly cracked pepper.

Baseball highlights played loud enough for me to hear as I peeled and sliced the plantains, but once I did, my mind floated away from the present and into the memory of making *tostones* with my mom. She had me standing on a stool next to her in the kitchen and learning her recipe before I even played football — which was saying something, since Dad had me in pads at the age of six.

The sound of the oil popping when I dropped the first plantains in made me smile, my stomach growling as I got out a bowl to mix the dipping sauce. I was so focused on the recipe that I didn't hear Mary walk down the stairs, didn't notice her at all until she was leaning through the window that separated the kitchen from the living room, her eyes closing on an inhale.

"Holy *fuck*, it smells good in here."

"Careful — don't get popped by the oil," I warned.

"Yes, *Daddy*," she teased, sliding onto the barstool on the other side of the window and resting her arms on the ledge. I had to contain my smirk and the way I fucking loved when she called me daddy — even if it was a joke.

I wondered what it would be like if it wasn't, if I had her pinned beneath me and obeying my every command to get the relief she so desperately wanted.

My cock twitched at the thought, and I pressed my waist against the kitchen counter to hide it as I focused on the sauce.

"What are you making?" she asked.

"*Tostones.*"

She sighed reverently, her chin balanced on the palm of her hand as she looked longingly at the saucepan. "Really makes the bologna sandwich I was about to make seem like dog food in comparison."

I chuckled. "You can have some, I'm making enough to feed a football team."

I peeked up at her just in time to see her face fall, and she plopped a notebook down on the counter in front of her, opening it to a blank page and popping the lid off the graphite pencil in her hand. "No, it's okay. I don't want to eat your food."

"Why?"

She shrugged. "Because I didn't pay for it."

"So?" I shook my head on a smile. "Stop being weird and just say thank you."

I thought I saw her smile, but her eyes were so laced with concern when she looked at me again that it was hard to say. "Are you sure?"

"Of course. Besides, *tostones* are meant to be shared. My mom would smack me upside the head if I kept them all to myself."

I finished stirring up the garlic dip and set it aside, still watching Mary curiously. I could only see the oversized t-shirt she wore, and her hair piled in a messy bun on top of her head as her hand started moving over the page, a charcoal gray filling in the white.

I wondered if she was wearing those tiny fucking boy shorts again, if I was going to have to sit on my hands to keep from tracing the dark ink that lined her thighs.

It had been enough to make me want to burn my eyes out, seeing her walk around without a bra and barely anything covering her ass over the last week. Not because the sight was one I didn't want to see, but because it was driving me absolutely insane to see her like that and not be able to touch her.

She was our fucking roommate.

She trusted us to make her feel safe and comfortable, not to ogle her when she was in her own home. I'd smacked Kyle more than a few times this week and reminded him just the same, but he pinned me with a glare that told me I didn't have room to talk with how my eyes followed Mary every time she passed by us with her nipple piercings pressing against the fabric of her thin tops.

The fact that she seemed slightly less annoyed by me now only made me want to press my luck, to sling one of my cheesy lines at her but with a little more intent. I wanted to make her laugh *without* rolling her eyes.

Almost as much as I wanted to see what she looked like when she came.

I scrubbed my jaw with an angry hand before pressing my hips even more into the counter before an erection could spring. "Can I ask you something?"

Mary didn't bother looking up from her sketch. "Hmm?"

"What's the story with your family?"

She blinked at that, the pencil falling limp in her fingers as she looked up at me. "What do you mean?"

"I mean, when all this happened with the house," I said, gesturing vaguely toward the direction her house was. "You didn't have anyone to call. Or if you did, you didn't want to."

"That's kind of a rude question," she said.

"Yeah, well, I'm an asshole, remember?"

"Or so you want the world to think."

Her words weren't sharp, but they hit me like a dart all the same. I didn't want to analyze how it felt that Mary possibly saw past the cocksure attitude to the real me.

She sighed. "I could have called my parents, but to do so would mean submitting myself to long, tear-filled lectures from my mom about how I'm wasting my life and good fortune."

I was still a bit shaken by her previous comment, but I blinked it away. "Why would she say that?"

"Because I'm pursuing a career as a tattoo artist instead of an acquisitions manager like my dad and older brother."

I let out a low whistle, pulling the plantains from the oil to work on flattening them with the *tostonera* my mom gave me when she moved me to NBU my freshman year. She considered it an essential. I didn't disagree.

"So you're *rich* rich, huh?"

"My parents are," she corrected.

"Does your dad feel the same way?"

"Kind of?" she answered with a sigh. Her sketch was taking shape now — two faces facing opposite directions but connected by the dark lines that made them. "He isn't as vocal as my mom, and I think he wants to try to support me. But I also think he secretly hopes it's a phase I'll grow out of."

I nodded. "That must be hard."

She paused over the nose of one of the faces, glancing up at me. "I could say the same for you."

"Me?"

Mary nodded. "I'm sure you feel pressure from your dad to follow in his footsteps, too."

"How do you know about my dad?"

Her mouth parted like I'd caught her red-handed in a burglary, but then she waved her hand over the page. "Come on, everyone knows Nick Parkinson."

"Everyone who follows football, yeah," I said, placing the plantains back in the oil to fry once they were flattened. "I just didn't peg you for one of those people."

She wrinkled her nose, focused on her drawing again. "I'm not, trust me. I hate football."

"That's just because you haven't played."

Mary cocked a brow at me.

"When these are done, I'll show you," I said, nodding to the pan.

She just shrugged, watching where her fingers sketched.

"I love football so much that it doesn't feel like pressure, really," I said after a moment. "It did when I was younger, but now, I feel like I have my own path."

"What changed?"

"I came to NBU instead of going to his alma mater in Alabama."

Mary paused at that, silence washing over us.

"You didn't want to go where he went?"

"No," I said with a heavy breath. "But I also didn't want to disappoint him. He loved his school, but I grew up here in Boston. We had Southern Alabama on the TV every Saturday when I was at his house, but Mom took me to my first college game, and it was NBU. It was one of those perfect fall days, you know? Cloudy and gray, cool with a breeze that rustled the leaves. I fell in love." I shrugged. "I just didn't know how to tell my dad that."

"What finally gave you the courage?"

My chest nearly caved in on itself. "Wise words from a friend," I said, almost whispering.

I dropped the conversation there, shaking off the memory as I plated the *tostones* for each of us, along with a side of the garlic sauce. I carried them into the living room, and Mary abandoned her sketchbook, plopping down next to me on the couch.

She was wearing leggings, thank the fucking Lord.

"*De la panza sale la danza*," I said, setting up the feast on the coffee table.

Mary tilted her head. "Did you just curse me out?"

"No." I chuckled. "It's just something my mom would say before we ate sometimes. *From the stomach comes the dance.* It basically means eat up to grow strong, or like..." I considered how to translate it. "You gotta eat well to live well."

"That explains why I'm a terrible dancer," Mary mused with a smile. "All the Easy Mac I've been eating."

"Still hot," I warned as she picked up a golden morsel, but she didn't seem to care as she skipped the sauce altogether and popped it into her mouth. Her eyes rolled back, a deep moan coming from her that made me grab a pillow and pull it into my lap. I pretended it was to use it as a table for my plate.

"Good, huh?" I teased.

"*Sofuckinggood,*" she said around a mouthful.

"Try the sauce."

She did, and that damn moan broke through again.

"Your mom taught you how to make these?" she asked.

I nodded.

"She's an angel. Please thank her from this starving artist." She dipped another plantain before looking at me. "And thank you, too."

I crooked a smile. "Anytime."

I could have watched her all night with that happy glow on her face as she ate my cooking, but I had a mission.

"Alright," I said, wiping my hands on my pants before I switched the TV over to Xbox and cued up Madden. "Eat up, and then I'm going to make you love football."

Chapter 12

MARY

I was almost uncomfortably full from the ghastly amount of *tostones* I had shoveled down, but it didn't stop me from jumping up and doing a little dance when I kicked Leo's ass at his own game.

"Suck it, bitch!" I said, flipping him off with both hands before I did a little hip wiggle and spin.

He barked out a laugh, tossing his controller down on the coffee table before he sat back on the couch and ran a hand through his hair. "Well, your attitude toward football changed quickly."

"Football still sucks," I argued, plopping down next to him. I crossed my legs and tucked my feet underneath me. "But it makes me happy to know there's something else I can beat you in."

"What's the first thing?"

"*Halo*, obviously. Also just being a decent human being."

I said it as a joke, but Leo's smile slipped, and he cleared his throat, gathering our empty plates. "Yeah, doesn't take much."

He took our plates into the kitchen before I could say anything, and I internally cursed.

"I was just kidding," I said when he came back, and I noted how he sat a little farther away this time.

I almost apologized, but then I remembered that he was an asshole who deserved to have his eyes opened to what a dick he'd been to me and to many other women in his life.

Then again, the way he'd been with me the last few weeks since I'd moved in, how he'd offered me a place to stay in the first place... it refuted the beliefs I'd had about him. He'd made sure I had somewhere to go. He'd done his best to make it comfortable for me here. He'd asked about my first skin, about my family...

He'd *cooked* for me.

I swallowed, the apology forming on my tongue when I looked at him and found this numb sort of expression on his face.

"No, you weren't," he said before I could get it out. "And I don't blame you for thinking that about me. You're far from the only one."

"You seem like that upsets you."

A breath of a laugh left his chest as he looked at me. "Wouldn't it upset you?"

"Yes, but my sole purpose in life isn't to make people think I'm some cocky playboy with thick skin."

"I do have thick skin," he said, almost defensively. "And yeah, I have confidence in who I am, in what I can do. But..."

He scrubbed his jaw.

"But what?" I asked.

He just shook his head. "Nothing."

I pivoted to face him on the couch, resting my elbows on my knees as I leaned closer. "But you don't want to play this role for life?"

Leo stilled, and then he frowned, pinning me with his accusatory gaze. "Why do you keep saying that?"

"Because I see right through you."

"Oh, yeah? And what is it that you see?"

If he'd have asked me this question a month ago, I would have smiled in victory as I spat out every nasty thought I'd had about him for the past seven years.

But tonight, I saw a glimpse of the boy he used to be, the one who confessed his fears to me in a hushed voice at two in the morning so he wouldn't wake his parents. I saw the same eyes I watched from across the cafeteria, the ones that glittered with every joke he said but then glossed over when no one was looking at him anymore, when he didn't have everyone's attention — which was rare.

"I see a man who wants to be taken seriously, but doesn't know how to do that without feeling vulnerable or weak."

Leo blinked, his nostrils flaring as his eyes searched mine. "That's not what I expected you to say."

"See? I can surprise people, too."

"It's almost like you might not detest me anymore."

I scoffed, leaning back. "You wish."

"Come on, admit it," Leo said with a playful smirk. "You kind of like me."

"About as much as I like getting pricked with a needle."

His brow shot up, and then his eyes were washing over every inch of my skin. "Considering how much ink you have, I'd say you like getting pricked with needles quite a bit."

I laughed — *genuinely* laughed, because I had not thought of that before I threw my little quip at him. I shoved him away, tucking my hair behind one ear. "Shut up."

"Don't worry, I won't tell anyone. You can still pretend to hate me."

I rolled my eyes, but then I found his gaze again.

And the way he stared at me, the way the silence of the house fell down around us, the way he wore that little smirk...

It was like pouring water over hot rocks in a sauna, the heat too much to bear.

I flushed, looking down at my hands in my lap. I was about to tell him I should go upstairs and get ready for work when he said, "It's cool that you game."

Relief washed over me at the change in subject.

"I've only known one other girl who did," he added.

Something about his expression changed then, his eyes almost... *sad*.

My heart picked up its pace in my chest. "A lot of girls game."

"I'm sure they do," he said. "I've just avoided them since high school."

Another loud thump of my heart echoed in my chest. "Why?"

Leo opened his mouth, shut it again, and then the muscles of his jaw were working under the skin as that silence fell over us once more.

"It's a long story that I don't want to get into," he finally said softly.

All of his little comments over the last few weeks started clicking into place, like puzzle pieces that had been lost under a couch cushion.

Was he talking about *me*?

I wanted to shake my head as soon as I thought it, because *obviously* it wasn't me. He was disgusted when he met me in person. He made fun of me. He let his *friends* make fun of me for the rest of our fucking high school tenure. It was clear that he didn't recognize me now — thanks to braces, my skin being clearer, and my baby fat turning into feminine curves I loved to show off.

He didn't know I was that girl he hurt all those years ago, but he damn sure knew that girl was *Octostigma*.

My stomach soured at the memory.

And yet, the way Leo looked right now...

Who else *could* he be talking about?

Did he meet someone after me?

And if it *was* me who made him look like that, that made him *feel* like that... *why?*

A thought I'd refused to let myself believe whipped through my head like a rush of wind.

Maybe he really didn't realize it was you that day. Maybe...

"Tell me what happened," I said before thinking better.

I had to know.

Leo frowned, looking up at me before his eyes showed how surprised he was that I actually wanted to know.

For a moment, I thought he was going to tell me.

But then the front door burst open and our roommates stumbled in.

I jumped back, not realizing how close I'd been to Leo until we weren't alone anymore. Leo didn't move, his eyes still on me, even when Kyle flopped down backward over the top of the couch and landed between us with a goofy smile.

"Well, if it isn't the party pooper and our hot new roommate."

Leo flicked his nose, which made Kyle yelp before he let out another peal of drunken laughter.

"What are you two doing sitting in the dark?" Braden asked, leaning his palms on the back of the couch as he peered over us questioningly. I could tell he was a little buzzed, too, because he smiled wickedly in the next moment. "Or do we wanna know?"

I hadn't even realized how dark the house was, how we hadn't moved to turn on any sort of light other than the TV. I didn't chance a look at Leo before I scoffed and stood up, unfastening my hair from the messy bun I had it tied up in.

"I was just kicking Leo's ass at Madden," I said as I pulled my hair up again, desperate to keep my hands busy so no one could see how they were shaking.

Braden and Kyle erupted in a chorus of *ooooh*s. Then, Kyle did a somersault off the couch and grabbed one of the Xbox controllers. "Me next, me next!"

"You want to get your ass handed to you, too?" Braden teased.

"If it's by her?" Kyle said, his eyes raking over me and fixating on where I knew my nipple piercings were visible under my shirt. "Gladly."

"You're a pig," I said, hitting him upside the head with a pillow. I couldn't help the smile that curled on my lips, though. "And I have to get ready for work."

"Boooo, call out of work!" Braden begged, his hands clasped together.

I just ruffled his hair like he was my kid brother. "I'll see you guys tomorrow."

"Not fair," Braden said with a pout, plopping down where I had just been on the couch. "Leo gets to have all the fun."

The boys keyed up a new game on the screen, the two of them yakking away about some girls they'd apparently been trying to talk to at the bar.

I paused when I was at the bottom of the stairs, everything in me pulling like a magnet toward Leo. I wanted to look back, to confirm what I felt, but I didn't have to.

Because he hadn't said a word since they came home.

And I knew without looking that he hadn't taken his eyes off me, either.

I stood there for a moment, feeling the burn of his gaze on my skin.

Then, I took a breath, lifted my chin, and climbed the stairs without giving myself the satisfaction of proving I was right.

Chapter 13

LEO

"Are you sure you don't want to come home for the holiday?" My mom asked, and even through the phone I swore I could smell the *arroz con pollo* she was cooking. "It's been years since we've gone down to Harborfest for the fireworks."

My stomach growled as I threw my duffle bag in the trunk of my car, wrapping up an early morning Pee Wee practice.

"You know I want to, *Ma*, but we're having a party at the house."

"Mm-hmm," she said, and again, I didn't have to see her to know the look she was giving me, how one hand would be on her hip, and the other pointing the spatula at my nose. "I know you better behave yourself, *mijo*."

"I always do."

She laughed at that, and the sound made me homesick.

I was young when my parents split, so I didn't really have a choice on who I would live with. I remembered when I was around nine or ten wishing that it would have been my dad. I wanted to be playing football all the time, wanted to hang out with him in his impressive basement with the pool table and ninety-eight-inch TV and the constant crowd of guys that seemed to always be there hanging out. He shot the shit with Super Bowl-winning athletes like it was no big deal, with a cockiness that said he belonged in that circle even though he never got a ring himself.

I wanted to soak up his energy until that confidence lived in me, too.

But as I grew up, I realized how much my mom did for me, how she was always the parent when Dad was so often the friend. And when I told my dad I wanted to go to NBU, I felt that friendship we had rub raw, saw the disappointment in his eyes, like I'd let him down.

I never had the guts to tell him how many times he'd done the same to me.

He loved me in the ways he knew how. I was old enough to understand that now, to give him grace. He never wanted to be a father, not that young, anyway, and clearly he never wanted to be a husband, either. His dreams were dashed by an injury, a career in pro ball cut short. Fortunately, he had a big enough reputation that he was still able to use that name, to start a training center outside of the city and be invited on as a guest announcer for ESPN and Fox and whoever else. He found a way to still wrap his life around that sport, even when life threw him the hardest curveball it could have.

Football was what made him happy.

But I knew for my mom, it was always me.

She'd loved me so fiercely it almost suffocated me at times, but it was the purest, most special kind of love — the kind that's truly unconditional.

She was the only one I ever broke down in front of after what happened in high school, the only one who knew I'd had my heart broken. I didn't have to tell her who it was or what had happened — the fact that I was showing any emotion other than joy was enough for her to know I was hurting.

I still remember how she held me as I sobbed like a fucking baby, and then she made me dinner and ran a bath for me. We never spoke about it again, never really spoke about it in the first place.

But I knew from that moment on, no matter what I went through, she would always be there.

"We got the date for senior night," I told her as I slipped into the driver seat and fired up the engine. "November nineteenth."

"Did you tell your father?"

"Not yet," I said. "I wanted to make sure you would come first."

She sucked her teeth as if even insinuating that she wouldn't was an insult. I waited until my phone connected to the car speakers before I set it aside and continued.

"I just mean... if he comes, too. I don't want to make you uncomfortable."

"I still love your father, Leo. I always will. And I can put up with him for a few hours." She clicked her tongue. "Now, whether or not he'll be able to stand how *guapa* his ex is at forty-five years old is yet to be seen. Might have to restrain him and those jealous little cleat chasers who still follow him around."

A smile split my face. "Alright, *mamá, cálmate*."

It was slow traffic moving through the campus, some sort of holiday market going on. I was just about to turn and take the back roads to get off campus quicker and take the roundabout way home when I saw Mary.

There was no mistaking her, not even in a thick crowd of people.

She had on a pair of cut-off jean shorts, the ripped edges dripping over her thighs like webs and letting her tattoos peek through. Those shorts barely contained her ass, and the thin, red, spaghetti strap top she'd paired with them showed a sliver of her stomach. She was walking slowly, looking at all the booths before she paused at one, turning enough for me to see there was absolutely zero chance she had on a bra with that top. A navy-blue bandana with white stars framed her hairline, and the whole picture was nothing short of a patriotic fantasy come to life.

I bit my knuckle before my hands found the wheel and turned a hard left into the parking garage.

"I gotta go, Mom. I just remembered an errand I need to run before tonight. I'll call you later this week?"

"Whenever you have time. Enjoy your summer, that's what I want most for you."

I smiled as I pulled into a parking spot. "*Te quiero.*"

"*Te quiero mas, mijo.*"

I hopped out of my car as soon as I parked it, all but jogging toward the booth I'd spotted Mary at. While most of Boston was flocking down to Harborfest already, the entire city was full of events on our nation's birthday that meant you couldn't find a street within miles that didn't have *something* going on. How could we not make a big deal of our nation's independence, with so much history weaved throughout each and every block?

I pushed through the crowd, muttering *excuse me* as I did. I could have just waited and saw Mary at home later. She knew we were having a party tonight — was looking forward to it, it seemed. But the truth was I hadn't had the chance to be alone with her since that night I cooked for her.

And something had shifted between us that night.

I didn't know exactly what it was, but she no longer seemed like she hated breathing the same air as me. Actually, it was worse — because she was avoiding me.

Any time I'd walk in on her doing yoga with Braden or gaming on the couch with Kyle, she'd maybe utter two words to me before making an excuse to leave the room altogether. She wouldn't meet my eyes, wouldn't take the bait when I teased her.

Maybe that's why I picked up my speed when I spotted her red shirt again, her long hair swept up in a messy ponytail that swung as she walked.

She slowed at a vendor selling candles, picking one up and inhaling deeply. I slowed my gait as I approached the tent.

"Getting that to cover up the stench of The Pit?"

Mary didn't seem surprised by my entrance. In fact, she smiled a little as if she'd known I was coming before setting the candle down and turning to face me.

She about knocked me on my ass when she did.

Her eyes were kohl-lined and smoky, her plump lips painted the same red as her tank top. It set the green of her eyes off even more, the way her dark lashes fanned above and below them, and she offered me an easy smile like we were friends.

"Figured the party tonight would undo all the pleasant scents I've managed to bring in over the last month."

"You're not wrong. There's a very specific odor that hangs around the next day. We could bottle it as *Bud Light & Debauchery*."

"So *four* candles, then," she said, piling them into her arms. But she only held them long enough to make the joke before she was putting them back down.

I noted that the bag on her arm was large, but mostly empty — like she was being very careful with what she purchased. After our conversation about her family the other night, I understood why. I didn't imagine she made much as a tattoo apprentice.

It was hard for me to wrap my head around, already working and having the responsibility of bills the way she did. My tuition was covered from my football scholarship, and Mom and Dad easily picked up the rest — including giving me an allowance every month for food, shopping, going out, or whatever else I could want.

I didn't know what it was like to struggle, to have to think twice before I bought something at the grocery store.

I made a mental note of the scents she had picked up before falling into step with her as she thanked the vendor and stepped out of the booth.

"So, you're not ignoring me anymore, I see."

Her brow arched, but she didn't bother looking at me as she said, "To ignore you, I'd have to actually think about you."

"Ouch," I said, covering my heart with a palm. The little smile that found her lips brought me more relief than it should have.

"You smell, by the way," she added with a wrinkled nose, assessing the sweat making my shirt stick to my chest. "I thought you didn't have practice today."

"Pee Wee."

She blinked. "What?"

"I coach Little League," I said with a laugh. "Well, I *help* coach — kind of like an assistant."

Mary frowned a bit, like she didn't quite believe me. "So, you just voluntarily give up more of your summer time to coach football to little kids?"

"I see I've surprised you again."

She wouldn't admit it, but I saw that I had in how she pressed her lips together against a smile. She turned away from me and toward a booth we were passing, and I tried not to care that she couldn't possibly believe I'd do something like volunteer.

"How many people do you think will come tonight?" she asked.

I shrugged. "Hard to say. It's summer semester, so not as many people as we have in the fall, that's for sure. But with it being the holiday, and given that we have a rager every year... it'll probably be a good turnout."

She nodded, pausing for a moment to look at a booth selling custom cutting boards.

"We don't have to have the party tonight," I said when we started walking again. "If it would make you uncomfortable to have all those people in your space."

"It's your house," she reminded me. "I'm shocked you haven't had a party before this."

"We usually would have, but..."

"Ugh, that makes me feel worse."

I nudged her elbow. "Don't. The truth is probably more that Kyle and Braden like to hang out with you and don't want to share with the rest of the team or anyone else."

I left myself out of the equation, but hoped she saw when she gave me a look that said *brown-noser* that I meant me, too.

"I'm sure it'll be fun."

"Do you drink?" I asked.

"That's a very forward question."

"I just haven't seen you in all the time you've lived with us."

She shrugged, fanning herself with one hand. I noted the bead of sweat gathering on her neck, wondered when it would start its descent along the ink that disappeared between her breasts. "It's not really my preference. I'll have wine with the girls sometimes, or a good cocktail, but I much prefer my buzz to be of the herbal variety."

Mary cocked a brow at me like she wasn't sure I'd catch the reference.

"Ah, how fitting. Mary loves the Mary J."

We ducked inside another booth with her smirking at me.

This one had free samples of different dips made from the spice packets they were selling. They sold it with direction to *just add sour cream or mayonnaise*. I tested a spicy red pepper one while Mary dipped a pretzel into a sour cream and ranch. She closed her eyes on a hum that reminded me of when she had my *tostones*, and I was almost jealous of the older gentleman who lit up behind the sample table.

"Good, right?" he asked.

"*So* good." Mary grabbed another pretzel and tried a dill one next. "How much are they?"

"Three packs for ten dollars," he said. "And just add to whatever base you want — mayo, sour cream, even Greek yogurt works."

I saw the hesitation in Mary as she reached for her wallet.

"You know what, we should get some of these for the party tonight," I said, fishing mine out of my back pocket before she could. I handed the man a twenty-dollar bill. "We'll take six."

Mary gaped at the transaction as if I'd just bought her a car.

The man grinned as he bagged up our choices, and when we fell back in line with the other people wandering the market, Mary slapped me hard across the shoulder.

"Ouch!" I rubbed the spot. "What the hell was that for?"

"For acting like I'm some sort of charity case."

"I was just being nice."

"Yeah, well, it's weird and I don't like it. So stop."

I chuckled, and then as the crowd started to thin where we were walking, I noticed she was on the side of the path closest to the street. I slowed my step until she passed a little in front of me before I came around the back of her and she had no choice but to scoot over closer to the tents and have me between her and the street, instead.

She gave me a look. "What was that for?"

"What?"

She wiggled her finger between us. "Whatever that little dance just was."

I shrugged. "You haven't heard of the sidewalk rule?"

"The *what*?"

"You know, the guy always walks on the side closest to the street."

Mary stopped walking at that, and when I turned, she pegged me with a bored expression before she blinked slowly like I was stupid.

"You're kidding, right?"

I pressed a hand to my chest. "I'm nothing if not a gentleman."

Her face warped with the restraint of holding back a laugh, and then she started walking again. "Please. As if your body would stop a car from plowing over me."

"It might," I said, puffing my chest a little. I smirked down at her over the top of my sunglasses. "You don't see what I do in the weight room."

She poked my side hard enough to deflate me and then smiled in victory when it worked, skipping a few steps ahead.

"You wanna be chivalrous?" she asked, spinning to face me as she continued walking backward. Her ponytail swung with the motion, and something tightened in my chest at the sight of her so light and carefree. "Go to a women's march. Vote for a female to take office. Read a book on feminism. Stop using *pussy* as an insult."

"Hey, I already learned that lesson. Only took you telling me once."

She leveled me with a look. "You're telling me you haven't said it since that day?"

"On my mom's life," I said, holding up two fingers in a solemn swear.

Mary just shook her head with a smile, whipping back around and giving me that glorious view of her ass in those cut-off shorts again.

And I reveled in the feeling that she might actually enjoy having my company.

We walked the market for about another hour before we were both sweating profusely and ready for air conditioning. Mary had parked in the same garage as me, so we walked toward it together.

We were almost to it when a scraggly, too-thin cat sauntered out from under one of the buildings and directly into our path.

I paused and said, "*Ick*," at the same time Mary bent and said, "*Aww!*"

She glared up at me as I barked out a laugh, and then she was holding her hand out and trying to woo the thing.

It was fluffy and mostly gray, but with a white chest and feet and a little spot on its head. When it flicked its tail up, I noted it was a girl, and she walked right up to Mary, sniffing her fingers for just a moment before she nudged her head into Mary's palm and curled her back to get every inch of affection she could.

"Well, hello, sweet girl," Mary cooed with a giggle, and when the cat weaved between her legs before quite literally knocking Mary onto her ass and climbing into her lap, Mary let out a loud laugh, her face lifting to the sky.

Her eyes landed on me next, and they doubled in size like a cartoon character, her long black lashes batting up at me. She was a complete contradiction in that moment — the tattooed, dark-humored artist turning soft at a cat curling up in her lap.

"Mary," I warned. "Don't even think about it."

"Leo," she pleaded, her bottom lip protruding as she held the cat up for me to get a better view. "Just *look* at her."

"I see her, and I'll say it again — don't even think about it."

Fifteen minutes later, I was pulling into a parking spot next to Mary.

At a fucking pet store.

Chapter 14

MARY

Palico sat purring in my lap a few days after the Fourth of July party, her warm body curled up into a little ball. Leo didn't stand a chance against me once I gave the little furball a name, and although he'd never admit it, I knew from just the past couple nights that he adored the thing as much as I did.

With one fingertip, I absentmindedly stroked the white spot on her head that led down to her little pink nose as I watched ESPN with Kyle and Braden.

I hated ESPN. I wasn't following a damn thing, really, just sitting there in a comfortable silence and letting my eyes gloss over. Even though it had been a few days, it seemed we were all still recovering from the party. I'd spent most of the night in my bedroom with Palico, anyway, getting her settled and making sure the noise didn't bother her too much.

That cat was as cool as a cucumber. She watched me most of the night with a bored flick of her tail as if to say, "You think this has anything on the streets of Boston, kid? I've been through worse. My question is why aren't *you* out there partying?"

So, once I felt like she was comfortable, I joined the rest of the rowdy crew downstairs. And while I spent most of my night talking to Giana and Riley and steering clear of the booze, we all stayed up until sunrise, and the lack of sleep alone made it hard to get into a routine again.

I had no idea how the guys did this during football season, especially on nights when they knew they had practice the next morning.

My phone aggressively vibrating on the coffee table woke Palico, and she begrudgingly stretched and sauntered off my lap when I leaned forward to see who it was. Hope bubbled in my chest at the sight of Margie's name, and I slipped into the kitchen to answer.

"Hey, Margie."

"Hey, kiddo," she greeted back, that smoker voice I loved so much filling my ears. Margie seemed less like a landlord and more like a crazy aunt who took care of you, but also was first in line to get you booze when you were underage.

"Tell me you have good news."

Her long sigh on the other end had all that hope deflating out of me in an instant.

"Well, the pipes are fixed."

I perked up. "Okay, that's great."

"Yeah... except, when they started working on repairing the walls and floors and ceiling, well... they found mold."

I closed my eyes, forcing a slow breath. "Okay... and so that means?"

"I'm sorry, kid. It's going to be a while."

I cursed under my breath, sneaking a glance in the living room where Kyle and Braden were kicked back on the couch and sprawling over the entire thing like their limbs couldn't take up enough room even if they tried. Their hair was mussed, sock-covered feet kicked up on the coffee table, and Palico had curled up right in-between them. Braden scratched under her chin as she leaned into the touch.

The sight warmed my heart.

I didn't think it was possible, but this disgusting jock house almost felt a little like home.

The issue with that was that it *wasn't* home, and I couldn't pretend it could be for much longer. Fall was rapidly approaching, and I knew I was on borrowed time before the room I was squatting in would be assigned to another football player.

"How long are we talking?" I asked Margie.

"It'll take a couple weeks just for them to remove the mold, but that's just the beginning. Not sure what the repairs will look like after. They have to rip up carpet, floors, walls..."

"Fuck me," I whispered.

"Try being the homeowner," Margie shot back with an unamused chuckle. "Insurance will handle most of it. But hey, I wanted to give you the chance now to break the lease. I didn't think it would be necessary with just the pipes, but now..."

"I don't want to," I said instantly. "I mean, that is, if you think I'll be able to move back home soon."

"Define *soon*."

I chewed my bottom lip. "Let's just see how the next few weeks go and go from there. That okay?"

"You realize you're being sweet to me when I'm the reason your ass is homeless right now?" She laughed. "Of course, it's okay by me. I'd rather keep you than have to find another tenant. I just don't want to get your hopes up on how soon you can get back in."

I nodded. "Well, I have a place for now. Hopefully it won't be much longer."

Margie paused. "You sound happy, kid. You sound good."

I fought back the smile threatening to break loose and shrugged. "I'm okay."

"Good. Alright, well, I'll be in touch."

With that, I ended the call and made my way back into the living room. I chuckled to myself at the sight of Braden and Kyle both passed out, Palico curled up in the space between Braden's legs and sleeping, too.

I left them be, checking the time on my phone and making my way upstairs to start getting ready for a night at the shop.

I heard music coming from Leo's room as I passed it, and considered knocking and seeing what he was up to. But I shook off the thought. In fact, I pinched myself for having it at all. I hated how I'd somehow gone from ignoring him every time we were in the same room to wondering what he was doing, what he was thinking. I'd lit up like a fucking schoolgirl when he found me at the market the other day, and even though I pretended to be annoyed with him, the truth was that I wasn't. Not anymore.

And *that* was the new source of my annoyance.

I slipped into my room, quietly shutting the door behind me. I stripped off my shirt and pulled on a bralette, something to give the girls support without restraining them. I'd just shimmied on a pair of black jeans when a familiar scent found me.

I inhaled, eyes fluttering shut on the enticing mixture of coffee, bourbon, and sandalwood.

Then, my eyes shot open, and I blinked before turning to find a candle burning on top of my dresser.

A candle *I* didn't light.

Or purchase.

I stared at it for a moment like it was a figment of my imagination before crossing my room. I lifted it, careful not to grab it where it was too hot or tilt it so the wax would put out the flames. And when I read the label, when I recognized where it was from, I sat it back down in a numb sort of awareness.

Did he…

Did he buy this candle for me?

I blinked again, and this time, I saw a brown paper bag behind the candle. I reached inside and found three more just like it — all scents that I'd been looking at when Leo found me at the market. There was also a small, folded note.

To cover the stench — though I doubt it will work.
Love, Leo

A rush of heat flooded through me, my stomach lifting on the wings of a thousand butterflies.

I covered my mouth where a smile was already curling.

Then, my hands rolled into fists, and I stomped my foot with a frustrated growl before I whipped my door open and stormed down the hall.

I didn't let myself stop and think before I twisted the doorknob on Leo's room and burst inside without so much as a knock. It was only then that I paused, not because good sense had come to me, but because I was now staring down at a very sweaty Leo wearing very little clothes.

He was repping out pushups, and he finished his set with just a glance at me and furrow of his brow. Then, he hopped up to his feet like it was easy, swiping a towel off the back of his desk chair and mopping his face with it. He let it hang over his shoulder then, his hands on his hips, bare chest heaving and slick with sweat.

My mouth parted as I followed each bead that gathered and slid down the mountains of muscles covering his body — his pecs, swollen and smooth and round, his abs, hard and defined, all the way down to the deep-cut V that disappeared under the band of his shorts.

I didn't mean to wet my lips, didn't mean to take so much time as I slowly lifted my eyes up to find his, pausing on where his chains stuck to his chest on the way. His mouth seemed just as dry as mine, and I thought I saw him bite the inside of the lower one before he arched a thick, dark brow.

"Need help finding your shirt, roomie?"

Chapter 15

LEO

Mary was a vision of wrath and desire in my doorway, her brows bent in rage while her breasts heaved against the barely there scrap of fabric containing them. The button and zipper of her jeans were undone, too, the lacy fabric of her forest green thong peeking through the V-shaped opening.

When she saw my eyes stick there, her face flushed with color and she hastily zipped and buttoned her jeans before folding her arms over her chest, as if that could hide her curves from my view.

"No," she spat through her teeth. "What I *need* is for you to stay the hell out of my room."

I held up my hands. "Hey, I've respected that rule since the moment you put it into place."

"Oh yeah? Then why is there a fucking candle burning on my dresser? Because I sure as hell didn't put it there."

I smiled at that, folding my arms under my chest. The way Mary's eyes flicked to my pecs told me my upper body pump was distracting, and that made me smile wider.

"It's a gift."

"One I didn't ask for."

"Well, that's typically how gifts work. Otherwise, it would just be a transaction, wouldn't it? You ask for something, I get it for you." I waved my hand over the space between us. "Doesn't seem as fun."

Something washed over Mary, smoothing the line between her brows. I took that, along with the stretch of silence, as an invitation to explain.

"I saw you looking at them at the market," I said. "And I saw how you put them down, likely because you're trying to save. I listen when you talk to me, contrary to what you might believe."

Her jaw tensed like she was grinding her teeth together.

"So, I peeked at what scents you had picked up and went back the next day to get them for you."

She blinked, quiet for a long moment before she whispered one word.

"Why?"

"Why not?" I shrugged. "I wanted to do something nice."

Again, there was that softening, one that made me want to cross the distance between us and wrap her in my arms. I couldn't explain it, but I wanted so desperately to hold her and watch all that tension melt, feel her relax in my hold and rest her head against my chest and whisper *thank you*. I wanted to know what it would feel like to show her a little kindness, a little care, and her actually accept it.

The need was so strong I almost succumbed to it, but at the subtle shift of my body, she hardened again, her spiky shell snapping back in place.

"I don't need your pity," she said, taking two full steps toward me and pointing her finger at my chest.

"It's not pi—"

"*Or* your gifts," she said, cutting me off. "Stop being nice to me."

I pressed right back into her space, making her back down only an inch, but she stood her ground just enough that my chest brushed hers. The metal of her piercings hit the top of my abdomen and I suffocated the groan I wanted to let loose at the touch.

"Why?" I challenged, staring down at her over the bridge of my nose. "Because it makes it harder to hate me so damn much?"

Her mouth parted, eyelids fluttering so softly I questioned whether they did at all before she narrowed her gaze and pressed harder into me. "Trust me — *that* is always going to be easy for me."

"And why is that, exactly? What did I do to earn such passionate disaffection from you?"

She opened her mouth like she was ready to scream the answer at me, and I willed her to do it. I *wanted* the fight.

Give me that fire, I silently begged.

But the ire and passion drained out of her, her face relaxing, expression blank in an instant — like she decided I wasn't worth it.

She pulled away, taking all the heat and tension with her as the cool air of my room swept between us.

"Stay out of my room," she said pointedly, and then she spun on her heel and blew through my door, slamming it closed behind her.

Chapter 16

MARY

My spoiled mood only soured more as the night went on.

The shop was typically my refuge, the one place where I felt safe and at ease to be one-hundred percent myself. I looked forward to my shifts. Hell — I came in even when I wasn't scheduled to. I didn't care if I was cleaning or sketching or studying an artist, every minute in the shop felt like it was meaningful, like it had purpose.

Like *I* had purpose.

But tonight, about the only thing I felt was annoyed.

Sifting through my feelings felt like too much work. *Why*, exactly, was I so upset that Leo bought me some damn candles? It wasn't a big deal. He saw that I liked them, and he went back and got them for me. I should have been appreciative. I should have smiled and thanked him.

Instead, I wanted to throttle him.

I didn't know which option upset me more — the one where he took pity on me and my low cash fund and decided to be a savior by purchasing me a bunch of stupid candles, or the one where he actually *wasn't* showing pity, but kindness, and thoughtfulness.

Okay, it was definitely that one.

The fact that he could possibly be a good human being went against everything I'd believed about him since that summer in high school. When he did things like this, it was almost like he was that boy I talked to until early in the morning, the one who had layers he didn't let anyone else see but me.

I much preferred believing he was a self-centered asshole.

My hand hurt from how hard I'd been gripping the writing tool I used on my iPad, and I flexed my fingers as I leaned away from the screen and studied what I'd drawn. My aim was to create an underwater-themed sleeve, and I'd achieved it.

The issue was that it looked like every other fucking tattoo artist in the world.

I bit back a huff as I tapped the menu, and I was a second away from trashing the entire thing when my wrist was snatched in a fierce grip.

"Whoa, whoa," Nero said, frowning at me and then the screen. "I know you weren't about to delete this."

"It's garbage."

His hand softened where it held my wrist, and I almost thought I felt him smooth his thumb over my skin as he released me and grabbed the pen out of my hand.

"It's very good," he argued, and his eyes studied the screen for a long moment before he tapped the butt end of the pen to where I'd drawn coral reef connecting the massive stingray on the upper arm down to the sand and shells of the forearm. "This isn't you, though."

I sighed. "I know."

"So why'd you draw it?"

"Because I don't fucking know what else to put there."

Nero frowned more as I crossed my arms like a child and sat back in my chair. He dropped the pen to the desk. "What's wrong?"

I looked at him, at the screen, then at my shoes as I sighed. "Just a bad night."

He nodded, then rounded until he was standing behind me. Without warning, his gargantuan hands wrapped around my shoulders, and he began to knead the tense muscles.

I wanted to sigh with how good it felt, those massive fingers pressing into my sore muscles. A groan I didn't want to release came out without permission, because it felt *good* to be touched, and my muscles needed the release.

But when his hands swept over me in a slower motion, when I felt the heat of him behind me, my body went rigid.

Nero was my boss — my *married* boss — and him rubbing my shoulders felt a whole lot like it shouldn't be happening.

"You need to relax," he said, his voice low from where he stood above me. I still hadn't unfolded my arms, and even as he worked the muscles, I only tensed under his touch. We had always been friendly with each other. Flirty? Maybe occasionally.

But he'd never touched me, not like this.

And everything about it gave me the ick.

"You're so focused on finding your style that you're suffocating your creativity and any chance it has of showing you what it can do."

That made me soften a bit.

He wasn't being weird. He was just trying to calm me down, to guide me as his apprentice. I blamed my bitter attitude and general annoyance with men at the moment for assuming the worst.

If Nero only knew the main reason for the knots of stress in my neck were from my roommate and my rather inconvenient feelings about him.

"It's just confusing," I said, deciding to focus on what I *did* feel regarding my apprenticeship and stay away from any other thoughts swimming in my head. "I feel like I'm ready to start with my own clients, but I also feel like I have nothing to offer that they can't find from someone else."

"And what's wrong with that?"

I frowned up at him, and he squeezed my shoulders once more before rounding me and plopping down on the stool to my right. He grabbed the edge of my chair and rolled me over to him, until I was almost in-between his spread legs.

"Everything you want will come in time," he promised me. "But you're holding yourself back waiting for perfection when the truth is that you just need to practice. You've worked on several skins now," he reminded me. "All of which have been beyond happy with your work. So tell me — why aren't you?"

I could barely focus on anything he said because I was in-between his legs, and his hands were on my knees now, holding me in a way that was far more intimate than a boss and employee.

"You're right," I said with a sticky voice, trying to slowly back out of his touch. "I'll... I'll focus on relaxing."

"Good," he said, and then he eliminated what little space I'd managed to put between us. His eyes searched mine, and then he reached out and tucked my hair behind one ear. "You're talented, Mary. And fucking beautiful, too. That combination will take you far in this career."

My skin crawled at his close attention, stomach roiling violently as I chanted *no no no* over and over in my head.

I looked up to Nero. I *respected* him. Everything I'd learned in the last year had come from the same hands still squeezing my knees.

When he leaned in just a centimeter, I panicked, hopping up and breaking all contact.

"Fuck, man," I said on a laugh, running my hands through my hair. "What a night. Nothing an edible can't fix."

Nero chuckled, slipping back into the persona of the boss I knew as he braced his hands on his knees and stood. "Get out of here and go wind down. It's slow, anyway, and I can clean up."

"You're sure?" I asked even as I started packing up my bag. I had to get out of there. *Now.*

"I'm sure. I'll see you tomorrow. And hey," he said, grabbing me by the shoulders and hauling me up to look at him again. I fought the urge to squirm out of his hold. "It's going to be okay. You're doing great. And you'll have your own spot in this shop before you know it."

My heart did a somersault.

If he'd said this to me even ten minutes ago, I would have leapt into his arms.

Now, I wondered if he meant it, if I really was ready, if I deserved to have my own chair and clients to fill it.

Or if he just wanted in my pants.

"Thanks, Nero," I said.

I squirmed out of his hold without another word and darted out the door, trying and failing to calm my breaths as I fumbled for my keys on the way to my car. Once I was inside, I locked the doors as if that could keep out the questions assaulting me.

What the hell was that?

Was he... hitting on me?

I shook my head even as I thought it, sure I was wrong.

Then, I shook my head at myself for not trusting in my gut that I knew was the only thing I could really rely on.

But to actually believe he *was* hitting on me? What would that mean for my apprenticeship, for the last year of my life, for my future, my *career*?

What about his wife?

It made me sick to even consider, so I banished all thought with a squeal of my tires out of the parking lot and a twist of the volume knob on my stereo. I blasted The White Stripes, rolling down all my windows and letting the cool evening air waft in.

I'd just taken maybe my first calm breath all night when my phone started ringing.

Mom.

I groaned, head dropping back against the headrest. I considered not answering, but I knew well enough by now that if I didn't, she'd call repeatedly until I did, or threaten to report me as a missing person to the cops.

With a tap of my thumb, her voice filled the car.

"Are you in some sort of trouble?"

I smiled at the somehow comforting shrillness of her worry. It made me feel at home. "Hello, Mother. To what do I owe the pleasure of a late-night phone call from you?"

"Don't be smart with me," she warned. "You never answer if it's before noon, and I know you're probably working at that *parlor*, anyway." She spat the word *parlor* as if I'd been working in a brothel. "Or are you even working at all?"

"What's that supposed to mean?"

"It *means* that we got a past-due credit card statement in the mail today with your name on it."

I froze.

Shit.

I prided myself on never using the credit card they set up for me when I left the house at eighteen. I hadn't wanted it, but Dad had practically begged. He wanted to know I had it if I ever needed it, no matter how much I assured him I could do it on my own.

Since that day, I'd only charged a few things to it, paying it off immediately and letting it collect dust in my wallet the rest of the time. But when everything went down with the pipes and the unexpected move across the street, I had broken down and charged gas and some groceries. I meant to pay it off as soon as I got my paycheck, but I'd forgotten.

And it was with this notice that I realized I hadn't checked my mail since I moved to The Pit.

"*Fuck,* sorry, Mom. I meant to—"

"Don't curse at me, young lady!"

"I didn't curse *at* you, I cursed *to* you."

I heard her going off on the other end, but it was softer now, the sound far away as if in a cave that I was only catching the echo of. *You worry us to death, Mary. I don't understand why you won't just come back home. Or go to college, for goodness' sake. You won't let us help, you won't—*

It sounded like a hand was smothered over the phone, and then after a long pause of silence, the sound cleared, and a deep voice bellowed my name.

"Hey, Mare Bear."

I almost cried at the sound of my father's voice. "Hey, Dad. I'm sorry about the card. I'll pay it as soon as I get home, I'm on my way now."

"It's all good, I already took care of it."

My neck heated. "You didn't have to do that."

"You're our daughter, we're supposed to take care of you."

I ignored the sting in my chest. "I'll wire you tonight. Just tell me what the overdue fee was."

"I'll send it right back if you even try."

"I don't need your money, Dad."

"Hey, I'm not asking for anything in return."

He shot the words out like he knew that's why I was insistent, and I couldn't even lie and say it wasn't. Last time I'd asked for their help, they'd offered it along with a set of conditions — move back home, get a regular job, enroll in college, *get my life together*. I'd expected it from Mom, but with Dad... it hurt.

"Are you going to come home to visit anytime soon? Your mother and I miss you."

I snorted. "I highly doubt she misses anything about me."

When he didn't respond, I sighed.

"Maybe you and I could grab lunch this week. I can come downtown to the office? We haven't had your favorite Thai place in a while."

"Okay," Dad said after a pause, and I heard the hurt in his voice, how he wished things were different between me and Mom.

He wasn't the only one.

"I'll have Matthew join us, too. He's doing big things, just closed a deal on an e-commerce app that we were in a head-to-head battle over."

The first genuine smile of the day found my lips then. "That's my big bro."

I could tell Dad was smiling, too, even though I couldn't see him. "He'll be excited to see you."

My heart ached, wondering for a split second if I should have followed in my brother's footsteps, if I should have joined the family company right under him and Dad. I could have been finishing up my degree this year, just twelve months away from a six-figure salary that would only exponentially grow.

But the thought didn't even have time to stick before my creative energy was beating it right out of me.

I would have been miserable.

The truth was, I'd rather be broke and doing what I love than rich in some passionless job.

Of course, after tonight, I had a sinking feeling in my gut that the last year of my life might have been wasted on a man who wanted to fuck me more than he wanted to help me make a career.

My mood depleted again as I turned onto our street, and when I saw cars lining both sides of The Pit and lights flashing from our living room, I groaned.

A fucking party.

Great.

"I gotta go, Dad. I'll text you about lunch."

"We love you, Mare Bear."

"Love you, too. And... thank you," I said sincerely. "For the card thing. It won't happen again."

"No sweat," he said, and I knew for him it wasn't. Even with the overdue charges, my bet was that bill couldn't have been more than a few hundred bucks. My dad spent more than that on dinner most days of the week.

I parked at my old house, casting a forlorn look at it and wishing more than I had in the last six weeks that I could just open the door, climb the stairs to my room, pack a bowl, and be alone.

Instead, I dragged my feet across the street to The Pit.

Chapter 17
MARY

No one noticed me when I walked through the door. Not that that surprised me, considering half the cheerleading team was there as well as a dozen or so sorority sisters. I spotted Kyle and Braden in the kitchen lining up shots with a group of girls gathered around them, and while a lot of the team was there, I noticed Zeke and Clay weren't, which meant Riley and Giana wouldn't be either.

As much as I loved those girls, I was glad I didn't have to put on a happy face and pretend I wanted to party when it was the absolute last thing on my mind. Thank God they both had boyfriends they were obsessed with.

I weaved through the crowd up to my room, smiling when I found Palico curled into a ball on the clothes I'd left on my bed.

She yawned and stretched when I quietly shut the door behind me, and I petted her until she was satisfied before stripping out of my clothes and jumping in the shower. I didn't do the whole hair-washing and leg-shaving song and dance, just rinsed off and sighed with contentment once my sweatpants were slipped on. I grabbed the biggest t-shirt I had next, not bothering with a bra, and popped a blueberry-flavored edible in my mouth before flopping down on my bed.

I hadn't seen Leo on my way up, and I wondered for a moment if he was in his room with a girl already.

Then, I angrily shoved the heels of my hands into my eyes before putting on my headphones to drown out the noise of the party.

And my brain.

For a while, I sat propped up in my pillows with my iPad, drawing as Palico purred where she was tucked in by my side. When the edible started to hit, I felt all the tension of the day melt out of me, and my drawings became more fluid, more free.

Somewhere around one in the morning, I stood and stretched, cracking my back with a few quick twists before I stared at the door that led down the hall. A small part of me wanted to join the party now, but the larger part didn't want to put on makeup or wear anything with underwire or zippers involved. I could have gone to sleep, but I wasn't exactly tired.

My ears hurt from my headphones, so I took them out and opened my window, savoring the cool breeze and gentle quiet of the night. Then, before I could even think about what I was doing, I shoved the window all the way up and crawled out onto the roof.

The room they'd given me overlooked the garden, and I crawled only a few feet above my window before I sat my ass right on the cool shingles, crossing my bare feet under me and leaning back on my palms. The party was loud enough that the music and laughter spilled into the night, but it was softer out here, farther away, and the gentle high I had from the edible made me feel weightless and happy.

For the first time all night, I felt at peace.

"You found my spot."

I jumped, nearly toppling off the roof when I whipped around and found a shadowed figure hunched a little higher on the roof. I'd no sooner caught my balance before the shadow edged into the light from the streetlamp, and Leo's hand shot out to make sure I didn't fall.

He had no right to look as good as he did in the moonlight, and I knew my high only made him appear more appetizing. His hair was somewhat styled, but tussled by the wind, his eyes were glossed over and tired but somehow enticing, too. He wore a light pair of denim jeans I wouldn't allow myself to focus on too long, and a sweater that he'd shoved up past his forearms to bunch at his elbows.

Why did his forearms turn me on so much?

I wanted to pull one of those arms into my lap and draw all over it, wanted to tattoo it, to mark him permanently with my art.

I shrugged him off once I had my balance, pretending like I didn't need him to gain it. "You *would* be out here."

I didn't say it with the vitriol I spat at him earlier, but rather in a disappointed kind of sigh. I should have known the peace couldn't last.

I was already making to scoot my way back down the roof and inside when his hand caught the crook of my elbow.

"Don't leave."

My skin burned where he touched me, and I followed the lines of his forearm up to where the sleeves of his sweatshirt had been shoved up. I couldn't lift my gaze any higher, but I didn't move, either.

"I'll go, if you want to be alone."

"No," I said when it was him who started to move. "I didn't realize it was your spot. I'll go."

"I don't own it. You live here, too."

"It's fine, I was just..." I quieted, not sure exactly what I was trying to do.

"How about we share?" he offered with a smirk, settling in beside me. "And if I start to piss you off, which we both know is likely, just say the word and I'll go."

"Or I could push you off the roof."

"That is another option. Not *my* favorite one, though it's probably yours."

The corner of my mouth lifted just a bit as I sat back on my palms again, eyes on the sky and then the garden. I didn't know why it made me happy that Leo would rather be on a rooftop than inside partying, but it did.

I blamed the edible.

"I'm sorry about earlier," he said after a beat.

I slowly turned to him, but he kept his eyes on the roof, his knees bent and elbows balancing on them.

"With the candles," he clarified, still not looking at me. "I overstepped."

I sighed, and tried once again to blame the weed when I said, "You don't need to be sorry. It was *me* being a brat. You did something nice and I..."

"Didn't know how to accept it?"

I swallowed, cracking my neck in lieu of an answer.

"*I'm* sorry I barged into your room and screamed at you like a psycho," I said. "It's just... been a weird night, I guess."

"I kind of liked you screaming at me," Leo said, arching a brow and finally looking at me. "It was hot."

I tongued my cheek before shoving him hard enough to knock him down the roof if he hadn't been braced for it. He laughed, steadying himself, and then we both fell quiet again.

"What happened?"

"Hmm?" I asked.

"You said it's been a weird night. Why?"

I sighed at that. "Well, my parents called, which is never a good thing. And I'm *pretty* sure my boss hit on me tonight, so now I'm questioning if the past year of my life has been a waste."

I chuckled with the admission, trying to make light of it, but when I looked at Leo, his expression was stone cold, jaw tense, brows in a firm line over his eyes.

"What did he do?"

I blinked, then barked out a laugh when I realized he was serious. "Calm down, Mr. Chivalrous. It wasn't anything overt. I'm sure I'm overthinking it," I said, even though I felt the ickiness of that lie sliding into my gut as I turned back to the garden. "And I can handle it."

Leo didn't seem happy with that response, but to his credit, he left it alone, brooding to himself instead of saying whatever it was he wanted to say.

"I also got a call from Margie earlier," I said after a while.

Leo's expression softened. "And?"

"And on top of the water issue, they found mold."

"Shit."

"Yeah."

"Well, you can stay here as long as—"

"We both know this room isn't going to be vacant for much longer," I said, meeting his eyes.

He swallowed, not confirming but not denying, either. Fall camp would start soon for the team, which meant whoever was taking Holden's old room would be moving in — probably within a week or two.

"It's fine, I'll figure something out," I said. "Like I said, I can handle myself."

A strong wind whipped over the top of the house and down over us, making me shiver as I tucked my knees into my chest. This was what I loved most about living in New England, how the summers could bring blistering heat but also nights that felt like fall.

"Fuck, *hermosa*, you've gotta be cold in that," Leo said, as if he just noticed I was wearing a t-shirt. To be honest, *I'd* just realized I was *only* wearing a t-shirt, sans bra, because of course. I folded my arms over my chest in an effort to hide my piercings, though I wasn't sure why.

Then, without another word or a chance for me to respond, Leo ripped his sweater overhead and handed it to me.

I looked at it, at him, back at the sweater, and then laughed.

"What?"

"Are you seriously offering your sweater to me right now?"

His mouth flattened. "Are you seriously being so stubborn you won't take it even though you're clearly freezing?"

"I'm fine," I said, internally cursing the goosebumps that broke on my arms at the exact moment that lie found its way into the night. "And besides, it wouldn't fit me."

"What are you talking about?"

I gestured to my body. "Have you seen me? I'd stretch it out."

"Shut the fuck up and put on my sweater."

My mouth popped open. "How da—"

"Woman," he seethed, cutting me off, and then his hand shot out and grabbed me by the wrist. He shoved my hand through one of the arm holes before doing the same to my other, all while I struggled to break free without flailing so much that I pitched myself off the roof.

When I wouldn't sit still, he hastily yanked the thing over my head and then grabbed the neck hole and pulled me so close I could smell the sweet, heady notes of tequila on his breath when he said, "You can either wear this sweater or I'll use it to tie you down and warm you up with my body heat, instead."

There was a challenge in his eyes, one punctuated with that cocky smirk I hated so much. But I found it impossible to fight back with his hands on me like that, with his breath whispering over my lips.

I swallowed, shoving him away and relenting as I tugged the sweater the rest of the way on. "There. Happy?"

"Very."

Leo sat back with a victorious smile, and I shook my head, hating that while I was irritated, I was also fighting back the urge to swoon.

I'd always wanted a guy to give me his jacket.

So what if it was a sweater instead. It was still Leo's. It smelled like him, like a spicy body wash and lush green grass on a hot summer day. I inhaled that scent on a sleepy-eyed smile, and then a laugh bellowed out of me before I could stop it.

"What?" Leo asked, watching me with an amused smile.

"Nothing."

"You never giggle, so don't tell me that was nothing."

That made me laugh again. Or was it the edible? Everything felt so warm and lovely now that I had his sweater on, now that my high was really settling in.

"Nothing, it's just…" I bit my lip, but it didn't stop me from spilling what I know I would have kept locked up if I were sober. "When I was younger, I used to fantasize about a guy giving me his jacket."

Leo's smile crept up. "Really? You?"

"Yes, *me*," I said defensively, smacking his chest. "I specifically dreamed about it being a letterman jacket, about a guy liking me so much he wanted me to wear something that claimed me like that."

I shook my head at the stupid admission, cheeks flushing.

Then, I sobered on the memory that it hadn't been just *any* guy I'd fantasized about.

It had been Leo.

I found myself exasperated by how easily my brain took me back to the past again, by how frequently it had been doing so lately. Before I could say another word, though, Leo hopped up and was carefully moving up the roof.

"What are you doing?"

"Be right back," was all he called over his shoulder before disappearing.

I blew out a breath, and the longer I was alone, the more I debated sneaking back inside. I hated that I wanted to be there with him, that I loved the fact that he was up here with me when he could be inside with any other girl on campus.

"Don't be a fool," I chastised myself, and I was already starting to peel off his sweater when I heard him fumbling down the roof to me.

I turned just in time for him to open a huge jacket and wrap it around me from behind.

Not just a jacket.

His letterman.

I froze when the weighted fabric cloaked me, my heart pounding in my ears.

"What are you doing?" I thought I heard myself ask.

I glanced up at Leo, who only shrugged and tucked the jacket tighter around me. "Making dreams come true."

My breathing intensified, heart quickening its pace until it felt like just a flutter in my chest. I looked down at where the navy-blue wool hugged me, fingers deftly tracing the leather accents, the buttons, every little piece all the way up to our school's letter.

I knew without confirming that his last name was sprawled across the back.

For a moment, I was fifteen again, floating on the cloud Leo Hernandez built just for me. I was living on angst and butterflies until his name lit up my screen, dreaming about his voice, smiling every morning when I saw a text from him waiting on my phone.

"It looks good on you," Leo said, his voice all a part of the foggy haze.

But when I lifted my gaze to meet his, I realized I was smiling.

And when his eyes fell to my mouth, when he swallowed and glanced back up at me like he wanted... like he wanted to...

I plummeted down to earth again, landing with a painful *splat*.

Hastily, I shrugged the jacket off my shoulders, ripping his sweater overhead next. I couldn't breathe, let alone speak as I started fumbling my way down the roof.

"Mary, wait."

Leo abandoned the layers of him I'd shed on the shingles and chased after me. He passed me easily, blocking my window before I could climb through it.

"Move, Leo."

"What happened? Why do you shut down any time I try to get close to you?"

I was so dizzy I nearly fell off the roof. "Please, just move."

Leo let out a frustrated breath, but to my surprise, he did as I asked, sliding out of the way and even offering a hand to help me inside. I ignored it, of course, but once my feet were planted on the cold wood floor of my room, he pressed his hands on the window ledge and leaned in, keeping me from shutting the window.

"Why do you hate me so much?"

I was still having an internal freakout, but thankfully my instincts kicked in and I scoffed. "I don't care about you enough to hate you."

"I'm serious," he said, not deterred. "You're nice to the other guys. Friendly, even."

"Yeah, well, they aren't complete pigs."

"And I am?"

I met his eyes then, and instantly regretted it. He looked like he wanted to crawl through that window, through *me,* like he wanted to rip me open until he could see everything I was hiding.

"Just because you ask doesn't mean I have to answer," I said softly.

I reached up for the window, ready to close it, but Leo didn't budge.

"Can I have a second chance to right whatever it is I did wrong?"

I stared at the floor so I wouldn't have to stare at him, and my heart thumped loudly with the desire to tell him yes.

But then I latched onto the truth in his question.

He still didn't even know what he'd done.

He still didn't realize who I was.

"Goodnight, Leo," I whispered.

I held my shaking hands on the window frame, listening to the way his ragged breaths matched mine until he finally, wordlessly, backed out of my room.

I slid the window shut without another glance in his direction, pulling the blinds closed before I had the chance to change my mind.

Chapter 18

LEO

"Are you sure this isn't too much?" Braden asked, surveying the table spread.

Kyle had definitely understood the assignment, and used it as an excuse to stay in the kitchen most of the day while Braden and I deep-cleaned the house. The folding table that was typically sticky from beer and littered with red Solo cups was now cleaned and covered by a white tablecloth and copious amounts of food. Everything from bruschetta and chicken kebabs to a mushroom risotto and pesto skirt steak spread out like a buffet. We even lit candles to give it an elegant touch.

I slid my hands into my pockets, looking around at the house that was cleaner than it had been probably ever. "Considering what we're about to suggest to her, I don't think so."

"She's never going to go for it," Braden said.

I didn't argue, because honestly, I felt the same. If Mary wanted to cut off my head when I bought her candles or offered her a jacket when she was cold, there was zero chance she'd be open to what we were about to propose.

The memory of last week on the roof made my jaw tense, and I was sick of how many times I'd replayed every second, wondering what triggered her to blow me off. It seemed no matter what I did to try to build a bridge between us, it only pissed her off more. I liked when we joked about it, when I teased her and she gave it right back.

But sometimes when she looked at me, I saw actual disdain.

And it killed me that I didn't understand why.

Clearly, before she moved in with us, she thought I was a player, an asshole, just another cocky athlete who thinks he's too good for everyone. And that was the persona I painted, the image that got me any girl I wanted and earned me the respect of teammates before they'd even set foot on the field with me. My reputation made up their minds about who I was before I even entered the room, and that made it easy to keep a top spot, to intimidate those who considered battling me for my position and scare the shit out of anyone on the opposite team who had to try to defend me.

But Mary had lived with us for a month and a half.

Couldn't she see through the bullshit façade by now?

From all the little comments she loved to drop, I knew she could.

And yet still, she couldn't stand me.

It pissed me off as much as it made me determined to change her mind.

The memory of her in my letterman jacket soothed me like a balm, making a smile curl on my lips when the picture came to mind. Her cheeks had flushed such a pretty shade of pink, her eyes sparkling a bit when she held it tighter around her. And seeing my name on the back of that jacket, like she was wrapping *me* around her, like she was mine to claim...

I shook out of my thoughts when the front door blew open. Mary, Giana, and Riley piled in, their arms linked as they tried to catch their breath from laughing.

It was a sight I wasn't used to, Mary all carefree and silly like that. She was red-faced from laughing so hard, hair a wave of gold where it fanned over her shoulders, and fuck if she wasn't an absolute knock out in a brown velvet dress that was so short, I was absolutely positive she'd show her ass if she bent over in it. Its thin straps hung loose on her shoulders, and I let my eyes rove all her exposed skin, appreciating how she could wear the simplest dress or shirt and shorts and still turn heads because of the ink and piercings that covered her from head to toe.

That, and the fact that she should have to wear a sign that said *dangerous curves* to warn the poor suckers who walked into walls daily from gawking at her.

Giana and Riley both had shopping bags on their arms, and they tossed them onto the bay window cushion as Mary dabbed at the corner of her eye where a tear had formed from laughing. Then, she straightened at the sight of me.

Her smile fell, which felt like a sucker punch right to the gut. I wasn't a source of her joy, I was a thief of it.

She glanced at the table, at our roommates, back at me, and then to the girls.

"What the hell?" Riley said, pointing her finger at the table. "What's this?"

"Why does it smell weird in here?" Giana asked, nose scrunching.

"It smells clean," Mary said.

"Exactly," Giana agreed. "Weird."

Kyle rounded out of the kitchen with a casserole dish of some sort in his mitten-covered hands, and he plopped it down on the only free space left on the table before hanging his hands on his hips like a proud Mom at Thanksgiving. "What does it look like? We cooked."

The girls blinked in unison, and while Riley and Giana exchanged confused looks, Mary only looked at me.

"What's going on?" she asked softly.

"Can't we do something nice for our roomie?" Kyle asked, walking over to throw his arm around her.

Giana pulled at the fabric around his waist. "Are you wearing an *apron*?"

"Every good cook wears an apron."

"Okay… doesn't explain why *you* are wearing one," Giana mused.

"I cook all the time, fuck you very much, and I'm damn good at it." Kyle stood tall, defensive.

Riley folded her arms, her brow arching in suspicion. "Are you trying to kill us or something?"

"Jesus, Novo," Braden said, shaking his head at her.

"What? Given our history, I think it's fair to assume," she said, gesturing between her and Kyle.

"This isn't about you," he spat back at her.

"Then what's it about?" Mary asked.

That made us all grow quiet, and I ran my hand back through my hair before grabbing my neck. Someone had to rip the Band-Aid off.

Since she already hated me, I figured I was best suited for the job.

"Blake Russo got assigned to the house," I said.

There was a beat of silence, and then Giana deflated, and Riley cursed.

Mary just stood frozen.

"Oh," she said after a minute.

"We tried to push off the date," Braden said. "But with camp around the corner and summer training picking up, Coach wants him to get settled."

Mary nodded, and then snapped her mask into place and waved us off with a breath of a laugh. It was almost magic, how she hid her hurt so easily, like she had been doing it all her life and it was as second nature as breathing. "Hey, it's all good. I appreciate you guys letting me stay as long as you did. I'll figure something out."

"Well, actually," I said, stepping forward. "We were thinking you should stay."

Mary frowned. "Stay? But you just said—"

"In my room."

Once again there was a long beat of silence, and then Riley barked out a laugh. "Yeah, okay. Nice try, Leo."

Giana leaned into her side like she wanted to whisper, but we still all heard her when she said, "Oh, my God. This is one of my favorite tropes. Two people who hate each other, one bed…"

"I'm not staying in your room," Mary said loud enough to snuff out Riley's laugh.

"Why not?"

She scoffed like I was an idiot.

"You can have the bed, I'll take the couch."

"You can't sleep on the couch," she said.

"I've done it plenty of times."

"Yeah, he'll be fine," Kyle said, clapping me on the shoulder. "He's got a young back. Come on, Mary. You can't leave. We love having you here too much."

"At least not until your place is fixed," Braden interjected. "Besides, what about Palico? She needs you."

Mary looked between them and shook her head on an incredulous laugh. "Guys, I can't kick Leo out of his room."

Braden waved her off. "He'll be fine."

"What about my stuff?" she asked.

"I have plenty of room," I cut in. "And I promise, I'll only go in there when I have permission from you. I'll grab what I need for my day the night before and keep it down here so I don't wake you. I can share a bathroom with Kyle."

"He can put some of his stuff in my room if he needs to," Braden added. "We'll make room."

Mary's brows furrowed where she watched me, like she couldn't understand for the life of her why we would even suggest this.

"We don't want you to leave," Kyle said sincerely. "We're like your big brothers now. We want to look out for you and make sure you're okay until your place is ready."

I had to bite back a snort at that because the last thing I thought of Mary as was a sister.

"Pleeeeeease," Braden said, and he dropped to his knees, clasping his hands together. Giana and Riley laughed. Kyle, too. Even I cracked a smile at the sight.

Mary let out another laugh of disbelief, looking between all of us like we were insane. Her gaze snagged on me, and her smile slipped.

"You're sure it's okay?"

That was all the confirmation my roommates needed to celebrate a victory.

Before I could answer, Braden jumped up and leapt into the air with a holler while Kyle picked Mary up like she weighed nothing, tossing her over his shoulder and spinning around while she laughed and cursed at him to let her go. She covered her ass with her hands but it was a poor attempt, considering how much of that blessed ass she had, and I had just enough decency left in me to look away and down at the floor as I hid my own victorious smile.

"Alright, come on, let's eat," Kyle said when he dropped her feet back to the ground. "I made a fucking feast."

"I'm still not sure I trust that this isn't poison," Riley said as she approached the table warily.

Kyle grabbed her and pulled her under one arm, giving her a noogie while she struggled to break free. She socked him hard in the arm when he did, and I smiled at the two of them somewhat getting along, especially after the past few seasons. Kyle had really grown on all of us, like a stray dog you just couldn't help but love no matter how mangey he was.

As if she sensed the commotion was over, Palico sauntered down the stairs to join us. Mary bent to pull the gray ball of purring amusement into her arms. She stroked her fur, listening to Braden detail how he'd found a container of something questionable under Kyle's bed while he was cleaning and it had started growing a colony. There were mixed reactions of disgust and laughter, and then everyone was sitting and piling food onto their plates.

Mary stiffened before she sat, her hands on the back of a chair. She crooked her head just a little to the side, then lifted her gaze to meet mine.

I tried to smile, tried to assure her with one look that everything was going to be fine.

But inside, all I could think was that I was completely fucked.

Because within the week, that girl would be in my bed.

Chapter 19

LEO

The last bit of summer flew by in a heated haze.

Between shuffling our house around, Blake moving in, fall camp starting and Pee Wee wrapping up, I barely had a spare minute in the day to shit, let alone anything else. As exhausted as I was, being busy had been a good thing.

It kept my mind off obsessing over my roommate.

Mary officially moved into my bedroom just a few nights after we presented the option, and while sleeping on the couch had been a pain in the ass — and back — it wasn't nearly as difficult as pulling on a t-shirt and smelling her all over it.

She'd invaded every inch of my room and bathroom.

Mary was everywhere. Her hair, her scent, jewelry and lotion and nail polish, too. While she'd done her level best to steer clear of me, it was impossible to make it through even one day without her on my mind.

We'd at least found some sort of peace treaty in it all. While we were both busy and hadn't spent more than a moment or two together since that night on the roof, she was back to cracking jokes rather than throwing daggers at me with her eyes. She might not have been my best friend, but she at least seemed grateful for me sacrificing my space for her.

I tried not to get jealous when I saw her doing yoga with Braden or fucking around in the kitchen with Kyle. I did my best not to stare too hard when Blake got curious about what she was drawing one day, leaning over her with a curious smile while she looked up at him like she loved that he asked.

It was clear she didn't want anything to do with me.

But leaving her alone was possibly the hardest play route I'd ever had to run.

That's why I was thankful for the five AM wakeup calls, for padded practices, film meetings, strength training, and conditioning that left me just awake enough to shower before I'd collapse only to do it all again the next day. This was what I lived for — that feeling of fall, of football consuming every inch of my life. Some athletes crashed under this pressure, but I thrived. Pack my schedule with more than a normal human being can handle and I'll show you the impossible.

Still, even *I* was thankful for the little break coach gave us halfway through camp.

It was Saturday, and he'd not only let us out of the stadium early, but given us the next morning off, too. The reason?

The North Carolina Panthers were playing their first preseason game, and there was a high chance we'd get to see Holden on the field.

The Pit was packed by kickoff, half the team and some of their girlfriends littering our couch, chairs, bean bags and every inch of the floor they could find around the television. Even Mary had rearranged her schedule at the tattoo shop so she could be home for the game, and she sat right in the center of the floor on a massive bean bag with Riley and Giana on either side of her.

They'd been pounding seltzers since about noon, so while I was surprised they were all still awake, I wasn't surprised they were giggling and making jokes about how football pants should be illegal.

It felt like a Super Bowl party rather than a preseason game that didn't mean shit, but for us, this game was more significant than any we'd seen before.

This was our quarterback, an NBU alum who actually made it.

It was proof that, maybe, we had a chance in hell of going pro, too.

I tried not to watch Mary from where I was in the kitchen as the second quarter got underway. It had been practically impossible while sitting in the same room as her, especially seeing her so relaxed and happy and buzzed, if not already drunk. I remembered how she used to be at our parties last year, sour and closed off and usually looking for the first excuse to bolt.

Now, she looked like she really felt at home, like we were family.

"Man, I'm fucking *beat*," Zeke said, groaning a bit as he joined me in the kitchen and hopped up to sit on the counter. He squinted, massaging his neck with one hand while the other held his beer. "Am I getting old, or is Coach riding us hard this camp?"

"We're a championship team now," I reminded him. "More to prove."

Clay sauntered in to join us, and I tossed him a beer out of the fridge when I saw he was empty-handed. Zeke lifted his beer once our cans were cracked open, and the three of us tapped them together before taking a long pull.

"Feels weird without Holden," Clay said.

Zeke and I nodded, and I felt that mixture between nostalgia and nausea sweeping through me again. I wondered if it would be with me all season, if I'd constantly be caught between soaking up our last year together at NBU and reminiscing on all we'd done together the last three years.

"Hard to believe we'll all be going our own ways soon," I said.

"Eh, different teams, maybe, but we'll all be pro," Clay offered with a confident shrug of one shoulder.

I cocked a brow. "You realize the odds of that are pretty slim, right?"

"And *you* realize you're in the company of the best college football players in the nation, right?"

I chuckled, lifting my beer in a salute. I loved that he was confident, and with his talent, he should be. His confidence was different from mine — it wasn't cocky and half a joke. It was calm and sure, as if it'd already happened.

Still, I couldn't quiet that realistic voice inside me whispering that only one-point-six percent of college football players make it to the NFL.

"I, uh... I actually don't know if that's what I want."

Clay and I both whipped around when the words left Zeke's mouth.

"What?" Clay asked. "The fuck are you talking about, man? That's been your *only* goal ever since I've known you."

"Long before that," I chimed in.

"Yeah, I don't know," he said, grabbing the back of his neck. "I still want a career in football, of course, but... I was leaning toward coaching, maybe."

Clay and I were both too shocked to speak.

Zeke checked behind him before looking at us again and lowering his voice. "I just... I don't know what's next for Riley."

That sucked the air out of the room.

"She wants to go pro as bad as the rest of us," he continued, shaking his head. "But, I mean, we all know there's never been a female drafted to the NFL."

"Fuck, man," Clay said, running a hand through his hair. "My stupid ass never even thought about that. I've been running my mouth about going pro all camp like a fucking asshole."

"It's fine, she's used to it," Zeke said. "When she first came on the team, I don't think she wanted anything past college, you know? She's got a career in art curation waiting for her easily. And she'd be damn good at it, too. But something has shifted over the last two seasons." He paused. "She got an agent, and let's just say the agent is not-so-gently suggesting she consider sports broadcasting if she wants a career anywhere near the sport she loves."

"He doesn't think she has a chance at all?" I asked.

Zeke scoffed, meeting my gaze with an incredulous look. "Come on, man."

I nodded, falling silent. Riley only started playing football because of a promise she made to her brother, but fuck if she wasn't the best kicker I'd ever played with. She loved the game, she was a great teammate, and any team would be lucky to have her.

It pissed me off that she might not even be considered.

"I'm sorry, man," Clay said, squeezing Zeke's shoulder. "But I don't think she'd want you to hold yourself back just because the NFL hasn't opened their eyes yet. She will make a way for herself and you know it. If anything, it'd piss her off to hear you talking like this."

Palico strolled into the kitchen then with a croaky meow, which made us all chuckle. Clay bent down to scratch the little thing under the chin.

"He's right," I said. "You were born to play ball, Z, not coach on the sideline."

Zeke nodded, but didn't have anything more to say. I could see it in his eyes that he felt one thing above all else.

He didn't want to leave her behind.

But I also knew that no matter what came next for them, they'd be together. Something about that made my chest sting, and I rubbed the spot absentmindedly as I changed the subject. "My biggest question is are you two going to take the route Holden did and put a ring on it before the draft? Because I need to know now how many suits I need to be saving up for."

They laughed me off, but I didn't miss how they both fell into a quiet contemplation. They were head over heels for their girls. I wouldn't be the least bit surprised when they made it official and claimed them for life.

"Speaking of which..." Clay arched a brow at me. "What the hell is going on with you and your new *roommate*?"

I surprised even myself with the casual coolness with which I took a sip of my beer. "Well, she hasn't tried to kill me this week, so that's nice."

"You two look like you're sixty seconds or less from fucking in the nearest closet," Zeke said.

"Yeah, right. She'd sooner be a nun," I combatted.

Clay leaned toward Zeke. "Notice how he didn't say *he'd* sooner do anything else."

"You're blind if you don't see that she wants you, too," Zeke added. "The tension is tight enough to snap, man."

"That's just because she despises me," I said with a heavy gut.

I couldn't help the way my eyes drifted to Mary through the kitchen window then, and one look at her buzzed, sleepy, overjoyed smile made me ache with the desire to pull her upstairs and hold her down until we settled whatever the storm between us was.

Before the guys could razz me further, someone shouted from the living room.

"Holden's going in!"

"Oh, shit!" we said in unison, and then we were scrambling out of the kitchen and fighting to be the first back in front of the TV. When we got to the living room, we stood frozen, slow smiles spreading on our face.

There he was, Holden Moore, jogging out for his first play as an NFL quarterback.

"I'll be fucking damned," Clay said in soft admiration.

I had to clear my throat to swallow down the emotion that overwhelmed me in that moment. I was so fucking proud of my friend, I felt like I could burst.

Of course, I'd never admit that, and to everyone around me, I looked calm.

"Bro's been skipping leg day," I said loudly, which earned me the chorus of laughter from my teammates that I wanted.

Mary's head dropped back against the bean bag, her lazy eyes zeroing in on me. I could see then how drunk she was, and she hiccupped before offering me a goofy grin and a look that told me she saw right through me.

It was as confusing as it was hope-inducing.

"Look, there's Julep!" Giana cried out, pointing at the TV where they'd panned to Julep in the stands. Mary dragged her head back up, the moment gone, and we all watched to see Julep wearing Holden's jersey, her hair pulled into a ponytail, the brightest smile I'd ever seen on her face, and that impressive rock glistening on her finger.

For the rest of the quarter, we were all transfixed by the screen, watching as Holden moved the Panthers down the field. I could tell he was still adjusting to the league, which we all knew would be night and day different from playing here at NBU. But he looked like he belonged there, like he wouldn't be on that bench for long.

In his second drive, he took them all the way down for a touchdown, and we all went fucking insane.

The energy really was like a Super Bowl by the time halftime rolled around, and everyone jumped up, running off to either use the bathroom, grab snacks, or refill their drinks. I had to take a leak so bad I was bouncing, and I cursed when I saw the guest bath downstairs had a line. I skipped upstairs to Kyle's room, but he was using his and told me to fuck off, which told me it would be a while.

Hesitantly, I knocked on my own bedroom door.

It was quiet inside, and after a bit without response, I slowly cracked the door open to find the room dark and vacant. I slipped inside, shutting the door behind me and making a beeline for the bathroom.

I groaned with relief when I finally started pissing, and then I looked around, a smile curling on my lips as I took in the disaster my bathroom had become. There was makeup on the counter and in the sink, hair products still plugged in with the cords strewn everywhere, about a million hair and face products that I couldn't begin to guess the purpose of, body spray, jewelry, and more.

A little Mary Bomb had gone off, and I couldn't even pretend like I didn't enjoy sitting in the rubble.

I washed my hands and pulled out a fresh hand towel to dry them, and then slipped back into my room, ready to head downstairs.

I stopped dead in my tracks at the sight of Mary with her shirt half-yanked over her head.

The fabric trapped her arms and head as she struggled against it, little grunts of frustration popping out of her. When she finally got it off, she threw it to the ground like it had greatly offended her, letting out a horse-neigh of an exhale.

In just a thin bra and her lacey, layered skirts, she looked up to find me staring at her.

She didn't scream, didn't jump in surprise, didn't throw things at me in an effort to banish me from the room. It was almost like she expected me, like she hoped to see me there. I held her gaze in an effort to not devour her body, to not treat myself to the sight of the metal piercing her nipples or the freckles on her abdomen or the ink across her chest and shoulders and arms.

With a lazy tilt of her lips, she shrugged. "Don't tell anyone I pulled an Irish goodbye."

The words were a slur of consonants and vowels I could barely make out, and a laugh bubbled out of me, softening the tension. "Your secret is safe with me."

Mary pouted then, her impossibly plump lip poking out as she reached behind her for what I presumed was for the zipper of her skirt.

"Can you help me? I gotta get outta this," she said, and then she spun around with the skirts flaring and backed up until she hit me.

I caught her and my balance before we both tumbled back onto the bed, my hands finding her now-bare waist.

I swallowed, running my knuckles down the smooth skin of her back on a groan I hoped she didn't hear.

"Uh, maybe I should go get Giana." The words burned my throat as I said them.

"Noooo," she whined, letting her head fall back against my chest. "She'll make me stay down there and I just wanna go to sleep. You do it," she insisted, and then she reached around in an effort to show me the zipper of her skirt, but ended up just dragging her hand over my cock, instead.

Jesus fucking hell.

I stifled a moan at the feel of her palming me, and she was so oblivious that she just let her hand fall back to her thigh with a slap, one of those horse-like exhales leaving her again.

I couldn't help but laugh at that.

"Thought you didn't drink much," I said as I unfastened her skirt and tried to think of road kill and politics and anything else but the fact that I was undressing Mary, that she *asked* me to do it.

"Welp, you are a bad influence."

"Me?"

When the skirts loosened around her hips and fell to a puddle at her feet, she sighed with relief, and I dragged my eyes up to the back of her head so I wouldn't stare at her ass in the little thong she was wearing.

She spun around and nearly fell into me again, her hands pressing against my chest. "Yes, *you*."

I sipped a fiery breath with her half-naked and in my arms, and then she slowly slipped away, flopping down onto her bed.

No.

My bed.

She struggled with the covers for a moment before she was buried underneath them, and I watched her thrash around for a minute until suddenly her bra went flying over my shoulder.

Fuck. Me.

Now, Mary was topless, in nothing but a lacy scrap of underwear, wrapped up in my sheets with her emerald, glazed eyes and lazy smile peeking over the covers.

I forced a slow inhale, an equally slow exhale, and shoved my hands into my pockets to keep from doing anything stupid.

"C'mere," she said, reaching a hand out long enough to pat the bed.

I swallowed. "I don't think that's a good idea."

Mary kept her eyes on me as she maneuvered under the covers again, and then she peeled her thong out from under them, letting them dangle off a finger for one second before they dropped to the floor.

She all but purred as she cozied into the sheets even more. "So much better."

Each breath was more ragged than the last from my aching chest. I needed to leave. I needed to turn out the light and close the door and take my ass downstairs right fucking now.

But I was rooted in place.

Mary pulled the covers up to her face, inhaling a deep, dramatic breath before she flopped around and sighed just as deeply. "Ugh," she groaned. "Why do you have to smell so good?"

I arched a brow.

"Your sheets," she said when I didn't answer, tugging them up farther and wrapping herself up like a burrito. "*God,* they smell so good. And your sweaters, too."

"You've been wearing my sweaters?"

She shot a hand out from under the covers with her index finger pointed up. "Technically, you gave me one to wear first, so it's in the rules that it's okay to wear them whenever I want to now."

"Is it now?"

"Uh-huh." She nodded up and then down sharply, matter-of-factly, her eyes closing like she was going to pass out right then and there.

"I didn't realize we had a rulebook."

She peered at me over the covers. "We do, but you keep breaking all the rules."

"How so?"

"Buying me candles, giving me your jacket." She thrust her hand toward me. "And why do you have to look at me like that?"

"I'm just listening."

"No, you're standing there all stoic, but I see it."

I swallowed. "What do you see?"

Mary watched me for a long moment before she sat up, weight on the palms of her hands, the covers just barely catching on the swells of her breasts and keeping her nipples hidden from view. Her long hair spilled over those swells, over the sheets, her eyes heavy and dazed.

"I see that you'd devour me," she whispered. "If I said the word."

My cock jolted in my sweatpants, every muscle in my body straining with the effort to restrain myself from doing what she'd just assessed. She was naked in my fucking bed. Even God Himself would give in.

"You should get some sleep," I managed to croak out, turning before I said *fuck it* and went against the rational voice in my head reminding me she was drunk and had no idea what she was doing.

I heard her flop back into the mattress, and I flicked out the light, turning back just in time to watch her roll onto her side. I opened the door and Palico bounced in, skipping past me and bounding onto the bed. Mary smiled, eyes closed as she ran her fingernails over the cat's neck while it kneaded the covers before curling in next to her.

I let myself watch her only a second longer before I turned out the lights.

"I wish you remembered."

I froze at the words, frowning in confusion as something sharp and hot zapped through my spine.

I turned slowly. "What?"

But Mary was already asleep.

Her mouth had fallen open in a little *o,* soft snores coming from her chest, hair fanning over her face.

After quietly shutting the door, I took a few steps before standing still in the hallway, one hand finding the wall as if I'd teeter off-balance and spiral down the stairs without holding myself steady.

My heart pounded. My thoughts raced. My breath was shallow and short.

Sleep wouldn't find me that night.

I'd toss and turn and sweat overthinking every single second of what happened in that bedroom.

But the next morning, when Mary dragged herself into the kitchen in an oversized t-shirt and shorts, her hair a mess and last night's makeup on her face, she'd smile at me. She'd smile, and groan about needing greasy food and a bottle of Advil, and sketch in her notebook while the rest of our roommates ambled into the kitchen, too.

She'd laugh when they commented on how drunk she was last night, and they'd take her jokes about how weak their game was with the few girls they'd invited over and failed to land at the end of the night.

They'd tell her she was a blast, that they were glad she stayed, that she was part of the family now.

And she'd blush and laugh and tell them she didn't remember a thing after the first quarter.

Chapter 20

MARY

"Oh, my God — *please* show me how you do that," Giana said after I lined my left eye.

"Do what?"

"That perfect cat-eye thing. Mine always goes up too high or angles out too low and I can never get them even, either."

Riley popped open her tube of mascara. "That's why I skip eyeliner altogether."

"Yeah, well, not all of us can look as effortlessly golden and gorgeous as you without a single ounce of makeup on, Riles," I pointed out.

"Shut up, you're both gorgeous," she shot back, but I didn't miss the way her cheeks tinged pink with a little blush. Something told me that being the only girl in a male-dominated sport probably meant she didn't get compliments on her feminine energy much, but she radiated it, and deserved to know.

Giana smacked my arm and held out her liner with a look that said *back to the subject at hand, please*.

It was Chart Day, which I had zero knowledge about other than apparently it was the day Coach announced who was playing what position. Riley kept saying something about a depth chart and Giana had been up to her nose in media work all week. But tonight, they were dragging me out along with the rest of the team to celebrate the true kick off of the season.

Part of me had wanted to argue, but it was so quiet compared to that part of me just two months ago. Yes, I was tired and really just wanted to smoke a bowl and watch a movie, but at the same time, I was excited to go out with everyone.

I was happy that I had girlfriends who wanted to drag me out of the house, that I had the obnoxious yet somehow adorable roommates who treated me like a sister, that the team as a whole had embraced me. For the first time, I felt like I had a community outside of the tattoo one.

I felt like I belonged.

The fact that I hadn't really felt that comfortable at the shop ever since what happened with Nero also added to my excitement to go out and blow off some steam. Nero hadn't tried anything weird since, but I felt the difference, the way he watched me less with guidance and more with expectation. I swore I felt the other girls in the shop watching me differently, too — like they thought I was excelling too fast or getting special treatment.

That was supposed to be my home, my refuge. That shop had been my source of comfort for years.

Now, it had flipped, and my comfort came when I unlocked the door to this house at the end of each night.

That thought struck me, and a little smile spread on my lips as I talked Giana through winging her eye.

"What are you smiling so goofily about?" she asked.

Before I could answer, there was a soft knock on the door.

"Come in!" Riley called without hesitation.

The door opened slowly, and I peeked out of the bathroom just in time to see Leo hesitantly lean his head in.

My stomach flipped at the sight of him, especially once he saw that no one was indecent and let himself the rest of the way in. He wore a cream button-up shirt with the sleeves rolled up to his elbows, showing off those forearms I swore were the source of every fantasy I had. The neck was unbuttoned, his necklaces visible through the V of the collar, along with the muscular swells of his pecs. The jeans he'd paired with the shirt hung deliciously off his hips, and I followed the line of them down to his bare feet.

Fuck me... why is him barefoot wearing jeans so fucking hot?

I took my time slowly trailing my eyes back up, and my gaze snagged on his dark hair, on the way it framed his golden eyes, and the devilish smirk he wore so well.

"I just need to grab some shoes," he said, and it was then that I realized he'd been busy checking *me* out while I was pretending not to take in every inch of him.

For a moment, we just stood there, eyes locked on one another while I held that stupid tube of eyeliner in my hand. There was a fuzzy memory in the back of my brain, one of him being in this room two weeks ago when I was drunk and half-asleep midway through Holden's preseason game. I couldn't remember what was said, but my body viscerally reacted to the memory, like it would always remember even if my brain never did.

Shaking it off, I cleared my throat and pointed toward his closet.

"Of course, go ahead."

He nodded his thanks, but his eyes didn't leave me until he dipped inside the closet to grab the shoes he was looking for.

"I think we're going to call an Uber soon. Are you girls about ready?" he asked when he was upright again.

"We'll meet you there, just finishing up," Riley said, and I hadn't even noticed that she and Giana had both been standing in the doorway of the bathroom.

"Cool," Leo said to her, and then his eyes were on me again, his smile slipping. He swallowed, gaze washing over the length of me. I tried not to cower under the heat, focused on squaring my shoulders as he took in my favorite, earthy-green dress that made my tits look incredible and showed off all my thigh tattoos, too. I'd found it at a thrift store while shopping with Julep, giving up seven of my hard-earned dollars to buy it. I hadn't even added the leather jacket or my favorite black boots yet. It was one of my favorite outfits to go out in, one that made me feel like a bad-ass bitch.

The way Leo was looking at me, I knew I'd landed the look.

He coughed a little before heading for the door. "Alright, well, we'll see you there."

When he was gone, I squeezed past Riley and Giana into the bathroom and went back to my lesson on the perfect cat eye. But I barely got two words out before Riley cut in, smacking the tube out of my hand.

"Bitch, we don't care about the eyeliner. What the hell was *that*?" She pointed to the door Leo had just exited out of.

"What?" I asked with a shrug. "He needed shoes."

"Oh, I think what he *needs* is a healthy dose of you in that dress," Giana argued.

My cheeks flamed so fast I hoped my makeup hid at least a little of the red I knew was finding my skin. "Shut up."

"*You* shut up and tell us everything," Riley said.

I screwed up my face at the paradox of what she'd said, but they were already dragging me to the bed. They sat me down and stood above me, arms folded and waiting.

"You guys are being so weird, nothing is going on," I said.

"Bullshit," Riley shot back. "You can't have one of my teammates look at you like *that* and feed me the lie that it's nothing. Zeke and I kept our shit hidden for weeks before anyone knew. I know what hiding it looks like."

"Ditto," Giana said, holding up one finger. "And you don't even have the guise of pretending you're dating to cover you."

I sighed. "It's... nothing. Really. We haven't done anything."

Riley arched a brow. "But you want to?"

My heart squeezed. "It's complicated."

"Welp, no time like right now to unravel it," Giana said, and she hopped into the bed with me. "Spill."

I was already opening my mouth to make up some lame excuse or brush them off again when something kicked me hard in the chest. It came from the inside out, like the very essence of who I was refused to let me flee.

And I realized that I *wanted* to tell them.

I'd never told *anyone* — mostly because I didn't feel close enough to anyone to tell. But here were two girls who'd become my friends — my *best* friends — and they were asking. They wanted to know what was going on. They wanted to help.

So, I took a deep breath, and I told them everything.

I told them about that summer, about how I'd fallen so hard and completely for the version of Leo I knew online. I told them about his texts and our late-night phone calls, about the times he wished so badly to know who I was. Then, with a tight throat, I told them about the day I revealed myself, how he'd rejected me, and finally, how I'd blocked him and killed any connection we had left. My voice grew a little shakier when I told them he had no idea who I was now, that my appearance had changed so much thanks to braces, my skin clearing up, and how I'd grown into my curves.

Various reactions crawled across their faces as I spoke, from shock and excitement to anger and hurt and everything in-between.

When I finished, Riley took a deep breath as Giana hopped up from the bed. "Okay, wait, so let me get this straight." She held up her hand and ticked off fingers as she said, "You two were basically in love as teenagers, you told him who you were and he rejected you, then the dummy didn't even remember who you were when you moved in across the street, then you ended up becoming roommates, and now he's been being nice to you, giving you his jacket to wear and buying you candles and looking at you like he wants you so bad he has to sit on his hands to keep from acting on it, and through all this," she said with a wave of her hand around the room. "He still has zero idea who you are?"

I shifted on the bed. "I mean, I think *love* is a strong word for what we had when—"

"Bah," Giana said, waving me off in a huff. "Whatever it was, it's strong enough that it's had you in a grip all this time. And maybe Leo, too."

"I've never seen him date anyone seriously," Riley added.

I snorted. "Yeah, but that's because it's *Leo*. He'd rather bang anything with tits and legs than be locked down."

"You sure about that?" Riley asked, and the three of us fell silent, considering.

After a moment, Giana clasped her hands together under her chin with her lashes fanning over her big eyes. "God, this is like—"

"Do *not* start listing off your smutty book tropes," I warned her.

She pressed her lips together, face turning red like she would burst if she couldn't get them out.

"I can't fucking believe this," Riley said with an incredulous smile. "When are you going to tell him?"

"I'm not."

They both balked at that. "What the fuck do you mean, *you're not*," Riley said, and Giana shook her head with the same notion.

I stood and brushed my hands over my dress. "Look, he doesn't remember who I am, which just shows how insignificant I was to him. And even if he *did* remember, he was a complete asshole to me and ruined my entire high school experience."

"It sounds like his friends did that," Giana pointed out.

"Yeah. And he stood idly by and let them. He didn't stand up for me. And when he saw what I looked like in real life, he decided I wasn't worthy of his time anymore." Just remembering it had me seething, and I was thankful for that anger, because it had been so absent lately that I wondered if it had evaporated altogether.

That anger was a blessing. It saved me from being stupid.

"He's a prick and I'm over it," I said with finality I only half felt.

At that, Riley and Giana folded their arms in sync. "Sure, sure, that's why you two were all eye-fucking just a second ago," Riley said.

"Don't you think he's changed since then? Grown up a little?" Giana added. "Maybe he deserves a chance to explain."

I chewed the inside of my cheek as that foggy memory of the preseason game surfaced again. I knew we were talking about *something* when I climbed into bed, when he was about to leave the room...

God, what was it?

For the life of me, I couldn't remember.

"Look, things with Leo are just too complicated and hold too much pain for me to rehash. Okay? It's a lot easier for me to remind myself of all the reasons I hate him than it is to think of how he might have changed."

Giana's face crumpled at my admission.

"For now, we have a good thing going. We're friendly and cohabitating. That's all I want. And," I added, swiping my jacket off the back of Leo's chair. "To go out and have a good time with my girls tonight."

They didn't look pleased with my insistence to drop the subject, but fortunately, they did.

And after quickly applying lipstick and last-minute touches, we were out the door and on our way to the bar.

Chapter 21

LEO

I felt like an unexploded bomb ready to detonate at the slightest movement.

Something lethal stirred in my veins as I drank at the bar with my teammates, a little too attuned to the door as I waited for Mary to walk through it.

I couldn't place my agitation, couldn't figure out how I'd managed to be completely fine around Mary until tonight. I'd survived that night in my room with her naked in my bed, kept my hands to myself and didn't push her when she said she didn't remember a thing. I had been content to live in this somewhat stable peace between us, knowing that was all I'd get from her.

But seeing her in that dress tonight, watching the way she took me in, how her skin tinged pink... it had wired me up tight enough to combust.

I had to have her.

At the very least, I had to shoot my shot, to tell her that I wanted her and not back down. I wouldn't let her hide, either. If she didn't want anything to do with me, she'd have to say it to my face — and the way she looked at me, I knew even if she could get the words out, they'd be a lie.

I was usually up for playing the cat and mouse game. I found it fun, enticing, and loved to lick my chops before finally devouring my prize in the end.

But with Mary, I didn't have the control to play the game any longer, to act unaffected by her.

I was completely fucking feral.

The chamber around my ribs eased up a bit at the sight of her swinging through the door with Riley and Giana, the three of them running straight to the bar for drinks. I took a long pull of mine as I watched them, taking in Mary in that goddamn dress again.

I'd seen her wear it before, but it was when she lived with Julep and wanted nothing to do with me. Back then, I'd taken one quick look and thought *damn*. But now, I knew what that body looked like in baggy sweatpants and a loose-fitting t-shirt. I knew what she looked like with messy hair and no makeup on.

And for some reason, that made my blood pump even harder to see her all dolled up, to know both versions of her.

I vibrated with a possession I had no right to feel.

"So, are you actually going to make your move tonight, or are you going to make us suffer through another month of the awkward tension between you two?"

I blinked, tearing my gaze away from Mary to find Braden smirking beside me. He drained the last of his beer with an expectant gaze.

"None of us are stupid, Hernandez."

"We're not blind either," Kyle added from where he was in a game of darts with Blake. "Although, sometimes I wish I was so I didn't have to witness you pining so damn hard."

Braden chuckled, hand reaching up to squeeze my shoulder. "For our sakes as well as yours, tell the girl how you feel."

"If you don't, I'll move in first thing in the morning," Kyle added with a smirk before he threw the dart and hit a perfect bullseye.

"If you want to keep that hand you just threw with, you'll reconsider."

He and Braden both laughed at my threat, sharing a look like they'd won just by me admitting his little comment got to me.

I shrugged Braden off and turned back to find Mary again, steeling myself to go over and talk to her. But when I found her, she wasn't with Giana and Riley anymore.

She was with a guy.

Not *just* a guy, but a group of them, and some girls, too. I didn't have to look them over more than once to make an educated guess that they were her co-workers, every single one of them covered in ink and metal.

The one talking to her was tall and massive, with long hair pulled into a bun and a thick beard. She laughed at something he said, which made the hair on the back of my neck stand up, my blood pumping a bit harder.

Then, he put his hand at the small of her back.

All the noise of the bar muted at that contact, my eyes sticking to where his palm splayed over her skin. I noticed a couple girls standing to the left of them noticed the intimate hold, too. One of them narrowed her eyes, nudging her friend and nodding toward where the guy was softly, almost imperceptibly, pulling Mary a little closer.

I nearly broke a tooth with how hard I gritted my teeth, and I spun away from them before I could torture myself with watching any longer.

Who the fuck was *that*?

She'd never mentioned a boyfriend, or even anyone she had a crush on at the shop. In fact, the only time she'd talked about a guy was when she said her boss hit on her.

Wait, was that her boss?

I snuck a look over my shoulder, trying to remember if she'd said anything about what he looked like — but she hadn't.

And it didn't matter who he was.

He had his hands on her, and that alone was enough to make me consider jail time.

I forced an inhale, blowing out my frustration and stepping up to take the next game of darts. I just needed to wait until she was with Riley and Giana again, or alone, and then I could go talk to her. I didn't need to be a fucking asshole and storm over now, especially not when I was seeing red with that guy so fucking close to her.

My plan worked — for about an hour.

But when I'd played enough darts to make my arm burn and had another bucket of beers only to find her still surrounded by the same group, I lost patience.

Fuck it.

I weaved through the crowd with her as my target, ignoring Clay when he tried to call me over for shots, and a girl I'd fooled around with last season who tried to catch me by the arm as I passed her. I had just slipped her off of me when Mary turned mid-laugh and saw me approaching her.

Her smile stayed in place.

She didn't turn away from me, didn't give me a look that said she didn't want to be bothered or go back to whoever she was talking to. She just held my gaze as I made my way toward her, smiling and tucking her hair behind one ear.

It was like the parting of the sea, the way the crowd seemed to move for me then. And all the music, the conversation, the laughter and sound of glasses clinking together — it all faded into the background the closer I got to Mary.

By the time I reached her, she'd all but turned away from the group she was with, and the guy talking beside her paused at her lack of focus, following her gaze to where I stood.

God, she was breathtaking.

The green fabric of her dress hugged her in all the right places, showing me every spot I could grab her and hold onto. It set the emerald of her eyes ablaze, too — and those irises flashed with curiosity the longer I stood there.

"Hey," I said.

Stupidly.

She smiled down at her boots before peeking up at me through her waterfall of hair. "Leo, these are some of my friends from work."

Mary gestured to the guys and girls around her, who all tipped their chins at me as she rattled off their names.

"This is my boss, Nero," she finished, and sure as shit, it was the guy who'd been blatantly hanging on her all night.

His jaw was hard as he extended a hand for mine. "You must be the roommate."

"One of them," I said, reminding him I wasn't the only guy looking out for her in this bar. I probably should have felt intimidated by how he towered over me, but I didn't, and I squeezed his hand just as hard as he squeezed mine. "No one to tattoo tonight?"

"Had some appointments cancel, so some us decided to take the night off," he said, then smiled down at Mary before throwing his arm around her. "Just serendipitous that we ended up at the same bar as Mary J here."

I thought I saw Mary's smile slip into something a little more uncomfortable, thought she looked a little stiff where he held her against him. That bomb inside me started ticking again.

"Nero was just telling me that he thinks I'm ready to start bringing in my own clients."

My anger subsided a bit at her words, and I smiled genuinely at her. "No shit?"

"She's *been* ready," Nero said, beaming. "Every skin she's had walked away happy. But now, she'll have her own spot."

I didn't take my eyes off her. "That... amazing," I said, wishing I had better words for the pride swelling in my chest for her. "Congratulations, Mary."

She flushed. "Thank you."

I felt that same hold on us that we'd both succumbed to in my room earlier, like we didn't give a shit that anyone else was around us. We just stood there, staring, waiting for the other to say the first word.

I wasn't going to lose my shot this time.

"Can we talk?" I asked.

But Mary didn't get the chance to answer before Nero was all but putting her behind him like he was some sort of barrier. "Actually, we were just about to play a game of pool and Mary's on my team."

"I'm pretty sure Mary can answer for herself," I said, still keeping my eyes on her.

She opened her mouth to speak, but he cut in again before she could.

"And I'm pretty sure you don't need to be an asshole about it."

"I'm not being an asshole, I just asked if we could talk," I said, finally looking at him.

He laughed. "Yeah, I bet you want to *talk*. Your face tells a different story."

"Nero," Mary said, tugging on his sleeve. She looked like she couldn't believe he'd just said that. "It's fine, I'll just be a second."

"No, it's not fine," Nero sneered. "Because this guy is pretending to be a gentleman offering you his bed when it's clear as day he has another agenda."

"That's fucking rich, coming from you," I shot back.

Mary's eyes grew wide. "Leo," she scolded.

Her co-workers were tuned in now, and I saw a few of them share questioning glances at my comment. The two girls who'd been watching Nero's hand on Mary's back earlier seemed particularly intrigued, and it made me wonder if Nero wasn't just a creep to Mary.

"What?" I asked Mary, but my eyes were still boring into Nero's. "Don't want them to know that your boss crosses the line and puts you in uncomfortable situations when no one else is around?"

I barely got the words out before Nero was rushing me like he was ready to fight. We met in the middle, chest to chest, both of us seething as his friends crowded behind him and my teammates began to flank my sides. Clay and Zeke were the closest, and knowing they had my back only kicked my confidence up another notch.

"That's *enough*," Mary said, slipping between us and shoving me hard until I had no choice but to step back. "What the hell is wrong with you?!"

"*Me*?" I almost laughed, but when I looked at her and saw sincere anger, my mouth hung open in disbelief. "Really?"

"I think you've outstayed your welcome, kid," Nero said from over her shoulder. He crooked a smile at the word *kid*, and when I looked back to Mary and found her staring at the floor, avoiding eye contact, and not saying a fucking word in my defense...

I realized he was right.

What the hell did I expect?

Mary hated me. She'd made that much clear from the moment we met last year when she lived with Julep. It didn't matter what I did to prove to her I wasn't who she thought I was. Even now, she tolerated me at best, shutting me down any time I tried to cross the line she'd drawn between us.

But that night, in my room...

She was drunk.

She was drunk and didn't even remember a second of it.

I tongued my cheek, nodding as I stepped back, all the while willing Mary to look at me. I pleaded silently for her to stop me, to take my side, to stand up for me and for herself.

But she didn't.

And when I couldn't bear to watch her reject me any longer, I turned, blowing through the crowd for the exit so I could detonate without taking anyone down in the carnage with me.

Chapter 22

MARY

Leo hadn't made it five steps out the door before I shoved through it, too.

"Leo!"

He didn't stop, and I had no idea where he was even *going* considering he was storming into a parking lot full of cars that didn't belong to him. We'd all taken Ubers. He didn't have anywhere to run, to hide.

"Leo, damn it, stop," I called again, and this time he paused, fingers rolling into fists at his sides before I saw him take a deep breath. His hands relaxed a bit, and he dragged them through his hair before keeping them there on top of his head, back still to me.

The lot was empty, save for a few smokers hanging out outside the bar. They didn't pay any attention to us as I hung my hands on my hips, waiting for Leo to say something. His back muscles tensed enough for me to see even through his button up, as if *he* had a right to be the angry one right now after what he just pulled.

"What the fuck was that?" I asked when he didn't speak.

Slowly, calmly, Leo turned around.

He pinned me with an inescapable gaze.

"*That* was me trying to talk to you, and then standing up for you when you wouldn't do it yourself."

"You're joking, right?" I threw my hand toward the bar. "*That* was you making a fool of me in front of everyone I work with."

"Because I told the truth?"

"Because you interjected yourself into my job, my *career*. Do you know how hard I've worked for respect at that shop? Do you realize what you could have ruined with those little comments you made?"

"I didn't ruin anything," he said confidently, pointing behind me to the bar. "*That* guy is the one ruining shit. And in case you didn't realize it yet, he isn't going to let you go. He wants a piece of you and is damn sure he'll get it."

"Oh, and you can see all that by meeting him *one time*?"

"I knew before I met him. I knew when you told me on the roof what happened between you two."

"But you weren't there when it happened! I don't even know if anything *did* happen." A frustrated breath puffed out of me. "I... I probably read too much into it, and nothing weird has gone on since, but *now*—"

"Don't do that," he said, shaking his head. He took a tentative step toward me, his eyes softening a bit. "Don't second guess yourself like that creep wants you to."

My words stutter-stopped in my chest, and I swallowed, folding my arms over myself. "Look, what happens to me is none of your business."

"What if I want it to be?"

Silence.

Silence that was so deafening I felt it in the very core of who I was.

It fell over us a like a parachute, drifting down slowly until we were encompassed completely and hidden from the rest of the world. My pulse reverberated through every cell in my body, the air between us a living thing. And when Leo took another tentative step toward me, his Adam's apple bobbing hard in his throat, I lost the ability to breathe.

"Say something," he pleaded.

My heart thundered in my ears as I shook my head, and I had to look down, away from him.

For a moment, Leo stood still, waiting.

Then, he growled in frustration, whipping around until he was storming away from me again.

"Leo," I said, his name cracking my voice.

I gasped in surprise when he turned on me again, pulling at his hair before his hands thrust toward me, his eyes wild. "I can't fucking do this, Mary!" His breaths shook through the words. "I want you. I know you know it, too."

My heart shuddered to a stop.

It was one thing to assume it, but to hear him say it...

"I didn't—"

"Don't lie," he said, his voice calmer now, softer. He took another step toward me. "You know it. You can feel it. *You* want me, too, but for some reason you keep playing this fucking game."

I was shocked silent, but inside, I felt the volcano whistling and searing and roaring to life. Each word he said spawned it on more, the taste of ash on my tongue as it simmered and stirred.

"Damn it, woman," he said, shaking his head.

My chest was on fire. My breaths were hot steam.

"I'm mad about you!" Leo gripped his hair again before his hands stretched out toward me. "Can't you see that?"

"You were once before and you don't even remember!"

There it was.

The eruption.

My eyes brimmed with tears, nose stinging as I lifted my gaze to meet his. My breaths were so haggard now that I pressed a hand against my aching ribcage as if I could soothe it, as if I could tame the molten lava burning me from the inside.

There was no going back now.

Leo just tilted his head to the side, frowning, confusion washing over him. "What?"

I shook my head, turning it to the side to focus on a random car instead of the stupid boy standing in front of me. The motion set two fat tears cascading down my cheeks, and I swiped them away, folding my arms over my chest.

"Two weeks ago, in my room..." Leo breathed the words slowly. "You... you said you wish I remembered..."

I closed my eyes again, tears burning behind my lids where I refused to set them free.

It felt like an eternity passed, but when I chanced looking at Leo again, he was ashen.

Every line in his face had softened, his eyes wide, jaw slack. He stared at me, but it was like he wasn't seeing me at all.

It was as if he was in another place, another time altogether.

"You..." he croaked, and then shook his head, deftly blinking before his eyes found mine. "Stig?"

The nickname was just above a whisper when it left him, but it felt like a knife to my chest.

I swallowed.

I nodded.

And then I let out a gasp of a sob as he charged me and swept me into his arms.

● ● ●

LEO

An entire city crumbled inside of me, burying my aching chest and stammering heart in the rubble as I reached for Mary and pulled her into me.

My next breath burned even more than the last as I crushed her to my chest, but I held her only a moment before I was pulling back to look at her. I swept one hand through her silky hair, cupping the back of her head as my eyes searched every curve and line of her face. I took in her freckles, her glossy wintergreen eyes, her trembling lips.

My other hand ran along the line of her neck, her skin hot to the touch as I traced her collarbone and then up to her jaw. My heart was in my throat as I smoothed my thumb over the apple of her cheeks, memorizing the bridge of her nose as I traced it, committing her plump lips to memory when my thumb found them next. Her breath was as shallow as mine, the warmth of it ghosting over my fingertips as I took her in.

I choked on the first clean breath I'd taken since I lost her.

Wrapping her tightly in my arms again, my hands went from her hair to her back, over her arms, up to frame her neck and hold her even closer so I could feel that she was real, that she was here.

It was a dream and a nightmare all at once.

"How?" I whispered, not sure if the question was to her or myself or the universe. I pulled her back, framing her arms with my hands and letting my eyes wash over her before I crushed her to me again. "*How?*"

I never wanted to let her go.

I never *would* let her go.

I'd already decided, my arms tightening around her, chest swelling with that possession that had built before I even knew who she was.

How did I not know who she was?

My mind raced with memories of that summer, of how she left me with no explanation, of the pain I thought I'd never escape. How could she be *here*?

And if she knew it was me... why didn't she say anything before?

I frowned as I thought through the last year and a half, from the comments she slung at me when she lived with Julep to every waking moment she'd lived at The Pit. My brain hurt as I tried to piece it all together.

I wish you remembered...

Her words echoed in my soul, but I couldn't make sense of any of it.

I didn't realize Mary was crying until she sniffed, pressing her hands into my chest and putting space between us. She folded her arms over her middle again, like she wanted to shield her most vulnerable places from me.

"I... I don't understand," I finally managed, aching to pull her into me again, but I refrained. "Mary, you knew it was me all along?"

"Of course, I did."

Shock slammed into me, my jaw hinging open. "I... why didn't you say something? Why..." I swallowed, and then the questions I had buried for so long tumbled out unbidden. "What *happened?* Where did you go? Why did you ghost me?"

It was her turn to look confused. "*Ghost* you?"

"Right after school started," I reminded her. "I logged on and saw your username but then you just... disappeared. I called you, but you didn't answer. My texts wouldn't go through. I..."

Mary blinked at me, anger simmering in her green eyes. "Are you playing some sort of fucking game right now?"

The way she looked at me, like I was some sort of villain...

It killed me and confused the ever-living hell out of me, too.

"What? No," I started, but she cut me off.

"You rejected me," she spat, and I didn't miss how tears welled in her eyes again, but she didn't let them fall. "I told you who I was. I gave you the drawings you asked me to make for you. I... I put *everything* on the line, and you took one look at me and decided I wasn't enough."

I was so desperate to hold her I couldn't fight it anymore.

"Mary, I would never—"

But she yanked away from me before I could touch her.

"You did," she seethed, but her anger was snuffed out by pain. "You *did*, Leo. Do you seriously not remember?"

I shook my head, so confused I couldn't do anything but blink at her.

"Pimple-faced porn freak?" She lifted her brows, waiting.

I frowned, tracking through my memories, because something she said did trigger a distant something. I closed my eyes, reaching for it. Whatever it was was so foggy, so minuscule in my filing cabinet of memories that it was like searching for a crumpled-up receipt lodged somewhere between thousands of pieces of paper.

My head ached from how hard I tried to reach for it.

And then, I remembered.

It was hazy, a day I hadn't thought twice about even when I was younger. But I vaguely remembered a girl giving me a notebook at school after practice. I had no idea who she was. I couldn't recall a thing about what she looked like — the color of her hair, what she was wearing — nothing. And I *definitely* didn't know her name — not even then.

All I remembered was feeling uncomfortable, just wanting to walk away before any of the douchebag guys on my team could make it any worse for either of us.

The reality of what it really was hit me so hard I stumbled backward.

"Oh, God," I managed, shaking my head. I lifted my gaze to Mary's. "That was... *you*?"

"Fuck you, Leo," she said, spinning on her heel. She stormed away from me, but I chased after her, rounding her and blocking her from going anywhere else.

"Mary, I swear on my mother's life, I didn't know."

"You're telling me you saw what I drew you and it didn't click? Me and you, an Xbox controller, the stars?"

I didn't. I didn't remember a single thing about what was in that notebook.

"I... I don't know what to say. I was an idiot, a fucking *kid*, okay? I thought you were some random girl with a crush on me and I was afraid my friends would make your life a living hell so I just blew you off. I mean, I didn't know it was *you* but—"

"They did," she said, her bottom lip trembling. "They *did* make my life a living hell. And you did nothing about it."

"I didn't know." The words were a cry, a plea.

"So, you didn't see the fucking flyers they printed out of my face and my drawing? Didn't catch the nickname they gave me that I never escaped?"

This time, I *really* couldn't place what she was talking about. "What? When?"

"Right after it happened!"

I frowned, shaking my head, and then I grabbed her arms and held her so she'd look at me, so she'd see the sincerity in my eyes when I told her the truth.

"Mary, I didn't notice anything that entire fucking year. Okay? I was *sick* over losing you. I was... I don't even know, *paralyzed* by the loss of you. I barely passed my classes that semester. I had the worst season of football of my entire life. I spent every waking minute that I wasn't at school or at practice trying to find you."

She tried to scoff and brush me off, but I held tight, carefully bringing my knuckles to her chin and tilting it up to look at me again.

"I never would have hurt you on purpose," I swore, and I prayed she felt it, that she believed me. "But I'm sorry I did. I'm sorry, Mary. I'm so, so fucking sorry."

Her face warped, like my words had speared her, and I knew without much rumination that she had to have been waiting years for me to say them. While I was missing her, wishing for her, she was trying to recover from the ugliest side of me. It killed me to even consider, to know those guys I'd called friends had made her suffer.

That *I* had made her suffer.

I'd hurt the one girl I'd ever cared for, all without even knowing it.

My stomach rolled at the thought, and I had to hold her. I had to hold her and pray that she felt who I really was, that she'd believe I never would have done this to her had I known.

I pulled her into my chest, squeezing my eyes shut as the overpowering feeling of having found her settled over me. She was stiff in my arms at first, but then she melted, her hands fisting in my shirt. I squeezed her tighter, wanting so badly to kiss the crown of her head, but refraining only because I knew I had a long way to go to earn back her trust.

If I ever even had it in the first place.

"You really didn't know?" she asked, her voice muffled by my shirt.

"I *swear*, Mary. I had no idea. If I had, I would have pulled you into my arms and claimed you for everyone to see."

She sniffed, burying her head in my chest. "No, you wouldn't have."

I pulled back on a frown, sliding the pad of my thumb along where a tear had streaked her cheek. "Are you crazy? You meant *everything* to me."

"I saw it on your face when we met, though. I wasn't good enough for you."

I tilted her chin again, finding her gaze with my own. "You were *too* good for me. I was an idiot for not seeing that it was you." The truth of that hit me like a tidal wave, the fact that I'd put us both through years of misery all because I didn't realize…

I shook my head, determined not to dwell on the past, on mistakes I couldn't take back.

She was here now, and I had the chance to fight for her.

I'd die before I'd let her slip through my fingers again.

"Come home with me," I said, searching her glossy eyes. "I know I have a lot to prove to you, a lot of pain to heal, a lot to explain." I swallowed. "Let me start tonight."

Mary rolled her lips together, eyes flicking between mine.

Mercifully, she nodded.

And when I took her hand in mine, the piece of me I'd been missing for years quietly snapped into place.

Chapter 23

MARY

I woke late the next morning, my body aching as if I'd run a marathon, throat scratchy and eyes puffy and raw. Leo and I had stayed up until almost dawn. We'd talked a little, but were both so drained from the emotions we expelled outside the bar that, mostly, we just existed together, like neither of us could believe we'd found our way back to each other.

I knew I couldn't.

I never considered telling Leo about what happened. To me, that ship had sailed, and I'd firmly put him in the box of assholes never to be trusted again. I knew he didn't realize who I was now, that I'd lost weight and fixed my teeth and cleared up my skin in a way that made me look like a completely different person.

But last night, when the truth did come out... I never expected him to say he hadn't known it was me all those years ago.

I'd considered it, once, that night he cooked *tostones* for me. But it had been such a brief, stupid thought that I'd shoved it away as soon as it made itself known.

I couldn't believe I was right.

My head still spun with everything he'd revealed to me the night before as I winced and pushed myself up to sit against the headboard. I didn't remember Leo even leaving the room. What I did remember, what I'd never forget, was the look on his face when he swore to me he didn't know it was me the day I'd thought he rejected me.

All this time, I thought he knew.

I thought he took one look at me and was disgusted.

So I'd blocked him, burned him, removed him from every inch of my life and made sure there wasn't so much as a crack for him to weasel his way back in.

I felt sick now that I realized if I'd have just talked to him, if I'd have just asked him to explain why he blew me off... I would have found out that he didn't. Not really.

What would have happened then?

What would our lives have been if he'd known it was me?

Maybe he still would have rejected me. Maybe he was lying last night when he said he would have held onto me and never let go. How could he say that, when he didn't even really remember what I looked like or who I was?

But maybe...

Maybe we would have been together.

Would we have dated, held hands in the hallway? Would I have worn his jerseys at the games and had his jacket wrapped around me late at night?

Would we have broken up, gone our separate ways after a young love burned out as it so often does?

Would we be together still?

I groaned, digging the heels of my palms into my eyes and pulling my knees up to my chest. I was so nauseous I didn't want to chance moving any more than that.

There was a soft knock on the door, and then before I could answer, it creaked open just enough for Leo to look in. He paused at the sight of me, something unreadable in his expression before he nudged the door the rest of the way open.

My heart surged in my chest, a mixture of longing and warmth combatted by fear.

His hair was an absolute mess, likely from the amount of times he ran his hands through it last night. Even with his eyes red and swollen like mine, he looked like a cozy dream in his sweatpants, sleeves ripped off the old, tattered NBU t-shirt he wore, his rib cage visible through the gaping holes and his necklaces gleaming around his neck. He had a mug of coffee in each hand, the liquid steaming as he carefully walked over and handed one to me.

My stomach settled just by having him near, by seeing that he wasn't going anywhere, that he knew who I was now and he didn't run.

"Thank you," I whispered, voice still raw.

"Figured you had to be as tired as I am," he said, hesitantly sitting on the edge of the bed. He watched me take a sip, my eyes closing on a hum.

The coffee had hazelnut creamer in it.

"I hope you like that flavor," he said. "I remembered you mentioned that you missed the creamer your dad always had at home, but I couldn't remember what it was."

"Toffee," I said. "But this is wonderful. Thank you."

My heart squeezed at the thought of him waking up early and going to the store to get creamer for my coffee.

"Did you get any sleep?" he asked.

"A little."

He nodded. "Yeah, I didn't get much either."

I stared at where my fingers curled around the mug, and the realization that he also knew just how I liked my coffee — more creamer than anything else — made me want to smile as much as it made me want to curl up in a ball and sob.

"I wish I could crawl inside your mind right now," he said softly.

I let out a breath of a laugh. "It's not a pretty place."

Leo watched me for a moment longer before he set his cup on the bedside table, taking mine next and doing the same. He wrapped my hands up in his, the warmth of his skin defrosting my icy digits.

"I've thought of a million things I want to say to you," he said. "But I feel like none of it is enough."

I stayed quiet, letting him work through the fog in his head that I knew had to feel as thick and heavy as mine. Just the fact that he was here gave me more hope than it should have. I wanted to curse myself for being stupid, for believing him, but then I realized that was the part of me that convinced myself Leo was this pig-headed asshole for the last seven years.

Now that I knew the truth, it felt like trying to untangle a web so thick and sticky it latched onto my soul every time I tried to sift through it.

His eyes skated back and forth between mine. "I wish I could tell you what you meant to me back then without sounding like a complete psychopath."

I chuckled. "Hey, I held a grudge against you for seven years. I think it's *me* who's the crazy one."

"I haven't felt for any girl the way I felt for you."

His words simmered like warm honey in my veins, but I laughed them off, looking down at where his hands intertwined with mine. "Oh yeah, none of the hundred or so?"

"I'm serious," he said earnestly, and he dipped his head until I met his gaze again. "I... I can't believe I hurt you."

I had to look away again at that.

"All this time I thought..."

He didn't finish the sentence, and when I looked up at him again, he was watching where his thumb drew a line on my wrist, his brow furrowed, a deep line etched into his forehead.

"How do I prove to you that I've changed?" Leo lifted his eyes back to mine. "That I'm more than what you think I am, what I used to be."

My heart twisted, the force so powerful I squirmed beneath it.

When I thought back over the past few months in this house with Leo, I couldn't think of a single thing I wanted him to change. His kindness was more than I deserved, even when I tried not to see it or to convince myself it was all for show. I wanted so desperately to believe he was this awful human being... and I'd successfully convinced myself of it for so long.

But now, to know the truth...

I sucked in a breath, desperate to lighten the mood, to bring back the ease with which we used to tease each other.

"Oh, I don't know. I guess you can start with tattooing my name on your chest," I joked.

But when I looked at Leo again, his face was dead serious.

"Okay."

I barked out a laugh, shoving him away playfully. "I was kidding."

"I'm not."

"You're not getting a tattoo of my name."

"I don't care what it is. Ink me with whatever you want."

I licked my bottom lip in amusement, folding my arms over my chest. "Do you have any tattoos?"

"Not one."

"You realize they're permanent?"

"Yep."

"And that they hurt?"

He sucked his teeth at that. "Come on, now — I get thrown to the ground and pummeled by three-hundred-pound defensive linemen on a regular basis."

I chewed the inside of my cheek, watching him for a sign that he was bluffing — but found nothing.

"You're really serious."

"I really am. Come on," he said, standing and holding his hand out for mine. "Let's do it."

"Now?"

"Right now."

I barely got another laugh out before he was hauling me up out of bed.

Chapter 24

LEO

Every ounce of cockiness I had drained out of me the second the needle buzzed across my sternum.

Mary had started whatever she was inking into my flesh on my upper chest, and while it had stung, it was manageable — an almost pleasant, little bite of pain that had me feeling like I could sit in this chair all day without so much as a little squirm.

Now, it felt like she had a vibrating knife in her hands and was dragging it through the skin *and* bone, gutting me like a fish.

I hissed in another breath that I held until she took a little break to drag the folded paper towel in her hands over my skin, and I swore that hurt almost as badly as the tattoo itself. My flesh felt raw, almost like I had a fresh sunburn and she was rubbing sandpaper over it.

"You're such a baby," she said on a laugh, and the easy way her lips curled told me she was enjoying seeing me in pain.

Not that I blamed her.

"It feels like you're scraping the bone."

She laughed again, but I was too busy holding my breath to join her as she started in again. "Just don't focus on it. Talk to me, tell me a story or something."

"You expect me to form sentences right now?"

I gritted my teeth, and then let all the tension go when she removed the needle for a break again.

When I wasn't writhing in pain, I was memorizing everything about the way Mary looked in this moment. Her hair was piled in a messy bun on top of her head, eyes still a little red and underlined in dark circles from our night together. I liked seeing proof that it happened on her face, that it wasn't a dream. I liked even more that she was marking me permanently, that she was real and I was about to have proof of her existence forever.

Her hands were covered by black gloves, and I'd watched with fascination as she got everything set up for us — from the stencil I told her I didn't want to see as she transferred it from the paper to my skin, to sanitizing the needles and setting up her station before she powered up her gun and got to work.

She was in her element, and it was a completely new side of her.

I'd seen her sarcastic shield she wore so effortlessly, heard her sling teasing insults with ease. But in this shop, she held herself differently — chin high, shoulders relaxed — calm and confident in a way only someone truly comfortable with themselves and what they do can be.

Inside, she might have been a nervous fucking wreck for all I knew.

But from my perspective, she was a pro.

There'd been a little tension when we first walked into the shop — especially when Nero had seen me step into his space. But I didn't give a shit about him or whatever had transpired between us the night before. Now that I had my chance to fight for Mary, I was willing to put everything on the line — including my pride.

On our way over, she'd explained to me how much that upset her — the way I acted toward Nero at the bar. In her eyes, it wasn't me standing up to a creep for her. It was her career in jeopardy, her reputation on the line.

That, I understood.

So, I'd walked right over to him and apologized, shaking his hand and explaining that I was out of line. It didn't matter that I still wanted to ram my fist right into his fucking nose, or that I still felt like the position he put Mary in was fucked. This place, and therefore these people, were important to her. So I'd respect him and keep my mouth shut.

For now, at least.

Any time I looked over to where Nero had his own client, I caught him watching us. I was sure Mary would see it only as a tattoo artist watching his apprentice and making sure she didn't fuck up.

I knew better.

The needle vibrating my chest again made me grit my teeth. "You talk," I managed. "Distract me."

"What do you want me to talk about?" she asked calmly, smiling a bit as she wiped the mixture of ink and blood away from my skin. When she smiled like that, so effortlessly, it tugged on a string tied to the deepest part of my gut.

How did I not know it was her?

The thought had played on repeat in my mind all night and all day, too. I racked my brain mercilessly, rummaging through it in my desperate attempt to remember that day, to remember *her*. But I couldn't — not more than I had last night, anyway.

It was so cruel, how her life had plummeted that day because of me, and I hadn't even noticed. And my life had shifted, too, but it was because I lost her. I lost her by my own fucking hand.

Thinking of how my team had treated her after, how I had been so broken I hadn't even noticed...

And even if I did back then, I didn't care. I *couldn't* care about anything or anyone other than the girl online who'd left me like a ghost in the night.

It was all so gut-wrenching, it made it hard to think straight.

Inhaling a breath back to the present, I tried to look down at what Mary was carving into me, but she covered it with her hand.

"No peeking!"

I chuckled, letting my head fall back against the chair again. "Your username," I said. "*Octostigma*. What the hell does it mean?"

Her smile bloomed. "In ancient Greek, *stigma* is the word for tattoo."

"No shit?"

She nodded. "Kind of fitting, considering the overall view of tattoos over the centuries." She dipped the tip of her needle into a cap filled with black ink, which she'd explained to me was a way of reloading the ink, before she started again.

"And the octo part?"

"I just think octopus are cool as shit."

I smiled. "Explains why you draw so many of them."

"Well, they expel ink, so obviously that attracted me to them," she explained. "Dreams of being a tattoo artist and all. But they're also super fucking intelligent. And two thirds of their neurons are in their fucking *arms* — and they are arms by the way, not tentacles."

I held my hand up in mock surrender. "I'll never make the mistake again."

Her eyes twinkled a bit as she smiled and continued working, and I had to admit, listening to her talk was helping me not to focus so much on the pain.

"They have three hearts, which I thought was pretty rad. But I think the connection I really made was with the fact that with three organs pumping blood into them, and eight arms that essentially all have a mind of their own — they must feel pulled in so many different directions, you know? Like they're made up of too much to be confined into one little being."

She paused, wiping my skin, her eyes floating up to mine.

"I could relate to that, feeling like eight people at once, especially at that time in my life."

"And so, you were *Octostigma*."

She smiled in confirmation, sitting back in her chair and cracking her neck. "Want to take a little break?"

"Nah, I'm good. Keep on with the torture."

Mary rolled her eyes, but then dipped the needle again before resuming her position over me.

I let my gaze drag over every centimeter of her face, noting how she had a line between her brows from concentrating. Everything else was smooth, though, and serene.

Again, I searched and searched, waiting for some sort of recognition to hit me, for my stupid brain to piece the girl tattooing me now with the one who bared her soul to me when I was a dumb teenager. I waited for it to hit me, for me to suddenly see that young girl's face, how her hair was styled, what notebook she held, the drawing, *any* of it.

But I couldn't place her.

I couldn't remember anything specific about that day, about that moment that had seemed so insignificant to me, but had meant everything to Mary.

Well, that was a lie.

I remembered that day, but not for the same reason. *My* life shifted later that evening, when I logged on and Mary immediately blocked me, when I called her and she didn't answer, when all of my texts went unanswered.

I never noticed how my friends reacted to the girl who showed me her notebook because I was too busy obsessing over the girl who wiped me out her life for seemingly no reason.

The reality of it all made me want a time machine so badly I'd kill for one.

"Stop looking at me like that," Mary said, bringing me back to the present.

"Like I'd devour you if you said the word?"

The gun paused over my skin, and she went white before her eyes shot to mine. "What?"

"That's what you said to me," I reminded her. "When you were drunk off your ass during the preseason game."

"No," she said, pulling away and covering her mouth with one hand. Her eyes doubled in size. "No, please tell me you're kidding."

"Nope," I said with a victorious smile. "To be fair, your assessment was spot on." I let my eyes trail a blaze over her skin, from where her own sternum tattoo met the swells of her breasts down to where her hips made a delicious heart shape from her waist.

When I slid my gaze back up, her face was flushed, but she dipped the needle in ink and took position again. The pain had ebbed a bit, almost like my body had adjusted to the invasion.

"Well, *that* embarrassing tidbit aside, I meant the way you were looking at me just now." She peeked up at me only a second before her eyes were back on where she was working. "Like I remind you of everything you regret."

I swallowed down the urge to tell her that was partly true.

"So, back to the devouring look, then?" I asked, arching a brow.

She smiled and shook her head, focusing on the tattoo and not saying another word.

It took five hours total for Mary to leave her mark, and when she finished, she wiped away the excess ink and blood with a proud smile on her lips. She looked a little tired, but in the way only an artist could be after completing another masterpiece, like she left a little bit of her soul in me.

I loved the thought of that, that no matter what happened next, she'd always exist in me in some way.

"Okay," she said, sitting back and admiring the piece. "Ready to see it?"

Carefully, I swung myself off the table, following her to the full-length mirror attached to the wall near her station. She blocked my view of myself, turning around to face me and biting her lip as her eyes scanned where she'd just inked me.

"I hope you don't hate it," she said, and her actual concern made its way through the joke she tried to hide it with.

"Step aside, Stig," I said, grabbing her by the arms and shuffling her out of the way. I didn't miss the way her cheeks reddened at the nickname, how her smile bloomed with it, too. But when I saw myself in the mirror, my focus shifted entirely to the ink on my chest.

Every muscle in my face went slack, awe striking me like a lightning bolt.

"Holy shit, Mary."

The skin was still a bit red and angry from being stabbed a million times over the last five hours, but underneath the slight swelling was the most bad ass octopus tattoo I'd ever seen.

The dark ink of the outline was clean and precise, but the shading of the head, of each tentacle, of the little suckers and the textured skin — that was what stole the show. I would never say it out loud, but it was far better than what I'd expected.

It was the kind of tattoo I'd presume to get from an artist who had been practicing for decades, not one who didn't even officially have her own chair yet.

I lifted my fingers to trace the ink, but she slapped my hand away.

"Do not put your grimy hands on my fresh tattoo," she said. "It'll get infected. I need to put a second skin on it, but I wanted you to see it first."

I shook my head as I took in every detail in the mirror, stepping even closer. It wasn't small, but it wasn't gigantic either. The head sat right in the middle of my sternum, with the arms stretching out over my pecs and down to touch the top of my abdomen.

"Adding to your list of regrets?" Mary asked from where she stood behind me.

My eyes found hers in the mirror, and I swallowed. Emotion gripped my throat in a tight vise.

"It's perfect," I said.

The corner of her mouth lifted, but then she looked down at her hands, shrugging. "I haven't done a chest piece before. The sternum was a little harder than I thought, and the shape—"

"It's perfect," I said again, and this time I turned to face her, and without a second thought about who was around us or the fact that I shouldn't have felt comfortable enough to do it, I slid my hands up to frame her face, tilting her eyes to meet mine. "I know you've been worried about your style, but I can tell you confidently that you have nothing to worry about. Because this tattoo is sick. It's bad ass. Fucking incredible. *Maravilloso*," I said as her eyes teared up a bit. "And I love it."

A victorious smile found her then. "Really?"

"Really. But I hope you realize what you've done, because now I want you to mark every last inch of my skin."

She laughed at that, pulling out of my grip and walking back to her station to start cleaning up. "Tattoos are addicting."

But as she cleaned my piece and covered it with a second skin, giving me all the aftercare instructions, I watched her with the truth vibrating through my chest.

It was her who was the addiction.

Chapter 25

MARY

After grabbing a quick bite to eat, Leo and I dragged our asses back to The Pit. The exhaustion from the night before combined with the adrenaline crash from tattooing had me yawning every two seconds, and one look at Leo when we kicked our shoes off at the door told me he felt the same.

It was quiet in the house, and I checked the time on my phone. "A little early for everyone to be asleep already."

"Tomorrow is our first real practice with the depth chart set," Leo reminded me. "Coach will start kicking our asses at the crack of dawn."

"Guess that means you should get some sleep, too."

"Shouldn't be an issue," he said around a yawn.

"Do you want the bed tonight? I feel so awful that you're still on the—"

Leo cut my words off with a roll of his eyes before he reached out, snagged my wrist in his hand, and tugged me into him.

"I'm fine, Stig," he said with a smirk aimed down at me. "And I like having you in my bed."

Chills erupted from where his breath whispered along my lips all the way down my spine.

His body pressed against mine, his hold on me so comfortable and confident, like he'd done it a million times, like I belonged nowhere if not in his arms.

I swallowed when he brushed my hair out of my eyes, tucking it behind one ear.

"Is it okay that I call you that?"

My heart skipped a beat before picking up double time. All I could do was nod, because all my awareness was zeroed in on where one of his hands held my waist, the other cradling my jaw.

Suddenly, I wasn't tired anymore.

I watched as Leo's throat bobbed with a thick swallow, like he just realized how close we were, too. He slowly slid his hand behind my neck, pulling me into him for a hug.

"Thank you for tonight," he said softly.

I closed my eyes, inhaling his scent as my fingers curled in the fabric of his t-shirt. I couldn't be sure how long we stood there like that, but I knew when he finally put space between us, I felt so dizzy I had to brace a hand on the wall to keep from falling.

"Well," I said. "Goodnight, then."

Leo shoved his hands in his pockets. "Goodnight."

I climbed the stairs in a daze, somehow managing to brush my teeth and wash my face before stripping out of my clothes and throwing on the largest t-shirt I owned. I crawled into bed, ready for exhaustion to take me under, but as soon as my head hit the pillow and the distinct smell of Leo surrounded me, every cell in my body buzzed to life again.

A deep inhale of him had my eyes closing, and I curled up in the sheets only to huff and throw them off me in the next breath. My nipples peaked under the cool air, adding to my already-over-sensitized nervous system as I stared up at the ceiling.

"Go to bed," I told myself, like saying it out loud would give me the restraint I needed.

But it didn't.

Instead, my breathing intensified, eyes racing over the lines of the ceiling fan above me. He wasn't even there anymore and I could feel his hands on me, feel the way he surrounded me when he pulled me into him, how he sighed into my hair like holding me was all he ever wanted.

I could see his eyes, the way they heated when they took in my dress last night, how they dragged over me so slowly my skin burned with every centimeter of that stare.

I could hear him, all around me — his laugh, the stiff breath he held when I was pressed against him, the deep baritone of his voice when he verified what I felt to be true at the shop — that he wanted me.

All of me.

He knew who I was now. He knew me past and present, the girl he hurt and the woman who grew strong despite him.

I pressed a hand to where my heart thumped loudly under my rib cage, waiting for good sense to find me and give me some reason why I couldn't have Leo, why I *shouldn't* let him have me.

But that voice had quieted.

I no longer heard the girl of my past screaming in pain, no longer felt her constant reminder of what he'd done to me. A softer version had moved in, one armed with the truth about that day, about everything that had happened since.

And now, all I could think about was the past couple of months, about late nights with him and the guys, video games and parties, him cooking for me, the candles, the rooftop, the jacket, last night at the bar, today at the tattoo shop.

He'd offered me a place to stay when I had nowhere to go.

He'd given up his *bed* for me without thinking twice.

My heart kicked so hard I sat upright.

Because now, the one overwhelming thing I felt was that I wanted him in that bed with me.

I didn't let myself overthink it, didn't consider how it might hurt in the morning. I threw the rest of the covers off me and scrambled out of bed, all but tripping over my bare feet as I lunged for the door. I yanked it open so fast the air blew my hair back.

And then I froze, because Leo stood waiting on the other side.

His jaw was a hard line, the muscle of it ticking under the skin as he stood perfectly still. All he had on was a pair of black sweatpants, and my eyes trailed the hills and valleys of his tan abdomen before they snagged on the fresh ink marking his chest.

My ink.

My art.

Mine.

The word echoed inside me the longer I stood there, hand still wrapped around the doorknob. Leo's hands were balled at his sides, like he'd been restraining himself to keep from knocking. His eyes flicked between mine with ragged breaths leaving his chest like he was in absolute agony.

The entire universe teetered precariously in that moment, the stars and planets stalling as if one wrong move from any of them would alter destiny's plan.

Slowly — *so* achingly slowly that my chest seized with the pressure of watching it — Leo lifted his hand. He stretched it out, toward me, his eyes following the movement until his fingers found my t-shirt. He caught it right above my hips, and we both stopped breathing with that one singular touch.

Then, he twisted his fist in the fabric and pulled me into him, catching me as we collided in a kiss that shattered time.

It was like a first breath and a last all at once, how we both inhaled together, our lips melding with a firm, delicious pressure that sent heat all the way down to my toes. My chest loosened with relief all while my heart surged and swelled and came alive.

He was everywhere.

His hands ran roughly up the length of me, a deep groan vibrating my lips as he traced every curve until he held my face in his grip. I felt that groan like my own heartbeat, his body pressing into mine, backing me up one heated kiss at a time until we were in his room and he kicked the door shut behind us.

Back back back, he pushed and invaded until my spine hit a wall and he could properly surround me, caging me in as if I'd ever want to escape now.

So many times I'd imagined what it would feel like to kiss him, to feel want radiating off him and know it was for me. Not just when we were younger, but here in this house, when I felt that tension so tight between us that one long-lasting look could have snapped it.

Now I knew that nothing I could have dreamed up would have ever compared to reality.

"You have consumed me for months," Leo breathed against my neck, maneuvering my head so he could kiss along the column of my throat before working his way back to my mouth. "*Por años.*" A bruising kiss punctuated that anguished confession before he pressed his forehead to mine, our breaths hot and frantic between us. "I couldn't sleep one more night without making you mine."

I whimpered at the words, at the way he sealed them with another punishing kiss that jolted me to the core. His thumbs held my jaw steady, fingers curling around the back of my neck possessively and holding me to him as he coaxed my mouth open and swept his tongue inside.

Another moan, another jolt — this time hotter and wetter and pooling between my thighs. I squeezed them together, as if that could bring relief, as if I could do anything to spare my body or my heart from the hurricane that was Leo Hernandez as he crashed upon the shores of my soul.

"You couldn't either, could you?" he asked, nipping my bottom lip. "You were coming to find me."

"Yes," I breathed.

"Tell me you want this, too," he begged, and for a moment, he held me still, eyes searching mine. "Tell me you need me."

My chest rose and fell in time with his, every breath louder and hotter than the one before it. With my eyes on his, I wrapped my hand around his wrist, guiding him away from where he held my face. I dragged his hand over my collarbone, over my chest, over the swells of my breasts, savoring the groan he let loose when his thumb brushed over the metal piercing my right nipple. Down, down, down, his palm surveying my hips and ass until I swiped his hand up and under my t-shirt and guided him where I needed him most.

"I think this speaks louder than words," I said, lining my fingers behind his as I pressed him to my core, slicking both of us with just how badly I wanted him.

"Fucking *Christ*," he cursed, and then he was kissing me again, pushing me so hard against the wall with his body that I felt pressure everywhere. But none of it compared to where he spread my legs wider with his thigh, skating one digit through my wetness before dipping the tip of his finger inside me.

I gasped, arching into him, and he visibly shook at the contact, burying his face in my neck as he toyed with my entrance before pressing just a little more inside.

"Sweet, perfect fucking pussy," he praised. "Wet and ready for me. I should just turn you around and fuck you against this wall right now. I'd slide inside you so easy, fill you to the fucking brim."

"*Yes*," I said, the word a breath and a plea.

Leo smiled against my lips, but then his hand withdrew, and I shuddered at the loss.

"No," I whined.

"If you think I'm going to fuck you without worshipping this perfect fucking body first, you don't know me at all."

"Fuck now. Worship later," I managed before wrapping my arms around his neck. I climbed into his arms, surprised that he lifted me so easily, that he held me like I didn't weigh more than he did.

He held me sturdy with one arm wrapped around me, and it had pulled up my t-shirt just enough to expose the bottom half of my ass. Leo's lips curled up again as he reared back and laid his palm against the exposed skin with a *slap*.

"I've played by your rules all summer," he growled. "Tonight — you play by mine."

I didn't have an argument left in me when he tossed me back into his bed, the scent of him invading me once again. But this time, it wasn't just the sheets. It was his hands bracing either side of my head, his triceps flexing under my fingernails, his hips pressing into my middle, thighs spreading my own for him as he settled between them.

"*Te ves tan bonita en mi cama*," he said, eyes raking over where my hair splayed out over the pillow. "You look so fucking pretty in my bed."

Then, he leaned back on his knees, grabbed my t-shirt in a fist again, and pulled me up until he could peel the fabric up and over my head. He tossed it somewhere behind him and then wrapped his hand around my neck, gently guiding me down until I was splayed naked in the sheets under him.

He squeezed, just a little, enough to make my toes curl before he dragged his palm flat down my neck, sternum, stomach, and *just* the top of where I ached for him before he sat back on his heels again. He shook his head, licking his bottom lip before he pinned it between his teeth, letting his eyes sear every inch of my exposed skin.

Instinctively, my knees folded in toward each other, and I was on track to cover my stomach when Leo caught my wrists.

"Oh, hell no," he said, shaking his head. "*Fuck* no. You've been teasing me for months in those little boy shorts, wearing no bra, giving me just enough to drive me fucking insane."

He moved my hands until they were above my head, then sat back again, gently pressing his fingertips against the insides of my knees until I had no choice but to spread.

"Open these legs wide for me, baby." He pushed and pushed until my hips hit their maximum, until I was completely at his disposal. "Let me see my girl."

His words were like little prods of electricity, so filthy and yet so *hot* I couldn't help but squirm with need beneath him.

I watched him smirk as he took in every inch of my body, and I didn't feel self-conscious then, didn't feel like I was too heavy or curvy or too *much* in any way. I felt like a goddess, like a prize he'd won in the fight of his life, like he could do nothing but sit there and rake his eyes over me and be perfectly content for life.

His eyes snagged on my breasts, and he groaned, bending until he was leaning over me again. "These fucking tits," he swore, balancing on one palm while the other cupped my right breast. "*Tan perfecta.*"

He tested the weight of it, another growl of appreciation at how it wouldn't all fit in his hand. He circled my nipple with his thumb before flicking it over the rose gold bar that spiked it, and he didn't know how that metal was like having an exposed nerve, that the slightest touch felt like a waterfall of pleasure.

I bucked my hips, arching into his touch with a moan of ecstasy.

"Mmm, so that's the spot, huh?" Leo mused, and he gently rolled the metal between his fingers as I whimpered again. "Let's add a little heat, shall we?"

He lowered himself, eyes cast up at me until the moment he covered the swell with his tongue, running it hot and flat up and over and around where I wanted him most before finally delivering. When he did, he swirled the tip of his tongue around the metal, and I heard it lightly click against his teeth before he sucked and gave me the warm, wet pressure to push me closer to the edge.

I loved my clit to be played with as much as the next girl, but for me, it had *always* been about my tits. And the way Leo worshipped them, the way he palmed and massaged one while his mouth devoured the other, it was like having a vibrator held on the perfect spot. Add the fact that it was Leo Fucking Hernandez who was bringing me those little shocks of pleasure, and I was a goner.

"More," I pleaded, and my hips writhed beneath him as I threw my head back and focused on where his mouth sucked my nipple. "So close."

He stopped immediately.

I couldn't help the involuntary shudder that ripped through me, or the way I cried out, reaching for him. But Leo caught my wrists again. He kissed each palm before sliding my hands into his hair.

"Not yet."

I could have cried if it weren't for the fact that he started kissing me again — first, my lips, then a blazing trail all the way down to my hips. He sucked and nipped at the skin from hip bone to hip bone before pressing a feather-light kiss to my clit, the cool metal of his chains just *barely* brushing against the hot, sensitive skin as he settled between my legs.

I shivered again. "You are the fucking *worst*."

"Hate me again?" he teased, and the motherfucker licked my clit so subtly, just a quick lashing of his tongue that it did nothing but cool my already-sensitive bud.

"So much."

"That so?" he asked, and this time he ran his tongue along my entrance, up and *over* my clit, licking everywhere but where I wanted him to.

"Leo," I begged, squirming.

"*Fuck*, I love it when you say my name like that." He rewarded me with a brief suck of my clit that made my legs quake around him. "When I let you come, that's all I want to hear."

"You don't own me," I said, trying to scoff even as I writhed beneath him.

"Oh, but I do, *cariño*," he said, and his eyes stayed locked on mine as he swept his tongue up the length of me. "And you own me, too."

Those were the words dancing in my head at a dizzying speed as he lowered his mouth, contrasting the brief connection he'd given me before with an all-encompassing sweep of ownership. He covered me with his wet heat, lapping and licking and sucking all while his hands wrapped around my thighs and held me in place so I couldn't move away, so there was no break, no relief from the sensuous torture.

As expert as his tongue was where he worked me, that wasn't what drove me to the edge. It was looking down at his head buried between my legs, watching the fervor with which he delivered each pleasurable lash of his tongue. He ate my pussy like it was a goddamn privilege, and it was *that* vision that made me peak.

"Ohhhh, *fuck,* Leo," I cried, and each word was long and melodic like I was singing him a fucking song, writing an anthem in his honor. It was all the affirmation he needed to reach one hand up and find my breast, and he held the weight of it while his fingers rolled around my piercing.

I combusted.

I didn't come in the cute, show-worthy way porn stars do. No, I flew apart at the hinges, legs violently shaking and body twisting in the sheets like that orgasm was an exorcism. It burned me from the inside out, and I cried out Leo's name over and over and over until every last wave had passed through me and I was bone-heavy and limp.

I didn't realize how hard I was breathing or how fast my heart was racing until I came crashing back to earth, and I ran a hand over my slick forehead and into my hair, shaking my head.

"Holy shit."

Leo chuckled against my core, kissing me there one last time before he crawled his way up. When he took my mouth with his, I tasted myself on him, and I lit up like a fucking Christmas tree at the fact.

"That was something," he murmured against my lips.

I flushed, burying my head in his neck, but he tilted my chin with his knuckles until I had no choice but to look up at him.

"Don't hide. That was fucking hot, Stig."

I rolled my lips together as another blush heated my skin. Then, I dragged a nail down his chest, carefully avoiding his fresh ink, and loving the way he broke out in chills at my touch. I drew that line over each swell of his hard abdomen before tucking my fingertip in the band of his pants.

"I want these off."

At that, he smirked, climbing off me and standing by the bed. He kept his eyes on where I was still sated and spread out in the sheets as he slowly stripped his sweats off and kicked them away once they were around his ankles.

I sat upright with wide eyes, my jaw damn near hitting the floor.

Because straining against the black fabric of his briefs was a thick, massive length that I was almost certain my pussy could not handle.

I'd seen the outline of him through his sweatpants and shorts around the house. I *knew* he was packing, but I thought it was in the normal way, in the *that's a nice dick* kind of way.

I was *not* expecting a fucking anaconda under those pants.

His cock twitched a little under my stare, and my pussy fluttered as if the bitch could actually take that beast.

"Mary?" Leo asked.

I blinked, dragging my gaze up to his. "Mm?"

He smirked, and I knew he was reading right through me in that moment. But he only held his chin a bit higher, biting the corner of his lip like my orgasm had only been the appetizer.

"Come here," he said. "I want you on your knees."

Chapter 26

LEO

Mary was too fucking pretty as she crawled out of the sheets, her cunt still dripping for me, breasts swollen and pink from my hands and mouth. Her hair was a mess, and I didn't miss how wide her eyes still were as she strolled over to me, catching my gaze before she dropped to her knees.

Fuck me.

That sight alone was enough to make me bust.

She looked up at me, every curve of her catching the soft rays from the light outside her window. It slipped through the blinds in little slats of gold, painting her in stripes of shadow and light.

I arched a brow, and without another cue, she turned her focus to my briefs, sliding her warm fingertips into the bands before dragging them down my hips. They caught on my ass, on my erection, and she yanked harder, pulling the fabric to my ankles as my cock sprang forward.

I'd seen the look before when a girl saw my length for the first time. In some ways, I found it to be a curse. I'd had girls walk out, or others who would try but we couldn't ever get past them taking the first half of me. Guys always slung jokes about massive cocks, but few knew the burden of actually having one.

But watching Mary as she took me in, her worry faded, and her lips curved up in anticipation like I was a challenge she couldn't wait to prove she could handle.

She licked her lips, reaching out to take my cock in her fist. I groaned at the first contact, at the feel of her hand wrapped around me as my cock jerked from the touch. I was so fucking gone after hearing her scream my name that I was two pumps away from coming. It took every ounce of focus and control I had not to.

"I won't be able to take you all the way in my mouth," she said, looking up at me through her lashes like she was ashamed of that fact.

If she only knew that those words and this view of her tits under my cock were enough to make me blow without so much as a lick.

"You're in control," I said instead, and I slid one hand into her hair, guiding her mouth to me.

She opened, swirling her tongue over my tip and coating me in her saliva as I groaned and let my head fall back. It was so fucking good, so fucking sweet after wondering what it would be like for so long.

I looked back down through heavy lids just in time to watch her dive, stretching her mouth open as wide as she could and sticking her tongue out, too. She took just under half of me in before she choked, and I hissed at the feeling, the sound, the view of her hair twisted in my fist and my cock in her mouth.

"Use your hands," I coached, and she obeyed like the good girl she was, wrapping one hand around me under her mouth before the other came up and covered the rest of me. For a moment, I was completely wrapped in her warmth, and I savored that brief stillness before I said, "Now, slick your hands and use them with your mouth."

Again, she did exactly as I said, her eyes floating up to meet mine as she pulled my cock out of her mouth. She rolled her hands up and over where she'd been sucking me, wetting her palms before she dragged them down my length again.

"Oh, *fuck*," I groaned. "Just like that."

I loved how much she preened under that praise, how she took me in her mouth again with even more eagerness. She sealed her hands together and that top hand to her mouth, and then she worked them in time together, pumping and twisting and sucking in a perfect rhythm that made me see stars.

My toes curled, spine burning with the need to release. My balls were already so tight, and one glance down at her, one millisecond watching her tits bounce as she worked me had me ready to pull out of her mouth and paint her with every last drop of my release.

Against every urge in my body, I pulled her hair, pulled her off me, and slowly helped her stand. I hissed when she fully released me, and then laughed at her pouty lip once she stood in front of me again.

"Not yet."

I grabbed her hand in mine and dragged her back to the bed. Crawling in first, I situated myself so I was seated against the headboard, and then I pulled her on top to straddle my lap. It was all the restraint I had left to pause a moment and reach in my bedside table drawer for a Magnum. I slid it over my length, taking my time since Mary was watching the movement with her lips parted like my cock was the prettiest thing she'd ever seen.

"Come here," I said when it was affixed, and I grabbed her hips in my hands, squeezing the softness there and lifting her until she was balanced on her knees. She braced her hands on my shoulders and lowered just an inch, my crown lining up at her entrance.

Then, I took a breath, and loosened my grip on her hips, letting her take control.

If she was going to try to take me all the way in, she needed to move at her own pace.

"It's yours, baby," I told her. "Take it."

She bit her lip on a moan, rolling her hips until I fit into her seam. She sank just an inch and we both shook, moaning, her eyes fluttering shut while I kept mine open and fixed on where she was taking me.

"Leo," she breathed when she sank down a little more, and my name on her lips had me desperate to feel her.

I leaned forward, grabbing her and pulling her into me for a kiss. I wrapped my arms fully around her, holding her tight to me as I flexed my hips just marginally, enough to slide a bit farther in. She was still fucking soaked from me, but when she hissed, I knew I was stretching her open.

My forehead hit hers, and I bit back a groan as she lowered down a bit more. When she winced, though, I cupped her face and made her look at me.

"We can stop."

"Fuck you," she said, and as if to prove a point, she lifted onto her knees and dropped down even lower.

I was three-fourths of the way in now, and the way she dug her nails into my shoulders as she lifted and dropped back down, again and again, slicking me with her desire as she stretched herself open for me — it was ecstasy.

"You feel so fucking good," I told her, moving my hands to grip her ass. "I want to fill you. I want you to sit this sweet ass all the way down."

She whimpered, wrapping her arms around my neck and kissing me hard. Up and down, her ass bounced in my hands as she rode me, slow and smooth, taking in just a centimeter more each time.

Then, on a breath, she tucked her pelvis, shifting to the perfect position to let me all the way in.

"Oh fuck," she cried. "Fuck, *God*, Leo."

Each word was a sip of air as we both stayed perfectly still, her adjusting to the feel of me while my cock throbbed inside her. I held her there for a long time, kissing along her neck, her jaw, up to suck the lobe of her ear into my teeth. I trailed my fingertips over her back, soothing her, patient and waiting.

She pressed onto her knees, the cool air sweeping over my slick cock, and then she slid back down again. This time, she tucked her pelvis as she lowered, taking me in one fell swoop that made us both cry out.

"*Mierda*, Mary," I breathed, my lungs on fire at the sight of her as she lifted and did it again. Her tits bounced when she hit my lap, and I grabbed them in two handfuls, playing with those torturous barbells through her nipples.

She relaxed a bit when I did, rolling her hips and grinding her clit against my pelvis with me deep inside. When I realized she was going to come again, I took control, letting her brace herself while I slowly flexed my hips, working her from the inside while my fingers played with her piercings and she ground herself on me.

"One more, baby," I whispered in her ear. "One more for me."

A mixture of a whine and a moan left her, like those words were both permission and a command she didn't want to follow. But her movements became more erratic, hips gyrating, and then she came in a beautiful, chaotic symphony of shaking limbs and loud moans, her walls squeezing around me.

I covered her mouth with one hand, muffling her the best I could but loving the noises too much to snuff them out altogether. By now, if the other guys had heard, they'd heard. Still, I didn't want anyone else to hear those sounds that were just for me.

"Oh my God," she panted, collapsing on me. "I can't move."

I chuckled, kissing her hair before I carefully maneuvered us. I rolled her off me and onto her stomach, and then I crawled on top of her, balancing myself above her as I positioned my crown again. She was even more wet, and I slid in a bit easier, though she tightened the farther I pushed.

"I'm almost there," I promised, and I withdrew before pushing in a bit deeper, savoring how her full ass rippled when I did. "But I can stop if—"

Mary silenced my offer by backing her ass up and taking me deeper inside, her pussy walls tightening around me like a fucking glove.

"Please," she begged, arching so my chest aligned with her back, and from above her, I could watch her tits pressed against the mattress as well as I could see my cock disappear inside her again. "Come inside me, Leo."

My next curse was just a breath as I picked up the pace. I didn't care that I had a condom on, those words lit me up with possession, with the idea that she wanted me to spill inside her. Balancing on one palm, I snaked my other hand up under her, squeezing her breast before I slid it up higher and wrapped my fingers around her throat.

She arched into me, gasping in pleasure, and I squeezed a bit tighter, holding her still while I flexed and pumped and took.

"God*damnit*, Mary," I grunted, and then fire ripped from my toes up to my balls, from my head down to my cock, all the blood and awareness rushing to that one place. I busted hard enough to blacken my vision, and Mary's moans only coaxed me on more. Every time I thought I was done, the orgasm would keep coming, draining me in the most powerful climax of my fucking life.

"Ho...ly... shit," I breathed as I pumped, still squeezing her neck until I felt my cum leaking out of the condom.

Fuck.

I quickly rolled off her and over onto my back, and Mary looked surprised for only a second before she saw my cock twitching, more cum than the condom could handle dripping out of the edges of it.

She wet her lips, and then peeled the condom off me and took me with her mouth and hands again, sucking me dry as I shook and convulsed under her. It was almost too fucking much, my cock as sensitive as an exposed nerve, but I kept coming, kept climaxing, filling her mouth even after the condom.

When I was finally spent, Mary sat back on her heels and swallowed, smiling at me wickedly.

"Fucking hell," I said on a laugh, running my hands back through my hair.

Then, I reached forward and grabbed my girl, pulling her into the sheets with me and wrapping her up. She giggled as I clutched her in my arms, throwing a leg over her for good measure.

"Are you caging me, sir?"

"You're damn fucking straight, I am."

She laughed again, but then gasped, pressing against me so she could look at my chest. "Your tattoo!"

"Is fine," I finished for her. "I made sure not to rub it or put pressure on it."

She took a moment assessing it for herself before she believed me, and then she laid back in the sheets, her sated eyes heavy where they watched me.

"Do you need food?" I asked.

I thought she tried to laugh, but she only closed her eyes on a sleepy smile, instead. "Pee, then sleep," she answered.

I let her peel herself out of bed to clean up, doing the same myself. I put my briefs back on and helped her into her t-shirt, and then we climbed into bed again, and I pulled her into me, folding myself around her with her back to my chest and my legs slipping into the curve of hers.

She slipped away quickly, her breaths turning long and slow.

And I kissed the back of her neck knowing I was ruined for anyone else.

Chapter 27

MARY

Panic slipped into bed with me the next morning.

The sheets were otherwise empty, so I felt the arms of anxiety like a straitjacket as they wrapped me up tight and held me against my will.

"Oh, God," I whispered to myself, hand against my heart as I rolled over and stared up at the ceiling. It wasn't even dawn yet, the room still cast in a calm darkness. "Oh, *God*."

I slept with Leo Hernandez.

I slept with Leo *fucking* Hernandez.

I slapped my forehead, shaking my head even as I tried to calm myself down. *It's fine*, I tried to convince myself. *Everything is fine*.

But I couldn't squeeze my eyes shut hard enough to block out the abrasive thoughts as they punched me from every angle.

I felt like a fool.

Yes, Leo had seemed genuine in his apologies — both for the past and the present. And *yes*, he'd let me tattoo him, marking him for life. Also, *yes*, I'd wanted him. I'd wanted him in this bed with me, wanted his hands and mouth all over me, wanted all of him inside me.

But now that I was alone in the aftermath of my decisions, I couldn't drown out the loud voice inside me saying it could all be a lie.

What if he *did* know it was me all those years ago? What if he *was* disgusted when he saw me? What if he was so embarrassed he blew me off in front of his friends, but was so selfish he pretended like it didn't happen when he tried to call me that night? What if he wanted to have his cake and eat it, too?

And what if he knew it was me when I moved across the street? What if he saw how I'd changed, and so he continued playing dumb, all while making me his next conquest?

How many times had I witnessed him relentlessly pursuing another girl — whether it was a cheerleader or a sorority girl or some random partying at The Pit?

How was I supposed to believe him when he said he never felt for any of them the way he felt for me when that was *years* ago? We were in high school. We never even *held hands,* let alone anything else physical. And judging from his performance last night, I *knew* he'd had plenty of experience.

My stomach turned with that thought, even though I had no right to feel any sort of way considering I was far from a virgin myself.

Still, even as my anxiety warned me away from Leo, I felt a possessiveness over him that I couldn't fight. Why was it so hard to believe that he'd had me on his mind all these years, if I'd felt the same way about him?

I *wanted* to believe him.

I wanted to live in the world where I was the source of Leo Hernandez's desire, where he meant it when he said he wanted to make it up to me, that he wanted me to be his.

But how could he?

How could someone who looked like him, who had talent like he had and a future in the fucking NFL want anything to do with *me*?

I was wound so tight that I jumped when the bedroom door creaked open, and Leo slipped inside, already dressed for practice with his gym bag slung over his shoulder. He dropped it at the door before crossing the room in three wide strides and climbing into bed with me.

It was a betrayal, the way my heart calmed when he was near, how my breathing leveled out just at the sight of him. When his scent surrounded me, I sighed with relief, like his presence was grounding me to the reality I wanted to believe.

"Did I wake you?" he asked, nuzzling his nose in my neck as he curled around me.

I shook my head, but didn't answer, and I felt myself stiffening in his arms as my anxious thoughts crept back in. Leo noticed immediately, frowning as he propped himself up on his elbow and looked down at me. His brows furrowed with one look at my face.

"I woke myself," I said, just above a whisper.

"You look like you saw a ghost."

I hated that my eyes welled with tears, that my skin burned with the restraint to hold them at bay. But it was no use. One tear slipped out of my eye and down to my ear before Leo swiped it away with his thumb.

"Hey," he said, searching my eyes. "What's that about?"

That only made me shake my head harder, and I covered my face with my hands so I wouldn't have to look at him, so he couldn't look at *me* while I fell apart.

When I didn't take my hands away, he covered them with his own. "Talk to me," he pleaded.

My chest was so tight I thought I'd burst.

"Leo! We gotta go, man!" Kyle called from downstairs.

Leo cursed, but I just inhaled a steadying breath before wiping my face clean and pushing him gently. "Go. Don't be late for practice, I'm fine."

He gave me a look that said *bullshit*.

"I'll *be* fine," I amended.

He shook his head, sweeping my hair from my face. "I don't want to leave you like this."

For a long moment, Leo's eyes flicked between mine, the concern growing in his features. And when he looked at me like that, it made it so easy to believe every word he'd said was real.

"Last night was..." He swallowed, thumbing my jaw. "Everything. It was everything to me, Stig."

I nodded, leaning into his palm and closing my eyes. The motion set two more tears free, and Leo let out a pained sigh.

"Please, tell me what's wrong."

"Leo!" This time it was a chorus from our roommates, and I shoved him more forcefully toward the door.

"Go. We can talk later."

Leo cursed again before taking my hands in his. He kissed each knuckle before leaning down and pressing a long, promising kiss to my lips.

"Whatever lies your brain is telling you, don't believe them," he pleaded. Then, with his hand holding mine until he had no choice but to pull away, he jogged out the door and down the stairs, grabbing his bag off the floor on the way out.

Once I heard the front door shut, my heart went into double time again.

See? Everything is fine, my brain tried to assure me.

No, it's not, my heart combatted.

Back and forth like a rag doll in the jaws of a pit bull, my emotions tore through me, and I had no choice but to lay there and let them for what felt like hours.

It was all I could do to eventually peel myself out of bed, shower, and drag my ass downstairs to make coffee. I couldn't stomach the thought of food. All I could do was watch the clock until it was a decent time late in the morning, and then I immediately texted the group chat between me, Julep, Riley, and Giana.

Me: S.O.S.

Less than a minute passed before my phone was ringing, and I answered the video call request to find a sleepy Julep staring back at me.

"Mary? What's going on?"

"Are you still sleeping?" I asked, checking the time. It was half past eleven.

"I was up late working on wedding stuff, and then I was too wound up to sleep so I poled for a while," she explained, rubbing the sleep from her eyes as she sat up more in bed. "What's up, why the S.O.S.?"

Riley joined the video chat next. Her ponytail swung behind her as she walked through the locker room out into the hallway. I realized then she was probably in the middle of practice or about to watch game film.

Giana came on last, and she was at the stadium, too, in her office. It was dark enough that the phone screen reflected on the lenses of her glasses.

"I'm sorry," I said. "I know it's a weird time of day, everyone's busy. Riley, you're at practice. Giana, you're at work." I shook my head. "Just call later, I'm fine."

"Absolutely not," Giana said, holding up one threatening finger. "I swear to God, if you hang up this phone, I will beat you with a book."

If I wasn't so paralyzed by anxiety, I would have laughed.

"We have twenty minutes until meetings start," Riley added. "What's going on, Mary?"

"Um… well…" I dropped my head back against the kitchen cabinet behind me. "I slept with Leo last night."

"What?!" They said the word all together, all at once, and then Julep burst into confused laughter while Riley and Giana did various versions of happy dances.

"I *knew* it!" Giana said with a fist pump. "You two looked less than thirty seconds from eating each other outside the bar the other night."

"This explains why Leo had a monster practice this morning," Riley added with a smirk. "Little shithead has been a walking ego all day."

"Okay, one," Julep said, holding up a finger. "I feel like I need some background because last I knew, you hated the guy. And two," she added. "Why do you look more like someone who got mugged rather than railed last night?"

Again, I wanted to laugh, but instead, my lower lip wobbled. "I wish I knew. I just… I'm a mess," I whispered, and then cursed when I started crying again.

"Oh, babe," Julep said, and I knew if she was with me, she'd have one hand petting my hair by now. "There are always big emotions after the first time. I freaked out when it happened with Holden, too."

I nodded but couldn't help but feel like my freakout was much more warranted than hers had been. Sure, Holden had been off limits for her, but there was no question *ever* about how he felt for her. We all saw it clear as day.

With Leo, we'd all seen him throw himself at every girl with long hair and a nice rack.

My stomach sank, and I felt two seconds away from vomiting.

The girls all gently consoled me until I got it together, and then Riley let out a sigh. "Honestly, I'm really glad you called. I'm not in the best shape either. My agent has pretty much confirmed that I have zero chance of being drafted, so it looks like this will be my last season playing football."

"I'm so sorry, Riles," Giana said softly. "I've been out of it, too. I'm in the biggest book funk of my life."

Julep snorted. "No offense, G, but I don't think that counts as an actual problem."

"Do you know what it feels like? Have you ever gone through a slump when you couldn't pole, when you didn't *want* to pole?"

Julep frowned at that. "I have, actually. It's the worst."

"See?! I haven't read more than a page since I finished that Elsie Silver cowboy romance two weeks ago." She pouted. "I'm ruined."

"Wow, so all of us are on the struggle bus?" Julep asked with a laugh. "I guess it only took one of us admitting it for the rest of us to follow suit."

"What's wrong with you?" I asked.

"Oh, other than planning a wedding on my own since my fiancé is working twenty-four-seven now that the season has started, and the fact that I graduated four months ago and still don't have a job?" She shrugged. "Not much."

"You know what we need," Riley said. "A girls' night."

"No," Julep said. "Not just *any* girls' night. *The* girls' night."

Riley, Giana, and I frowned in confusion, but Julep just grinned and waggled her brows.

"You bitches down for an impromptu bachelorette party?"

Chapter 28

MARY

My text to the girls had been the equivalent of the Bat Signal.

Julep packed a bag and caught the next flight into Boston. I picked her up at the airport just as Riley and Giana were finishing up at the stadium for the day, and we were all shocked when Riley was so quick to blow off her class that night and Giana didn't show up at the hotel with a book in her hand.

We checked into a hotel entirely out of my price range downtown, thanks to Holden and his big signing bonus, and after smothering each other in hugs and getting all dolled up, we piled into a cab and headed to an unknown location of Julep's choosing.

When the cab dropped us off, we stared up at the sign with mixed emotions.

"Oh, hell no," I said.

"Hell *yes!*" Giana combatted with a squeal and little claps of joy. Her eyes were that of a kid on Christmas morning.

Riley was quiet, but crossed her arms over her chest like she wasn't thrilled with the idea either.

But one look at Julep told me we weren't getting out of this.

"Come on, babes," she said, linking her arms through ours. "Time to introduce you to chrome therapy."

I was still groaning as she dragged us inside the pole studio, which was mostly dark save for some party lights. Loud, beat-driven music greeted us, along with the owner of the studio, who was wearing nothing but a black high-rise thong and triangle swim top along with high heels that were at least eight inches tall.

"Welcome to Spintensity," she said with a wide smile. I noticed then that she had some impressive ink on her thighs and shoulders, and she seemed to appraise me with the same appreciation. "I hear we're celebrating a bride tonight?"

Julep did a little spin and a curtsy. "That would be me."

The instructor whistled, looking Julep up and down. "Does your future husband realize how lucky he is?"

"If you saw him, you'd be saying I'm the lucky one," Julep combatted.

"Doubtful," she said with a smile. "I'm Joany. I'll be your party guide tonight. I take it from the notes that you're seasoned," she said, pointing at Julep before her finger dragged over the rest of us. "And you three are fresh meat?"

"The freshest," Giana said excitedly, stepping forward like a sacrificial virgin. "Can you teach me how to climb the pole?!"

Joany laughed, exchanging a look with Julep before she waved us farther inside. "We can try. But first, let's get you three changed into some shorts and start with walking around the pole."

I thought she was kidding, but after she walked us through the studio set up and we each stood behind our pole of choice, that was exactly how the class began — by walking. Joany and Julep made it look effortless, of course, both of them strutting sexily in their heels. Riley, Giana, and I, on the other hand, were barefoot and still looked like we were the unstable ones.

It was so embarrassing it was hilarious, and we all laughed and teased each other as Joany attempted to show us how to look sexier while we circled the chrome.

When we moved on to spins, Riley shocked us all — thanks to her upper-body strength and a core that should have been illegal. Joany walked us through beginner spins with names that confused me even more — Fireman, Goddess, Hollywood — and Riley did each one without more than just a simple demonstration.

Giana and I, on the other hand, were banging into the pole hard enough to leave bruises.

Still, the laughs came easy, and the more we worked on spins and tricks and dance moves like body waves and twerks, the less Leo was on my mind. Soon, I was completely wrapped up in the experience with the girls, in celebrating when they achieved something and laughing together when we all failed.

We were all sweaty and sore by the end of the ninety-minute session, but Giana was determined as she squeezed tacky grip out of a bottle and into her hands, rubbing them together with her eyes laser-focused on the bell at the top of the pole. Apparently, it was a tradition and an honor to ring it once you were able to climb to the top.

"Okay, so you're going to want to really squeeze your knees together and use the power in your thighs to hike you up the pole," Joany explained as she demonstrated climbing. "Once you've extended your legs, switch your arms and now your bottom arm becomes the top one, and you use that upper body to lift your knees to your chest, squeeze, and repeat."

She did a couple climbs before sliding back down and gesturing for Julep to go next. Of course, *that bitch* climbed while the pole was spinning, her long hair flowing behind her and her body moving with all the fluid grace of a gazelle. It was mesmerizing to watch.

Infuriating, too, because when you had a friend that gorgeous and talented, it was hard not to hate her just a little bit.

We all clapped when she was on the floor again, and then it was Riley's turn. She struggled a bit in the start, but once her muscles understood the assignment, she repeated the movement Joany had showed us until she was all the way at the top. Her movements were more athletic than Julep's, which made sense considering who she was, but her smile was the biggest I'd ever seen her wear when she rang the bell as the rest of us cheered from below.

Giana was next, and the poor thing could barely pull her chest to the pole while her legs and arms both shook with the effort it took to get her there.

"It's okay, it takes most girls a few classes before they can climb even that much," Joany tried to encourage her.

But that little bookworm was nothing if not driven by a challenge, and I watched her eyes narrow in concentration and determination at Joany's words before she hiked herself a little higher. It was a struggle the entire way, but she made it, hooting and hollering like a banshee as she rang the bell at the top before sliding back down.

"Alright, my inked queen," Joany said to me next, waving a hand toward my pole. "Let's see what you got."

I watched her for a solid second before I laughed, because she *had* to be joking. But she didn't return the jest, and the rest of the girls watched like they actually thought I could climb the pole, too.

"You're kidding, right?" I asked, pointing at me and then the pole. "You really think my fat ass can get up this thing?"

"Hey!" Giana slapped my arm. "Don't talk about my friend that way!"

"I didn't say it was a bad thing," I defended, rubbing my arm. Then, I grabbed the ample curves at my hips and over my stomach, my thighs, my ass, giving them all a squeeze and jiggle. "I'm just saying ya girl is thick and there isn't any way in hell I'm getting to the top of this pole."

"Size doesn't mean shit in this sport," Joany said. "Stick thin or curvaceous as hell, you can do anything you set your mind to."

Julep smacked my ass. "She's right. So go on, get to climbing."

"You have a lot more faith in my arms than I do," I mumbled.

"It's not all arms. Squeeze the knees and engage the thighs, remember?" Riley said, and I gave her a look that said *traitor*. She only smiled saccharinely back at me.

With a sigh, I gave in trying to fight them on it and decided I'd prove my point. I reached up and wrapped my hands around the chrome, fixing my shin to the front of it like Joany showed us before I engaged my shoulders and lifted the other leg. Instantly, I slipped back down to the floor.

"Okay, I tried, let's move on."

"Ah, ah, ah, not so fast," Julep said, and she held out the bottle of grip until I opened my palm and let her squeeze some into it. "Try again."

My grip was infinitely better with the white goo she'd given me rubbed into each palm, and this time when I lifted my leg, I stayed put. With a grunt, I pulled my chest to the pole, switching hands before I tucked my knees up to my elbows and squeezed again.

I looked down at the ground, at how far away from it I was, and smiled.

Holy shit.

I'm climbing a fucking pole.

I tried to get a little higher, but my arms gave out, and I ended up slipping almost down to the bottom again.

This time, though, I didn't give up.

I set my brow with determination and focused on the bell mocking me from the top.

I was going to ring that motherfucker.

"Go, Mary, go!" Giana cheered with a little clap as I reached up the pole again. The rest of the girls joined in encouraging me as I climbed, slowly but surely, up and up and up.

Sweat ran down my back and dampened my hair the higher I got, and every muscle in my body burned — my shoulders, my back, my arms, my legs, my fucking invisible abs. Everything had to be engaged, and I hadn't used my muscles that intensely ever before in my life.

Sure, yoga had its days, but I tended to stay away from the power flows and spent my time on my mat enjoying longer, deeper poses.

Not tonight.

Tonight, I was shutting out every voice in my head saying I couldn't do it, and I was inching myself higher and higher up a chrome apparatus.

The last bit was the hardest, and I gritted through the pain and the desperate plea my body was giving me to stop as I reached up and grabbed the ribbon tied to the bell, ringing it like crazy. The girls went nuts below me, and I looked down with a victorious smile and a surge of adrenaline coursing through me.

I slid down fireman style, and when my feet hit the floor, I was immediately wrapped up in a group hug as the girls bounced around me. We laughed and cheered until we were breathless, and when they pulled away and high-fived me, every cell in my body went from buzzing to absolutely still.

I couldn't explain what happened next.

One second we were celebrating and Joany was popping a bottle of champagne for us to toast our accomplishments.

The next?

I was sobbing.

The emotion bubbled up from my chest, making each breath shorter until the first cry escaped my lips. I wasn't even sure what it was that had me choked up. Was it Leo and everything fucking with my head in that regard? Probably. But it also felt... bigger. *More*. Like I had just faced every fucking trauma that had ever held me down and I'd ripped each one to shreds.

Julep hugged me tight, and when she pulled back, she framed my arms, her eyes bright and shiny, too.

"Pole therapy," she said.

Then, she slid a champagne flute into my hand, and with tears still drying on my cheeks, we clinked our glasses together and proceeded to get absolutely tanked.

Chapter 29

MARY

"I swear to God, there's nothing better than Cheetos when you're drunk."

Giana punctuated that statement by shoving a complete handful of the orange chips into her mouth, half of which landed in her lap and the floor around her. She crunched and groaned her approval with a smile.

We'd slammed shots at a night club until we all realized we'd rather be back at the hotel in our pajamas, which was where we were currently, sucking down a bottle of tequila and devouring the various snacks we'd had brought up.

Well, all of us except Riley, who chose to stay sober only because she didn't want to die at practice the next day. Giana was able to get the day off and so was I, and Julep didn't fly back to Charlotte until the following afternoon, but Riley couldn't escape Coach's wrath with the season starting up, and therefore was our sober spirit guide.

"I don't know, I think this pizza wins my vote," Riley argued as she twirled a hot piece of cheese dripping off her slice around one finger before popping it in her mouth. "I've been eating so clean all through camp, I forgot what a good greasy slice tastes like."

"You look fucking insane," Julep said in the way of a compliment. "Like, more ripped than I've ever seen you."

"Well, I am insane," Riley said. "Because I thought if I could put on some weight, build muscle, and level up my kicks, I'd have a shot at the draft." Her eyes softened, losing focus somewhere beyond her slice of pizza. "What a fucking joke."

She took a bite while the rest of us offered her sympathetic looks of understanding.

"They're idiots," Giana said.

"Is there any other way you can play?" Julep asked. "Like a women's league or something?"

I smiled a bit at Julep offering a solution, because this time last year, that girl was a walking rain cloud with no optimism or silver lining to be found. Holden had changed that.

"Actually, kind of," Riley said with a shade of hope. "The Women's Football Alliance. It's a minor league, and the pay isn't great, but... the Boston team is really good. They've already reached out with some interest."

"See!" I said, nudging her knee.

Riley smiled on a nod. "Yeah. It's cool. It's just..."

"You should be able to play in the NFL," Julep finished for her. "You should be able to at least have the chance."

Riley shrugged, but we could all feel her agreement in the air. It was a tricky situation. To play on a field full of massive grown men could be dangerous for her. But as a kicker, would she really have that much contact anyway? And she wasn't just a good kicker, she was the best one playing college ball right now.

But because she was a woman, she didn't even have the chance to prove she could handle it.

I couldn't imagine her frustration.

"Anyway, how's the wedding planning?" Riley asked Julep.

"It's great," Julep said with a bright smile as she picked up a piece of chocolate. "If spending hours on seating charts and flower arrangements is your cup of tea."

"Sounds fun!" Giana said, which made us all snort.

"It's fine," Julep added, without the sarcasm this time. "Mom has been helping a lot — which is... weird," she admitted. "And also nice. I just wish Holden could help, too. And he *wants* to, but even riding the bench, the team gets ninety percent of his time. And I'm *happy* for him. He's living his dream. And I know it's just the season where he'll be like this. I'll have a little more of his time come February."

"That's why you planned the wedding for April, right?" Riley asked.

Julep nodded. "Yeah. And he helps when he can, but he's tired after practice or games, and let's be honest — what little time we get together, we're not spending on filling out our registry."

Giana waggled her brows at that.

"Does it ever freak you out?" I asked, trying not to project my own insecurities but failing. "Him on the road, all the women throwing themselves at him both in person and online..."

"It's hard sometimes," Julep admitted honestly. "I mean, any woman who says it's not is lying. It doesn't matter that I trust him, that I know he'd never do anything with anyone else. It's still sharing, even if he's not a participant. He's part mine, and part the rest of the world's, too."

I nodded, a thick lump in my throat at the fact that it would be the same with Leo. Then, I mentally slapped myself for even thinking that far ahead when we'd literally *just* slept together. But I couldn't help it. He'd been so engrained in my past, threaded through the very fabric of my being for so long... and now, he was in my present, saying things and touching me in ways that made me think he wanted me.

That was as exhilarating as it was terrifying.

"I'm excited for you," I told Julep. "It's going to be perfect. And tag us in if you need us. We're here to help."

She smiled her agreement, and after sucking a shot from the bottle of tequila, she handed it to me. "Okay. We've got the feelings tunnel lubed up. Are you finally going to tell us why you sent an S.O.S. text or are we going to have to hold you down and tickle it out of you?"

I winced as I drank from the bottle, even though it was nice tequila. We didn't have a lime to polish it off with, so it burned every centimeter on the way down.

"I wish it was easy to explain. I feel like a crazy person," I admitted.

"Why don't you just start talking and see what comes up?" Giana offered.

So, I did.

I had to fill Julep in on why I had spent the last seven years hating Leo, since the other girls had heard the backstory before we went out the other night. Once she was caught up, I proceeded to tell them about the bar, about the scene he made with Nero and the blow up that followed when I chased him outside. When I told them about the tattoo, they freaked out and demanded photos, and then, I told them about what happened when we got home.

Although, I left out all the details, because my friends didn't need to know I peeled a Magnum off Leo's gargantuan cock and licked him clean.

"And then," I said with a sigh, picking at my nails. "I woke up, and he wasn't there, and I just... completely freaked out."

"He wasn't there?! What the fuck, that asshole!" Julep raged.

"Well, he was still *there*, but he wasn't in bed. He'd had to get ready for practice," I explained.

"Oh," she said, and then was confused, which made sense because so was I.

"It's just, I woke up and everything crashed down on me. I have been hardwired for *years* to hate this guy. I had the worst impression of him. But then, over the last couple of months, I've seen the other side, the side I once knew and..." I almost said *loved*, but grew quiet instead. "I've seen glimpses of the boy I knew before everything went to shit," I landed on. "And... I don't know. It made it hard to remember why I hated him, until he did something that reminded me, then I was on fire with anger and the desire to shove him off the roof."

Giana snickered.

"I feel like a yo-yo stuck in an endless cycle," I continued. "And then, to find out that all this time, I'd been punishing him, punishing *myself* for something that didn't even really happen... at least, not the way I imagined. He didn't know it was me that day he rejected me." I paused. "But then again, it was still *me*. It doesn't really matter if he didn't know it was me, the girl he talked to online, does it? Because he took one look at *me,* the girl standing in front of him with a notebook full of sketches, and found me wanting."

"So, is that what it's about then?" Riley asked. "Are you still upset by what he did that day?"

"Yes," I said, then immediately shook my head. "No. I don't know. I guess that's part of it." I paused, thinking, trying to make sense of it all. "I guess I'm just... scared."

"That he'll hurt you?"

"Yes," I admitted softly. "What if he lied and he did know it was me, but then he saw what I grew into and made me his conquest?"

"Leo wouldn't do that," Giana said earnestly.

"You don't think so? Look at all the girls we've watched him relentlessly pursue, from cheerleaders to water girls. But does he ever end up with them?" I didn't give them a chance to answer. "No. They fuck, and he moves on. I mean, you guys saw the article over the summer. *The twenty-seven exes of Leo Hernandez.*"

Giana looked like she wanted to say something, but bit her tongue.

"I don't want to be the butt of another joke," I told them, voice shaking. "I *can't* be."

The girls were quiet for a moment before Julep crawled over to where I sat on the floor. She wrapped me in a hug, resting her chin on my shoulder.

"It's okay to be scared," she told me.

"Thank you."

"But it's not okay to punish Leo for a crime he hasn't even committed."

I frowned as Julep pulled back to look at me.

"I get that he has some groveling to do to make up for the past, but it sounds to me like he's all too eager to do that, if you let him."

"It sounds to *me* like he's crazy about you," Giana added. "And that your brain is trying to freak you out by holding fast to what it believed about him for years instead of letting the reality of who he is *now* shine through."

"But do people really change? Can I really trust that?" I asked.

"Have *you* changed since you were fifteen?" Riley asked. "I know I have."

I swallowed, knowing she was right, that they all were, but my stomach was too sour to admit it.

"What if he hurts me again?" I whispered.

Giana crawled over to join me and Julep, sliding her hand into mine and squeezing it. "But what if he *loves* you?"

My eyes flooded with tears, and I searched her gaze for a second before a laugh burst from my chest. "Jesus, Giana. You really do read too much smut."

"No such thing."

Riley came over to join in the group hug. "Look, at the end of the day, it doesn't matter what we think. But, for what it's worth, I think he deserves a chance. I know what it's like to deny someone the opportunity to prove they're good, that they've changed... and I regret that time I wasted with my heels dug in on my perceptions. Give him the chance to surprise you."

I nodded, my chest still tight even as a breath of relief left it.

Because I *wanted* to give him a chance.

"Maybe I just needed to hear y'all say I'm not stupid for wanting to try, that I won't get my heart shattered in the process," I said.

"You might," Julep replied, but her smile was one that said that wasn't what she believed would happen. "If you do, we'll be here to get you through it."

Riley and Giana nodded their agreement, and I chuckled, wiping my face. "You know, I never had girlfriends before you," I admitted.

"Me either," Julep said. "Other than my sister."

"Fictional characters have been my only friends for years," Giana added.

Riley poked her thumb into her chest. "I hung out with my brother and *his* friends, that's how much I was terrified of making my own."

"What does that say about us?" I asked.

"You know how they say you have to wait for *the one*?" Julep asked, looping us all together again. "Maybe it's like that for us. We had to wait for the right girls to be our besties."

"We're soul mates," Riley added.

We grouped in for another hug, and then Giana sniffed, and I soothed her back. "Aw, G, don't cry."

"No, I'm not," she said, leaning back and wiping her nose. "It's the book funk."

I blinked. "Your book funk is making your nose run?"

"It's like having the flu!" she defended. "My body doesn't know how to function without at least two fictional stories playing out in my brain at all times."

That made us all laugh, and as Julep and I started cleaning up and Riley climbed into bed to get as much sleep as she could before practice, Giana went into full detail about the book that had caused her funk — getting particularly dramatic over something about a cowboy hat rule — and how she had tried every known remedy to get out of it without success.

By the time we all crawled into the sheets and turned out the lights, it was just past midnight.

I rolled over and set my head on Julep's pillow. "Thank you for coming to my rescue."

"Always," she promised.

"You're getting *married*," I sang with a wide grin, poking her ribs under the covers.

She did a little happy dance and squealed, then we both fell silent, and minutes later, she was sound asleep — along with Riley and Giana.

I, on the other hand, stared up at the ceiling and counted down the minutes until morning.

Chapter 30

LEO

Before my alarm went off the next morning, I woke to the feel of a warm, lush body wrapping around me.

"You're in my bed," a groggy voice whispered in my ear.

I hadn't realized how much tension I'd been holding until it all leaked out of me the second I heard her, the moment I felt her against me.

I smirked, rolling over until I could see Mary's sleepy smile as she balanced her chin on my chest. She was careful to avoid my fresh tattoo, her eyes skating over it like she was making sure I was following her care instructions.

"*Your* bed?" I repeated.

She nodded, and I chuckled, not fighting her on it. Palico hopped up on the bed like she'd been waiting for Mary to show, and we both smiled as Mary ran her hand along Palico's spine, the cat arching into her touch. She only stayed for a moment before hopping off the bed again — likely because she knew Kyle would be up any minute, and was always first in the kitchen.

Which also meant he was first to feed her.

I settled my gaze back on Mary. She looked tired and a little sad, her eyes a bit red, the skin a bit ashen. I wondered if her night had been as long as mine.

Yesterday had been chaotic. I felt alive during practice, energized from my night with Mary and flying high on just the thought of seeing her again at the end of the day. But when she didn't answer any of my texts, that high turned into a desperate low, and it was all I could do to make it through my evening classes before speeding back to The Pit.

Only to find she wasn't home.

There was a note on the bed, something about an impromptu bachelorette party for Julep. And while that alone wasn't a reason to worry, the way she'd been that morning when I left, how she'd fought back tears, and how my texts had gone unanswered — the combination made me sick to my stomach.

I wanted to talk to her, to call repeatedly until she answered and told me what was wrong. But I knew Mary enough to know that if she was asking for space, that was what she actually wanted. So, I waited.

And here she was, back in bed with me.

I swallowed, brushing her hair from her face. "How was it?"

"Ridiculous," she said with a smile. "We went to a pole studio."

I arched a brow. "Got any video? My spank bank could use a refresh…"

"You're disgusting," she said on a laugh, pinching my ribs. I just chuckled and pulled her into me, kissing her forehead once she was resting in the crook of my arm. We were silent for a moment, my fingers running through her hair as hers curled into fists over my stomach.

"I missed you," I admitted.

Her entire body softened in my arms at that, and she leaned up again, her eyes soft under bent brows. "I'm sorry."

"For what?"

"For running."

"Is that what that was?"

She sat all the way up, folding her legs under her and staring down at her hands in her lap. I pushed until my back was against the headboard, so I was sitting up with her, too.

"I'm fucking terrified, Leo."

Her voice was a wavering whisper, and I felt her words like a hundred needles through my throat. "Of me?" I asked.

She nodded, and a piece of me died.

"I woke up yesterday, and the first thing I thought was that I'd been made a fool of."

I moved to hold her. "Mary, I—"

"Let me finish," she said, holding up a hand to stop my advance. "I was overcome with panic that I had been some kind of conquest for you, that you'd known who I was all along and I was just another game, another notch on your headboard."

I shook my head harder with every word she said, fighting the urge to interrupt her and tell her she was wrong.

"But," she continued on a sigh. "I know that's just my own insecurity."

She was quiet for a while, and I tentatively reached over to take her hand in mine, to soothe her and let her know I was there, that I was listening.

"You... you're Leo fucking Hernandez," she said on a laugh. I smiled a little, too, but it slipped quickly when I realized she was saying that as if it were a curse. "You could have any girl you want, any fit, *hot* girl in the world." She shook her head. "It doesn't make sense that you'd ever want me."

"Are you insane?" I couldn't help myself this time. I grabbed her by the elbows and made her look at me. "You are the most beautiful, the most entrancing woman I have ever laid eyes on. And you're witty, and smart, and talented, and creative, and brave."

She snorted, shaking her head.

"You are," I told her. "And *fuck*, Stig, you are so goddamn sexy. Without even trying. You've driven me out of my mind since the moment you moved across the street."

"And now you've had me," she said, her eyes meeting mine with a despair. "So, what more is there? What could I possibly have to offer you?"

I closed my eyes against the pain those words sent echoing through my chest. Without a word, I tugged her wrists until she had no choice but to go where I led her, which was right into my lap. I pulled her to straddle me, letting my hands trace every curve of her until I held her face in my palms, her focus on me.

"I hate myself because I know that I'm part of the reason you feel this way about yourself."

She tried to look away from me, to shake her head, but I held her still.

"No, it's true and we both know it. *La cagué.* I fucked up. And it doesn't matter that I didn't know it was *you*, that it was my girl I was hurting that day after practice in high school. Because it was *you*, the girl I didn't know but should have wanted to, the girl who was brave enough to approach me when I had such asshole friends and every eye in school on me."

"I don't blame you for not giving me a second look. I was—"

"As beautiful then as you are now," I said before she could finish. "It was *me* who was *el idiota*. Me. Okay? And I will spend every second of every day on my knees to make it up to you."

Mary waggled her brows. "On your knees, hmm?"

I cherished that smile, that lightening in her mood, but I wouldn't let this go until I knew I'd made myself clear. I slid my fingers back into her hair, my thumbs lining her jaw as I met her gaze.

"You want to know what you have to offer me?" I asked. "*Todo. Everything.* A chance to start over. A chance to be myself. A chance to have what I've always wanted. You offer laughter and adventure, spontaneity and challenge, *life*," I said. "You infuriate me," I added with a smile. "In the best possible way. You make me want to be better, and you make me mad with the need to touch every inch of you until I can map your body out with my eyes closed."

Chills broke on her skin, and I pulled her closer, resting my forehead against hers.

"I'm sorry I hurt you. I'm so, so fucking sorry. But I'm here. And I want you, Mary, *you*. All of you. Exclusive. No bullshit, no wondering what's next, no games." I looked at her again. "I've never felt anything for anyone else but you — even when I didn't know it was you all along. You're fucking *it* for me."

She choked on a sob, nodding and leaning into my palm.

"This is the real thing, Stig. You and me, right here, right now. I want it. I want *us*."

"I want us, too."

She barely got the words out before I was swallowing them, savoring them, devouring every syllable before my mouth crashed down on hers. I wrapped her in my embrace as her own arms threaded around my neck and held me to her, deepening the kiss. She held me there like I'd disappear if she opened her eyes, like this kiss was our last.

"I'm yours," I promised her. "I'm not going anywhere."

She nodded against my kiss, but still clung to me as if I were a dream.

My alarm went off on my phone, and I blindly felt for it and shut it off before tossing it across the room.

"You need to go," Mary tried to tell me, breaking our kiss. "You can't be late to practice."

"I have just enough time."

"To what — get dressed?"

"To make you come," I said, grinding my hips against where she was straddling me. She whimpered a bit as I nipped at her bottom lip. "And *then* get dressed."

I didn't give her the chance to argue before I was slapping her ass and helping her off my lap. When I had her standing, I stripped her between kisses, shedding a layer for her and then me, back and forth until we were both bare.

"God*damn*, Mary," I said appreciatively when she was naked, scanning her with my eyes and hands both. I took in every curve, every inch of softness, every piercing and stretch of ink across her skin.

And now, it was mine.

She was mine.

I pulled her into me with possession humming through every vein, and she hissed when I ran a hand roughly between her thighs.

"Fuck," she cursed, lurching away. "Damn pole kisses."

I blanched. "What?"

"I'm... I'm bruised, from the stupid pole," she explained, gesturing to her thighs. I glanced down, and with the soft light of dawn starting to break through, I could see a shadow of the bruise she was referencing. I could also see it wasn't the only one she had.

"Damn, baby," I said, frowning as I traced a circle around it. I was careful not to touch it as I guided her back to the bed, laying her in the sheets and propping myself between her legs. Then, I kissed my way down, stopping when I started noting the bruises again.

I pressed my lips lightly to the first one, and Mary moaned.

"Does it hurt?"

"A little," she confessed, but the way she writhed under me told me it was the good kind of pain.

I smirked, running my palm flat and warm over her stomach, her hip, skating my fingers through the maze of bruises until they slid up and ran the length of her wet center.

She arched into the touch, and when just the tip of my finger dipped inside her, I kissed that bruise again, a little harder this time.

I was rewarded with another, louder moan, her fists twisting in the sheets.

"My little masochist," I teased, and then I slid my finger all the way inside her, biting down around her bruise at the same time.

"Yes," she breathed, shuddering under my touch.

It was maddening, how sexy she was, how much she turned me on when she spread her thighs wider for me and peered down at me over the swells of her heaving breasts. I hated how much I was under her spell just as much as I loved surrendering to it, like a dying man taking his last breath before letting the earth take him back.

"You've got two minutes to fuck my hand and come for me," I told her, curling a second finger inside her. "Can you do that for me?"

"No," she said, panting.

"No?" I repeated with a challenge, working my fingers inside her as I lowered my mouth to her clit. She bucked her hips when I sucked her into my mouth, and the moan she let out told me she was lying.

"I mean, I can," she amended, panting. "But I want *you*."

Her hands reached blindly for my hips, and the way she was tugging at me, I understood what she meant. My cock twitched at the invitation.

But I wanted this morning to be about *her*.

"You want me?" I teased her, slowly crawling my way up her body as I kissed and sucked and licked. "What do you mean?"

"I want *you*," she said again, and this time she wrapped her hand around my shaft, pumping me once, slow and long and torturous.

I fought back my groan, smiling down at her. "Be specific."

She paused, narrowing her gaze. "You're such a pompous prick."

"And yet, you still want me to fuck you into this mattress, don't you?"

I loved how she reacted in a mixture of anger and desire, pushing me away with her hands even as she chased me with her mouth. Her kiss was hard and impatient, and then she wrapped her legs around me and dug her heels into my ass.

"I want your cock inside me," she said against my lips, and I finally let my groan free, reveling in the filthy words as they rumbled out of her throat. I wrapped my hand around that neck of hers just so I could feel the vibration the next time she spoke. "I want you buried so deep I feel you in my gut."

"That's my girl," I praised, and then I reached down to fist my cock and drive it inside her.

I wanted so badly to plow all the way in, but even as wet as she was, I still knew better. I didn't want to hurt her. With restraint, I sheathed myself a quarter of the way before pulling out and flexing in again, just a little deeper.

"Oh, *fuck*, yes, Leo," Mary cried out, digging her nails into the flesh of my back as I found a rhythm, inching myself inside her. It was pure fucking ecstasy, the way she wrapped around me warm and wet and tight.

That's when I realized I'd forgotten a condom.

"Shit," I cursed, but as if she read my mind, Mary dug her heels in deeper.

"Don't you dare stop," she threatened, and then she wrapped her arms around my neck and tucked her pelvis to take me deeper, fucking *me* as best she could on her back.

Her eagerness sent all the blood in my body rushing straight to my balls, and before I could come, I pulled out of her, pressing my forehead to hers.

"Fuck, this was not my plan."

"To fuck me before breakfast?"

"To come after three pumps inside you," I said, smacking the side of her ass. "Now, turn around and grab the headboard so I can rail you properly."

Mary obeyed, looking back at me so sweetly when she was braced that my chest ached. I sidled up behind her, fisting my cock again until I lined it up with her entrance and pushed inside. This time, she was wet and stretched, and so I slammed all the way in, knocking her against the headboard and it against the wall.

"More," she begged.

"You love taking this cock, don't you?" I asked, licking behind her ear as I flexed deeper. "Touch yourself while I fuck you. Play with those sweet tits."

Again, she obeyed, and she let out a feral moan when one hand twisted her nipple while the other slid between her legs to rub her clit. Her legs started trembling where they held her upright, and I took her weight with my hands on her hips.

Someone called my name from downstairs.

"We're running out of time," I told her. "Come now or you won't come at all."

She mewled, as if I'd *actually* leave without getting her off now. Coach could make me run laps all fucking day and I'd do so happily if I had the sounds of Mary's climax as a soundtrack replaying in my head.

"Need more," she panted. It was sexy as hell, how she unabashedly spread her legs and plucked at her nipple while she circled her clit. Her cheek against the headboard and my hands at her hips were all that kept her steady while she chased her orgasm.

I was deep inside her, and she was touching herself in every place that worked her to the edge. There was only one place empty, and I took a real fucking risk when I went for it without so much as a casual conversation about whether it was okay or not.

Sliding one hand from her hip, I ran a palm over her ass, smacking it softly before I settled my thumb at the tight opening above the one I was balls-deep in now.

"Yes," she begged. "*Yes.*"

With that permission, I slicked my thumb in the wetness between us before gently pressing into her.

I didn't push all the way in, just slipped the very tip of my thumb into that tight entrance, but it was enough. Mary cried out and shook like a fucking earthquake as she rode out every last second of her climax. The sight of her trembling and breaking apart for me was all I needed to find my own release, and as soon as Mary collapsed, I pulled out of her, spraying the swells of her ass and filling the dip of her spine with my cum. Black invaded my vision as I pumped myself dry, and Mary arched her ass up like she wanted to make sure every drop landed on her skin, like it was wasted if she couldn't feel it.

"Leo! We're going to leave your ass!"

It was Kyle who screamed this time, and I laughed or groaned or some combination of the two as I carefully maneuvered off the bed and into the bathroom. I ran the shower hot, then peeled my girl out of the sheets where she was still lying limp with my seed slowly dripping down her skin.

I pulled her into the shower, washing myself off her before I planted a long, deep kiss to her lips.

"No shower for you?" she asked, trying to pull me inside.

"I'll shower at the stadium. Coach will have my ass if I'm late."

"I tried to tell you."

"And I told *you*," I said, slapping her ass and reveling in the little yelp she gave me. "I wasn't leaving until you came."

"You win."

"Damn fucking straight, I win."

I growled the words against her mouth, and then she wrapped me up and held me to her, my cock coming to life again at the thought of taking her in this shower.

But the front door shut downstairs, and I cursed.

"You need to clean your tattoo," Mary said.

"I promise I will."

"I mean it. If you fuck up my work, I'll—"

"You'll *what*, exactly?"

She tried to pull me into the shower with her, but I heard the car fire up outside, and I really was about to get left if I didn't get a move on.

"Let me go, you insatiable woman," I teased, kissing Mary one last time. "I promise I'll clean it and be as careful as I can at practice."

She begrudgingly let me go, and I let myself take in the sight of her in that shower with the steam rising around her before I hurriedly cleaned myself up and pulled on my joggers and hoodie before running down the stairs. The guys were already backing out of the driveway when I caught up to them and yanked open the back door, sliding in like I was a robber and they were the getaway car.

They all pinned me with annoyed glares, but then Kyle let out a fizz of a laugh that set the rest of them laughing, too.

And I didn't care that they cracked jokes the whole ride in, or that by the time I showered and made it on the field, I *was* a little late and had to run laps to make up for it.

I smiled the entire time.

I couldn't wait to get back home.

Chapter 31

MARY

I had never been so thankful for a day off in my life.

Between the emotional rollercoaster of yesterday, staying up all night drinking with the girls, and then Leo ravishing me this morning — I was exhausted. I'd barely made it through the shower before I'd collapsed naked and still damp in Leo's bed and slept until almost noon.

I texted the girls an update, which they responded to with a thousand emojis that varied from eggplants and water splashes to heart eyes and wedding bells. It made me smile, and that smile was latched in place permanently when I got a text from Leo after practice.

> **Leo:** Only had to run ten laps. Proceeded to have the best practice of my life afterward.

> **Me:** Hmm... sounds like I should be part of your training program.

> **Leo:** Deep in you, and then deep in the end zone? I like the sound of that.

I spent the rest of the day cleaning up the house, which was an absolute pigsty. I swept and mopped and changed Palico's litterbox and, because I felt generous, I grabbed the guys' laundry when I went down to do my own. Other than that, I relaxed and rested, watching movies and doodling tattoo outlines on my iPad from the couch while Palico purred in a little ball next to me.

I was just folding up the last load of laundry when the guys barreled through the door like a pack of wild animals.

"Mary!" Braden called, slinging his bag onto the bay window bench I'd *just* cleaned. He wrapped me up in a hug and spun me around before I could yell at him. "We've missed you."

"One of us more than the rest," Kyle added with a smirk, tossing his bag on top of Braden's. He paused at the sight of clothes piled on the couch. "Wait — did you do our laundry?"

"Some of it," I said when Braden put me on the ground again. I pointed at the bay window. "And I just cleaned, so take your bags upstairs, you animals."

Blake had been about to add his to the pile, but he paused, letting it swing mid-air before he pointed at the stairs. "I was just taking mine up."

"Uh-huh," I said with a smile. I turned back toward Braden just in time to see him mouthing *mommy* to Kyle as he pointed at me.

I rolled up a pair of his briefs and pegged him in the face with them.

"Wait, are you off tonight?" Kyle asked, checking the time on his Apple watch. It was just past eight. I didn't know their full schedules, but I did know that they tried to line up their afternoon and evening classes as much as they could so they could all ride together.

"I am."

"Madden tournament?!" Braden asked, waggling his brows.

"You guys really want an ass-whooping that badly, huh?" I teased as I folded the last of my shirts. But the jokes and challenges the guys replied with were blurry in the background, because Leo swung through the door.

My entire body buzzed to life at his nearness, at the sight of him all roughed up and tired from a long day. He dragged himself inside, wearing his full NBU Football sweatsuit, and I didn't hide the way I ogled how those pants highlighted a very specific part of him. I let my eyes trail the length of him slowly, taking in his messy hair and freshly tan skin and honey eyes that were glinting with amusement as he took in the sight of me, too.

He was biting one of his chains absentmindedly, like it was just a normal habit and not an instant reminder for me of the *other* things he could do with that mouth.

As if he sensed that seeing that chain in his mouth did something to me, he grinned, his tongue catching the silver before he let it fall to his chest again.

He looked so cozy, like he was made to hold me on the couch in that moment. I wanted nothing more than to have him wrapped around me, to have his scent invading my brain and making my mind fuzzy.

But we hadn't talked about how we'd handle this with the roommates.

I hesitated, staring at him while he hovered at the door. But he just kicked it shut behind him before dropping his bag to the ground and crossing the room to me in smooth, unbothered strides. He crooked that smile I used to hate to love so much, and then he scooped me up, pulling me into him in a warm, all-encompassing hug that made me tingle from head to toe.

A heavy sigh left him once I was in his arms, like he'd been waiting all day for this moment, and he held me tight for a breath before he pulled back and kissed me — not on the forehead or the cheek or a quick peck to the lips, but a possessive, demanding kiss that I had no choice but to open up to. His tongue against my own sent a different kind of vibration humming through me, but he broke away before either of us lost control.

"How's my girl?" he asked sleepily.

I smiled, heart skipping a beat. "Better now."

Leo's eyes searched mine, and I loved how happy he looked, how happy *I* felt in that moment. I wanted to bottle it all up, to stash it away somewhere where I could take a shot whenever I wanted to.

"Did I hear we're playing Madden?" he asked after a beat.

"Apparently the guys want an ass-kicking. Who am I to deny?"

"I hope you're not looping me in with *the guys*, because it'll be me kicking your ass — not the other way around."

"He talks a big talk, but can he back it up?" I teased, tilting my head and tapping my chin with one finger.

There was a devilish challenge in Leo's eyes that told me I'd pay for that comment later.

I couldn't wait.

"Are you going to tell her your big news or just make us watch you two make out all night?" Kyle said.

I arched a brow at Leo. "Big news?"

He grinned, but his cheeks tinged pink. Was Leo Hernandez... *blushing*?

"You're looking at NBU's new Captain."

My jaw slackened. "Wait... *really?!*"

I didn't even think before I leapt at him, and he caught me just in time for another long, deep kiss. When I pulled back, I slapped him on the arm.

"How long have you known? Why didn't you text me and tell me?"

"Because I wanted to see this face in person," he said, tapping my nose.

I shook my head, still smiling. "Wow. Congratulations, Leo. I'm... I'm so happy for you."

He somehow stood even taller, and then he pulled me in for a hug, holding me tight.

"You can show me just how happy you are later," he said low under the shell of my ear.

I shivered.

With a squeeze of my hip, he skipped upstairs to drop off his stuff and shower. Blake passed him on the way down, and when I moved all our clean clothes to the dining table so we could have the couch, I turned to find the three of them smirking at me with their arms folded over their chests.

I sighed, waving my hand over the space between us. "Alright. Go ahead. Get all your jokes out now."

"Who, us? We would never," Blake said, taking a seat on the couch and firing up the Xbox. Palico hopped up on the arm of it, and he pulled her into his lap without a second thought.

"No, no, we're happy for you," Braden added, sitting in the armchair.

Kyle was suspiciously quiet when he flopped down in the beanbag, and I took a seat in the middle of the couch next to Blake, saving a spot for Leo. Kyle handed me a controller while Braden set up the first game, and I actually thought I got away without their smart-ass remarks about me and Leo.

But then, Kyle stretched, casually turning to his roommates. "Hey, did y'all hear some sort of... *thumping* sound this morning?"

"Yeah, come to think of it, it's been a couple mornings now," Braden said, tapping his chin. "Sounded kind of like a *thump, thump, thump* against the wall."

My cheeks flamed, but I ignored them, fighting back my smile as I picked my team for the game.

"Maybe it's a plumbing issue," Blake added, and I tongued my cheek, shaking my head and still ignoring.

"I don't know," Kyle said. "Might be a ghost. I could have *sworn* I heard some moans and screams."

"Must be haunting Leo, then, because I *definitely* heard it screaming his name," Blake added.

I finally succumbed to my laugh, bopping Kyle on the head before I threw a pillow at Blake and elbowed Braden in the ribs since he was closest. They all laughed, too, just as Leo joined us and plopped down next to us.

"What'd I miss?" he asked.

"Oh, nothing," Blake said. "Just debating whether The Pit is haunted or not."

I rolled my eyes, but my heart was light as a bird, the wings of it fluttering in my chest and making it impossible not to smile.

I'd never felt more at home.

Chapter 32

MARY

It surprised me how easy time slipped away after that.

Leo and the guys were busier than ever with the season starting up, and I was working at the shop almost every night. Now that I had some experience, Nero had me taking on the walk-ins.

In two weeks, I'd tattooed everything from the inside of bottom lips and fingers to the tops of feet and knees. I had a printout of my designs that some people stumbled in and chose from, signing legal paperwork that swore they weren't drunk, and I also had very specific design requests that were mostly script and images printed off Pinterest. Those were my least favorite.

My *most* favorite were the clients who found me on Instagram and booked an appointment with me, giving me vague instructions but allowing me to have creative freedom.

There'd only been two so far, but one had been a five-hour upper back piece where a girl around my age let me draw up a tree with striking roots and branches, along with leaves that tested my shading skills. The other was a man in his fifties who wanted his first tattoo — a thigh piece — and it was an ode to his brothers in the military, a sloth in a bar eating nachos. It was apparently an inside joke with them, but I didn't care either way. It was hilarious and challenging and made me so happy as I created it, both the sketch before he got there and the actual piece on his skin.

The Rebels took on their first home opponent on a warm Saturday afternoon. I had sweat running down my back along with the rest of the student body, and for once, I was upset that my friends were so successful. I would have given anything to have Giana or Riley in the stands with me instead of on the field, or for Julep to give up her job hunt and wedding planning to get on a flight and come sit with me. But as soon as the coin toss was over and the game began, I didn't care who was in the stands.

All I could do was focus on Leo.

It was one thing to see him in his practice gear, the mesh jersey with the padding underneath. It was another completely to see him all suited up, wearing the white home uniforms with crimson letters and numbers blazing against it in contrast. HERNANDEZ stretched across his upper back in all caps, the number thirteen underneath it, and that jersey was tucked into pants that should have been illegal for how they hugged his ass. I assumed he was wearing some sort of protection around his manhood, because otherwise, those pants would leave nothing to the imagination. Even with whatever he had on underneath, it was impossible not to notice the giant bulge.

It made me and every other girl in the stands salivate when he jogged by.

But as much as I loved checking him out, it wasn't his looks that held me enraptured once the first whistle blew. It was his talent. I hadn't seen him play since high school — had avoided it at all costs, actually — but to see how fast he was now, how massive he was as a running back when most were smaller, how he could plow through defenders and give them stiff arms like they were nothing more than little kids trying to block him... it was breathtaking. It felt like the equivalent of seeing a leopard in the wild, the muscles and speed a phenomenon you couldn't tear your eyes away from.

They won the game by twenty-four points, and I got the pleasure of celebrating with Leo later that night.

When I wasn't at the shop and Leo wasn't at the stadium, that was how we spent our time — tangled in the sheets. There was still so much to talk about, so many things I wanted to know about him and that I wanted him to know about me. But with the limited time we had together, we were both starved whenever we had the chance to be alone. We'd barely make it through pleasantries before we were stripping each other, exploring new ways to make the other come unraveled.

For the first time in longer than I could remember, my life felt... balanced. Peaceful. *Blissful*, even. I didn't even care that Miss Margie had called and regretfully told me she didn't have an update on when I could move back home. It was the last thing on my mind, actually. Not even sassy comments from my mom when I called home could wipe the smile off my face.

Early one afternoon, I was parked in Leo's chair in front of my PlayStation I'd set up with his monitor and mine together. It'd been a hectic week at the shop, so I was treating myself to some R&R time by playing Cyberpunk 2077. I'd also treated myself to a ten-milligram blueberry gummy, so I was deeply entranced in the game when Leo's door swung open and scared me half to death.

"Fuck!" I cursed, and I spun in my chair, wielding the controller over my head as if that could protect me against whoever the intruder was.

Fortunately, it was just Leo, smirking at me like the devil himself.

"Did I catch you masturbating?"

I blew out a breath, my heartbeat steadying out. "No, but you nearly gave me a heart attack. What are you doing here?"

I knew the schedule pretty well now that we were into the season, and no one was due home until after five today. Leo had his Rehabilitation Science Techniques class tonight and shouldn't be home until after nine.

"My first class got canceled," he answered, leaning a hip against the doorway. "And I don't have to report to the weight room until four.

I nodded, running a hand back through my hair and pressing one hand to my chest. My heartbeat *was* settling, until I looked back at Leo and found his gaze dark and hungry crawling over me. He'd once again hooked one of his chains in his mouth, his tongue and teeth toying with it as he fucked me with his eyes.

I looked down at where I was sitting with my legs open in a very unladylike stance, wearing nothing but boy shorts and one of Leo's t-shirts.

"I like when you wear my clothes," he said, dropping his chain from his mouth and crossing the room to me. I saw evidence of exactly *how much* he liked it pressing against his shorts as he ran the back of his fingers over my shoulder.

"You're not worried about me stretching them out?" I asked.

He almost growled, hands clapping down on the arms of the chair and caging me in as he dropped his mouth to mine.

"Woman, if you don't stop with that shit," he warned. "Besides, even if you did, it only seems fair, since stretching *you* out is my favorite pastime."

The words vibrated through me before his mouth descended, and I inhaled the kiss, dropping my controller on the desk and wrapping my arms around his neck to pull him closer.

But Leo broke the kiss, even as I whined, and grabbed the controller again. He slid it into my hands and spun the chair to face the screen.

"Play," he demanded. "And do your best not to die."

With that, his lips curled up, and he sank onto his knees between my legs.

When I didn't do anything other than stare at him, Leo grabbed the hem of my boy shorts and yanked them down my thighs. I lifted to help him, but once they were off, he smacked the side of my ass that he could reach and pointed at the screen.

"Focus, or I stop."

That was all the motivation I needed.

But even as I started playing, my eyes on the screen, all my focus was zeroed in on where Leo was kissing a trail up my thighs. I spread them wider for him, sinking down in the chair a bit, and he smiled against my center before running his tongue long and hot and flat from my entrance to my clit.

I moaned, eyes rolling back, thumbs stilling over the toggles on the controller. Leo teased my clit with the tip of his tongue, and when I bucked against his mouth, wanting more, he pulled completely away.

"No," I whimpered, peering down at him through my heavy eyelids.

"If you want me to play," he said, drawing a line along my inner thigh. "*You* have to keep playing."

God, I didn't know if this was more hot or aggravating. Both, I decided, as I began moving my character around again. I was more focused on just walking around the Westbrook District than taking on any missions because I knew I'd fail them with Leo between my legs.

I slowly weaved through the streets toward my apartment in Megabuilding H10. I could pretend I was checking my stash there before a mission — Leo didn't need to know. All *he* needed to do was keep whatever magic he had going on with his tongue.

I ran my bike off the road when he sucked my clit a little harder, and I was all but ping-ponging off the walls once I made it to my apartment building because he'd just slid one thick finger inside me. He curled it, hitting that perfect spot inside me as I moaned and sank deeper, opening wider, needing more.

"Come on, baby," he breathed against my core, licking one long, slow swipe of his tongue in time with his finger inside me. "Can you fuck my fingers and stay alive, too?"

I moaned against the challenge, hiking one foot up on his desk so I could open wider for him as he slid another finger inside me. My hips rocked into his touch, and when I glanced down from the screen to watch where his messy head of hair was buried between my legs, I all but whimpered at the sight.

It was so fucking hot, to have this strong, powerful man on his knees just to please me.

Add in the fact that I had a PlayStation controller in my hand and it was heaven on earth.

Until he stopped again.

This time, he pulled his fingers all the way out, sitting back on his heels and wiping my wetness from his lips.

"Leo," I whined.

"You know the rules."

"It's impossible."

He gave me a look, and I huffed, tossing him the controller. He barely caught it before I stood and gripped him by the arm, hauling him up with his help.

"If it's so easy, *you* try," I challenged, and then I stripped his shorts and briefs off in one fell swoop, his cock springing forward, already hard and ready for me. I pressed him down into the chair with one hand against his chest, and then I kissed him hard, trailing my lips down every ridge of his abdomen until I was on my knees and settled between his legs.

I looked up at him through my lashes, finding him with a waiting grin before he turned his gaze to the screen and started playing.

I had no idea what he was doing, but I loved the way the clicks came slower as I kissed around his shaft, how his breathing intensified when I rolled my tongue around his tip like a lollipop. He groaned when I took just an inch of him in my mouth, his head falling back, and I pulled off him instantly.

He dragged his head back up, eyes on me, and I just smirked and pointed to the monitor.

He returned my smile, taking the challenge and focusing on the game again. But when I grabbed his thick cock with both my hands and spat on him, using my palms to slick him and work him in slow, methodic pumps, he groaned loud enough to make the house crumble.

"If you want me to gag on it, pay attention," I told him when he looked down at me.

He cursed under his breath, but as soon as he turned his gaze back to the screen and started playing again, I rewarded him with my promise. Pressing up higher onto my knees so I had a better angle, I took him in my mouth, slicking him with my tongue an inch at a time and working him in time with my hands. After a few slick pumps, I dove down, taking him as deep as I could and holding him there until my gag reflex had me pulling off.

"Fuck it," he said, and I'd no sooner had his cock out of my mouth before I was hiked up and thrown onto the bed.

I smirked in victory as Leo made quick work of his sneakers and shorts that were still around his ankles. He ripped his shirt overhead next, and before he could reach for me, I stopped him, running a fingertip over the ink stretching across his chest.

The tattoo was healing nicely, just a few places still scabbing now. I noted a couple spots where I wanted to touch up once he was fully healed, but I was proud of that octopus, of my first big piece on human skin.

I loved even more that it was on Leo.

"Are you done admiring your work?" he asked, grabbing the hem of his shirt — the one I was wearing. "Because I'm growing impatient."

I barely nodded before the shirt was peeled over my head. He groaned his approval at the lack of bra underneath, his hand palming one breast while his mouth clamped down around the piercing on my other.

I hissed, arching into his touch. I was ready to lie back in the bed and let him fuck me cross-eyed, but he pulled me up to stand, instead. His mouth devoured mine as he walked me backward toward the bathroom, blindly turning on the shower before we both tumbled inside.

The water was cold at first, and I gasped against it, but then it ran warm, dampening our hair and sluicing over our bodies in thick rivulets.

I didn't have time to adjust to any of it before my back was pressed against the cold tile, one leg was hiked up, and Leo pressed his crown to my entrance. It was still soaked from my saliva, and one thrust of his hips had him halfway inside me, had me seeing stars and digging my nails into his shoulders.

"Filthy fucking girl," he cursed against my neck, biting it as he retracted and pushed just a little farther in. "I'm not going to last with you so wet for me."

"Let's see if you can set a record, then," I challenged, tucking my pelvis so I took more of him inside me. "How fast can you come, Leo?"

He groaned, free hand fisting in my hair and yanking until I had no choice but to look up at the ceiling, to expose my neck for him. He kissed and sucked the skin along my throat as he hiked my leg higher and slammed into me. Once, twice, three times, each thrust rocking me harder against the wall. I couldn't find grip on anything but him, so I held on tight, riding him with just the toes of my standing foot to steady me as he found his release.

Leo let out a vicious moan, pulling out as he rasped, "Knees."

It was a command, one I heeded with pleasure, landing on the tile in front of him. I grew even wetter at the sight of him pumping his cock, the water from the shower head sliding over his chest and abdomen, droplets dripping from his hair and off his nose as he stared down at me.

"Open," he managed, and just before he busted, I opened my mouth.

Rope after rope of cum rained down on me, slicing across my tits and neck and face, some of it landing in my mouth as I savored every last drop. It was so fucking hot watching his abs contract as he flexed into his hand, and I couldn't wait any longer. I reached between my legs and circled my clit as he painted me with his climax, and I found mine easy enough, moaning and shaking as I fucked my own hands.

Leo cursed, barely finishing before he pulled me up to stand. I was mid-orgasm, ready to cry at being interrupted, but he hiked my leg up again and thrust inside me, sparking it back to life. Then, he rubbed me with his expert fingers, kissing me and swallowing my moans as the orgasm caught life again and rocked through me. I shook so hard I couldn't stand on my own, Leo pressing me against the wall to hold me, but he didn't relent until I was completely spent and sagging in his arms.

We stayed like that for a long time, panting and clinging to each other until we found the strength to stand again. The water had run a bit cold, so Leo turned it all the way up, the hottest it would go. Then, he grabbed my shampoo, squeezing a dollop into his palms and rubbing them together before he made me face away from him.

The water ran hot and delicious down my back, and then Leo's large hands were in my hair, massaging my scalp as he washed it. I moaned, letting my neck relax, the sensation almost as good as the orgasm that preceded it.

And suddenly, the moment turned from feral to something so tender that tears stung my eyes.

It was silent but for the water slapping at the tile by our feet and our breaths still evening out. Leo washed and rinsed my hair before repeating with conditioner, and then he lathered his hands up with my body wash.

Those hands started at my shoulders, massaging and kneading until they trailed down my back and over my arms. He turned me gently then, his eyes finding mine through the steam as he washed my hips, my thighs, and tenderly between my legs. And I didn't hide. I didn't pull away or fold my arms over myself or do anything to shield my body from his view.

I felt safe with him.

I felt wanted.

He ran his palms over my breasts next, my nipples hardening under his touch. I glanced down to find his cock hardening, too, but he didn't move his gaze from my eyes.

Slowly, he pulled me into him, his forehead resting against mine as he continued his slow strokes all over my body.

There were so many words that hung between us, emotions too strong for either of us to look directly at.

They were like the blinding sun or a car crash or both at the same time.

Instead, Leo dropped his mouth to mine, kissing me long and deep as his hands worked me all over. When he palmed my ass and rubbed the thick swells there, his cock twitched against my stomach, and I wrapped my arms around his neck and threaded my fingers into his hair.

We kissed for what felt like another eternity.

Then, I turned around, and he slid inside me again, taking me until the water turned cold and we both came again.

Chapter 33

LEO

By the time October swept through Boston, the leaves turning bright yellow and orange and the skies growing more and more gray, I felt like I was on top of the world.

The Rebels were off to a killer start to the season — one we weren't sure we'd have after losing some of our best players to graduation last year. But we were 5-0, winning all three of our home games and the two we'd played on the road. Another fight for the championship was within our grasp, and the entire team seemed focused, tuned in, alert and ready.

My father had surprised me at the stadium after our fourth win, along with a man named Leonard Bowden, who wanted to be my agent, and Coach Lee. I apparently had eyes on me for the draft, and it seemed everyone had forgotten about the little article about my girlfriends that came out over the summer. I'd been as squeaky clean as a college athlete could be, and I saw it in Coach's eyes as much as in my father's.

They were proud of me.

Hell, *I* was proud of me, too. My grades were excellent, I was performing the best I ever had on the field, and when I wasn't in school or playing ball, I was with Mary.

We'd had parties at The Pit, of course — it was tradition, after all. But I swore, the entire team had their eyes on the prize, and none of us got out of line. In fact, most of the time, we were kicking people out by one so we could get sleep.

It felt a little like growing up, like we were going through our own changing of the seasons just as fall washed over us in all its glory.

Mary had been just as busy as the rest of us, her hours at the shop increasing now that she had a steady stream of clients. I knew it was only a matter of time before she was offered an official position at the shop.

I had mixed feelings about that.

Of course, I was proud of her — happy for her — but I was also still wary of Nero. It didn't matter that he'd seemed professional since that night at the bar. Every time I visited Mary, I felt his eyes on me, on *her*, and it made the hair on the back of my neck stand straight up like he was a predator and I needed to be prepared for him to pounce.

So, I kept my guard up, kept my eyes on Mary to make sure she was safe.

And at the end of every night, no matter how late it was, Mary climbed into my bed.

God, it was easy to get lost in that girl.

Whenever we were together, everything else slipped away. I was completely wrapped up in her smile, her laugh, her tired eyes, her wandering hands, her lush lips and soft, inviting body that I was sure I could never tire of — no matter how many times I had her. And I was insatiable. Early in the morning before practice, in the middle of the day any chance I could rush off campus, late at night when she came home from the shop — whenever I could take her, I did.

It was never enough.

On the Sunday after our win over the Rhode Island Trojans, we both had the day off for the first time in a month. After we spent the morning waking up slowly together and the afternoon having brunch and playing games with the roommates, I gave her instructions to get dressed and be ready to go on a date by six.

"A date?" she asked, one brow arching as she wrapped her arms around my waist. "Where are we going?"

"That's for me to know and you to find out," I said with a swat against her ass.

She yelped, biting her lip against a smile before she pressed up on her toes and kissed me. "How dressy should I get?"

"Wear what you would wear on a date in high school."

That made her blink in confusion. "Uh... I never went on a date in high school."

"Then I guess the options are endless."

It took me all of twenty minutes to get ready — a shower, shave, deodorant, and pulling on my favorite pair of joggers along with an old hoodie with our high school football team's logo on it.

It took Mary two hours.

I didn't rush her, just relaxed on the bed with Palico and watched as she showered and dried her hair — not before putting more products in it than I owned, though. She listened to Tame Impala as she moisturized her skin and did her makeup, dancing and singing in-between applications. Then, I didn't even try to hide my smile as I watched her try on ten different outfits before finally settling on one. She'd gone through everything from a tight dress and leather jacket to jeans and a bodysuit, but she'd landed on my favorite of them all — leggings, an oversized sweater, and boots.

"You look perfect," I told her, letting my hands float down to rest on her hips. It should have been a crime, the way those leggings hugged her ass, and she chuckled and shoved me away the longer I stared and appreciated the view.

"I'm trying to match your vibe," she said, tugging on the strings of my hoodie. "Since I have no idea where we're going."

"One more thing," I said, and then I ducked into my closet and pulled out my letterman jacket, draping it over her shoulders.

She rolled her eyes, but it didn't stop her cheeks from flushing a beautiful shade of pink, or her hands from clutching it to her and making sure it didn't fall off. She pulled it snug around her shoulders, and my chest tightened almost painfully as I stared at her, wondering if it could have been like this all those years ago if I hadn't had my head so far up my ass.

I swallowed, snatching the car keys off my desk. "Ready?"

Only Kyle and I had cars, Braden and Blake usually hitching a ride with one of us or catching the train to campus. Mary had her car parked across the street. We hopped into mine — a gift from my dad when I graduated high school — and Mary kicked her shoes off as soon as we were buckled in and on the road. Her feet were on my dash in the next moment, tapping along to the beat of *No Me Quieras Tanto* by José Luis Rodríguez — one of my mom's favorite songs.

I couldn't swallow down the knot in my throat, not as I smiled at her or slid my palm to rest between her thighs. Just the sight of her bopping along to a song I'd heard my entire childhood had me imagining the first time she'd meet my mom. I knew Mom would love her, knew they'd get along right off the bat and probably be ganging up on me within an hour. I could picture it all — them sitting together at my games, Mom teaching Mary how to make *gazpacho* at Christmas — I could even see Dad proudly showing her all his trophies and awards in his basement, happy to explain all the rules of football to her if she was ever confused while watching me play.

I held tight to her the entire drive, one hand on the wheel and the other on her, my thumb grazing lazily over her thigh. We were both quiet, content to listen to the music and just be together, although I didn't miss how Mary grew more and more confused with every turn.

When I pulled into our high school's parking lot — one that had been unlocked just for me by special request to my old coach who I still had a good relationship with — she laughed.

"Please tell me you're kidding," she said, looking at the old brick building and then back at me.

I just smiled and cut the engine, rounding to open her door before holding her hand tight in mine and walking us toward the football field.

So many memories flooded back to me as soon as I opened the gate that led to the field. When my sneakers touched the grass and the distinct smell of fall drifted up to my nose on a breeze, I closed my eyes and inhaled it, feeling like I was seventeen again. Sometimes I missed it, that dramatic and yet simple time in life. My biggest worry was the game on Friday nights. I was looking forward to college, knowing I still had years and years left of playing ball.

Now, my future was uncertain.

I shook off that thought as I held Mary's hand tighter and walked her over to the bleachers, climbing up several rows before I took a seat and pulled her down next to me.

The sun had already set on our drive over, but the cool, violet light of dusk still clung to the clear sky over the field. It was freshly painted and groomed, the season underway, and the only reason the lights flicked on overhead was because I'd asked Coach to do so.

"I feel like this is trespassing," Mary said, sliding her arms inside my letterman and crossing her arms against the chill of the night. "Are we allowed to be here?"

"Please, I'm like a celebrity at this school."

She rolled her eyes. "So they did this just for you, huh?"

"For us."

"Uh-huh. I can guarantee you, not a single teacher or faculty member remembers my name."

My smile slipped, gut sinking when I thought about how different our high school years had been. I moved closer to her, sliding my hand between her thighs again and holding tight.

For a moment, we just looked out over the field, listening to the sounds of the city. We were about a half hour from downtown now, the trees more abundant than buildings, but it still had the feel of the city, like Boston bled right into Weston and they were one.

"I used to be here every morning and afternoon," I told her. "Every fall. In the spring, I'd do track just so I could stay on the field in the off season. And then in the summer, it'd all start back over with camp."

Mary turned to face me, listening intently.

"My dad was in these stands every game. Mom, too. Never sitting together, though," I added with a weak smile. "I can still close my eyes and hear the sound of the whistles, the cheers from the stands, and my dad's voice barreling over all of it."

"I came to a game once," Mary said. "I sat in the very top back corner."

"You did? When? What year?"

She looked down at her nails. "It was the season opener after we met," she said. "Well, we hadn't *met* yet, but…"

I let out a long exhale, tilting her chin with my knuckles and pressing a soft kiss to her lips. "I'm sorry."

She nodded. "I am, too."

"What the fuck do you have to be sorry for?" I asked with a laugh.

"I didn't tell you who I was," she said with a shrug. "I mean, in my dramatic teen head at the time, I felt like I did. But I didn't really. I shut you out without giving you a chance to explain. If I would have just picked up the phone when you called that night…"

"I might have fucked it all up even worse," I finished for her. "Listen, I *hate* thinking about the years I missed with you. But at the same time, I wonder if it all worked out the way it was supposed to."

Mary shot a brow up.

"Not the horrible things my friends did to you," I amended, wrapping her cool hands in mine. "I'd go back and kick them all in the dick if I could."

That made her laugh.

"But I mean… what if we weren't ready for each other yet? What if I needed to grow up a little?" I paused. "Maybe I didn't deserve you yet and the universe knew it. But then, when the timing was right… it delivered you right across the street."

Mary crooked a smile. "Leo Hernandez, a believer in fate?"

"If fate is what brought you to me, I'm not only a believer — I'm a worshiper."

She shook her head, but leaned into me, her head on my shoulder. "I saw about a dozen girls wearing your number on their shirts that night I came."

"Am I a pig if I admit I used to love that shit?"

She chuckled. "No. I can only imagine what it felt like."

"It's nothing compared to seeing you in the stands now."

"I don't have your jersey, though," she said, leaning up and balancing her chin on my shoulder to look up at me. "Need to change that."

Everything in me beamed at the thought of her in my jersey, at just the idea of what she'd look like with my number on her chest.

"I brought you here because I wanted to share a little of my life before you came back into it," I said. "I wanted to tell you what was important to me before I found you again. And I want you to tell me about you, too. I want to know how you spent your days, your nights, how you ended up in the house across the street, how you found your way to the shop, what your parents are like, your brother. Everything."

Mary shifted uncomfortably, sitting up with her eyes on the field. "I don't think my story will be as light as yours."

"So, let me sit in the darkness with you."

I watched the stars come out in Mary's eyes as she told me about her life. Some of it she came out with easily, like how her older brother worked at the firm with her dad and how she found Nero's shop when she turned eighteen and could finally get a tattoo without a parent's sign off. I was surprised to hear she'd worked at various restaurants after high school, spending most of her money on tattoos until she was ready to move out of her parents' house. That was when she got the apprenticeship.

She'd moved to the house across the street from us to be closer to the shop, and it really did feel like fate to me that out of all the houses in that part of town, she moved into the one so close to me.

Other things, I had to pry out of her, like who her friends were (to which she said she had none really before Julep) or how she kept quiet when she knew it was me across the street (with great restraint and a desire not to go to jail, she'd answered with a sarcastic smile).

I shared my life with her, too — opening up about my complicated relationship with my dad, my high respect for my mom, and my desire for her to meet them both. I told her a few stories about being on the team in high school and how excited I was when I got the scholarship to NBU, even though my dad hated it.

"It was because of you, you know," I said softly, fingers trailing over her leg. "I wouldn't have had the courage to choose NBU if I'd never have met you."

"Yes, you would have."

"No," I assured her. "I was content to go to Southern Alabama, to be what my dad wanted me to be. But when I met you, when I heard you talk so fearlessly about how you went against the grain with your parents, how you were so fearlessly yourself... it inspired me." I swallowed. "After I lost you, it felt like a way to honor what we had, to stand up for myself and choose the school I wanted to go to instead of bending to my father."

Mary smiled, her brows bending together. "I love that, Leo."

I squeezed her thigh.

With a sigh that sounded like a laugh, Mary scrunched her nose like she didn't want to admit what she was about to. "I actually *did* bend to my mom's will after what happened between us, though."

I balked. "Do tell."

"Remember the deal I made with her to get *Resident Evil*?"

I squinted through the years, reaching through the filing cabinet of my mind for the memory. When it hit me, my jaw slackened. "No," I said with a smile splitting my face. "You didn't."

"Oh, but I did. You're looking at a certified debutante. I wore the white puffy dress and everything."

"Okay, I *demand* a photo."

I had to tickle her mercilessly before she finally relented, pulling out her phone and thumbing to a photo of her looking horribly uncomfortable in a white dress that corseted her at the top and flared off in a puff of cloud below her waist. Her parents stood behind her, their hands on each of her shoulders, proud as could be.

But my eyes snagged on the girls in the photo, how they held so much pain and sadness even at that young age. She looked like she wanted to crawl out of her own skin, out of the life she was forced into. I realized distantly that, not too long after, she did. She made a new life, one of her own.

The longer I stared, the more I willed the memory of that fateful day to come back to me. But even seeing a photograph of her back then, I couldn't see her clearly in my mind.

It killed me.

"It's okay, you can laugh," she said, ripping the phone from my grasp before I could look too long.

I shook my head, quiet for a minute. "I should have been there with you," I said. "Should have been your date."

"I'm rather glad you didn't have to witness my terrible attempt at dancing," she tried to joke.

I turned to face her, pulling her closer. "I mean it. I know I've said I'm sorry a thousand times now but… I am." I kissed her knuckles. "Thank you for giving me another chance."

Her eyes softened, and she nodded. "I'd be lying if I said I wasn't still scared."

"That's okay," I told her. "One day at a time, I'll stay. I'll be here for you. And I'll prove to you that you don't have anything to be afraid of."

I love you.

The words blew through my mind as strong as the October wind, surprising me even though I'd felt them humming under the surface for weeks.

"What?" Mary asked, sensing the shift.

I swallowed the words down, burying them in my chest for now. I knew it wouldn't be long before they'd crawl their way out, but Mary had just admitted to me that she was scared — of me, of us. The last thing she needed was me to throw that at her.

"Nothing," I said.

Mary narrowed her eyes but didn't press. Instead, she bit her lip against a smile. "You know... I always wanted to make out under these bleachers."

I arched a brow. "Did you now?"

"I'm ashamed to admit how many times I fantasized that it'd be you."

"Well, shit," I said, pulling her to stand. "I'll be damned if I miss an opportunity to play out one of your fantasies."

I dragged her down the bleachers with her laugh singing sweet on the evening breeze, and when we were alone under the shadow of the bleachers, I pressed her into a dark corner and kissed her until her lips were swollen and both of us were desperate to get back home.

On the drive back, I was once again overcome by the high of life in that moment. We rolled the windows down and let fall sweep in, Mary's hair blowing everywhere as we sang Breaking Benjamin songs so loud our throats were raw. I soaked up every drop of laughter, reveling in the way it felt to hold her hand and the steering wheel at the same time.

I was on a winning streak — in every possible way.

And with every whispered invocation against Mary's skin that night, I prayed it would never end.

Chapter 34

MARY

"**W**HERE'S MY BIRTHDAY BOY!?"

The door to The Pit burst open early on the morning of October twenty-first, and in blew a petite, gorgeous woman who I only had to glance at once to know was Leo's mom.

She had warm brown skin and jet-black, shoulder-length hair that swung in silky strands around her face as she kicked the door closed behind her. She was holding a homemade something in her hands — perhaps a cake? — and her purse was nearly as big as she was as she adjusted it on her shoulder. It was her smile that gave her away, along with those golden eyes that were wide and bright.

They grew even wider at the sight of me.

"Oh," she said, a little out of breath as she tried to cover her surprise. "Hello."

I shook off my nerves, thankful I'd actually decided to get dressed this morning before coming downstairs.

I didn't usually, but maybe it was the universe's way of showing me a small kindness, because for some reason I'd pulled on a hoodie and my leggings.

"Hi," I said, matching her smile. "You must be Mrs. Hernandez. Here, let me take that," I offered, reaching out to take the pan covered with Cling Wrap out of her hands.

"Please — call me Valentina," she said, letting me take the dessert. Once I had it in my hands, I realized it wasn't a cake, but rather several oversized pastries with a ruby-colored jam oozing out of them and powdered sugar dusting the top.

I looked back up to find Valentina studying me with an arched brow, like she was waiting for me to explain my presence. But before I could, a stampede of boys barreled down the stairs, Leo at the forefront.

"*Mamá!*" he said, and then he scooped his tiny mother into his arms and spun her around while she laughed and squeezed him just as tight.

"*Feliz cumpleaños, mijo*," she said when he sat her feet back on the ground. She grabbed his face in her hands and kissed both his cheeks.

The rest of my roommates enveloped her next, and I used the distraction to slip away, quietly tucking myself into the corner. I was ready to make myself disappear completely, but Leo's gaze snapped to me, and he smiled so wide and carefree that it felt like a blast from the past, like I was seeing him in high school again.

His hand shot out for mine, and I balanced the tray of pastries in one hand as I slipped my other into his.

"*Mamá*, this is Mary," he said, pulling me close.

"Ah, so this is the girl who's stolen my son's heart," she mused.

I flushed furiously, but Leo only kissed my temple and nodded. "The very one."

Leo's mom nodded, crossing her arms as she appraised me. Then, she clicked her tongue and shook her head. "She's too pretty for you."

I laughed, and Leo smiled like this was normal for them. "*Lo sé.*"

"Come on, Mary," Valentina said next, looping her arm through mine and shooing Leo away. "Help me plate these *pastelitos de guayaba* and I'll show you how to make coffee."

"Oh, I know how to make coffee," I said.

She arched that brow at me again, looking at Leo who held up his hands in surrender.

"Be easy on her, *Mamá,* I want to keep her."

Valentina sucked her teeth, but then smiled up at me. "Trust me. You don't know how to make it how *I* do. But I'll show you. Come."

The boys were in a tizzy at Mrs. Hernandez being at the house. They cleaned as quickly as they could as I joined her in the kitchen, and I chuckled to myself as I heard them fantasizing about the guava pastries she'd brought with her. I worked on plating one for each of us as Valentina pulled a can of coffee out of her purse and got to work at the coffee pot.

When Leo said he wanted me to meet his mom, I didn't exactly have a *surprise birthday* meeting in mind.

But once I got past my nerves, it was so easy to talk to her that I felt like she was my own mother — you know, if I had a mother who actually talked to me, that is.

Valentina couldn't ask enough about me, it seemed. She wanted the story behind each one of my tattoos, wanted me to show her my entire portfolio. Then she pleaded with me until I showed her pictures of me and my family and demanded that I come to the house next time Leo did so she could return the favor by blessing me with embarrassing baby pictures of Leo.

That I was excited for.

The boys stole most of her time at the table once we were seated, especially since they had to run out the door to practice soon. I watched Leo licking powdered sugar from his lips while laughing at a story his mom told us about how he'd gone around calling people *bicho* — which meant *dick sucker* — because he'd heard her say it under her breath after getting off the phone with his father so many times. It made my heart squeeze seeing him so happy, and I loved that I was a part of his birthday this year.

I wondered if, maybe, I'd be a part of it *every* year now.

When the boys had to run out the door to head to the stadium, Leo pulled me into his arms and melted me with a warm kiss.

"I can't wait for my birthday present tonight," he whispered in my ear low enough for only me to hear.

"Who said you're getting one?"

He just smirked and made sure his mom wasn't looking before he swatted my ass and skipped out the door.

When Valentina and I were alone, we cleaned up the coffee cups and plates from breakfast. I managed to ask her a few questions before she was desperate to know more about me, and she looked so sad when she told me she had to get going or she'd be late for work.

She wrapped me in a fierce hug when I walked her to the door, her eyes a bit glossy when she pulled back. She held me there in her hands, like she was debating her next words.

"He loves you, you know," she said after a moment. "My son."

Heat rushed over my neck, and I smiled, looking down at the floor as my hair fanned over my blushing cheeks. "I don't know about that."

"I do," she said. "And I'm his mother, so I know better than anyone."

I swallowed down the knot in my throat when she pulled her hands from me, adjusting her purse on her shoulder and opening the front door.

"*Ten cuidado con su corazón*, Mary," she said with a smile. "Be careful with his heart."

"I will," I promised, all the while smoothing a hand over my own heart to soothe the way it was aching.

Valentina nodded like she knew I would even before I told her, and then she pressed up on her toes to kiss each of my cheeks and made me promise we would both come see her soon.

Later that night, after I was done at the shop and Leo was home from his evening classes, we sat in bed together while he unwrapped his present. He was silent when it was finally revealed, running his hand over the navy-blue velvet cover of a thick sketchbook.

His eyes found mine, and then he looked back to the book and opened to the first drawing.

It was a simple doodle, one of some of the flowers that bloomed in the garden over the summer before the weather had grown too cold. The next was of Palico, curled up in a blanket.

When he flipped the page, it was a scene — of that first morning where Kyle made pancakes. Leo stood in front of me, shirtless and hot as ever, one hand absent-mindedly toying with his chains as I scowled at him over my plate that held that smiley-face chocolate chip pancake. Kyle and Braden laughed at the interaction between us.

Leo's face split with a wide grin as he took it all in, and even more so as he flipped through and found more and more scenes waiting — everything from quiet mornings playing video games to sensual nights of us in the sheets. He stared particularly long at the one I'd drawn of us sitting on the roof, his letterman draped over my shoulders.

"This is incredible, Stig," he breathed, finally looking up from the pages and finding my gaze.

"It's not much," I combatted. "But, as you know, things are kind of tight. I thought—"

"It's better than anything money could buy," he refuted before I could finish.

Then, the notebook was on the bedside table.

And Leo was laying me down in his sheets.

Chapter 35

MARY

When I was eleven, my parents surprised me with the best gift ever.

I had a feeling it was going to be the best gift ever, because they'd sent me away to stay the night with my cousin, saying they needed to prepare my birthday surprise. I could barely sleep that night, and the next morning, I declined breakfast, desperate to race back to my house and see what it was.

I walked in to the corner of my room being completely converted into an art studio.

They'd set everything up — the brand-new desk, a dozen different-sized sketchbooks, pens and pencils and markers of all shapes and sizes and widths and colors and depths. The cherry on the cake was a brand-new tablet, one already set up with a drawing program.

I'd sobbed, clinging to my father and thanking him incessantly.

"It was your mom's idea," he'd whispered.

I was so shocked when I turned back to find my mother with tears in her eyes, and then I was clinging to her, crying a hundred *thank yous* into her shirt as she held me tight.

That memory curled around me like fog as I headed toward the shop, that same impatient, giddy feeling settling into my bones. Because just like then, I had a feeling I was walking into good news.

I had a feeling I was walking into a permanent job offer at the studio.

It was Monday, and the shop was closed, but Nero had asked me to come in for a couple hours. He'd assured me no toilets would be cleaned, and I'd laughed, all the while bouncing left to right just *knowing* there would be a job offer waiting for me.

Leo had thoroughly enjoyed watching me tear through dozens of outfits before landing on The One Where I Got Promoted. He was walking out the door to head back to campus for class after sneaking home with just enough time to make my toes curl before he had to go back. I couldn't wait for the end of the night, where we'd both be home celebrating together.

As I drove, I imagined what I'd be walking into. I wondered if they'd already have my space set up and decorated, my name and photo on the wall. I wondered if the rest of the crew would be there, too, with signs and balloons and a cake. *Welcome to the team!* they'd all say.

I was truly floating by the time I parked, and I rode the cloud into the shop, hanging my coat and scarf along with my bag on the hooks by my temporary chair. It was quiet, but a smile still split my face.

"Hello?" I called.

"Back here!"

I followed the sound of Nero's voice to the back office. His brows were furrowed as he worked on a design on his iPad, but he grinned ear to ear when I walked in, setting it aside. "Hey, Mary J."

He was up out of the chair and halfway to me before I could tell him that I did *not* want that nickname. I'd heard it enough as a kid to have to ever hear it again as an adult. But his smile was so big when he wrapped me in a bear hug that I figured I could save that for another time.

Nero's hands stayed on my arms as he pulled away, and he looked me up and down from head to toe. I'd landed on one of my favorite black blouses that was form-fitting but modest, along with dark skinny jeans, and black pointy-toed boots with a three-inch heel. It was simple, and yet the way each piece accented my curves and lines, it made me feel powerful.

"You look... stunning," he said, still holding on.

"Thanks," I replied, blushing a little. Not because of his eyes, but because I was having flashbacks to putting on this outfit and having Leo immediately strip me out of it and bend me over the desk in our room.

Our room.

I tried not to linger on that thought.

Clearing my throat, I stepped out of his grasp and pretended to tidy up some files on one of the desks. "So, what do you need help with?"

"I called you in to have a talk, actually," he said, gesturing to one of the chairs. "Have a seat."

I couldn't wipe the stupid grin off my face as I did.
This is it. I'm getting my own chair.

I sat down as calmly as I could, crossing my legs as Nero sat across from me. He rolled the chair until his knees almost touched mine, then leaned back and folded his hands together over his chest.

He really was a vision — all that dark hair on his head and face, the dark ink on every inch of his skin. It made me feel a bit stupid for how I overreacted with his comments a couple months before. He could have any girl he wanted, and he had bagged one of the hottest ones I'd ever laid eyes on. His wife was a smoke show.

He was just a flirty guy. And ever since that night at the bar with Leo, Nero had been nothing but professional, as if he realized that what he'd said could have been taken out of context, that he might have made me uncomfortable.

Now, I came into work and did my job and he left me to it.

I could get used to that — a flirty, good-looking boss who trusted me and left me alone.

"I've watched you really come into your own over the last month and a half," he said, an easy smile on his face. "Whether it was a simple line of script on a forearm or a complicated custom piece on a back, you've treated every client the same — with respect. You've given them your full attention and made them feel important, which is the best thing you can do in this industry. You already have people wanting to come back — not to this shop, but to *you*." He shook his head. "Most artists wait years for that kind of loyalty."

I beamed under his praise, my skin so warm I pressed my palm to my cheek. "Thank you."

"You can thank yourself. You've worked hard for this. You took every hour of your apprenticeship seriously, and you've really honed your skill, your style. I think you have a bright future ahead of you." He paused. "I think you have a bright future *here* — if you want it."

I had to cover my mouth with my hand to keep from squealing. "Really?"

He chuckled, standing. "Yes, really." He walked over to the fridge and pulled out two beers, handing one to me. He cracked his open and tapped it to the edge of mine before I did the same. "Drink up, Mary. This is your official job offer to work at Moonstruck."

An elated, singsong laugh burst out of me — which made Nero grin wider. He took a long pull of his beer, and once I was done freaking out, I sipped mine. I didn't really like beer, but I wasn't going to turn down a celebratory drink from my boss.

"Thank you," I breathed. "I... I'm shocked."

"You can set your own schedule with the clients you book online, but at least to start out, I want you here in the shop a dedicated three nights a week for walk-ins. You'll pay me rent for your chair and anything you make over that is yours. Rent will cover our basic supplies, but if you decide you want a special gun or brand of ink, that's on you."

I was nodding along feverishly as he spoke, abandoning my beer to take notes in my phone. I didn't care if I barely made enough to cover renting the chair — I was *hired*. I was officially a part of the shop. I would have my own chair, my own space, my own clients.

I could barely sit still.

Nero stood when he was done, opening his arms. "Welcome to the team."

I leapt up, crashing into him and wrapping him in just as fierce of a hug as he gave me. He picked me up a little, spinning us while I chanted *thank you thank you thank you* over and over again.

Nero chuckled when he stopped spinning, and he slowly dropped me back to the ground. It felt a little uncomfortable how my breasts smushed up against his chest and every inch of him on the way down.

I laughed it off, though, and once I was standing again, I tried to pull out of his grasp.

But he held me tighter.

"Congratulations," he said, looking down at me over the bridge of his nose. His breath smelled like he'd had maybe more than just that one beer. "I'm really happy you said yes."

I laughed a little uncomfortably, again trying to break out of his grasp, but he held tighter, inhaling like I was a scented candle.

"You know," he said, his eyes falling to my lips. "There is a way you could properly thank me... for the apprenticeship, the job..."

My stomach instantly soured.

Joy and elation were replaced by panic and revulsion as Nero stroked the side of my cheek with his knuckles. The propellers inside me started to whir, that fight or flight sensation pulsing through me.

"It's been torture, having you working under me all this time with an ass as sweet as yours," he said, as if that was a compliment.

No, I pleaded with the universe. *No, please, no, don't let this happen.*

He hadn't crossed a single line since that night where I'd thought I'd read too much into his compliment.

Now, he was about to cross them all.

"Before you sign the paperwork and become an employee, let's take this momentary break in contract to have some fun," he proposed, intensifying his grip. "What do you say?"

Warning bells rang so loud in my ears I could barely hear my own voice when I replied. "I don't think that's a good idea."

"Oh, come on," he chided, and when he pulled me into him, his erection pressed into my belly.

I nearly gagged.

"I see the way you look at me. You've had a crush on me ever since you walked through that door as a fresh teen to get your first tattoo. It was adorable then, but you've really grown up..." He sucked in a breath like it was hurting him to restrain himself. "I promise, I can handle *everything* you bring to the table."

His hands swooped down to grip my ass firmly and rub me against him, and I'd had enough.

I grabbed his shoulders, locking my eyes on his like I was giving in, my mouth on track for his...

And then hiked my knee up hard and fast right into his balls.

Nero doubled over, coughing and cursing as I backed away and out of reach.

"I'm sorry," I said, ignoring how pissed off it made me that I was apologizing for hurting him when he was being a gross pig. But as sick as it was, I still wanted that job.

He's just drunk, I convinced myself.

"It's just... You have a wife. I have a boyfriend," I added. *Was Leo my boyfriend?* He sure as hell was more than my friend at this point. "And... and I respect you. I don't want anything like this to come between us."

Nero had been bent over and red-faced the entire time I spoke, but he slowly stood upright again, spitting as if I'd hit him in the mouth and drew blood.

He stared at me with the most horrific expression I'd ever seen in my life.

His eyes were wild, but also dead — how they could be both at the same time, I had no clue. The veins in his neck pulsed and bulged, and for a moment, I thought he might attack me. I balled my hands into fists, preparing to fight.

But he just stared at me for a long moment, and then, he let out a slow breath, running his hands through his hair and turning away from me like he'd just remembered who he was.

"It's all good," he said with his back to me, and he started fiddling with some papers on the desk.

"Okay," I whispered, clearing my throat. "So... we're good here? Do you want me to just come back tomorrow when the shop is open to talk about next steps?"

"Yeah," he said, the response short. He grabbed the iPad he'd been working on and sat in his chair again, eyes on the screen and not on me.

I swallowed, backing away from him like he was a snake. I made it to the edge of the office before I turned, and as soon as I did, he struck.

"Actually," he said, making me pause. "Maybe this is a bad idea."

Ice slid through my veins as I spun to face him again. "No. Nero, don't—"

"Yeah, I just don't think you're a good fit, now that I really think about it," he said, not even looking at me as he threw the words like ninja stars. "Your style, if you can even call it a style at all, is more amateur than what we're looking for. I don't want to risk the reputation of the shop."

"You just said I had clients already wanting to rebook," I defended, trying to stay calm as tears welled in my eyes. "You said—"

"I was trying to be nice. No one has called to rebook, Mary." He paused his drawing to make sure he looked at me when he said that last part. "I thought maybe you had a little potential, but I think I was making a decision with my dick rather than my head. You know how that is."

He looked back down as I grappled to remain standing upright.

"Can't help it, it's a bad habit for me. Easily distracted by a pretty face and a nice set of tits."

Each word sliced another ribbon off my skin.

"Honestly, kid — I'm not sure this is the career for you. I just haven't had the heart to say it."

Kid.

He was saying anything he could to kill me now.

I tongued my cheek, shaking my head and trying to find the will to speak. "Please, Nero. Don't do this," I croaked when I finally found it.

He sniffed, shrugging. "Sorry, I just think this is best." He paused to look at me one last time. "Oh, and if you were thinking about any other shops in the area, I'd be careful about what you say about your time here."

It was a threat and a promise both, the assurance that if I ran my mouth, I'd never work in Boston. He'd see to it.

Nero didn't look at me again. Not as I stood there in disbelief, not as I numbly dragged myself out of the office, and not as I put my coat and scarf back on and slipped into the cold.

In the span of twenty minutes, I'd been promoted, assaulted, fired, and denounced by a man I'd looked to as inspiration for years.

I took ten steps toward my car, and then I vomited.

Chapter 36

LEO

Driving home from campus, I had a hard time not speeding with all the excitement flowing through me. Coach had called me into his office for a quick meeting before class, one where he told me the Minnesota Vikings had their eyes on me.

Now, I didn't know one fucking thing about Minnesota other than it was damn cold, but the fact that a team knew my name, that I was on their radar, that I could be the missing piece in their offense that took them to the next level… it lit me up like nothing else in the world could.

The only thing I could think about was telling Mary.

I knew she'd have good news, too — a permanent position at the shop. And while I still had Nero on my radar for being a creep, he'd left her alone ever since that first time she'd told me he'd made her feel some type of way, and I knew this job was one Mary wanted more than anything.

I couldn't wait to meet her good news with my own, to collide at the door as we both burst at the seams to tell the other every single detail. I couldn't wait to take her upstairs and celebrate afterward, too — and I'd take my sweet ass time, regardless of the early wakeup call waiting for me in the morning.

My tires squealed a little bit when I pulled into the drive, and I noticed Mary's car was already parked across the street. I all but skipped through the front door, hiking my bag up my shoulder and taking the stairs two at a time. I slung my bag into the corner as I opened the door to my bedroom — our bedroom? — and kicked my shoes off before pouncing on the bed where Mary was curled into a ball.

"Wake up, sleepyhead!" I started kissing all over her neck and shoulders, making them obnoxiously loud with my grin against her skin. "We have celebrating to do."

But when Mary rolled over, everything inside me turned to ice.

She didn't meet me with a face-splitting smile. She wasn't jumping up and down and throwing herself on me as she spilled every detail of her job offer.

Instead, her face was red and puffy, eyes swollen, lashes wet.

She'd been crying.

And instantly, I was ready to kill.

"What happened?"

She shook her head, trying to pull me down into the sheets with her. "Forget it."

"Absolutely not." I pulled her gently until she was sitting up, her legs folded underneath her. I took her hands in mine and waited.

"He fired me."

"*What*?!" I shook my head, jaw slack. I was completely dumbfounded. "How... *why* would he do that? You've been an apprentice for over a year. You've been *killing* it with your own clients for two months!"

"Which is why he offered me a chair of my own," she said.

I blinked, confused. "Huh?"

She bit her lip against a wave of tears, finally meeting my gaze after taking a deep breath. "He offered me my own chair. Then, he gave me a hug, and proceeded to grind his erection into me and say he could think of a way or two to *properly thank him*."

My soul left my body.

It hovered above us, listening as Mary continued, saying that when she'd turned him down, he'd taken everything back and fired her. I thought I also heard her say she kneed him in the balls, but I couldn't even find joy in that.

My body was detached, a numb sort of fire crawling up my spine. My jaw ached with how tight it was, throat constricting with the need to scream.

That was it.

I was going to jail tonight.

Mary was still talking when I slid off the bed and wordlessly slid my sneakers back on.

"What are you doing?" she asked with a sniff.

I couldn't breathe, couldn't think straight enough to answer her past the red-hot anger seeping through my every pore. Distantly, I heard my mom's voice as if she were in the corner of the room.

Cálmate, mijo. Think.

I could even hear my father and Coach, as if they were one person, their arms crossed over their chests as they shook their heads.

Don't do it. You're risking your career.

I glanced back at Mary, and she blinked, recognition falling over her.

"No," she said, loud and firm as she jumped up and ran to me.

"Someone needs to put that piece of shit in his place."

"Leo, don't!" Mary begged, her hand reaching out to snag my arm.

"He's not going to touch you like that and get away with it."

"It's fine. I'm handling it. There are other places I can work."

I shook my head. "That doesn't excuse what he did."

"I know it doesn't, but I'm... figuring it out."

She shook her head, tears still staining her cheeks, and I had to tear my gaze away because it hurt so badly to see them.

"Leo," she said, squeezing my arm. "Look at me."

When I did, I was breathing like a fucking beast — nostrils flaring, jaw so tight I thought I'd bust a tooth.

"I am asking you not to do this," she said. "*Please*."

But I couldn't listen.

I ripped out of her grasp and flew down the stairs as fast as I'd come up them, the thrumming of my heart in my ears drowning out the rest of Mary's pleas.

MARY

When I pulled up to the shop, it was too late.

Leo had been too fast, like there were squealing tires under him instead of legs as he raced out of The Pit. I'd gotten dressed as quickly as I could and run across the street to my own car, speeding toward the shop to try to stop him.

But I parked and barreled out of my car just in time to see Nero tossing Leo out, both of them bloody.

"Oh, my God!" The scream ripped from my throat before I had any chance of keeping it in. I ran to Leo, who was dragging himself off the ground with his murderous gaze still pinned on my boss.

Ex-boss.

"Wow," Nero said on a laugh, spitting blood out of his mouth and onto the pavement at our feet. "Real fucking mature, Mary, siccing your boyfriend on me."

He didn't give me the chance to respond before he shook his head and turned back to the shop.

"You're done in this town," he said, so low I thought I misheard him. But he whipped around and pointed a finger at me, his nose busted up and bleeding, eyes already turning purple. "*Done*," he reiterated. He pointed at Leo next. "And you're fucking lucky I don't press charges, you dumb sonofa—"

It happened so fast; I couldn't register it all.

One second Leo was beside me, puffing like a dragon, and the next, a sickening crack split the air and Nero was laid out on the ground. Leo had connected his fist right to Nero's jaw, making him spin around like a giant in a cartoon before he fell.

"If you *ever* so much as fucking look at her again, I'll kill you," Leo seethed, grabbing Nero by the shirt. He held him inches from his face long enough to land the threat before he dropped him back to the pavement.

And the sight of him standing over Nero and defending me like that both turned me on and pissed me right the fuck off.

"Leo," I ground through my teeth.

Nero blinked a few times, groaning as he stood. He spit blood again, and this time?

A tooth.

He picked it up with an amused grin, rolling the piece of white bone around in his fingers before shoving it in his pocket.

Then, he pinned Leo with a bloody grin. "I hope you enjoyed that because you just fucked your girlfriend — and not in the way I could, I promise you that."

Leo surged forward like he was going to hit him again, but I wrapped my arms all the way around him to stop him, my chest to his back, me hanging on him for dear life.

"I bet you would have been a lousy lay, anyway," Nero said to me as his final word, and then he was in the shop and locking the door behind him, a manic sort of laugh like he'd won ringing out in the air.

And he had.

He held all the power over me. I wouldn't stand a chance of landing another job in the city now, and Leo hadn't proven anything by knocking a tooth out, other than that Nero had enough power to upset both of us.

We'd shown our cards, and he'd played his ace.

For a long moment, we stood there, me wrapped around Leo and him breathing loud, shallow breaths, both of us staring at the door Nero had disappeared through.

When I finally released him, I shoved him hard.

"What the fuck is wrong with you?!"

"*Me*?" Leo spun to face me, his eyes still wild. "I should have killed him, Mary. He's a fucking scumbag and—"

"And I can handle my damn self!" I shouted, chest heaving. "I kneed him in the balls. I walked out of here with my head held high and at least a scrap of my dignity still in place. I don't need you swooping in like some fist-happy shining knight to defend my honor. I had a plan, which you've now shot to hell. Because now I'll never work anywhere in this city because I have a psychotic boyfriend."

Leo blinked, taking two long breaths. "Boyfriend?"

I chuffed a laugh, turning and striding to my car. The words that burst out of my throat without permission were immature and hasty, but I didn't care. "Ex, now."

"Whoa, whoa, wait," he said, catching up to me and taking me by the elbow to spin me toward him. "What do you mean *ex*?"

"You completely disrespected me," I screamed through my tears, chest tight. "I asked you not to. I *begged* you. And you did it anyway."

Leo's face leveled out more with every word. "Mary."

"No," I ripped my arm out of his grasp. "I can't believe you." I shook my head, tears blurring my vision. A short laugh chopped out of me. "Actually, I can. I really fucking can. I should have known better."

I hated myself before the next words even left my lips, but I wanted to hurt him. I wanted him to feel loss like I felt in that moment.

A small part of me remembered feeling this way before with him, seven years ago, when he hurt me and I was desperate to return the favor.

"You don't really care about me," I said. "You just wanted a prize, something to have on your arm and get in fights over. You didn't stop to think twice about what *I* wanted, how this would impact me and my fucking *dream*. I have worked for years for this. *Years*, Leo. Imagine if I did this to you, if I tore through the stadium and ripped a cheerleader off the top of a pyramid by her hair for ogling you or bragging to her friends in the bathroom how you'd fucked her into the next decade at a party last year."

Leo had completely sobered now, all the fight gone from him as he rushed me and pulled me into him. He held me tight, brushing his fingers through my hair.

"I'm sorry," he breathed.

His knuckles were bleeding.

So was his eyebrow.

"I'm so sorry," he said again when I didn't pull away. "You're right. I was stupid. I just—"

"Didn't think," I finished for him, sniffing and pulling away. "Yeah. I know."

He crumpled. "Stig, I—"

I held up one hand to stop him. "Don't you understand?" The realization hit me like a boulder, one that fell from a skyscraper and squashed me like a bug. I sniffed, searching his gaze. "I trusted you."

That nearly broke us both, and I tore away from him, needing to get away from his touch.

"I trusted you not to hurt me. You promised me I could."

"I would never hurt you," he said, voice booming.

"You already did."

His nostrils flared, jaw hinged tight as his eyes glossed over just like mine. But he didn't move, didn't try to touch me again, didn't try to argue. He just stood there waiting for me to absolve him.

And I couldn't.

"Leave me alone, Leo," I pleaded softly, bringing my eyes to meet his. "I need you to leave me alone."

He swallowed. "What if I can't?"

"Then you'll prove that you really don't care about me at all."

Twenty minutes later, I pulled up to Giana and Clay's.

They made up the couch for me without asking a single question, and Giana held me as I cried until I fell asleep.

Chapter 37
LEO

Twenty-four hours ago, everything was different.

My biggest worry yesterday had been football. We had an away game against our rivals in two weeks after our bye this weekend, and it was all we could focus on. If we won, not only would it be a rivalry win, but it would secure a bowl game for us.

Coach had also told me there would be multiple scouts at this game — scouts who had been visiting our campus throughout the season with their eyes on our seniors.

On *me*.

Yesterday, I was full of hope. I had sped home with nothing but excitement flowing through my veins as I rushed to tell Mary. Yesterday was a whole different world, a completely different universe.

Today, I woke up in hell.

Mary never came home last night, and she ignored every single text and phone call from me. The only solace I found came at almost midnight when Clay texted me and told me she was at his and Giana's place. I'd sucked in a breath of relief so fierce I'd nearly collapsed.

But even though I knew she was safe, I still couldn't sleep.

Because safe or not, I'd lost her all the same.

Every time I thought the words, my stomach would roll so violently I nearly puked. Then, I'd immediately shove the thought down, suffocating it before it had the chance to invade my brain again.

I didn't lose her.

I *couldn't* lose her.

My chest was on fire all night and well into the morning, even as I got myself ready for the day. All I could see was Mary's eyes when I realized what I'd done, the way she looked at me like I'd just proven every doubt she had about me correct.

And I guessed I had.

I didn't think about it from her perspective until it was too late. Hell, I didn't think about it *at all*. It was disrespectful to step in like some big bad motherfucker when she'd already told me she'd handled it. It didn't make anything better when I clocked that stupid *bicho* in the mouth. It didn't even make me feel better. All it did was piss me off more because he stood right back up, and then, he hurt Mary even more.

Because of me.

And to add more shit to the pile, Nero had me by the balls, too. If he went to the police, if he pressed charges… my career would be snuffed out before the flame had the chance to catch.

There was a bottomless pit of doom in my stomach with so much uncertainty. I didn't know if Nero really wouldn't press charges or if I'd walk into a media shit storm at the stadium. I didn't know if Mary meant *leave me alone* as in for the night or forever.

It couldn't be forever.

I convinced myself that somehow it would all be okay as I dragged my ass to practice. Despite how dead I felt inside, how hard it was to breathe not knowing where I stood with Mary, I managed to put it all away and show up for my team. I balled out at practice, and to everyone on that field, I was just fine. I was *better* than fine. I was on fire.

Everyone, that was, except for Clay, Zeke, Riley, and my roommates.

They all watched me like a bomb that would detonate with one wrong step.

When practice was wrapped and we were in the locker room, they cornered me.

"What the hell happened?" Riley demanded in a hushed voice. "Why are your knuckles scabbing and why did Mary sleep on Clay's couch last night?"

I filled them in as emotionlessly as I could, locking everything down because otherwise I knew I'd fall apart right then and there. And as a leader, as their captain — I couldn't do that in front of my team.

By the time I finished, they were all silent, their brows pinched together.

"Shit," Zeke said.

"Yeah," I agreed.

No one had time to offer a word of advice before Coach Lee's voice boomed through the room.

"Hernandez," he said, and all eyes whipped to where he was standing in the doorway of his office. He tilted his head toward it with his lips pressed into a hard line.

Fuck.

I closed the door behind me once I dipped into his office, and when I sat down across from him, we both sat there silent. Coach finally let out a frustrated breath and said, "We both know why we're here, so let's not fuck around."

I nodded solemnly. "How bad is it?"

"Fortunately for you, it should stay out of the press. The guy came here threatening to press charges or go to the news, but we had... help," he said carefully. "From some alumni who were eager to rectify the situation and keep you on the team."

I squeezed my eyes closed, cramping at even the thought of someone handing over their hard-earned money to save my ass. I also wasn't an idiot. I knew that probably wasn't exactly *il*legal, but was also likely very frowned upon.

"Giana did a quick scrub this morning. She said there's not even a whisper of it, so we should be fine. We had him sign an NDA once both parties were satisfied."

"And my parents?"

"You get the honor of telling them."

The way he said it, I knew there wasn't a choice to not tell them. Either I could, or he would if I took too long. I swallowed at the thought of telling my father, who would no doubt scold my ass for risking my career. But Mom?

She'd be heartbroken.

That was worse than any screaming Dad could do.

Coach let out another long breath, and then he shook his head, looking at me with such disappointment I wanted to curl into a ball and cry like a little boy. "What were you thinking, son?"

"I wasn't," I answered immediately, honestly.

Coach nodded, and then something in him softened a bit the longer he watched me. "You okay?"

"No," I said on a laugh, nose stinging. I sniffed it away. "I messed up. I'm sorry, Coach," I said, meeting his gaze. I hoped he felt how much I meant that. "I really am."

Coach Lee looked like he didn't know if he wanted to scream at me, make me run laps, or give me a hug. In the end, he settled on another nod. "Whatever is going on, figure it out. We need you for the game next weekend. And those scouts won't think twice before turning their backs on you if you're not performing at the level they want to see."

I nodded, and at this point, the souring of my stomach felt like it would be a new permanent state of being.

"You're on probation," he added.

I wasn't surprised. "Meaning?"

"Meaning if you fuck up again, there won't be a conversation. There won't be help. There won't be a way out of it." He leveled his gaze with me. "Focus, son. The rest of your life is at stake here."

After that, the day dragged by and happened in a flash all at once. I didn't know how I managed to stay alive long enough to ride home with the roommates at the end of it, all of us quiet and exhausted in the car.

No one said a word, but Kyle's eyes caught mine in the rearview mirror from where he was driving. He nodded, wordlessly telling me he was there, and Braden squeezed my shoulder from where he sat beside me. Blake glanced back at me with concern, but then offered me a pitiful smile, trying to give me hope that I didn't think could ever exist in me again.

That was, until we pulled up and saw Mary's car across the street.

Kyle barely put the car in park before I was rushing out of it and in the house and up the stairs. I burst through my door and felt the most relieving exhale leave me at the sight of Mary sitting on the bed.

Her hair was a wild nest piled into a bun on top of her head, and one look at her face told me she'd slept as shitty as me last night. Palico was laying beside her, flicking her tail at me like even she knew what a moron I'd been.

But Mary still wore one of my hoodies, and that sight along with the possible implication it held had me moving toward her.

The second I noticed all the bags and boxes packed up around the room, I froze again.

My eyes flicked from one box to the next, bouncing into my closet that was much less crowded now before sneaking a glance at the bathroom that was far too clean to have any trace of Mary left. Panic gripped my throat in a fist, and when my gaze met Mary's, I had no choice.

I fell to my knees.

I fell hard, with a crack of bone to wood that made Mary's eyes well with tears. She looked up to try to keep them from falling, but they seared down her cheeks, anyway.

"Don't go."

They were the only words I could say, the only ones that made sense in my scrambled brain. I could say I was sorry a million times, I could promise her the whole world — but the one thing I needed her to hear above anything else was that I wanted her to stay.

I *needed* her to stay.

"I'm going to live with my parents," she said, her voice a cracked whisper.

I closed my eyes, shaking my head, willing myself to wake up from this nightmare.

"I've overstayed my welcome here as it is."

I opened my eyes again. "You know that's not true."

"I don't know what's true anymore."

My jaw ached with how hard I clenched it.

"Look, this was a bad idea from the start," she said, not looking at me as she said it. But she stood, pulling Palico into her arms, and that made it feel so final that I could barely breathe. "Let's just... go back to pretending we left each other back in high school, okay?"

"I don't want to pretend," I said, climbing to my feet. My chest heaved as I stared at her. "I don't want to pretend I left you in high school because I didn't. I don't want to pretend like I didn't want you the second you moved across the street, even before I knew who you were. And I *refuse* to pretend that I don't want you now, more than ever, because I *do* know who you are."

Mary's face didn't show an ounce of emotion, but another tear slid down her cheek, landing silently on her shoulder. She clutched Palico closer.

I took the fact that she wasn't leaving yet as my last shot to make her stay.

"Can I hold you?" I asked on a desperate whisper. "Please?"

Her lip wobbled, but she nodded, and as soon as she carefully sat the cat back on the bed, I swept her into my arms before she could take another breath.

She clung to me just as fiercely as I held her, and I closed my eyes against the emotion strangling me as I crushed her to me — one hand in her hair, the other wrapped completely around her. I inhaled her, telling my poor fucking heart that this wasn't over even as I felt her slipping away.

"I'm sorry," I told her. "I shouldn't have gone last night. I was an idiot. I should have stayed with you, should have *been here with you.*" I shook my head, still holding onto her. "I didn't think. I fucked up. But I swear I will do everything to make it up to you. Please," I begged. "Stay."

Mary choked on a sob, clutching me tighter, and I held her to me until she pressed her hands against my chest asking for space. When she looked up at me, I wanted to die.

She was in so much pain.

And it was because of me.

"I need some time, Leo," she said, and her eyes didn't cower from my own. "This dream that I've worked for for... *years*... is just... gone."

She stuttered, and I wanted to hurl myself off the roof.

"I'm jobless. *Home*less. Broke." She shrugged. "I have no idea where to go from here."

"Let me go through it with you."

Something hardened her then, and she stepped even farther away, out of my grasp.

My heart shattered at the thought that that might have been the last time I ever got to hold her.

"I don't trust you."

The words slid through me like a hot knife, slicing me right in half like I was just a stick of butter.

"Mary," I tried.

"You have the game," she said, crossing her arms. "You need to focus on yourself, and I need to focus on me. All of this happened so fast. One day I was full swing in the life I'd created for myself, the one where I was living despite the hell you put me through. The next, I was in a heaven I never knew existed, wrapped up in everything that you are, that *we* are, together."

I wanted her to stop there. I wanted that to be the end. But she sniffed and continued.

"And now, I'm in hell again. Deeper, this time, because now I've lost the one thing that has always been mine despite what happened to me. I worked my *ass* off for this, Leo," she said.

"I know," I told her. I bit back the urge to remind her that it wasn't me who took it away from her. It was Nero.

But then I remembered that I'd made matters worse. She'd had a plan, she'd said — and I didn't doubt it. Mary was strong. She was smart. She could handle herself.

It was *me* who fucked everything up.

"We just… we need to take a break," she said with finality, picking up a duffle bag and tossing it over her shoulder. "My parents will be here in twenty minutes. Could you…" She swallowed. "Can you please not be here when they are?"

That gutted me.

Just a few weeks ago at our old high school football field, she'd told me she wanted me to meet them.

Now, I felt like a shameful secret being locked away in a closet never to be found.

"I'll do whatever you need me to do," I promised. "I'll leave. I'll give you space." I closed the distance between us, tentatively reaching out. When she didn't flinch, I slid my hands into her hair, framing her face, holding her gaze to mine. "But I will not give up on us."

She closed her eyes. "What if I need you to?"

"Then I'll leave you disappointed." I paused. "Again. Because I can't do that, Stig. I... *can't*." That last word left me like a guttural declaration of truth, one pulled from me against my will.

I didn't know if it was a laugh or a sob that came from her next, but I pressed my lips to her forehead, closing my eyes and praying harder than I had in my entire life that this wasn't the end for us.

"I love you, Mary," I breathed.

She stilled in my grasp, and I pulled back until I was looking down at her again.

"I love you," I repeated. "I may be a colossal fuck up. I may make mistakes. I may disappoint you and fall short in more ways than I measure up. But I love you, and that will never not be true."

Mary covered my hands with her own, closing her eyes again and leaning into my palm. She let out a slow exhale.

Then, she peeled my hands off her and stepped away.

"Right now, I have to love myself," she said softly.

My heart was a bloody, bruised, barely living thing — but I let her go.

I nodded. I held her gaze until I couldn't anymore. I turned and walked numbly down the stairs and right out the door without a plan of where I'd go next. I just walked and walked and walked until my body refused to walk any longer. I'd ended up somewhere in the North End, staring at people laughing and eating and drinking and enjoying their lives, all of them oblivious to the zombie among them.

Eventually, I texted Braden, and he came to pick me up.

We were quiet on the drive back, Braden driving my car because I knew I couldn't. When we pulled into the driveway, I looked at the door with a pit in my stomach.

"Did I lose her?" I asked.

Braden sighed, looking at the house and then at me. "She's gone, man."

And all the strength I'd been using to hold it together left me.

I didn't care that Braden was still there, that Kyle and Blake were now coming out of the house, too. It didn't matter if I *did* care. I was powerless against the emotional dam that split wide open inside me.

I somehow managed to push the car door open and stand up.

Then, I broke.

My roommates rushed to me. They weren't my friends in that moment. They weren't my teammates. They were my brothers. My family. And they held me while I fell apart.

"It'll be okay, man. She'll come back," Kyle said.

The air pulsed, because every single one of us knew that was a promise that wasn't his to make.

Chapter 38

MARY

The gray morning matched my mood perfectly, colorful leaves dripping wet from the way the clouds hugged them. It was quiet except for where the dew dripped down into the grass, a soft *pit, pat, pit, pat* that drew me outside like a magnet. The distinct smell of fall decay hung in the air, and I welcomed the wet morning with open arms. I was so sick of the sunshine, of the world continuing to spin on without a care.

I wrapped myself in a blanket and went outside on the back porch just so I could sit with the fog.

With the blanket wrapped around me, the scent of Leo that still barely clung to the hoodie I'd stolen from him wrapped around me, too. I closed my eyes and inhaled it along with the cool morning air, and just when I thought they'd dried up, my eyes welled with tears again.

It'd been almost a week since I moved out of The Pit and back home with my parents.

It was a last resort, one I'd only chosen after Margie informed me the house wouldn't be ready for me to move back in until after the holidays. She and I had both decided it was time to let me out of the lease, for us to go our separate ways while she fixed everything up. I couldn't wait in limbo any longer, and this time, I really didn't have a choice.

I had to go home.

It had killed my pride to make the call. I'd called Dad, of course, who didn't ask a single question. He just said he was on his way. And while hearing his voice, his concern, his *love* for me filled my aching heart with warmth, I knew when he pulled into The Pit, Mom would be with him, locked and loaded with a million questions.

I'd been right.

She'd been tight-lipped and quiet while we loaded up the SUV with my belongings — including Palico. The roommates had helped, minus Leo, who had left because I'd asked him to. I didn't miss the hard edge of my father's expression as he watched three male college athletes interact with his daughter. But Kyle, Braden, and Blake showed him and my mother both the highest respect.

They also gave me the best hugs of my life when it was time to leave, and I tried not to cry as we said goodbye.

As soon as we were in the car and on the highway, Mom started in.

She berated me with questions the entire drive home. *How in the world did you end up there? What were you thinking? You should have called us. You should have moved home. This is why you never should have moved into that decrepit house to start with. You should be in college, in a dorm room that's safe and passes a thorough inspection. How in the world did you end up with a cat? And what does that Margie character say of this? You better be getting your deposit back. I can't believe you've been living with men without our permission. You could have been killed, or worse—*

My father putting his hand on her knee had silenced her, and while he hadn't so much as looked at her when he did it, I watched Mom take her first real breath, cover his hand with hers, and fall silent.

Mercifully.

I'd slept in my old room, which was pretty much the same, except that it was painted brighter now, with a bed set only my mother would love, and there was a treadmill in the corner facing out of my favorite window — the one I used to gaze out of as I sketched. It wasn't any easier to sleep in here, not with memories of high school clinging to the space. I stared at the television that I used to play Xbox on with Leo, heart lurching every time.

I so desperately wanted to get high, but I didn't have any edibles on hand, and I knew I couldn't sneak a joint — not in my mother's house. It didn't matter if I walked down the street to smoke it, she'd find out.

So, I tossed and turned soberly through the night before Dad knocked on my door at two in the morning, his walking sneakers in hand.

We didn't talk as we walked, and unlike when I was younger, it didn't really help me sleep. But it did make me feel marginally better — less alone, at the very least.

And the next morning, I gave my mom all the answers she was looking for.

I also told her and Dad both about Nero.

Naturally, they wanted me to go to the police. They couldn't see reason, not even when I pointed out that it was his word against mine, that if I moved against him, he'd move against Leo and me both. Mom swore the law would side with me, which made me laugh because clearly she hadn't paid attention to any similar court cases in the last hundred years. Dad seemed to understand why I was hesitant, but he was like Leo. He wanted to murder Nero. And while my shot of ever working in Boston was already obliterated, I didn't want to poke the bear that had the power to annihilate my career completely.

It was only after I begged and pleaded with them through my tears that they agreed to let me handle it the way I wanted to.

That's the thing no one tells you about being a victim to harassment — that not only do you lose power during the assault, but afterward, too, when you're expected to follow rules put in place by people who have no idea what you've been through or what's at stake.

What my parents didn't understand was that I *needed* to take back control of the situation. I needed to be the one to decide what happened next, to determine how much I let this incident impact me and the rest of my life.

All I wanted was to wipe my hands of Nero and the memory and move forward.

I wanted to live on without ever thinking about him or that shop again.

And I never wanted to give him the satisfaction of thinking he'd so much as slowed me down, let alone stopped me.

After the dust settled, once the questioning was done and Dad convinced Mom to leave it alone, I was finally able to breathe.

But each breath was a fiery assault on my lungs, because now all I could think of was Leo.

It was sick, how I knew I needed space from him and yet I stared at my phone all damn day wishing to see his name pop up on the screen. I'd asked him to leave me alone, and he'd listened — even when I knew he didn't want to. He was giving me what I needed, and my masochistic ass was over here wishing he wouldn't, wishing that he'd say *fuck what you think you need* and burst through the door.

But if he did, I knew I'd be upset.

I'd take it as further proof that I couldn't trust him, that he didn't care about what I needed, what I asked of him. It would hurt me. It would piss me off.

And yet, not hearing from him at all killed me.

I was a chaotic disaster, one he didn't deserve to put up with. I was so angry with him, so betrayed by his actions — and yet, he was the only one I craved to make me feel better about it all.

The only one I knew could actually do it.

I'd beaten these thoughts around in my brain so much over the week that it felt like mush, and I sat outside in the cool morning fog with a dazed look on my face, my head floating in the mist, body on autopilot and just keeping me alive.

Someone opened the patio door, and Palico sauntered through it and right up to the couch I was sitting on. She hopped up, meowing before she nudged me as if to say, "*Let me inside that thing, I'm cold.*" I couldn't smile, but I did open up the blanket long enough for her to make her way in. I swore, she knew something was wrong. She'd been glued to my side since we first arrived.

I didn't know how long I had been sitting there when suddenly a hot mug of tea was presented in front of my face.

I blinked, coming back to earth and following the hand that held the mug up to find my mother staring down at me.

The older I got, the more I saw how much I favored my mother. It wasn't just her long, thick hair that I had, too, or her fair skin. It wasn't her plump bottom lip that matched mine, or the way our eyes were the same emerald green. It was that I saw the sadness that felt so at home in my eyes reflected in hers, saw the determination that filled me emanating from her, too. She held her chin high, her shoulders square, never afraid to say what she meant or to face anything that scared her.

I was more like her than I ever realized before.

When I didn't immediately take the mug from her hand, she nudged it closer, and I held the blanket tight around me with one fist as I reached my other hand out to take hold of the handle. Once I had it, Mom sat down primly on the couch next to me, sitting nearly on the edge of it as she daintily lifted her cup to her mouth and took a sip.

Our outdoor furniture was so spotless it looked like it belonged inside, the white cushions crisp and clean, the teak wood that framed it pristine and beautiful. I remembered when Mom picked out the set, when Dad had instructed the movers where to put it all just to have Mom change her mind and Dad and my brother had to move it all around again.

But once she had it the way she liked it, it never moved again.

It also never wore a speck of dust longer than a few hours.

I didn't have anything to say, not even to acknowledge my surprise at her joining me on the deck. She'd barely talked to me since I'd been home — mostly because I'd holed up in my room — and whenever she *did* talk to me, it was to press me for what I was going to do next, how I was going to move on.

As if I knew.

But I was thankful for the hot tea, the first sip warming me all the way down to my toes.

"Thank you," I croaked, my throat in shit shape after all the crying and late nights of no sleep.

Mom nodded, her back still ramrod straight as she took a sip of her own tea and then cradled the mug between her hands.

She looked out over the beautifully curated yard she'd created over the years — the garden that would make Holden have wet dreams, the man-made pond and fountain, the stone walkway through the beautiful trees and bushes and flowers. Birds and squirrels alike made themselves comfortable, eating the seed Mom put out each morning and swimming in the baths on hot days. This morning, however, it was quiet and still, the fog slinking in heavy patches through the space.

"So, are you going to tell me more about this boy?"

I let out a long breath, a moment of regret sinking in my stomach for having told her and Dad about Leo at all. But what happened between him and Nero was part of the reason I wanted to leave the whole situation alone, so it had to be said.

"I'd rather not," I confessed.

"Because I'm such an evil, emotionless monster that I wouldn't understand?" Mom assumed with a harsh laugh.

"Because I'm having trouble breathing without him in my life," I shot back. "And I don't really care to hold my bloody heart out for you to dissect."

Mom turned to face me, her brows hinged together. And for the first time in years, I saw genuine concern in her eyes, like she hated that I was in pain and she couldn't do anything about it. She'd used to look at me that way when I was sick, as if she'd rather be the one with the stomach flu than to see me go through it.

"Maybe talking about it will help rather than hurt," she offered.

I didn't respond. I'd talked at length about it to the girls, each of them listening and waiting for when I asked them for their advice. I was thankful they didn't just offer it without the cue, because the truth was I didn't know if I was ready to do anything about any of it.

Because if I was to do something, that would mean one of two things — either I'd forgive Leo and go back, or I'd not forgive him and leave him behind.

Both options made my chest impossibly tight.

"How did you meet?" Mom asked when I didn't speak.

A laugh of a breath left my nose. "Playing *Halo*."

She made a face. "That God-awful game we got you for your fifteenth birthday?"

"The very one."

I expected her to wrinkle her nose in distaste, but instead, it was like something clicked. She paused, then smiled, then sat back a little on the couch, relaxing next to me.

"Huh," she mused. "Well, that explains a lot."

"How so?"

"You were so weird that summer," Mom said. "The most emotional I'd ever seen you. I blamed it on being fifteen. That's when you really started doing your makeup. You'd steal mine, you little brat," she added. "I remember fretting to your father about how we had a teenager now and our real problems were about to begin."

"My wife, fretting?" Dad said, and I turned in time to see him swing out the back door with a coffee in his hand. He sank into the rocking chair across from us with a smile. "I can't imagine."

Mom shot him a glare, but a smile threatened the corner of her lips. Just that little interaction alone made my chest ache, made me clamp my hands together to keep from reaching for my phone to call Leo.

As if Palico sensed it, she nudged my knuckles so I would pet her, instead.

"But then…" Mom continued, frowning. "Not too long after school started, you *really* changed. And I don't mean in the petulant teenager way. I mean… you were hurt." She paused. "Your father and I knew something happened, but we didn't know what."

"And you didn't ask," I added.

Mom tilted her head a little higher. "Maybe we could have done better," she admitted. "But let's be honest — you've never been exactly easy to talk to." She waved her hand between us as if I was illustrating her point at this very moment.

And I supposed I was.

The fact that my mom was showing an actual interest in my life and not the one she wished I was living had me softening a bit. Maybe it was that along with being tired of feeling so alone even in a house with my family that had me opening my mouth and spilling everything.

I told them about that summer with Leo, about what happened when school started. I told them about the hell I went through with the teasing over that stupid drawing, and how I never lived down that awful nickname. Then, I fast forwarded to moving across the street from him, to this summer with the pipes and moving into The Pit and how, slowly, everything between us unfolded.

It was somehow colder by the time I finished, even though the sun was starting to clear out some of the fog. It was still a cloudy day, and when the sun dipped behind one of those clouds, I wrapped myself and Palico up tighter in the blanket with a sigh.

"And then, when all of this happened with Nero..." I shook my head, not wanting to relive it. "Leo didn't listen to me. He didn't stay when I begged him to, didn't take a second to think about what consequences his actions would have." Emotion had me struggling to swallow. "I lost everything I'd worked for in the blink of an eye," I whispered. "And in turn, Leo lost my trust."

Dad let out a heavy sigh. "I'm sorry, Mare Bear."

I nodded, not sure what else to say. Mom was quiet, and I didn't dare look at her for fear of the judgment I'd find. I opened my mouth to say that it would all be fine, I just needed some time, when suddenly...

Mom laughed.

Not a quick, sarcastic lash of a chuckle, either, but a full on, belly-deep, had to put her cup of tea down so as not to spill it laugh. She tilted her head up to the sky as it barreled out of her, and then tears were streaming down her face, and she was wiping them away as she laughed even harder.

I didn't laugh with her. In fact, I watched her like something I should be afraid of before casting a worried glance at my father, silently asking if she was having a stroke. Palico was so startled by it all that she skittered off my lap and used her paw to open the door Dad had left ajar, retreating inside.

"I'm sorry," Mom finally managed, the words a high-pitched squeak as she still struggled to catch her breath. She reached over and squeezed my knee with her hand, as if we were best friends just yukking it up together and I'd just told the most hilarious joke she'd ever heard. "It's just that you're so much like me, it terrifies me sometimes."

That made my other eyebrow shoot up to join the first.

She waved me off before I could even ask, wiping tears from her face as she sat up straight again. "Ask your dad what happened on our three-month anniversary."

I wrinkled my nose. "You guys celebrated a three-month anniversary?"

"Oh, we celebrated everything back then," Dad said with a smile that said he was reliving a memory. "Every day I didn't screw up my chance with your mother was a special occasion."

"And I didn't make it easy for him," Mom added.

"Imagine that," I mused.

My parents shared a knowing look.

"We had gone bowling," Dad explained. "And long story short, some Ivy League prick kept hitting on your mom, regardless of the fact that we were clearly there together."

"This guy was a smoke show," Mom said.

"Hey!" Dad frowned.

"*And* he was massive. At least a foot taller than your dad and a hundred pounds heavier — all muscle."

"I had muscle," Dad said, taking an angry sip from his coffee.

"Anyway, this guy just kept on, but I was handling it. Look, if I didn't want someone's attention, I wasn't afraid of them thinking I was a b-i-t-c-h when I told them to get lost."

"You can say *bitch*, Mom," I interjected.

She ignored me and continued. "But toward the end of the night, when I went to turn in our shoes, this guy caught me at the counter and put his arm around me. Your dad couldn't see straight, nor could he think straight, because he just ripped the guy off me and plowed his fist right into his nose."

My jaw dropped. "*Dad?*"

Mom looked almost proud as she nodded. "Oh, yeah. Laid him out flat and then we were thrown out of the bowling alley. We weren't allowed to go back, either. The guy tried to press charges, too, but luckily for us the judge could see they were just a couple of stupid kids."

"Not that the judge's verdict helped me with your mom at all," Dad piped in. "Because she'd completely written me off."

"I was so done," she agreed. "I told him I refused to spend my life with a pig-headed macho man who wouldn't respect me when I asked him to back off and let me handle myself."

My stomach turned with how familiar that sounded, and how being on the listening end of someone else's story made me feel a different way about that decision.

"But you took him back," I said, because clearly.

Mom sighed, smiling at Dad. "After taking a few weeks to cool down, yes, I did."

"What changed your mind?" I asked.

"I didn't really change my mind," she said. "I still thought he was a big dummy for acting that way and I told him that. But I realized that as much as I was annoyed by what he did, I also found it kind of sweet. I liked that he wanted to protect me. I liked that he cared about me so much that he couldn't think straight and that he'd literally punched someone in the nose."

I smiled a little, remembering how I'd felt seeing Leo lay Nero out on the ground. I'd been horrified, angry, and yet...

It had also been quite hot.

"What she's forgetting to say is that she finally stopped being so stubborn and ignoring my flowers and phone calls and desperate apologies enough to see that I was crazy about her," Dad said. "Literally. I loved her so much I did crazy things, like punch dudes twice my size."

"In the end, what I realized more than anything was that while it wasn't the way I wanted the situation handled, it *was* how your dad showed he loved me. He didn't punch that guy for his own satisfaction," Mom said. "He did it because he saw someone touching me when I didn't want to be touched."

"I saw my girl being threatened," Dad amended. "And I didn't care about anything else but protecting her."

"Ew," I said with a laugh. "That's so weird but also sweet?"

Dad beamed like I'd called him a superhero.

"Anyway," Mom continued, turning to face me. "All I'm saying is that maybe in a weird, caveman way... this was Leo showing his affection for you."

"He lost you once, remember?" Dad added. "Does it not make sense that, now that he had his chance with you again, he would be a little crazy at the thought of someone you trusted hurting you the way Nero did?"

I pressed a hand to where my chest felt like it was splitting in half.

Why did it make so much sense when my father said it? And why was I just now realizing that my stubbornness came from my mother — the very one I'd always dug my heels in to defy?

"Let me ask you this," Mom said when I didn't respond to them. "Do you still care about him?"

I nodded.

"And does it make you sick to think of losing him?" Dad asked.

My eyes filled with tears on another nod.

Mom chuckled, grabbing my arms in her hands and giving me a little shake. "Then forgive him, stubborn girl. And believe him when he says he's learned his lesson. Trust me — you can do much worse than a man who loves you so much he can't see straight."

That made me burst into tears, and Mom pulled me into a hug. Dad was enveloping us both in the next breath, and I felt like a little girl again. It gave me permission to fall apart.

When I could catch my breath again, I swiped the tears from my face. "I'm scared," I admitted.

"Well, obviously," Dad said. "Why do you think you pushed him away in the first place? This was never about the fight with Nero."

"It's about the fact that you're in deep," Mom chimed in. "And it scares you to death. So, to combat that fear, you pretend like you're in control. You push him away just to prove that you can."

"It's like you understand the feeling or something," Dad mused.

Mom nudged him with a smile.

Then, my phone rang.

It made all of us jump because I had the ringer turned all the way up. And when we all looked down to find Leo's name on the screen, Mom swatted my knee.

"Speak of the devil," she said.

I just blinked, heart in my throat as I stared at the photograph on my screen. It was us on the couch at The Pit, me in Leo's hoodie that I was still wearing now and him wrapping me up from behind. He was kissing my cheek while I laughed and tried to shove him off me. It was dark and grainy and blurry. It was him who'd taken the picture even though I'd threatened him not to.

It was my favorite now.

I picked up the phone with numb fingers, and Dad kissed my hair before grabbing Mom's hand and tugging her inside to leave me alone.

I tapped the green button on the screen to accept the call.

And then Leo was there.

He looked so good it hurt.

He must have just had a shower because his hair was slightly damp, a bit mussed, his jaw freshly shaven. There were dark bags under his eyes, but they lit up when I answered, and he sucked in a breath of surprise, dropping his chains that he'd been chewing on.

"Hi," he breathed.

My heart.

It squeezed so painfully tight I hiccupped.

"Hi," I said.

Leo licked his bottom lip, shaking his head. "I'm sorry, I... I know I said I'd leave you alone. And I am. I will," he amended. "I just..."

He swallowed, unable to finish the thought. And for a moment, we just stared at each other, as if the other wasn't real.

"Can you check your mail?" he finally said. "I sent you something."

I frowned, getting up and pulling the blanket snug around me as I padded inside. Dad always dumped the mail on the kitchen counter before Mom would sort through it, and everything was already in neat piles.

There was a large, thick envelope addressed to me.

I propped the phone against a candle and carefully opened it, pulling out a brick red jersey with gold trim sleeves.

"The rivalry game is in two days," he said as I unfolded it. I held it up, using it as a barrier to cover my smile when I saw that it was his jersey, the number thirteen and his last name sprawled across the back.

I lowered it, finding Leo staring back at me hopefully.

"I have a ticket waiting for you at will call," he said. And before I could reply, he hurriedly added, "You don't have to come. I understand if you don't want to. I just... I wanted you to know that you have a ticket." He swallowed, shaking his head. "No, I wanted you to know that I *want* you to be there."

I swallowed, looking down at the jersey in my hands with my parents' words circling in my mind.

"I'm sorry I went back on my promise to leave you alone," he said, the corner of his mouth crooking up a bit. "But to be fair, I warned you I'd likely leave you disappointed."

Someone yelled his name in the background, and he cursed just as Palico hopped up onto the table. I carefully draped the jersey over the back of one of our dining chairs and pulled the cat into my arms.

"I have to go," Leo said. "We're—"

The phone was snatched out of his hand then, and after a dizzying blur, Kyle was staring back at me.

"Mary!" He gasped. "*Palico!*"

That caused a scuffle behind him, and then Braden and Blake were flanking his sides, all battling to fill the screen.

"Palico!" Braden and Blake said in unison, and then they were all fussing over the cat, telling it how much they missed it while I bit back a smile and held her at the right angle for them to adore her.

"We miss you, too, Mary," Braden said. "I need my yoga buddy."

"And I need to know how you ever kept this place clean," Blake added grimly. "Because we're struggling here."

"Pancakes on Sunday morning aren't the same without you," Kyle added, and with each word they said, my eyes stung more.

"Miss you guys, too," I managed.

Leo wrangled the phone back, and after punching each of his roommates in the arm, he looked down at the screen. "Sorry about that."

I smiled. "It's okay."

Another long silence fell between us. I wanted to say something, but I didn't know what. I still hadn't sorted through all the thoughts swimming in my head, so I just stared at him with the fiercest longing in my chest.

"You're wearing my hoodie," he said.

I glanced down at where I held Palico in my arms, the blanket on the ground at my feet now. Then, I looked back at the screen and helplessly shrugged, still unable to put words to anything.

Of course, I'm wearing your hoodie, I wanted to say. *I'm pretending its arms wrapped around me are you.*

"Okay, well. I'll let you go," Leo finally said. He swallowed, opening his mouth like he wanted to say something else. But he closed it again.

"Good luck at the game," I managed.

He nodded, and just before the call was cut, I saw his face twist like it physically pained him to end it.

I sat Palico down then, picking up the jersey again and smoothing the fabric between my fingers. I brought it to my nose, inhaling, but it was brand new and didn't smell like anything at all, let alone like the player it represented.

But I remembered that smell, even without it being present.

Leo was a part of me — his scent, the way his arms felt around me, the vibration of his deep-chested laugh, the softness of his heart.

And I was finally ready to admit what I'd known all along.

I was terrified of him hurting me again, of losing him, of giving him my trust only to end up with a broken heart.

But I didn't have a choice in the matter.

It was a risk I would take, one I couldn't escape, because the alternative was to give him up now.

And I couldn't do that.

I loved him.

I *loved* him.

The realization shocked me so much I nearly fell over, but at the same time, it was as if it had been there all along. It was like my brain was saying, "Duh, bitch," while I grappled with the new discovery.

I still had so much to figure out. I still wanted to hold Nero responsible for what he did to me, for what he probably did to others. I still had to figure out where I went from here, what my future held.

But I knew that regardless of how any of that unfolded, I wanted to do it all with Leo by my side.

Something between a laugh and a sob ripped out of me, and I covered my mouth, shaking my head as I stared at the jersey still in my other hand.

Then, I picked up my phone again, dialing the group chat on a video call.

Julep answered first, and then Riley, with Giana's screen going black at first before her sleepy face came into view, her hair a wild bird's nest. When they were all there, I propped the phone against the candle again and held up the jersey.

"Alright," I said. "How the hell do I style this thing?"

I was met with a chorus of delighted screams.

Chapter 39

LEO

The South Hartford University's football stadium was so loud my ears were already ringing.

Our rivalry had grown over the years, and any time we came to their turf, we were greeted by loud jeers from their fans, a shitty locker room, and a team full of massive guys just itching to take us to the ground.

North Boston University was a tough team, but we were also trained to respect our opponents and the schools we visited. SHU, on the other hand, wasn't above playing dirty. They wanted to hurt us. They'd love to see one of us benched after a play where we were knocked down hard. And above everything, they wanted to win.

But so did we.

The locker room had been quiet after warmups, with our training staff taping up the last of the players as the rest of us bounced to stay warm. I could feel the nerves of everyone, especially Blake, and I'd jumped up on one of the benches to call everyone together.

"This may not be our house, but this is our win. Our season. Our chance to prove we're not a one and done championship team. Nearly everyone in this stadium wants to see us lose, along with most of the country. No one wants to cheer for the team that's already on top." I'd grinned then, hitting my chest. "But that's just too fucking bad for them."

The locker room had roared, and when Clay jumped up beside me and started a chant, we fired up past all the nerves, running through the tunnel and out onto the field like it was our university instead of SHU.

Our fans had shown up for us, rivaling the *boos* that came from South Hartford as we ran out. I loved knowing we were taking up almost half the space, that it wasn't a house full of their fans like it usually was. But when I quickly glanced at the NBU friends and family section and didn't see Mary, my stomach dropped.

Her seat was empty.

I tried to ignore it, mouth clamped shut as I jogged out with the rest of the team. I only had a moment on the sideline before it was time for me to join the refs in the middle of the field for the coin toss.

I chanced a glance again.

Still empty.

I couldn't shake off that second look. I stared at the seat with my heart beating loud in my ears.

I thought she'd come.

She'd answered my call. That alone had given me more hope than it probably should have. To see her still wearing my hoodie? That had me flying high. And she'd smiled. She'd told me good luck. She hadn't said she would be here but…

I'd stupidly believed without a doubt that she would be.

"Captain," the ref said, and I blinked, finding him and the player from the other team watching me like they saw just how stupid I was.

"Tails," I said when I realized they were waiting for my call.

The coin was flipped. We won. We deferred. And then, the game began.

Other than checking the stands every two seconds to see if Mary had shown, I was locked in and focused on the game. Calling it a game at all felt wrong.

It was a blood bath, a battle, a *war*.

Our defense held them to three and out on their first drive, and then with a sick return from Zeke, we managed to score with our first possession. That only fired SHU up more, and two plays into our next possession, Kyle was taken down in a ghastly tackle that had him rolling on the ground in pain.

It was a concussion. I knew without having to hear it confirmed.

Our training staff helped him up and he walked off the field, all the way back through the tunnel to the locker room. We knew he wasn't coming back.

And now, we were down our best tight end.

The momentum shifted to South Hartford, and they scored on their next drive before picking off Blake and getting a defensive touchdown, too.

It went on like this, back and forth, both teams grinding like it was the championship game right now instead of a rivalry. We were all beat up when we limped into the locker room at halftime, and we were down by ten.

I expected Blake to feel defeated already. He'd been picked off twice. He surprised me in the locker room, though, huddling the team together and reminding us what we were fighting for.

With us having first possession of the second half, we drove down strong and steady for a touchdown.

And still, Mary wasn't in the stands.

Defense was battling, trying to hold South Hartford to a kick when Zeke came and put a hand on my shoulder on the sideline.

"You okay, man?"

I nodded, but couldn't verbally assure him or myself. I was here. I was locked into the game.

But I also *wasn't* here, not really.

My head was wherever she was.

"It's not over," he said, a bit lower this time. "Maybe she just needs more time."

I tried with everything in me not to break down and cry when he said it.

With another nod, I faced him. "Let's just win this game."

"Damn right," he said, slapping my helmet before he jogged over to Riley.

The longer the game went, the more grueling it became, and the crowd was so alive with energy it was impossible not to buzz right along with them. I was having a monster game, and everything was going right for us — but we were still down by six by the time we got the ball back in the fourth quarter.

There was just over two minutes left.

It was do or die.

I pulled my helmet on, jogging out onto the field after Zeke got us the best return he could. Even with it, we still had sixty-three yards to drive down the field for a touchdown. A kick wouldn't win or even tie. It *had* to be a touchdown.

As I huddled with Blake and the rest of the offense, listening to him call our first play, I felt an all-encompassing Zen wash over me. It was like all the noise cleared out, the cheers falling mute, my breaths steadying, and even Blake sounded like he was whispering instead of shouting over the noise of the fans.

We have this, I said to myself, and I felt it deep down in my fucking soul.

Without thinking, I looked up over Blake's head to the empty seat in the stands.

But it wasn't empty anymore.

Mary was there now, her long blonde hair shining in the last bit of sunlight and giving her away. When she realized I was looking at her, she climbed up to stand in her seat, taller than the sea of fans around her.

She was wearing my jersey.

Even from the distance, I could make out her smile, and it made my heart skip a beat before it kicked back to life and raced like a motherfucking horse.

Slowly, her hands lifted over her head, holding a large white sign with black marker lettering.

Dibs on #13.

I couldn't contain it. A laugh that was something more of a cry rushed out of me, and Blake paused where he'd been calling the play. He followed my gaze over his shoulder, and then gave me a knowing grin when he turned back to the group.

"Let's win this," he said to us, and then he nodded his head at me. "Some of us have a girl to impress."

A few of the guys thumped me on the helmet, making smart-ass remarks that I took with the goofiest grin I'd ever worn stretching my face. They could hound on me all they wanted to. Nothing could get to me, not now that she was here.

We clapped our hands and sprinted to our spots on the line with seven seconds left on the play clock.

Just before the ball was snapped, I looked back up to Mary in the stands.

She had my number on her chest.

And my heart in her hands.

Chapter 40

MARY

I was so out of breath by the time I made it to my seat in the stadium that I was seeing black spots at the edges of my vision. After being stuck on the highway due to an accident that shut down all three lanes, I'd spent the last two hours cursing and praying and then speeding to get here with literally two minutes left in the game.

That didn't stop me from standing on my chair and making sure Leo saw that I was here.

I collapsed back down into my seat just in time for their first play of the drive. Before this season, I knew absolutely nothing about football — mostly because I'd avoided it at all costs, thanks to Leo. But after playing Madden with the guys and going to a few games now, I was picking it up.

It was the penalties that always confused me.

That's why when the whistle blew after Leo picked up an impressive nineteen yards and they called holding on the offense, I was confused, watching them move fifteen yards *back* instead of the nineteen yards Leo had moved them forward.

I cursed under my breath, looking at the time on the clock and the score with a pit in my stomach.

Maybe I was bad luck.

It *would* be the first rivalry game I attend that they lose.

"God, Leo Hernandez is so fucking hot."

I blinked, finding the source of the comment that snapped me out of my daze belonging to a girl sitting in the seat in front of me. She shook her head, her red ponytail swinging a bit as she nudged her friend. She was wearing Leo's jersey, too, but hers was an older version.

"We made out after the rivalry game last year," she said proudly. "Think lightning can strike twice?"

Her friend snorted. "I'll pray for you. I'm still in mourning that Clay Johnson is off the market."

The first girl sighed with her. "Yeah. That jagged pill will never be easy to swallow."

I couldn't bite back the smile that stretched on my face. I also couldn't wait to tell Giana. But more than anything, I couldn't wait to show that first girl just how wrong she was about where Leo would be after the game.

The ball was hiked, and Blake was sacked.

The crowd was a mixture of *ohhs* from our fans and cheers from South Hartford. I grimaced, looking at how we now had twenty-one yards to go on a second down with just over a minute left to play. SHU fans were already getting ready to celebrate their win, blowing air horns and pops of confetti. Neither were allowed at NBU, and now that I realized how annoying they were, I understood why.

I kept my eyes on the field, on Leo, biting my thumbnail and chanting a silent prayer.

Come on, come on.

The ball was snapped, and this time, Blake found a receiver — but they were still eight yards short of the first down.

And now, it was third down.

"Fuck," someone yelled beside me.

"We're toast," someone else said.

"Nah, we got this. We'll get the first here."

"There's less than a minute to play. We have the whole fucking field to go."

"God, walking out of here is going to *suck* if we lose."

The chatter was too loud to ignore, and when Coach Lee called a timeout from the sidelines, I let out as much of an exhale as I could, stretching out my fingers I didn't realize I'd been wringing together.

The team huddled around Blake, all of them talking adamantly. I noticed he and Leo were having a particularly heated exchange, and after a moment, Leo crossed the huddle and put his hands on Blake's helmet. He said something to him before tapping his own helmet against his quarterback's, and Blake watched him for a moment before nodding.

The team looked a little nervous as they clapped and got back on the line, and once again, my stomach tightened into a thick, knotted ball.

Leo lined up at the far edge of the field.

And as the play clock ticked down, he stood straight and pointed directly at me with a smirk I knew was there even through his face mask.

"Oh, my God!" the girl in front of me squealed, clutching her friend's arm. "Did you see that?! He pointed at me!"

I rolled my eyes, laughing to myself as Leo crouched back down. And when the ball was snapped, he took off down the field as fast and sleek as a leopard.

"Wait, what the fuck?" someone said.

"Why is our running back jetting down the field without the ball?"

"Fuck, O-line is crumbling. He's going to get sacked!"

"Wait!"

"Oh shit, it's a Hail Mary!"

It felt like the entire stadium — no, the entire *world* — fell silent the moment Blake launched the ball into the air. He was taken down to the ground as soon as it left his hands, and then everyone followed the ball as it sailed through the air toward the other side of the field.

The other side of the field where Leo was now sprinting.

The defense caught on too slow, most of the coverage on the receivers they thought Blake was trying to hit. No one noticed Leo until it was too late, and even though their fastest player caught up to him, it wasn't enough to block the catch.

Leo leapt up into the end zone and plucked the ball from the air, cradling it to him as he tucked and rolled. He controlled it the entire way, popping back up to stand and holding the ball victoriously with one hand.

Touchdown.

The stadium went ape shit. The team swarmed him, Braden and Clay picking him up and carrying him like a king as he celebrated. But then they had to get off the field, clearing it so Riley could make the game-winning extra point.

And she did.

There were only nine seconds left on the clock when we punted the ball back to SHU, but they couldn't do anything with it. And while all their fans sat in shock and disbelief at what had occurred, ours went absolutely insane.

The game had no sooner ended before the field was swarming with players, staff, and media alike. Leo had cameras and reporters all around him as he shook hands with some players from the other team, but he looked up and found me through the madness.

I smiled, standing in my chair again and holding up the sign I'd made.

He pulled off his helmet, and I saw the flash of his teeth before he was sprinting.

Leo shoved through the crowd, declining every microphone that was thrust in his face as he made a beeline for the section I was in. With a running start, he leapt over the concrete wall that separated the stands from the field, and then he was taking the bleacher steps two at a time.

My heart raced in my ears with every step.

I had only a second to laugh at the girl in front of me who about passed out thinking Leo was running to her before he barreled right past and into my row. He muttered *excuse me* to the people he had to shimmy past, all who were clapping him on the shoulder and congratulating him on the win.

After that, I was swept into his arms.

Leo crushed me to him, lifting me all the way off the ground as he did. I wrapped my arms fiercely around him, squeezing my eyes shut as we both exhaled in relief at finally being together again. I clung to him like he would disappear, and he held me tight enough to bruise. I faintly registered the fans cheering around us as Leo pulled back enough to capture my mouth with his own.

It was a kiss I felt all the way down to my toes. It stirred my desire as much as it soothed my aching heart. It was the feeling of coming home after a long trip. It was Christmas morning and a sunset on the beach. It was a night spent between the sheets and a day of perfect sunshine.

It was Leo, and it was me.

It was *us*.

I never knew how much power we held until that kiss showed it to me.

"I'm so sorry," Leo yelled over the noise, his chest heaving. He still held me so close, like he was afraid I'd disappear. "I'm so fucking sorry."

"I'm sorry, too," I yelled in return. "I'd just been assaulted, and I lost my job, and I…" My chest ached at how stupid I'd been. "I just took out all that fear on you, on top of already being scared of us. I took it out on you because I wanted to have control over something. I took it out on you because—"

"You never have to apologize to me," he said, shaking his head and silencing me with a kiss. "You can take anything out on me because you know what? I can handle it. I can take it. I can go to war for you, or *with* you, if it's what you need."

I choked on something of a laugh at that. "I'm a mess," I said. "And I hate to scare you off now that I have you again, but I'm afraid I'm like my mother."

Leo frowned, confused.

"I'm stubborn," I clarified. "And something tells me it'll only get worse with age."

Leo smiled at that, letting out a long exhale like he'd just remembered to breathe. He brushed my hair back, tilting my chin.

"No matter what life throws at us, what you throw at *me* — we will make it. Just stay," he said, kissing me again. "That's all I need. Stay, and I promise, no matter what happens, I'll make it right."

"You may regret those words one day," I warned him, knowing the chaotic disaster I tended to be.

But Leo shook his head, his lips finding mine as he lifted me again.

"Never," he promised.

And I believed him — with every messy inch of my heart.

Chapter 41

LEO

"I think you might actually rub my skin raw if you keep kissing me like that," Mary said, her sleepy smile the most beautiful thing I'd ever seen as I trailed soft, lazy kisses over her shoulder.

"I'm counting," I said, planting another. "And until I get to a thousand, you're stuck here."

She chuckled, pulling me back down into the sheets with her so that my next kiss was on her mouth.

I hadn't even had to say a word to Blake after the game for him to pack up his shit and leave the room we'd been assigned to at the hotel. He *had* cracked a joke or two to Mary on his way out, but I was thankful that he knew we'd want the night alone together, that he hadn't made a big deal of it. We were teammates, brothers, and I knew he'd sleep on a pullout couch in another room if he had to.

As soon as we were alone, it'd been a blur of clothes being shed. We were both so starved for each other that we skipped over foreplay altogether, and I was fucking her into the mattress within five minutes. We both came fast, sweating and panting and clinging to each other like we'd had our first sip of water after walking in the desert for a week.

But we were still thirsty.

I felt it in every long, slow, intentional touch from her as we laid in bed after our shower. Neither of us bothered to put clothes on again, and I reveled in the feel of her body pressed against mine, in the bite of metal from her piercings, the softness of her thighs sandwiching mine between them.

"God, I was miserable without you," I confessed into her neck.

She squeezed me tighter. "I was a mess, too."

"I thought I'd lost you again. I thought..." I shook my head, and then I was pulling her in closer, like even a centimeter of space between us was too much. "Have I apologized enough yet? Because I really want to say *I'm sorry* another million times. Oh! I could start saying it in Spanish. *Lo siento. Lo siento mucho.*"

Mary kissed my hair. "Save your apologies for the next time I'm a stubborn witch."

"Witch," I mused with a laugh, leaning up on my elbows so I could look down at her. "That's pretty accurate, considering the spell you have me under."

"Mmm," she mused, trailing her fingertip down my chest. "I wonder what I can use my powers to make you do..."

"I think at this point we know the answer to that is *anything.*"

Mary bit her lip, shaking her head on a long, sated sigh. She kept trailing lines on my skin, her expression softening. "So... what now?"

"What do you want?"

"To be together," she said, lifting her eyes to mine. "*Really* be together."

"As if there was another option."

She smiled a bit. "I just mean... I know there's a possibility of you getting drafted. And, if you do..."

I arched a brow, waiting. "Say it. What do you want, Mary?"

She glared at me, but her smile broke through. "You're such an ass."

"I just like to hear my girl confess how badly she wants me," I argued with a roll of my hips into her. I was covering her in kisses again as she wrapped her arms around me, her soft laugh the sweetest sound.

"Fine," she conceded, making me stop with a hand pressing against my chest. "I want to go with you."

"Say it again."

"I want to go with you," she said louder, pinching me in the side. "You cocky sonofabitch."

I resisted the urge to make a joke about just how cocky I could be — mostly because I was high off her saying she wanted to go with me if I was drafted.

When I was drafted.

"What else?" I asked.

She considered. "Well, I want to figure out a way to tattoo wherever we end up."

"You will."

Mary didn't seem as confident. "Before I can move forward, I have to deal with what happened with Nero." She curled into me a little then. "I think... I think I want to talk to the other girls at the shop, see if any of them went through what I did. My word against his isn't much, but if there are more than us?"

I nodded.

"And... God, it makes me sick to consider, but... I think I need to tell his wife."

"I'm with you," I said. "Whatever you want to do. And I promise not to punch the fucker in the face again. Or any other place — even though I still stand firm that he deserves a dick punch."

Mary laughed. "I have a confession."

"Mm?"

"I actually found it *really* hot when you laid him out."

My jaw dropped. "And you made me pay for it with weeks of misery?!"

"Just because it turned me on didn't mean I wasn't still pissed!"

"It turned you on?" I smirked against her skin. "In that case, I take back what I said about it never happening again."

I smothered her with another round of kisses while she squirmed, and I knew I could stay just like that, in bed with her, forever, and I would live the happiest life.

"I don't know what will happen with him, if anything. And I reserve the right to change my mind," she said. "But... I want to at least try. I don't want him to keep doing this to other girls."

I nodded, leaning up on my elbow so I could brush her hair from her face. "I'm with you. And, when you *do* have your own chair again, I have a long list of clients for you."

Mary frowned.

"The entire NBU football team."

At that, she laughed. "Right."

"I'm serious. They love your work. They all want in. So, when you have a chair again, you'll be busy."

"*If* I have a chair again."

"You will. In fact, when I get signed, you can bet your sweet ass that fat signing bonus I get will go to opening up your own shop."

Mary bit her lip. "I have always wanted to open my own... I was thinking maybe one with all female artists. A real bad bitch spot. Palico could be our shop cat."

"See? That asshole can't keep you down for long."

"I'd never use your money for it, though."

"Like you have a choice," I said. "Besides, it's our money."

"We're not married, Leo."

My tongue hurt from how hard I had to hold it back from saying *yet*.

"If you get a bonus, you should invest it."

"Nah, too safe," I said, but I was done talking, and I let her know with a slow trail of my fingers down her shoulder and over the swells of her breasts. Her breath caught when I thumbed her piercing, her nipple pebbling beneath the touch.

"What happens if you don't get drafted," she managed through a raspy breath. "And I never tattoo again?"

I shrugged. "We sell everything we own and move to a new country and figure out who we want to be next." I flipped her until she was on her back, until I was between her legs. "Wherever we go, whatever we do, you belong to me," I said, kissing along her jaw. "And I belong to you."

Mary grabbed my face in her hands, stopping me so I had no choice but to look at her.

"I love you," she said.

My chest squeezed, heart throbbing inside it. "Fuck, I love to hear that."

"I love you," she repeated, wrapping her legs around me and pulling me flush against her.

"*Te amo, cariño,*" I echoed, claiming her mouth with a hard, demanding kiss.

She opened for me then, letting my tongue sweep in to dance with hers as her hips widened. She was already wet, my cock sliding between her lips and making us both inhale on a groan. But I'd ravaged her once tonight in a frenzy.

Now, I wanted to take my time.

"Come here," I rasped, climbing off of her and the bed altogether. I stood at the edge of it, stroking my cock where she'd slicked me with her desire.

Mary's eyes were glued to my fist as I pumped, her breasts heaving, every curve of her on display in the sheets where she waited for my instruction.

"Lie on your back," I said. "I want your head right here."

I pointed to the edge of the bed in front of me, and she maneuvered herself down, shimmying until she was lying under me with her eyes cast up and waiting again.

She was so fucking gorgeous it hurt.

Her knees were together, as if she was suddenly shy, but her hands still roamed her body, plucking at her piercings and trailing every lush curve. I let my eyes roam slowly over every color of ink that sprawled her skin — black and blue and red and green, bright orange and deep violet. My chest hummed with possession as I did, like a king marveling at his riches.

"Scoot up," I told her. "Hang your head off the bed."

Mary did as I told her to, and I cursed at the sight of her throat arched, her body stretching out even more across the white sheets.

"Now," I said, carefully cradling her head in one hand as I fisted myself in the other. "Open that pretty mouth."

She did, sticking out her pink tongue as a welcome sign. I stepped in closer, guiding my crown to her mouth. I slicked it with her tongue in slow, torturous circles that elicited a deep groan from me and a desperate whimper from Mary before I slowly pressed inside, all the way until her lips had no choice but to wrap around me.

"Fuck," I cursed, closing my eyes and letting my head fall back at the sensation. I wasn't even a third of the way inside her, but the sight of her stretched out, the angle, the feel of her tongue as it swirled around me... it was enough to make me come right then.

Mary's hands reached for my ass to pull me in deeper, and I let her, flexing a bit more until she gagged. I pulled out then, letting her catch her breath. Then, I was hinging at the waist, my cock hard and hovering at her mouth, waiting for her to take it again, all while I kissed along her breasts, her stomach, until my tongue could reach her clit.

She shook violently at the first taste, and I braced my knees against the edge of the mattress to hold myself steady as she played with my crown again, matching my teases against her clit. I licked and she swirled, I sucked and she gagged. It was a sweet, sadistic game of cat and mouse, both of us teasing the other to see who would break first.

When Mary bucked her hips against my mouth, giving me no choice but to run my tongue flat and hot along the length of her, she shuddered beneath me, moaning around where my cock was in her mouth.

"Does my girl need more?" I teased, breathing against her before I licked her in a long, hot sweep again.

"Please," she begged, and she barely got the word out before I held onto her thighs and buried my face between them.

I ate her pussy like a starved man, licking and sucking and slowly inching one finger inside her to curl along with the rhythm my tongue was stroking against her. I couldn't even focus on the way she was teasing me, because my singular focus had shifted to her pleasure.

"Focus, baby," I told her with another flick of my tongue. "Can you come for me again tonight?"

A whimpered, "*Yes*," floated into the air like a spell.

Mary still licked along my shaft as I played with her, but when I curled two fingers inside and sucked her clit in the way I knew gave her the right amount of friction, I felt her focus shift, too. She was still sucking me, but it was lazy and slow, distracted, all while her hips widened, her knees stretching open, pelvis bucking up to reach for her release.

"That's it," I praised her. "Find it. I want these legs shaking for me. I want to hear you scream."

She moaned, and then she pulled her mouth away from my shaft so I could soak up every sigh and whimper and cry as I found the right spot to make her shatter.

My name was a repeated prayer on her lips as she did, and her hands fisted in my hair, holding me to her as she ground her hips against me. I grabbed her thigh tighter with my free hand, the other working inside her in time with my mouth on her clit. And only when she sagged into the bed like dead weight did I stop, carefully removing my fingers as she shuddered and clung to me like I was all that held her from floating off into space.

"Good girl," I breathed against her, pressing a light kiss to her clit that made her shake again.

"Fuck," she breathed, her eyes hooded as I stood again. But when she went to move, I pressed her back into the sheets.

"Not yet, *mi alma*," I said, sweeping her hair from her face. "I want to fuck that sweet mouth."

Mary licked her lips, coating them before she opened wide and stuck out her tongue for me again. She was already pulling me to her before I could wrap a fist around myself, like she was starved for *me* now.

I let her take control, groaning as she slicked me and took me in inch by blissful inch. She could still only get a little under half of me inside before she'd gag, but she used her hands and worked them in time with her mouth in a torturous rhythm that had me flexing into her, my toes curling on the hotel carpet.

"Hang your head off more," I told her, using my hands in her hair as a guide. "Arch for me, baby. Open your throat."

When she did, I palmed her breasts, squeezing the ample softness and toying with her piercings with each thumb. She squirmed under the touch, moaning around my shaft. It sent a vibration through me that made my knees buckle.

"Fuck, yes," I praised. "Just like that. Can you open more for me?"

She arched even more, and carefully, I moved my hands to her head. My fingers wound into her hair, and I stroked her in calming touches as I started to shift control to me, holding her still as I worked myself in and out of her mouth.

"I want to see my cock stretching your throat," I told her, still moving slow and easy. "I'm going to fuck you deeper, baby, and I want you to take it. Hold me deep as long as you can."

She moaned around me again, affirming that she wanted it, too. Her hands grabbed my ass to pull me in a bit more, but I still held the control. Slowly at first, I pulled her mouth off me and then slid her back down, watching as she arched and opened as much as she could underneath me. I groaned at the sight of my cock bulging in her throat when I pressed deeper, and even though she gagged, she still held me to her, telling me she was okay.

The deeper I went, the more I lost control, flexing my hips with every thrust into her. She moaned and gagged but never faltered, and the sight of her stretched out, her tits bouncing as I fucked her throat — it sent me.

I slid in deep, holding myself inside her as the first pulse of heat vibrated through me. "God*damn*, Stig," I managed on a breath, and then I was pumping my release inside her, small flexes of my hips stretching out the release as I felt every inch of her tongue on me, her throat constricting around my shaft, her lips tight and warm.

I shook, knees giving out, and made noises no grown man should make as I came. She soaked up every drop like it was hard earned, not letting me pull away until I was completely drained and near collapsing. Mary gagged a little when I finally did pull out, and then I was on the floor, and she rolled over onto her stomach, hair a wild halo around her as she smiled and wiped her lips.

"Damn," she said, breathless. "That was fucking hot."

I barked out a laugh, body still spasming. "You should have seen it from my point of view."

The little minx crawled off the bed and down onto the floor with me, and I hadn't even caught my breath before she was straddling me and kissing me hard with intent.

"Please tell me you can get hard again," she breathed against my lips. "Because that turned me on so fucking much."

I laughed against her lips. "You're insatiable."

"*Please*, Leo," she said, running her hand down to grip me. I didn't know how it was possible, but slowly, as she pumped me, I grew in her hand. "I want to ride you. I want to feel you."

I groaned, maneuvering us until my back was against the bed for support. That was all the confirmation Mary needed before she was pressing up onto her knees, lining me up at her entrance.

With her heated eyes locked on mine, she sank down.

She was wet and relaxed from her orgasm, from bringing me mine, and she took half of me in on that first flex, making us both see stars.

Mary moaned loudly, nails biting into my shoulders as she lifted and dropped down more. In four rolls, she had me all the way inside her, and she shook around me, her walls tightening, lips frantic where they met mine.

"Touch me," she pleaded. "I'm so close."

I palmed her breasts roughly, massaging them as she bounced wildly on my lap. When I rolled her piercings between my fingers and thumbs, she screamed, and this time it was loud enough for me to cover her mouth with one hand. I knew Coach wasn't stupid enough to think we never had girls in our room, but I didn't need him finding out about tonight — nor any of the scouts staying here, either.

Mary didn't care. She just rode me harder, tilting her hips so her clit rubbed against me as I flexed inside her. And then she was quivering, moaning, almost crying as she found her release. I didn't think I'd be able to join her, but watching her surrender completely, feeling her tighten around me without a barrier between us, hearing her sweet moans… it was too much.

I captured her mouth with mine just as the first of my orgasm caught, and at this point I didn't even know if I had anything to release into her, but my body clenched, and a delicious fire consumed me as I flexed and pumped whatever I did have left. Mary was still coming, too, and we moaned and held tight to each other, riding out the last of our climaxes before we both slumped into the floor.

It might have been a minute later. It might have been an hour. Somehow, at some point in time, Mary had crawled to stand and reached down for my hand, both of us moving slowly on our way to the shower. She'd run the water hot over both of us, and we'd taken turns washing each other between slow, promising kisses I knew I'd never tire of.

When we crawled back into bed, sore and sated and bone-tired, I curled myself around her, kissing her wet hair and inhaling everything that she was. My chest didn't ache for the first time in weeks. My breaths came easy. My heart was at peace.

"*Mi amor, mi cariño, mi cielo,*" I whispered against her neck between soft kisses. "I love you."

"I love you," she whispered back.

And in the quiet dark of that hotel room, I silently promised to never hurt her again, to never put her second to anything, to never let her push me away even when her defensive instinct told her to. I promised to do everything in my power to always make her stay, even when things got rough.

Mary Silver was finally mine.

It was the sweetest win of my life.

Epilogue

FIVE MONTHS LATER
MARY

Not a single one of us could hold our shit together when Julep walked down the aisle to Holden on April sixteenth.

It didn't matter that Giana, Riley, and I had helped her get dressed, that we'd already seen the way that elaborate cream lace hugged her body in a perfect hourglass shape. We still lost it when the doors opened at the back of the garden and she walked through them holding Coach Lee's arm.

The fact that *he* was crying might have been what made me lose it more than anything.

Julep's father beamed with pride just as much as he broke with heartache as he took the slow steps toward giving his daughter away. Julep's deep brown eyes were glossy, too — her hair swept up into a classic updo with curls and a thick braid, a small flower crown threaded through the strands, and a simple, yet gorgeous, pearl-drop necklace adorning her neck. She'd found the wedding dress at a thrift store, along with every accessory from her pearl-stud earrings to the designer high heels on her feet. Every piece was old and borrowed, and yet they looked as if they'd been made just for her.

And while everyone in that garden was transfixed by Julep, she couldn't take her eyes off Holden.

Sniffing back my tears, I glanced at where he was waiting for her, and immediately wished I hadn't. Because one look at him completely falling apart at the sight of his almost-wife made me cry again, too.

He was like a *GQ* model in his garnet tuxedo, the gold pocket square and trim making him look like an NBU legend. And I supposed he really was. The deep red against the lush green of the botanical garden was dreamy, like a fairytale. But he couldn't fight back his tears, and he pinched the bridge of his nose, shoulders shaking before he wiped his face and stood straighter with a smile like he couldn't believe he was so lucky.

That smile was aimed right at Julep.

When I looked back at her, she rolled her eyes on a playful laugh like she was making fun of him for crying, but she was a mess, too.

My eyes drifted to Leo then, who was standing behind Holden as his best man. He had the rings in his pocket and his eyes on me.

It was entirely unfair how he and the rest of the guys looked so good in their suits. We all knew they were hot in football pants and jerseys, but seeing them dressed to the nines was enough to make every girl in their vicinity feral. I wished I could say I was excluded, that I was immune, but watching Leo with that devilish smirk on his face and knowing I would get to strip him out of that suit later made my skin tingle with heat.

His eyes were hooded where they stared at me, as if he was saying without words that this would be us one day. I felt his possession in the air as if it were hands on my hips, and I bit my lip a little, tearing my gaze away from him to look down at my flowers before the whole garden of people caught on to our little show. Then again, I didn't have to look to know Zeke and Riley were eyeing each other the same way, and Giana and Clay, too.

When the music died as Julep reached the end of the aisle, there was a chorus of sniffles through the crowd, which made us all smile and wipe our faces and laugh a little at ourselves. Coach Lee gave his daughter's hand to Holden, who stared at her like every dream he'd ever had was coming true in that moment, and the ceremony began.

It was sweet and short, which didn't surprise me considering Julep hated being the center of attention. And when Holden dipped Julep back in a dramatic kiss to seal the deal, we all went wild, cheering and throwing rose petals over them as they walked back down the aisle.

Then, the party began.

Edison lights came to life as the sun went down, casting the garden in a beautiful glow as the band began to play and guests flooded to either the bar or the dance floor.

"I have to pee *so bad*," Giana said when we were free of our ceremonial duties, and she abandoned her bouquet on the wedding party table before practically running toward the bathroom.

"I need a shot," Riley chimed in. "I've never cried so much in my entire life."

"Besides when you realized how much you love me, right?" Zeke said, sliding up behind her. He wrapped his arms around her waist and pulled her back into his chest, and she smiled, leaning into the touch.

"Those were tears of frustration," she shot up at him.

"Oh, that's right. You were still pretending to hate me, huh?"

"Trust me — I didn't have to pretend very hard."

"Sure," Zeke said, nuzzling into her neck. She flushed and turned into him, and I looked away just as they started to kiss.

So much had happened in the last five months for all of us, it was almost dizzying.

The Rebels had gone on to have their first undefeated season since the nineties, sending them straight to the championship game. Sadly, they'd lost by a last-minute field goal, which had crushed all of us. But even with that loss, there wasn't a graduating senior who didn't get a call during the draft.

Every team in the NFL wanted a North Boston University recruit.

But while Clay, Kyle, Braden, and Leo had signed contracts with fat signing bonuses, Zeke had withdrawn himself completely.

It had shocked us all at first, but when he and Riley took us out to dinner and told us about their business plan, the only emotion we felt was ecstatic. They were working with the NFL to launch the Novo Football Coalition, a program dedicated to exposing young girls to football and giving them opportunities to play as they grew older. It was the first program the NFL was directly involved with that supported females stepping into the arena, and there was a partnership with the Women's Football Alliance to make a future in football for girls, too.

They had a long road to walk, one that we all knew would be bumpy and full of roadblocks. There were so many adversaries to women playing football in our country, but with Zeke and Riley behind the wheel, I had a feeling there was nothing they couldn't achieve. Maybe one day, there would be a Women's Super Bowl with two teams of bad ass bitches just like Riley.

I couldn't wait for that day.

We'd all told them we were there to help every step of the way, too. Some of the guys even forked over a big part of their signing bonus to help them get started. The first branch of their coalition was set to open in the fall right outside of Boston, and Riley's brother, Gavin, was to be general manager.

"There's my girl."

I bit my lip on a smile as Leo's arms wound around me from behind, his lips finding my neck before I was spun in his arms to face him. He trailed his eyes down every inch of me before making a deep noise in his throat.

"You in this fucking dress, Stig," he mused, shaking his head. "Remind me to keep you away from all roads. We don't need a car pile-up to ruin the wedding day."

"Shut up," I said swatting at him.

"No chance. Unless you think of a creative way to make me," he added with an arch of his brow. "Sitting on my face might work."

He kissed me before I could laugh at him, and I wrapped my arms around his neck, reveling in the way it felt to have him cling to me like I was all he ever wanted.

I was also now very distracted by the thought of following through on his invitation later.

Leo was drafted in the third round to the Minnesota Vikings. And while I was secretly hoping we'd end up somewhere hot and tropical, I was just ecstatic for Leo that his dream had come true. There was a high chance he'd end up starting in the fall, too, with how awful the Vikings' run game had been the past couple of years. They needed Leo, and he was all too happy to step in and step up.

As soon as he signed the paperwork, we were loading up a moving truck and heading to Minneapolis.

Leo's mom had moved with us, buying a place just outside the city because she couldn't bear the thought of being too far from her son. We'd welcomed her and the meals she loved to make for us, and my parents helped us move, too, before telling us we always had a place to stay when we wanted to visit Boston.

There was also a threat that we *would* be back for the holidays — and we were to bring Leo's mom with us.

Leo's relationship with his father was strengthening now, too, especially with Leo entering his career with the NFL. Nick was at our condo at least one weekend a month, running drills with Leo to prepare him for the season and walking him through everything he could expect once training camp started in the summer.

And as for me? I was busy renovating.

Because Leo *did*, in fact, buy me my first tattoo shop with his signing bonus.

Of course, the only way I allowed it was by him promising that he'd accept me paying him back once we were profitable. I still wasn't convinced he actually would, but I was thankful for the chance to try.

My emotions surrounding tattooing had been a tangled mess after what happened with Nero. Skill wise, I felt like I was bursting at the seams, like I had just cracked the code on my style and was so anxious to get started on my clientele that I would go insane if I didn't have my own chair. But mentally, I was shut down, afraid of my next move, of what might happen if I tried to work at another parlor in Boston while Leo and I waited to see what would happen in the draft.

For a while, I did nothing.

I allowed myself to come down off the crazy rollercoaster of everything that had happened, finding safety in Leo's arms. I'd moved back to The Pit, thanks to my roommates who were more than happy to welcome me and Palico back into their space, and I found my joy there with them through the holidays.

Once the new year rolled in, I decided it was time to pull myself out of the rubble and rebuild.

My first plan of going to the other girls at Moonstruck failed miserably. Half of them wouldn't talk to me at all, like I was a plague and if they so much as answered my texts, they'd be fired and blacklisted, too. The few I *did* manage to get a conversation out of denied Nero ever making them feel uncomfortable — even though I would have bet my life savings on them lying.

So, my final move was to tell his wife.

Arianna agreed to meet with me after I left an anonymous note with my phone number on the windshield of her car. I felt a little creepy reaching out that way, but I wanted her to know the story of what happened. She deserved at least that much. In the end, I couldn't control what happened to Nero. In a world set up for men to get away with shit like what he pulled, I didn't have a whole lot to work with.

I just had the truth, and the desperate hope that Arianna, at least, would believe me.

She'd been quiet when we met for coffee, and she wore dark sunglasses and a scarf that covered her head. When I'd finished, she cleared her throat and said she had to go.

I never heard from her again.

But two weeks later, there was a breaking news story about how Moonstruck Tattoos had been shut down after an anonymous tip to the police that the owner was laundering money for a local drug lord. Nero was arrested, his bail set so high he was sure to be stuck in jail until his court date.

He was served divorce papers while in custody.

I never did hear from Arianna again, and I could only grasp at straws when I tried to put the pieces together of what happened. But justice had been served, even if it wasn't in the way I wished it had been.

It was closure, and it set me free.

Now, all my time was spent at the shop, and I'd turned a drab, old brick building into my dream parlor, complete with an all-female crew of artists anxiously waiting for our grand opening.

I'd also instilled a little of my best friends into it — a pole for Julep, which she'd already tested and approved, a mini bookstore in the front corner for Giana, which she insisted on being the curator for, and an impressive art collection from local artists for Riley, each piece for sale with the artist taking all the profits. Palico loved spending her time there more than at our condo, since

I'd had a custom-built cat tree installed that consisted of various heights and textures.

There was also a gaming corner — a giant screen with an Xbox loaded with games for our clients and staff, alike.

That had been for me.

I just had a few final touches before it would all be ready, and we were planning to open the doors on the first day of summer.

"Alright," Giana said breathlessly when she returned from the bathroom. "Is the food out yet? I'm ready to *eat*."

"Me, too," Clay said salaciously, and he picked her up like she weighed nothing, scooping her and her long sage dress into his arms.

"You're a brute," she said through her laughter, but she clung to him with her rosy cheeks and let him carry her to the wedding party table where our dinner was being served.

The garden filled with cheers as Julep and Holden were introduced as husband and wife for the first time, and once they were seated at the table with us, the band played softly while the staff served a dinner fit for the president. Julep's mom had taken over so much of the planning that it didn't surprise me one bit. It felt like a southern ball, but with a boho touch.

Leo drew circles on my knee with his fingertips under the table, his other hand shoveling food into his mouth as we all talked and laughed through dinner.

It was the most bittersweet feeling, because we all knew that we wouldn't be together like this very often now that we were all spread out over the country. Riley and Zeke would be in Boston, Holden and Julep in

Charlotte, Clay and Giana in Denver since Clay had been drafted to the Broncos, and Leo and I would round out the stretch in Minneapolis.

Giana must have really been feeling it, because as our plates were being cleared and we were about to make our way to the dance floor, she started bawling.

"I'm sorry," she said, taking Clay's handkerchief when he offered it to her. She dabbed at the corner of her eyes, shaking her head, her wild curls bouncing with the movement. "I just... I love you all so much."

"We love you, too, G," I said, reaching over to squeeze her hand with mine.

"I bet some dancing will make you feel better," Julep said as she stood, and once again, I was breathless looking at her. She was the most beautiful bride.

"Psh, *I* know what will make her feel better," Clay argued, putting his arm around Giana. "A trip to the bookstore tomorrow. I saw you eyeing that little one downtown when we were on our way to the hotel."

Giana smiled up at him through bleary eyes. "You know the way to my heart."

"I think Clay only *pretends* like he does it for you when we all know what the kinky bastard really wants is more highlighted pages to re-enact," Zeke said with a smirk.

"Two birds, one stone," Clay confirmed. "Though at this point, I'm pretty sure we've done it all."

"TMI," Riley said, standing and folding her napkin before dropping it to the table.

"Well," Giana said, pushing her glasses up the bridge of her nose. "There is *one* trope we haven't tried yet."

"If you're referring to the reverse harem shit, I've already told you — I don't share." Clay looked almost murderous with that comment, which made us all laugh.

"No," Giana said with a laugh of her own. "Um… I was thinking more… accidental pregnancy."

Clay laughed, kissing her temple. "Yeah. Sure."

But the rest of us were frozen still.

Because Giana did not look like she was joking.

She watched Clay with worry etched in every feature, wringing her little hands in her lap. When Clay saw us all staring at her, he found her again, and his face went snow white.

He searched her eyes, a thousand questions in his, and then he trailed that gaze down to her stomach.

Giana unfolded her hands and smoothed them over her flat belly, framing it in a little heart.

"Wait…" Clay swallowed, his eyes snapping back to hers. "You're… You're really…"

"Yes," she whispered.

I clamped a hand over my mouth, tears springing to my eyes as Julep let out a little squeal. But no one moved, not as we waited for it all to sink in for Clay.

He blinked — once, twice — and then, he shoved back from the table, his chair grinding against the floor as he fell to his knees. He wrapped Giana in his arms, burying his head in her chest as his shoulders shook.

"Come on, guys," Leo said. "Let's give them a moment."

He nodded toward the dance floor, and we all followed, but not before the girls and I snuck another look back and found Clay's massive hands spreading over Giana's belly, his eyes thick with tears.

"I'm going to be a dad," he breathed a question up at Giana.

When she nodded, he broke entirely, and we all tore our eyes away, linking arms and letting out unnaturally high-pitched peals of laughter as we ran to the dance floor.

The band was a hit, transitioning from the soft music that had played through dinner into a broad range that pleased everyone from twenty-one to eighty. We danced in a circle, mostly around Julep and Holden, though we all took turns doing stupid dance moves in the middle. I laughed particularly hard when Zeke, Holden, and Leo did some sort of mime act that involved them stuck in invisible boxes.

We were all sweating by the time Clay and Giana joined us, and the guys wrapped Clay in a loud bear hug of congratulations while the ladies swarmed Giana. We fawned over her, taking turns touching her stomach even though nothing was showing yet. Julep said she hoped it was a girl. Riley tried to pester her for names. And I just gave her a high-five for finding a way to make a book-related joke about her pregnancy.

Soon, we were all dancing again, and more and more players joined us.

Braden and Blake started a train at one point, pulling me right between them and giving me no choice but to join. When we were dancing in a circle again, Kyle held up his phone to show us the photo he'd posted of all the guys in their tuxes before the wedding. It had half-a-million likes already, along with thousands of comments — most of them from women who were heartbroken Holden was wifed up now. He'd garnered quite the following after the starting quarterback for the Panthers was injured near the end of the season and Holden stepped in, taking them all the way to the playoffs. They went out in the first round, but once again, Holden was in the spotlight.

I had a feeling he'd live his entire life there.

When I was sweating so much I had to down an entire glass of water to keep from overheating, the band finally gave us a break with a slow song. They crooned out a beautiful rendition of "Scenic Drive" by Khalid and Alicia Keys, the male and female lead singers somehow making it sound even better than the original.

Leo took me by the hand as the first notes played, pulling me to the edge of the dance floor that was the least crowded. His hands found my hips and held me close as I threaded my arms around his neck.

For a while, we just swayed to the music, our eyes dancing over one another as soft smiles played at the corners of our lips. I'd never been to a wedding before, but there was something about being surrounded by such young, promising love that made me want to lean into Leo and tell him how much he meant to me in a hundred different languages.

As if he felt the same, he tugged me in even more, until I could rest my head on his shoulders and close my eyes as we danced. I inhaled his scent, his soul, intertwining mine with it and absentmindedly wondering what our wedding would be like.

There wasn't even a doubt in my mind now that it would happen one day.

"What's on your mind, *mi amor*?" he asked, his words low and sultry in my ear.

"Forever," I answered softly.

Leo pulled back on a smile. "With me?"

"And Palico."

"Of course," he said, but his smile leveled out as his eyes searched mine. "I can see it."

"Me, too."

"What do you think," he asked, nodding to the grand scene around us, the garden lush with plants and flowers and trees, the lights golden, the band more expensive than our mortgage. "You want something like this, too?"

I let out a long breath, considering. "Maybe," I said. "Or maybe, just you and me and a quiet beach somewhere far away."

"An elopement?" Leo asked, surprised. Then, after consideration, he nodded. "I could get down with that."

"Yeah?"

"Hell yeah. But," he said immediately. "You know there's no way we can get away without having my mom there."

I laughed. "Would never dream of it."

"But you do want to get married?" he asked, almost tentatively.

"I do."

"And kids?"

"Um…" I cringed. "Maybe we could be the cool aunt and uncle?"

"Oh, come on, Stig," Leo said on a low, throaty laugh, his lips pressing against the soft skin under my ear. His next words were whispered just below it, sparking chills down my legs. "Let me put a baby in you."

"Not tonight," I said, pressing a hand against his chest. "We have a fur baby, and a shop to open."

"Fair," he conceded. "But one day…"

"Maybe," I said, holding up a threatening finger. Leo grabbed it and kissed it, and my ovaries tightened like little traitors at the touch.

The music picked back up after that, and we rushed to join our friends in the center of the dance floor. We partied until well after midnight, Julep's dad paying the band and the event staff to stay later so we didn't have to stop. It wasn't until almost two in the morning that we finally gathered our belongings, the girls holding our heels in our hands as we walked barefoot out of the garden.

Holden and Julep left the venue under a parade of sparklers, ducking into a vintage car that took them to their honeymoon suite at the hotel. They were leaving for their honeymoon in the morning — two weeks traipsing through Europe.

Once they were gone, we all took the shuttle back to the hotel, hugging each of our former roommates when we were back in the lobby. We made them promise to come see us before the season got under way, and Kyle booked his flight right then and there to prove he would.

Riley and Giana tackled me next while Leo said his goodbyes to Zeke and Clay, more tears being shed before Leo and I rode the elevator up to our own room. It was so quiet compared to the wedding that my ears rang as we undressed, and then Leo ran a hot bath in the massive marble tub, both of us easing into the sudsy water with heavy sighs.

We got more dirty than clean in that tub, eventually toweling off and moving to the bed. With all the emotion of the night still clinging to us, we made love until dawn, not stopping to sleep until the sun started slipping through the curtains of our room.

When we finally did curl up in the sheets, Leo spooning me from behind, I inhaled a long, sweet breath before letting it out as I cuddled closer to him. I'd never felt such joy and happiness for people I loved before. I smiled wider with each passing thought — Braden and Kyle playing together for the Seahawks, Blake staying another year as quarterback to lead NBU, Riley and Zeke starting their coalition, Holden and Julep starting their marriage, Clay and Giana starting a *family*.

My heart was so full, I thought it'd burst.

And when I rolled over, pressing my forehead to Leo's and feeling his warmth radiating over me, the most blissful peace enveloped me like a blanket. A laugh bubbled out of me as I realized the most hilarious, beautiful truth.

I had everything I'd ever wanted.

All because I begged my parents to buy me *Halo*.

THE END

Thank you for reading Hail Mary, and the entire Red Zone Rivals series. As a special token of my gratitude, I've written a bonus scene with your favorite couple – Clay & Giana. Read it here. (https://kandisteiner.com/bonus-content)

As bittersweet as it is for this series to come to an end, I'm so excited for what's next...

A pro hockey romance series of interconnected stand-alones.

Football is my number one love, but hockey is a close second, and I'm over the moon to write some tropes I've been longing to write for years. Get ready for single dad, fake fiancé, teammate's little sister, and more.

Pre-order book one here (https://amzn.to/3Yx092N), coming summer 2023!

MORE FROM KANDI STEINER

The Red Zone Rivals Series
Fair Catch
As if being the only girl on the college football team wasn't hard enough, Coach had to go and assign my brother's best friend — and *my* number one enemy — as my roommate.
Blind Side
The hottest college football safety in the nation just asked me to be his fake girlfriend.
And I just asked him to take my virginity.
Quarterback Sneak
Quarterback Holden Moore can have any girl he wants. Except me: the coach's daughter.

The Becker Brothers Series
On the Rocks (book 1)
Neat (book 2)
Manhattan (book 3)
Old Fashioned (book 4)
Four brothers finding love in a small Tennessee town that revolves around a whiskey distillery with a dark past — including the mysterious death of their father.

The Best Kept Secrets Series
(AN AMAZON TOP 10 BESTSELLER)
What He Doesn't Know (book 1)
What He Always Knew (book 2)
What He Never Knew (book 3)
Charlie's marriage is dying. She's perfectly content to go

down in the flames, until her first love shows back up and reminds her the other way love can burn.

Close Quarters
A summer yachting the Mediterranean sounded like heaven to Jasmine after finishing her undergrad degree. But her boyfriend's billionaire boss always gets what he wants. And this time, he wants her.

Make Me Hate You
Jasmine has been avoiding her best friend's brother for years, but when they're both in the same house for a wedding, she can't resist him — no matter how she tries.

The Wrong Game
(AN AMAZON TOP 5 BESTSELLER)
Gemma's plan is simple: invite a new guy to each home game using her season tickets for the Chicago Bears. It's the perfect way to avoid getting emotionally attached and also get some action. But after Zach gets his chance to be her practice round, he decides one game just isn't enough. A sexy, fun sports romance.

The Right Player
She's avoiding love at all costs. He wants nothing more than to lock her down. Sexy, hilarious and swoon-worthy, The Right Player is the perfect read for sports romance lovers.

On the Way to You
It was only supposed to be a road trip, but when Cooper discovers the journal of the boy driving the getaway car, everything changes. An emotional, angsty road trip romance.

A Love Letter to Whiskey
(AN AMAZON TOP 10 BESTSELLER)
An angsty, emotional romance between two lovers fighting the curse of bad timing.
Read Love, Whiskey – Jamie's side of the story and an extended epilogue – in the new Fifth Anniversary Edition!

Weightless
Young Natalie finds self-love and romance with her personal trainer, along with a slew of secrets that tie them together in ways she never thought possible.

Revelry
Recently divorced, Wren searches for clarity in a summer cabin outside of Seattle, where she makes an unforgettable connection with the broody, small town recluse next door.

Say Yes
Harley is studying art abroad in Florence, Italy. Trying to break free of her perfectionism, she steps outside one night determined to Say Yes to anything that comes her way. Of course, she didn't expect to run into Liam Benson...

Washed Up
Gregory Weston, the boy I once knew as my son's best friend, now a man I don't know at all. No, not just a man. A doctor. And he wants me...

The Christmas Blanket
Stuck in a cabin with my ex-husband waiting out a blizzard? Not exactly what I had pictured when I planned a surprise visit home for the holidays...

Black Number Four
A college, Greek-life romance of a hot young poker star and the boy sent to take her down.

The Palm South University Series
Rush - FREE if you sign up for my newsletter!
Anchor, PSU #2
Pledge, PSU #3
Legacy, PSU #4
Ritual, PSU #5
Hazed, PSU #6
Greek, PSU #7
#1 NYT Bestselling Author Rachel Van Dyken says, "If Gossip Girl and Riverdale had a love child, it would be PSU." This angsty college series will be your next guilty addiction.

Tag Chaser
She made a bet that she could stop chasing military men, which seemed easy — until her knight in shining armor and latest client at work showed up in Army ACUs.

Song Chaser
Tanner and Kellee are perfect for each other. They frequent the same bars, love the same music, and have the same desire to rip each other's clothes off. Only problem? Tanner is still in love with his best friend.

ACKNOWLEDGEMENTS

My first thank you goes out to the communities of BookTok, Bookstagram, BookTwt and my Facebook group — Kandiland. This series has completely changed my life, and it's all thanks to you. Words cannot express how much it means to me that you take the time to post photos, videos, quotes, discussions, and more from the books you love — and that some of those books happen to be the ones I write. Thank you, and please know I never take any of your time, hard work, or love for granted.

To my husband, Jack — thank you for believing in me even when I threw my arms up and cried and said I SUCK AT WRITING AND THIS IS GARBAGE. You kept me going on days when I really didn't think I'd be able to. I love you.

Momma Von, thank you for instilling me with a fierce love of football, and for always being my biggest cheerleader.

This book would never have gotten done if it weren't for my dear friend and angel of an assistant, Tina Stokes, who took care of quite literally everything else so I could focus on writing. Thank you for taking care of me always and for loving my characters like they're your own.

To my sprint sluts, Lena Hendrix and Elsie Silver, I'm so glad we found each other and I look forward to our group chat shenanigans every day. Love you both.

Karla Sorensen and Brittainy Cherry, our little writing group was UNSTOPPABLE and I truly don't think I could have done this one without having y'all to pace with. I'm so blessed to be surrounded by amazing women and writers like the two of you.

Laura Pavlov, although our schedules never aligned (damn time zones!), I always looked forward to reporting back to you with word counts and hearing yours too. I'm so thankful for our friendship.

My early reader team for this book was expansive, and not without reason. I wanted to make sure I was doing justice in many areas, from Leo's Puerto Rican heritage to the video game culture. I also wanted to ensure that when readers left this series, their hearts would be full. None of that would have been possible without my amazing team.

Frances O'Brien, Gabby Vivas, Meagan Reynoso, Sarah Green, Lily Turner, Kelle Fabre, Samantha Warren, Jewel Caruso, Carly Wilson, Jayce Cruz, Allison Cheshire, and Janett Corona — THANK YOU, from the bottom of my heart. I love you all.

Nicole McCurdy of Emerald Edits — once again, you blew me away with your attention to detail and you helped me take this entire novel up a notch. My sincerest gratitude and respect.

Elaine York of Allusion Publishing — the fact that you literally edited this with a busted up hand??? You always prioritize me and make my deadlines work even when I put you through the ringer. Please don't ever leave me, and know that my love and appreciation for you knows no limits.

To Ren Saliba, thank you for sharing your photographs with me and allowing me to bring Leo, his lips, and his necklaces to life.

A big shout out to my friends at Valentine PR for spreading the word about this series and helping others fall in love with it. Nina, Kim, Sarah and the rest, I couldn't do this without you on my side.

Finally, to YOU, the reader. Whether you have been with me for ten years or you just found me, whether you've read only this book or a few or all thirty-three of them — you are the reason I am here doing what I love. I can never thank you enough, but I can promise to keep bringing you stories as long as my brain keeps dreaming them up.

ABOUT THE AUTHOR

Kandi Steiner is an Amazon Top 5 bestselling author and whiskey connoisseur living in Tampa, FL. Best known for writing "emotional rollercoaster" stories, she loves bringing flawed characters to life and writing about real, raw romance — in all its forms. No two Kandi Steiner books are the same, and if you're a lover of angsty, emotional, and inspirational reads, she's your gal.

An alumna of the University of Central Florida, Kandi graduated with a double major in Creative Writing and Advertising/PR with a minor in Women's Studies. She started writing back in the 4th grade after reading the first Harry Potter installment. In 6th grade, she wrote and edited her own newspaper and distributed to her classmates. Eventually, the principal caught on and the newspaper was quickly halted, though Kandi tried fighting for her "freedom of press."

She took particular interest in writing romance after college, as she has always been a die hard hopeless romantic, and likes to highlight all the challenges of love as well as the triumphs.

When Kandi isn't writing, you can find her reading books of all kinds, planning her next adventure, or pole dancing (yes, you read that right). She enjoys live music, traveling, playing with her fur babies and soaking up the sweetness of life.

CONNECT WITH KANDI:
NEWSLETTER: kandisteiner.com/newsletter
FACEBOOK: facebook.com/kandisteiner
FACEBOOK READER GROUP (Kandiland):
facebook.com/groups/kandilandks
INSTAGRAM: Instagram.com/kandisteiner
TIKTOK: tiktok.com/@authorkandisteiner
TWITTER: twitter.com/kandisteiner
PINTEREST: pinterest.com/authorkandisteiner
WEBSITE: www.kandisteiner.com

Kandi Steiner may be coming to a city near you! Check out her "events" tab to see all the signings she's attending in the near future:
www.kandisteiner.com/events

Printed in Great Britain
by Amazon